# DAY UNTO NIGHT

Tammy Jo Eckhart

Liminal Books is an imprint of Between the Lines Publishing. The Liminal Books name and logo are trademarks of Between the Lines Publishing.

Cover design by Cherie Fox

Between the Lines Publishing
9 North River Road, Ste 248
Auburn ME 04210
btwnthelines.com


First Published: October 2021

ISBN: (Paperback) 978-1-950502-59-2

ISBN: (Ebook) 978-1-950502-60-8

Library of Congress Control Number: 2021947833

# Glossary of Akhkharu Terms Used in this Novel

*Abum*: term of affection for a parent

*akalum*: human blood, or humans as food for vampires

*Akhkharu/Akh*: vampire

*Akhkharu Ilati!*: a religious exclamation that translates as "vampire gods," used to express intense emotion

*Allamudi*: a family of vampires known for their scholarly pursuits

*Alu-Bel*: the vampire who controls a city

*arammu-wardum*: a vampire's most beloved wardum

*arnum*: punishment

*Bel*: Lord or Lady

*Beleti*: Young Lord/Lady

*Belum/Belen*: the leader of a kataru or the eldest Akhkharu of a family

*bitum*: house where a vampire who controls land or a city dwells

*bubussunu/bu*: vampire blood

*dami/damu*: vampiric child/children

*ebebu*: formal ruling from a vampire over a wardum or a more powerful vampire over a subordinate

*ehus*: a training room in an Akhkharu's home

*ekallim*: house where the ruler of a vampiric family dwells

*esharra*: house where the vampiric ruler of a region dwells

*Gelal*: a family of vampires known for their sensuality

*Ilati!*: exclamation of frustration, *see* Akhkharu Ilati!

*Kalum*: priest in charge of powerful vows and sorrowful matters

*Kashshaptu*: a family of vampires notable for their use of magic

*kataru*: alliance of vampires

*kur*: land, the general region that one vampire, the Kur-Bel, controls

*Kur-Bel*: the vampire Lord or Lady of a kur

*mimmum*: humans held as property of a vampiric ruler

*patu*: the territory that a particular branch of a vampiric family controls

*Sarrutum*: a family of vampires that concerns itself mostly with power and manipulating large numbers of humans

*sekretu*: male/masculine humans used as food

*sinnis*: female/feminine humans used as food

*Shi*: vampiric parent

*Tamu*: a formal oath between vampire and wardum backed by the mystical force inherent in bubussunu

*Ummum*: the mother of all vampires, called alternatively Ningai or Charity

*wardum*: the living slave of a vampire

*Xul*: a family of vampires known for their violence and sadism

*Zagmi*: priest of joyous matters

# Beginning of the Old World

*"Bard is almost done; they are anxious to greet you."*

*I glance in the mirror at Jon, looking the same as he did the day I met him in the park nearly three centuries ago. I return his announcement with a childish smile, but that does not work as well as it used to.*

*"You are the Ummum," he reminds me. "The new ones have been chosen; they have proven their worth; it is their first night."*

*"They'll want to hear the entire thing again," I sigh, pushing back a lock of reddish-blonde hair that I may never grow used to.*

*"Tell them what you wish; let the others talk for a change. If they do not wish to, let Bard tell."*

*Once more my arammu-wardum's counsel is wise.*

*They are all sitting there, the five who head the families, their allies who aided in the final battle, their older children around them, and the newly raised seated in front. Shi and damu, family all, as I willed it. I catch my greatest ally's eye as he sits perched on the back wall around the garden, his presence revitalizing it. As He willed it.*

*After formulaic greetings, the pleading begins. "Please Ummum, please tell us how you created our world. Tell how Allamudi, Sarrutum, Kashshaptu, Gelal, and even Xul came to live in harmony with the mortals."*

*I hold up my hands, and the crowd quiets. "It is a very long story," I begin and then deviate from the normal pattern for this event. "I cannot tell it alone. Your Abum must tell their stories as well, or Bard will do it for them."*

*I have played upon their affections for their children; I have played upon their fears of the intermingling of truth and lies. One by one my dami agree.*

*Jon and Bard bring forth a chair, and for a moment my heart aches on seeing Bard's white hair and the wrinkles around his eyes. I have struck a deal, so I must keep it.*

*After a moment's pause, I speak.*

I remember running.

I remember their screams.

Father's, as they came to the farm. Father's, as they pushed him aside. Father's, as they stabbed him while I watched in horror from the window.

I remember their screams.

Brother's, telling them to get off our land, then crying out for Father, then crying for us all to run, but then there was nothing but a gurgle.

I remember their screams.

Mother's, ordering them out, then silence until she yelled for us to hide, then her cries to the goddesses to protect her until there was only a slapping sound, their laughter, and a gurgle.

I remember their screams.

Sister's, as she was pulled by her hair from beneath the bed, the sound of cloth being ripped, and her cries of anguish and pleas for mercy, then her command to me: "Run!"

I remember running.

I ran between their bodies as they did things to her that I didn't even have words for. I ran over the cold stone floor, slipping on the cooling sticky substance that dripped from my mother's still body. I ran over the door and my brother's cold mass trying to block it. I ran over the earth and grass, matted from my father's slaughter.

I remember running.

I ran until I fell into the Great Water, what you call the Euphrates, but we only called Puranum, and was carried until I could grasp a branch with my hands, tearing at it until my blood also covered the ground as I pulled myself up.

I remember my pain.

My stomach gave up the wonderful dinner Mother and Sister had made for us that night, as all I could see were blood and bodies in my mind. I retched until I was as hollow in my stomach as I was in my heart.

I remember my pain.

My hands were torn; my blood was dripping down my arms to soak my nightshirt. My feet were pitted by the rocks and twigs that I had dashed through in my haste to obey. My legs were aching from the run, my lungs were still gasping from the water, and my fingers felt like they were turning to ice in the black night.

I remember my pain.

My mouth opened and let out a scream that was primal and raw, that tore itself from my very depths. My throat burned until only a squeak came forth and I collapsed on the ground, shivering.

I remember them coming.

He floated down, his beard flowing and his eyes two bright stars, his crown jutting forth into enormous bulls' horns that made me tremble. The god An frowned down at me, heard my sorrow, and declared, "Time shall have no meaning for you, child. The strength of the stars themselves, my warriors, will flow through you, and your vengeance shall know no better from now until eternity."

I remember them coming.

She flew down on her great eagle wings, her majestic head turning to and fro like a lioness watching her prey, but I was not afraid of the first Mother of All. Ninhursag enfolded me in her wings and promised me, "Your five children shall live without fear of disease or old age, they shall offer you their protection and their loyalty, and they will praise you as they attempt to outshine you, but none shall. Your grandchildren will conquer those who dare stand in their way. You will be Ummum to eternity."

I remember them coming.

He rose from beneath the earth, the sacred hoe in one hand, a sheaf of grain in the other, his beard laced with vegetables and flowers, and I smiled. Enlil lowered his gaze to me and then nodded his head, deciding, "You will be driven to plant your seed far and wide, child. But you shall be wise where you plant it, determining the best vessels in which to lay it, the best hearts in which to plant it, and the best bodies in which to instill it, but this wisdom may not pass to all your children. When this happens, remember that the wise farmer reaches for his scythe of bronze to cull his harvest."

I remember them coming.

He washed forth from the river on the backs of a goat and a fish; in his hands was his great staff with the entwining snakes that bathed in the fountains that flowed from his shoulders, and I was hopeful. Enki smiled at me and declared, "Your food and drink will flow through you and make all your desires manifest and potent. Those with whom you share your life force shall serve you day and night until eternity with all their renewed strength and being."

I remember them coming.

He descended on a winged bull, the moon shining through him, his lapis lazuli beard glowing, flecks of gold in the dark blue hair. Nanna looked down on me as I cried and said, "Child, the moon will always guide you and lend you its strength, and your eyes will always find the light of it, even in darkest night, so that you may forever thrive where others fall. You shall use their fears and their weaknesses against them and make them your fortress."

I remember them coming.

He came as a ray of light, solidifying into a handsome man holding a scale in one hand and a scroll in the other as his eyes shone their bright light through me, making me sink to my knees. Utu frowned and lowered his eyebrows in anger. "Your soul demands retribution instead of trusting in your village chief and your city's king. But what was done was not just, and thus I will give you only this. Your life shall be hidden from my eyes, so that I cannot see your vengeance, for should I see it, I shall consume you with fire. Carry out your heart's desire, but never forget that you will reap what you sow."

I remember them coming.

She rode up on her jeweled chariot pulled by two fierce lions, a sword in one hand, a hitching ring in her other; her hair flowed like honey surrounded by the stars of the sky in her crown, her naked skin shone with the desires of all creatures, and I held my breath. Inanna stepped down and shook her head at me. "I hear your true heart cry

4

out, Child. As you have been polluted by blood, so shall it consume your essence. Through it and only it shall you gather strength and build desire; through it and only it shall you destroy your enemies and bind your servants. Through it and only it shall your power to avenge and protect grow."

The god of all waters stepped forward and turned his frightful eyes to his family, who vanished without further comment. I pressed my face to the Earth, but then as always, Enki lifted me up and bade me look at him as he spoke. "I see what you really want, little one. Never doubt that I do. Since I dislike some of their aid, I will ensure that you adhere strictly to their prophecies, but I will see you achieve your true heart's desire. I'm extraordinarily good at working around their rules. Call me when you need me, little one, and expect me at any moment."

Then he left me confused, as he often does, to struggle with all I'd been told. I would have children, though I was still a child myself and my body no longer felt the same. I would have servants as well, though I had never commanded one. They would help me avenge my family, if only I could acquire them.

My first two tries didn't work.

The first time it didn't work at all, and I was left with a dead body by the side of the road and the sun about to rise. I was clever enough to find a place to stay during the day, and my stomach wasn't complaining anymore, though by nightfall I was feeling a touch hungry. I could ignore it. Even with my father's position at the Temple in the village, there had been difficult seasons during my mortal lifetime when there hadn't been much food.

So, the second time I didn't feel so hungry that I couldn't stop, slit my own wrist, and press it to the man's lips. He was a man who did his job well and even had a family of his own, unlike most Temple dependents. I thought he could help me. He wanted to help me when he woke up, but he also turned away when I offered him the goat I'd captured and killed for his first feeding. He built a fire and cooked it, and then I knew that I hadn't done it right.

I prayed alone in the cave he found us. Burning a small piece of the goat to ashes, I prayed for guidance, but got no answer that night before the sun made me too tired to stay awake. The last thing I saw was my new servant standing at the mouth of the cave, nodding seriously at me, promising he'd watch out for me. I should have been afraid of him. My mother and sister surely would have been, and my father and brother would have warned me against men not of our family. When night fell, I found him asleep by the cave entrance and left him for a while to go think.

It was while I was walking and thinking that Enki came to me alone for the first time. Immediately I lay upon the ground, as the Temple priests and priestesses told us to do. Immediately I called him by every sacred name I knew and trembled. He only laughed, water dampening my body and clothes as he bent down and urged me to stand. "You are a very clever girl," the god told me with a twinkle in his eyes, but I was not fooled into thinking I was safe with him. While I found much of what the priestesses and priests said to be boring, I did listen to my family, and they had always pointed out repeatedly how fickle the gods are.

I followed where he led me, back to the riverbed, and then sat where he motioned. "Only one was a failure, so I'm impressed, Ningai."

Hearing my name made me weep. My father had been the last to call me that. It was a name that had caused jealous men to stare at him for giving it to his child, but he had thought it proper given his position as overseer. In a few minutes I controlled myself and focused on Enki again.

"Creating a slave first is a particularly good idea, too. Someone to help you while you take your time to find the right ones to follow your path, to assist you."

"I didn't plan it that way," I whispered, and this made Enki laugh so heartily that water sprayed from him.

"I know; that's why it is so perfect. You are doing exactly what you should be doing without knowing it. You are clever, and I do like clever," he added, narrowing his eyes just a bit.

Before I could worry about this, he stood up, so I did as well. "Your slave, though, may need reminders of his place, more of your gifts to fully make him yours. Your children will have no such inclination, so choose carefully, little one." With that he vanished in a puddle of water.

6

"There you are!" An unfamiliar voice made me turn around. The man I had tried to change last night was standing there, his face a bit pale with worry. "I was afraid you'd run off; you could get hurt around here, being all alone."

I could hear his heart pounding and the blood rushing through him, but instead of making me hungry as the first man had that first night, it made me feel connected to him, like the servants my parents were allowed to use the services of every now and again when the Temple decreed that my father had done a particularly good job at overseeing a harvest or clearing a new field. "You were worried about me?"

"Well," he said, looking away and then at his feet for a moment. "Sure, I mean, you are the only excuse I have for not being at my loom today. I'm not sure why I stayed with you; I mean, I think I have a woman and child of my own, though that seems like a dream," he added with a frown.

I frowned but then smiled as I realized he would be mine if he was forgetting his own life so easily. I took his hand in mine. "What is your name?"

"I'm called Amar," he replied as he let me lead him back to the cave.

Once he was sitting, I turned and cut my wrist again, a small cut that let the blood slowly pool. "I am called Ningai."

He blinked at me, and I could tell his mind was turning over the color of my hair, the cut of my dress, and the dyes in it, until he jerked back, and his eyes widened. "You're the Chief Overseer's daughter? No, I heard in the village that there was a fire; everyone died."

That made me angry, and without asking I found that I was able to pin him to the ground and hold my wrist against his mouth. At first, he resisted, but then he started lapping at the cut and drinking down my blood until I pulled it from him. They had covered up their crime with a lie, and that made me even more furious.

"What are you, Beleti?"

"Vengeance." Then I told him everything until the sun rose and I fell unconscious again.

Amar took me back to what remained of my father's house. The mud bricks were blackened, but they still stood; the furniture, doors and roof were all ashes, and the fences that had marked this small plot as his own were destroyed. I sat in the ashes of what had been my mother's chair and cried.

Amar sat on the floor next to me and watched. "We can't stay here, Beleti," he finally said softly. I looked up at him, my tears drying on my cheeks. "They may come back; these are not good men to have attacked the Chief Overseer and his family. You. I, I'm just one man; I can't protect you against them if they come in force."

He stopped talking and sighed. "Truth is, they could arrest me, take me back to the Temple, and punish me; I do belong there."

"You belong to me," I stated so firmly that I surprised even myself.

Amar grew a bit paler, but he smiled back after a moment, dipping his head and shoulders as I'd seen the lent slaves do toward my father and mother when they were sent here. "I'm not sure they will agree, seeing that you are a child, but it will be as you say, Beleti. But," he added, looking up at the night sky, "the sun will rise. You seem to need sleep then, and shelter. I don't know how I know, but I feel as if you shouldn't be out in the sun; is that true?"

I bit my lip. Honestly, I didn't know whether it was true, only that Lord Utu had told me that his light would kill me. I didn't tell Amar this, because I had a feeling that if I mentioned the gods, he might panic and run away. I felt that I needed him, or someone like him. I only said, "I can't be out in the sunlight."

He simply looked upward and waved at the sky. I smiled and went to the secret that I prayed the murderers had not discovered. The door looked solid against the floor, and the notch in it for a lever was not broken, so without thinking of how difficult it should be I lifted the door up to reveal my mother's storage space. She had told me many stories about how her own people had needed such storage, because they did not have the almost year-round harvest that we often got if the gods were generous and the nobles smart with their planning. Smoke billowed upward, trapped there from before, but it didn't bother me, even though it made Amar cough. "Are you sure that's safe?" he called after me as I jumped down instead of using the ladder, which had been rickety even before it had been damaged by the fire.

As above, my eyesight seemed to attune itself to the darkness very quickly, and soon I could count the jars of food my mother had preserved for us and stored here, much to my father's amusement and pride. I looked back as Amar landed on his feet in the space and looked around. "Amazing," he whispered, though at what I wasn't sure, nor did I ask.

"I can sleep down here, and there's food for you." I pointed to the jars and started naming what each contained. My mother had begun including me the past year when my sister became a woman, saying that soon her helper would be gone, and I would have to replace her. Thinking about it made my vision and hearing blur back to that night and the night before.

"Beleti?" I looked up to find Amar on his knees before me. "What is wrong? You were too still and quiet for a long time."

I made myself nod my head and pointed to one of the oldest jars. "You should eat from that one first."

"Aren't you hungry?" he asked as he broke the seal to find dried fish inside. "No? Or just not for this? Or do I want to know?"

"I'm not hungry right now," I stated simply as I climbed back up to watch the stars and think. That night I gave my wardum his first orders for the daytime, then I took a risk and let him shut the trap door on me so I could sleep.

He was worthy of that trust. The next night I awoke when he opened the trap door and smiled down on me. The moon was bright, and he knelt to offer me his hand to help me up. I stood up to find the roof half rebuilt. "You did a good deal of work," I praised him, but he waved it away with a hand gesture.

"Whatever you've done to me has made me so much stronger, faster – I can see better, hear better; it is amazing. I think you may be a god testing me," he added with a serious expression that broke into a smile when I handed him the fish jar from the cellar for him to continue eating.

"I'm not a god," I simply replied, then my stomach growled, and we both stopped dead at the sound. "No, I can't eat that," I decided when he held out the jar to me. I don't know how I figured it all out; it was as if I just knew that giving my blood to someone would change them and that I needed human blood instead of food, and that I was stronger than even my father in his youth. My first wardum seemed to know it, too.

"I'll go out with you then; it isn't appropriate for a girl to go out alone," Amar said, and when I looked at him with surprise he smiled. "You look like almost any little girl – well," and he motioned to his own dark hair, "not like most around here, but ..."

"I understand," I replied, placing my hand in his as I would have my father's or big brother's when we left our small farm. It was true that during the day, women and girls mingled freely with men in the markets, in the fields, or at the looms and temple shops. At night, though, the darkness gave bad men too much cover. The fact that I could see clearly would be well hidden as I held onto my servant's hand. We were both still dressed as we had been days before, but we would deal with that when my stomach was no longer demanding food.

My father's farm – my farm; I had to start thinking of it as mine – was not far from the temple or the markets. A man of his importance must be within easy reach should a priest or king call. Of course, he wasn't now, so I grasped Amar's hand more tightly. He responded by glancing down at me then looking around. "If anyone asks, I am your family's servant. I doubt anyone will recognize me, but you ..." He let the thought hang in the air.

"No, not many saw me away from the farm," I said, trying to reassure us both, as a guard forced us to stop at the entrance to the marketplace. I let Amar speak for us, but when the guard asked me a question, I found that my voice seemed to drive my will into him, and he blinked, staggered, and then let us pass into the area, now mostly deserted. Amar's hand was sweating a bit, but we walked around looking for a hapless person.

We found her by a wall. She was partly sitting and partly lying on the ground, and the smell of her blood hit me hard, so hard I had to bow my head and tighten my grip again on Amar's hand until he made a pained sound. His noise drew the woman's attention so that she scrambled to her feet.

She tried to brush back her hair with her hands, tried to smooth her torn skirts down, but mostly I could see the cuts on her arms and face, which were also bruising. "What do you want? If you have something to trade, we'll talk; otherwise keep moving." Her voice was trembling, but I got the feeling this was a speech she'd given hundreds of times.

"Sorry to bother you," Amar muttered, but I stepped closer to her, which made the woman step back further. "Bel, we should go," he whispered to me.

"I have food, water, and shelter to trade for your time."

The woman frowned and tried to pull her shawl around her tighter. "Tell your master that his daughter isn't nice, making fun of poor free women just trying to make a living."

"It's for my father – he's not feeling well; my mother is dead." The lies fell so easily from my lips; it's a trait I passed on to my servants and children. "He just needs a companion for a few hours, for dinner; he is so lonely," and again I felt my words defeat her worry and pull her toward me.

We took her home. She called herself Shag-ad, and she was a recent widow, childless, and thus alone. Rather than turn to the temple, she had turned to men she met on the streets. I didn't quite understand it really, except that all fathers needed mothers, though my own family had told me and my sister that only a family rite made that possible. Amar seemed to understand what she was talking about, and he went outside at one point, his face flushed.

When my father never appeared, she turned to me, her dark eyes glaring in anger. "I may be a poor woman and alone, but I will not sleep with a slave!"

I took her hand and pulled her to sit next to me. I crawled into her lap and put my arms around her neck. "I'm sorry I lied. I lost my parents. I'm so lonely," I whispered as I clenched her neck and laid my head on her shoulder.

She sighed and started to pat my back, but it felt forced, not like my mother or sister. She tried to escape when I held her and told her what had happened in this house, but my strength held her tight, and my mind held her voice silent until I finished my story. I paused a moment, and she spoke unbidden. "I know those men. They, some of them, came to me – they come to me. They've talked about it. They are very bad men," she added softly, a soft sound like weeping ending her words.

11

"I need your help," I whispered to her as I bit into her neck and drank for a moment. "Will you help me?" I pleaded when I paused, her grip on me tighter. At her nod I drank more deeply, my eyes attuned to her skin color, my ears counting the pounding of her heart. Then, when it all slowed down, I stopped and bit into my own wrist and held it to her mouth.

"What are you doing?" Amar's voice made me snarl back at him, and he scrambled out the ruined doorframe, his eyes wide as he saw my new nature revealed as never before.

"I want her to be my first," I replied. I smiled as I felt her grip weakening, then strengthening as she lapped at my blood. "Find someone disposable," I ordered then, and my words seemed to echo off the walls and spur my servant to his feet. As my mother had fed me, I fed her from the drunken homeless man Amar dumped on the floor. I cut his neck first and took a sip, then held him up to her trembling lips as Shag-ad's eyes widened to see clearly in the night.

Later she held me as my mother had held me in the storage space under the house. She listened to my story again, interspersing her own ideas with my desire for vengeance. She believed me, truly believed me, and I believed her when she said we needed more help.

My first told me that to fight men of power, we would need people of power, mortal power, not simply the type we felt running through our bodies. Shag-ad had never had much power, but she knew a woman who did, a Kashshaptu, a witch, whom she and her own mother had turned to repeatedly. She believed this witch also counseled the Temple itself, and there, in that most important place, we could find others to help us.

Amar was not impressed, but he said nothing as we went the next night to find this witch, who called herself Mammetum. She lived on the other side of the Temple in a place where the caves have jutted up from the earth. As we approached, Amar trailing behind and always looking around him, we could see a large bonfire not far from a small house. Around it were several people who appeared to be dancing and a bent-over woman who was striking the ground with her cane repeatedly.

12

"Those are the women who come seeking her guidance," Shag-ad told me as she carried me in her arms as my mother used to. "I came here when my husband died; she told me that exchanging my body would lead to an amazing gift," she added, and then kissed my cheek.

"Halt!" the old woman called out to us before we got too close. The people stopped dancing and stood behind her, and I could then see that they were all women, many of them with bruised faces or swollen bellies. "Stay," she whispered, and those with her obeyed as she hobbled toward us.

"The career has served you well," the witch began to say when she nodded at Shag-ad, who set me on my feet. As soon as I looked at the old woman, she stopped and took a step back. Then she hissed for her women to scurry inside the house, adding a word I did not understand then: Akhkharu, a word those same women spread among the mortals, which came to represent my children and their children and so forth.

"It has, Mammetum, it has indeed," Shag-ad said as she motioned for me to approach. Behind me, Amar made a sound but stayed where he was.

"What are you?" the witch asked me in a soft whisper that was her normal way of speaking. So, I repeated my tale for her, letting my tears spill forth again, drawing her to me, until she was sitting on the ground with us around her. "You saw the gods, child. They have blessed you or cursed you – only time will tell, and I am no priestess. I deal with the plants, the animals, and the souls of those who have passed beyond, which you have not and which you did only briefly," she told us, resting her eyes on my first for a moment.

"You can see that?" I asked, amazed because one of her eyes was almost as white as milk and the other seemed hazy as she stared intently at me.

"These are poor eyes," she said, motioning to them, and then swept her thin white hair up off her forehead to reveal a drawing of another eye, this one wide open, sharp, and clear, and radiating something my sight could almost see. "My true sight is here; that mark is merely a sign, a rite of passage, for to be in tune with the world you must suffer first."

"Some do not give you a choice," I replied with a frown.

13

"But you give me one," the witch stated as she rose with difficulty to her feet and looked back at the house. "The women of this village rely upon me when their men become drunk or jealous, or merely stupid. If I follow you, who will care for them?"

"Those who hurt her are here; we need not go far," Shag-ad stated. "I feel so much stronger, more alive than before. Perhaps if you let her become your mother, you too will be more than you are and thus able to give more to them."

The old woman frowned at the statement of being alive but then nodded slowly. "My time is near, and I have found no one worthy to teach my craft to since the last was taken from me."

On our coaxing, she told us her tale. She had had a husband and children. All had moved on; none of the children were gifted as she was and thus unable to hear the call of the wind, the cry of the herb, the scratch of the owl, or the whispers in the graves, so her loneliness was tenfold, she said, when she thought of the village without a wisewoman. She had found a promising young woman from among the Temple tribute years ago, and because she had the ear of the High Priestess, confirming my first's statement that this old woman might be our way into greater seats of power, she had been given the girl to raise as her own. The girl had shown many gifts, especially regarding healing and poisons, and Mammetum had invested years in her training. Then one evening when she went to gather herbs, she was beset by a group of men whose behavior sounded familiar to our ears. These men stole something precious from her as they had from my sister before killing her. The old woman found her the next day, dying and only able to tell her what had happened. In her grief she shut herself away until the women of the village came and begged her to reopen her door to them. Since then, she had been too busy aiding these women around her, who were now watching us from what they thought was the safely of her hut, to find these men and make them pay.

We sent Amar to the house to guard the women lest any of them see. Then I crawled onto her lap, whispered that she need never worry again, and took her life, only to return it tenfold. My first returned with a lamb, and we helped my second feed for the first time.

Then we could only stare for several minutes at what had happened. The witch's body changed. She stood upright, and her smooth, full face smiled with perfect, gleaming teeth. "You have returned me to my youth, Ummum," she declared, and it was the first time anyone called me that.

To us, our Temple was really impressive. The clay bricks had been handmade and dried in the sun – the entire city had helped, I was told – then they had started building: first one level, then another, indented and smaller than the first, then another, and finally the top, where the priestess would stand and look up at the stars. Later people called them ziggurats, as though they were magical, but to us they were necessary, the focal point of our entire existence. On each level there were trees and bushes, cared for by acolytes, postulants, and novices. The priests and priestesses were too busy keeping records, reading the sky, and talking to the gods. It had been built before there was writing, so all we had were the stories and the songs.

The current High Priestess was in charge; it was unusual for a woman to be in that position, but her father was king and her brother his heir – to marry her off would threaten that arrangement, so she served Nanna, who ruled the night. It was fitting, Mammetum said, that I should meet with her.

Meeting Lugul-Aya proved a bit more difficult than any of my other children.

With my power running through her, the witch was no longer recognizable to the Temple guards, though those who came to her for help saw this change as a sign of her power and not mine. She did not correct their mistake, and now I know that this was my first sign of problems to come. My first's lying with my wardum and taking pleasure and blood from him was my second sign, but as with all mothers I was blinded by my joy in creation, and like all children I needed them, so I pretended all was well.

It took a few weeks for both of them to master the skills needed to convince the guards to let us pass. Shag-ad coaxed one away from his place with her touch, and Amar knocked him unconscious. Mammetum spun an image in the other's mind, and he escorted us right

15

Day Unto Night

to the High Priestess's chamber. It was near the altar where they sacrificed animals; I could smell the new and old blood there, and it drew my attention far more than the columns that lined the central nave or the other temple dwellers who stepped out and watched our small group advance.

The High Priestess was beautiful – there is no other word for it – but unlike my second, whose beauty shone from her inner gifts, or my first, whose body swayed with grace, Lugul-Aya stood and demanded our admiration by her sheer confidence. Her children have always believed they should be so worshipped, and her words, demeanor, and smile should have been my third warning.

"I've been expecting you, child, or should I call you Ummum?" she said as she stepped down the few stairs and knelt in front of me. "My god has told me that you were coming. He has guided you to me, for I have what you need."

"You save us a good deal of explanation then," Mammetum said softly, having learned that her words could flatten trees and drive men deaf.

"And you are young, full of power, from someone even more young and full of power," the High Priestess replied, but she kept her dark eyes on me. She studied me for a moment, then reached out and ran a hand through my hair. "I can see your mother in you; no wonder the gods have blessed you."

She threw aside her veil and lifted her head. "Bring me across, and I will serve you as a loyal daughter."

"You presume a great deal," Shag-ad replied as she knelt next to me. "How do we know you have the moon-god's blessing? That you are the one?"

"If you are the one, then you know why I am here, not merely what I am here to do," I told her firmly.

That made her blink and sit back, letting her hair fall and her head nod a few times. She told me the story of my family's destruction; she even had the name of the man who had replaced my father, saying he had spoken to a minor priestess two moons back and was warned not to do the evil in his heart. But the High Priest, who held more authority than she, something that made her heart pound in anger, forbade anyone in the Temple from revealing this wicked deed to the city, saying it would disrupt our unity when we had enemies pressing us at all times. Men always claim there are enemies, even in times of peace, to hold onto their power.

Then Lugul-Aya told me her story of her thirst for justice. Having been only female, she had been denied her father's throne. That he felt he could give it away when my father had told me that most cities chose their kings by vote seemed the height of arrogance to me, and it was: later, his son, trying to take his position, had been cast out, and a trader who had arranged a lucrative agreement with two other cities had been elected by the populace.

She had tried to content herself with the thought of marrying a rich man or great warrior, guiding them with her wisdom, which she said far outshone her brother's, and Mammetum agreed, as did Shag-ad, though I was too young to know of what they were speaking beyond the words of my deceased parents and brother when they spoke of village matters. Then her father had declared that she should serve the entire city in the Temple. He had arranged, she believed, for the High Priest to claim he saw visions that said Ninhursag called for a priestess. Shouldn't she be content to serve the mother of all instead of becoming one herself?

Through her own cunning she had outlived that priest and convinced the king and new High Priest that Nanna was truly calling to her. You see, she loved to do her planning at night when others slept. I didn't know if this was the will of the gods or her own pride, but having faced them, I could not risk Nanna's blessings to me by casting out one who claimed to be his chosen.

After I took her life and channeled it back, she drank down one of the novices my first seduced for her while my second spun sleep in the minds of the others. She gave me a necklace of rare amber and bracelets of fine metal for her sisters, and then she took us into her chambers and gave us a new home that did not end my longing for the farm and my family, though I pretended it did.

With her new powers, Lugul-Aya quickly gained control of the Temple. Her drive caused desires in my first two, and soon each of them had several servants to protect and comfort them. I reminded them of my family and my goal, and they remembered their obligations, turning their mind to others who could aid us.


I did not like Enmul from the moment I first saw him. I never liked him, but my first told me that a mother cannot like all her children; she must only love them and try to guide them as best she can and use them as they should be. Being a mother is difficult, and being the Ummum more so, but it took me centuries to realize I hated it so. In no small part it is because of his children that I felt this way, though I do not feel that way now.

After a few nights, Lugul-Aya told me that her spies had learned that a great warrior had finally been cast out from the city's militia and had been hanging around the fields, wells and even Temple grounds, declaring the injustice of it all to any who would listen. My brother had spoken of becoming a city guard, though my father told him a surer livelihood was to follow in his footsteps. We do not have open conflicts with many other cities, but when we do, those who guard us are seen as the best of all men for a few weeks, until memories fade.

Shag-ad grew a bit pale when we learned this rejected warrior's name, Enmul, but she would only tell me that he was an exceptionally strong man with a temper. Mammetum said he was unmarried; she had only heard of his anger when those who were caught on the wrong side of his fist or dagger came to her for aid. This was before I learned I could search the minds of others so easily. Had I known, had I done it, I would never have ventured out to meet with this warrior in Lugul-Aya's company. The gods had claimed I'd choose wisely; perhaps I wasn't choosing as much as being guided by the adults I had changed. To consider that the gods were wrong or lied – let the new philosophers make such claims; I dare not.

Amar took me aside and told me that he had heard of this man, that he was so overcome with rage during battle that he did unspeakable things to the bodies of those he killed, even if he left them in pieces during the battle. I asked him how he knew, and he said that in the slave quarters of the Temple's pottery production center he had heard tales at night when they were left to themselves. I dismissed them as mere servile rumors and didn't trust my first wardum as I should have. I was young, I made mistakes, and I make no claim otherwise.

Enmul was a mountain of a man – even though my father seemed large to me, this man could have carried him as if he were a child. He recognized the High Priestess and stepped forward but did not bow, and I felt anger flash from Lugul-Aya, though she merely smiled and asked him to come inside with her to explain his grievance. He agreed with a cold smile and followed us into her private quarters, where my first two damu and my wardum watched hidden behind a curtain.

He told us of the last venture the city militia had made into the territory of another city not more than two days from here. The attack had been in retaliation against thieves from that city who had been raiding our grain supplies when the Temple said that a famine might be coming this season. The entire city, including the women and children, had come out of their gates to protest the appearance of our men and to refuse to engage in honorable battle or hand over the thieves. Enmul wanted to rush into the city and find the criminals, but he wasn't in charge; he told us he had been unjustly denied promotion for years now because the others were jealous of his prowess in combat. Again, I wasn't sure if this was the truth or merely pride speaking, but not knowing much about it, I simply sat on Lugul-Aya's lap and listened.

The captain in charge of his unit had agreed to meet with the city's council of elders and their king to discuss the charges. Enmul was ignored when he pointed out that going alone would be suicide, and he told us with a wide smile that he was proven correct when the captain's body was tossed over the locked city walls the next day. The entire guard then went mad, he claimed; all of them rushed the gates and began climbing, taking the city by enough surprise that more than half of them made it inside to exact their revenge.

Enmul claimed he had done nothing worse than any other guard, killing any man he encountered and taking the women when there was time. At this Lugul-Aya put her hands over my ears, and he laughed, saying it was hardly a topic for a girl to hear. Instead, she turned his story to those whom he felt most wronged by. One of the guards sounded like one of those who had come to my family's farm, and I slipped off her lap to look him in the eyes.

"They are bad men; they have no honor," I told him, and he nodded, slack-jawed and silent for the first time. I told him my story, and he continued to nod silently until I finished. Glancing at the High Priestess, he knelt in front of me and offered me his life. As I took it, it felt sour in my mouth, but I called him back again with my own blood at Lugul-Aya's urging.

Then he took the novice he was offered and sated his hunger before turning eyes burning with rage toward us. "Let us slaughter this entire city," he whispered, and behind him my damu and wardum stepped forward, crying out that I should listen to their words. The desire for vengeance is great – let none say I do not understand – and so we went to the house of this other warrior who had wronged him.

There I saw firsthand the crimes that Enmul committed as he took not only that man's life but his wife's and son's, ripping them to pieces, tearing off their flesh with his teeth, and crushing their bones underneath his feet before my shocked eyes. Only the other three stopped him before he could move on to the next house.

We went to the Temple, but soon the city dwellers came with torches and weapons, demanding he appear, for the city guards had seen him talking to the High Priestess and going inside earlier. As the crowds grew and grew, we knew those inside were firmly bonded to us and would not turn us in, but they threatened those who ventured outside, and so upon Mammetum's wise words we left and returned to my family farm.

As we waited quietly through the night, some of the wardum gathered information. They returned to us the next night to report that the city was on high guard now, convinced that a monster had been unleashed upon it. I cried for the first time in weeks then and let Amar comfort me as a father does a daughter, but I knew he was not my father, and it made me weep more.

The monster did not recognize my authority unless I used my will to force him; this unsettled the others, as did our exile, away from the markets and easy food for us and our servants. My first tried to soothe him, to control his rage, but he was able to resist her in ways no other man or woman could. My second talked with him, did a reading of his mind, and turned from him in disgust. My third attempted to use her words and those of the gods to control him, but he only grinned and agreed to bide his time until we had a plan to find the others we wished to kill. Our plans, though, he would not listen to, because we were "just women," and of course he would not listen to our slaves, though some held good positions in the city where some returned every day to learn all they could.

That is why we went looking for another man.

The problem was with the men we found. The ones my first found were men of passion and wealth, frankly too well off in the world to care much about revenge. The ones my second found were the occasional slave who was hoping for revenge against his master, but primarily she interacted with women, more so every night, it seemed. The ones my third found were also too connected, too well-to-do, and frankly already enslaved to her, so I rejected them all after she tried to bring one to our place and he lay stone dead on the floor of her room. That was when we knew that there would forever be this division between those who command the night and those who serve in it. I won't go further than to say that the ones my fourth found were unsuitable on all counts.

I ordered all my children to refrain from creating more of our kind or more servants until I gave them permission. I think they were frustrated that when I wished to, my will overcame their own, but I knew my words would be heeded.

We were three nights without a suggestion for a fifth dami to join my first four children, when Amar came to me saying that he had found a man clutching a heavy bag lying on the side of the road. I thought perhaps this would be my meal tonight, so I went out to see him.

The man was dressed in clothes that might once have been of quality, though now they were dirty and torn. The bag he held tightly to his body was bloodstained, and I could tell it was his own blood as well as that of two others. The bag itself was torn, and a tablet was sticking out of it. I had seen tablets in the tax collector's possessions, so I thought this might be one such agent of a city – but not ours; my father had known all such men, and I had seen them when we went into the

21

city and they greeted him. Thinking of that made me pause so I could control myself.

When I got closer, I could see the man was still alive; his heart was beating slowly, but bruises were developing on his body. "I'm thinking bandits, Bel," Amar explained as he knelt across from where I was crouching to examine everything.

"A man who isn't from here will have no loyalties to anyone else," I added with a smile.

"A man made of sticks and bones," Amar pointed out, lifting one thin arm, and causing the man to stir. "If he can count, keep records, read and write, he might serve well as another servant; your children have too many," he said with unhidden hostility. "He can't help you hold your place, Bel, not in this shape."

I said nothing, but my mind was busy. I simply stood up and ordered my slave to carry him home, then to tend to his wounds and give him food and drink. I took the bag, though the man clutched at it desperately, whispering that the gods had given it to him. I carefully laid it aside, easing his fears with gentle words like those my mother and Shag-ad said to comfort me. I couldn't read his tablets; that was a skill he would teach me later.

The next night, the man could talk a bit, and Amar reported he had eaten a bit and asked for his bag, but he had convinced him to simply lie still and be cared for until the lady of the house awoke. Now cleaned and half sitting up, I could see the man more clearly. He was not as old or as young as my others; he was thin, and his fingers were worn, as though he had done much delicate work with them. His eyes were still lively, though he narrowed them and had to lean in to see me clearly. When he did, he sat back and ran his hands over his head, only to frown when he discovered it was covered with stubble and not clean-shaven, as I guessed it usually was. This led him to frown at the growth of beard on his face, and finally he sighed, exhausted, and stared at me.

"My servant found you," I told him. "We brought you here; it isn't much, but we hope you are feeling better."

He smiled slightly. "Kindness from one so young in such a wretched world is rare to find," he said, and it sounded like a phrase he had learned and repeated, since it was said without emotion.

22

"When you feel better, you can tell us what happened," I said simply as I stood up, intent on finding dinner for the night and leaving Amar and him behind.

"Please, child, where are my tablets?" the man asked.

"Tablets? Ah, the things in your bag?" At his nod I picked them up, and he gaped in amazement that I could carry them so easily. I laid the bag by his side, and he opened it and counted out the tablets inside with a look of deep concern until he sighed again. "Thank you, thank you," he said, now with emotion in his voice and written on his face as he looked at both Amar and me. "You saved them."

"What are they?" I asked, hoping he might tell us his story now, so that I could decide to go out and find food or stay in and eat.

"The Truth," he said, and his eyes lit up. "This is the real Truth, of everything," he added when Amar looked at me in disbelief. "About it all, the creation of the world, the flood, the recreation, all of it."

"The Temple tells us all of this," I point out, sitting back down with a smile, knowing that he will be my meal and not a servant with such odd and dangerous ideas.

"No, no, this is the Truth; they do not know it," he insisted.

"How do you know it?" Amar cut in, then looked away when he realized he was speaking out of turn. I put my hand on his, for, as you know, I have never been one for strict formalities. Any decent servant who pretends to be my father in the mortal world must be allowed to speak his mind, or he is useless to me.

The man didn't seem concerned with protocols either as he smiled. "He told me. Ziusudra told me himself. I found him years ago and have been his student. He sent me out with history because, he said, a new race blessed and cursed by the gods had arisen, and they would need to know the Truth."

Another one who claimed to be sent by the gods! My head started to ache as I tried to reason out how likely this all was. "Why are you so special? Who are you?" I spat out, my voice quaking with fear.

"I am called Shulpae, and my teacher sent me here to find the first of them, a woman named Ningai," he said. Amar drew in his breath sharply, causing the man's sharp but short-sighted eyes to look at him.

"You know this name? It is unusual, and the people of other cities say a man of some importance here may have a daughter by that name."

I started to cry then, blood dripping from my eyes, making the scholar move closer to see what was happening as Amar scurried to my side and held me. Through my tears I told him my story. At first, he did not believe me, and he asked me questions about the gods. When I told him of their mien and form, their words and power, he believed. I did not ask of him further but simply slid onto his lap and had my dinner before calling him back to do the will of his new mother.

Vengeance sounds good.

With my five promised children created and strong in their own ways after a full turning of the moon, I got my vengeance. But whether they killed only the men who came to my father's farm that night or also others who tried to help them, I felt no less lost and cold inside. I was still without true father or mother, brother, or sister.

We stayed in this city, whose name is now lost to the past, for many years. Each of my children created their own, and those in turn created their own. I could never bring myself to try again to stay in the palace my damu had built for me on the old farm. I took no other wardum until Amar died – in an accident, I was told – but I knew, I knew then, that Enmul was not content to answer to a mere girl.

With my fifth's help I got my evidence, and I judged him harshly, casting him and his children out of the city, with a curse called down using the words Lugul-Aya supplied me and the gestures Mammetum taught me. They behave as monsters, so monsters they would be, infecting any they drank from and forbidden to make any more brethren on pain of death from the others.

For many years, my other children and their creations lived in harmony in our city. Other cities sent us tributes of fine men and women, of sheep and goats, of grain and cloth, of the finest stones and metals. We ruled all of the night, but the gods do not like the pride of once-mortals, and they cast us out of our own Eden.

The plague which drove us into this hidden kingdom came in the form of Xul, for how they behaved became how they were known. Enmul returned, his children more numerous than shoots of grain during a plentiful year. My curse had to be carried out, and so my children and their children attacked.

Those who survived scattered, huddled in the wagons of their slaves, while I stood still at the center, grasping my fourth's head as it turned to ashes in my hand. A mother should never have to kill her own, but as he cut down the last of his sisters, his brother long since turned to ashes by the hordes, I had no choice but to reach for my scythe of bronze.

I began to plan for a time when my descendants would calm down. I would find those who could see me for what I am, who could stand beside me, who would be what I've lost, what has been taken from me time and again.

*I pause in my telling to look at Enki perched upon the wall. I change the pattern again by saying, "But I was not alone on my quest; I had help from my greatest ally."*

Eckhart

# Day

# Day Unto Night

# Reviving Smoke

The thick gray smoke rose in an appropriately solid column above the offering of lamb and fish; the vapors from the boiling bowl of wine mixed with it but did little to dampen the smell of burning flesh on the breeze through the *ambulation*, the ornamental garden at the center of the villa I was currently residing in. Millennia of performing this sacrifice meant that I could feel pleased and reasonably certain that my God was as well, but my wardum Vibia's dark brown eyes showed confusion when I turned to her.

"This is a very unusual sacrifice, Domina," she said to me for perhaps the twelfth time this night. As I had discovered over my century among them, Romans were particularly difficult people to make blood-bound servants. Their pride and belief in their divine right to rule wasn't entirely new to one who has crossed as many kingdoms, empires, and peoples as I have in thousands of years. But they lacked a good appreciation of us, the Akhkharu, or *lamia* as they call us, thinking us merely spirits instead of flesh-and-blood creatures they should truly fear.

I should have been more forgiving, considering that she had not been with me long when she criticized my ritual. I should have been more understanding, given her background as one of the most powerful female religious figures in Rome. I should have realized that she saw a child kneeling by this offering, rather than the mother of all my people, trapped for what had already been almost three millennia in this body.

29

But I was too frustrated, because lately, every time I had tried to rescue another of my kind, saving the last shreds of her humanity before she became something else, something violent and sinister, I had been too late. We have souls, but they can be so easily and thoroughly corrupted that sometimes there is nothing worth saving. For some reason, the last one had been particularly painful for me. Like those who had voted for him I had believed his lies, until I found his dungeon and was forced to stake him through the heart. I will always pay for the foolish decisions of my first year as Akhkharu by continuing to fail at making a family for myself to live with me for eternity. But that doesn't mean I won't keep trying. Enki promised me my family, so I must keep trying. Mothers can be very single-minded, and children even more so, and I'm the worst of both.

When I frowned, displaying just the tips of my fangs, she paled, scooted back, and bent to the ground. "I am sorry to question you, Goddess," she whispered.

"Goddess?"

I looked up to see my God standing on my other side, so I quickly bowed to the Earth, but he only chuckled, sending drops of water out to land on me and the ground around me, causing sparks to rise from the fire into the smoke. "My Lord Enki, I am honored you came," I stated, using the old language that even I barely understood then, after so many years of not hearing it.

Enki just waved one hand, frowning, and waving it more as the toga he was wearing got in his way. "Never again will I accept anything from this damned people. So many villas burning, though, that we were all drawn like flies," he mused with a twinkle in his eyes. He told me once that he is the reason why we make burnt offerings, drawing upon the advice he gave to old Ziusudra, whom he saved from the Great Flood back before my mortal father was born, or his father, or his father's father.

I nodded and rose to my feet when bidden, my wardum rising with me. "From Sicily?" I asked politely.

My God nodded and then tilted his head, his eyes resting on my newest blood-slave. "Indeed, the Sicilians are having another bout of slave rebellions. But who is this?"

I believed it was an unnecessary question, but I answered anyway. "My Lord, this is Vibia. She simply goes by Vibia," I added when he arched an eyebrow. Roman females may have had fewer names than their males, but normally she would have had a marker for her family. She had told me that her false conviction for sexual misconduct had brought disgrace upon them all and begged me not to make her tell me their cognomen, though I could have guessed it from her first name had I cared to.

"A bit young to be a mother figure, isn't she?" Enki said as he moved to take hold of her chin and look more closely at her. I saw the water drip from his hand onto her chest, which heaved in fear.

"Domina, I do not know how to respond to your nephew's presence," she stated, too afraid to look away, if I read her pounding blood correctly.

At her words, my God stepped back, laughing out loud for a few seconds before bending his face near hers. "Who do you think I am, slave?"

"Mercury," she replied softly, her eyes searching for mine.

"Leave us now, Vibia. I wish to speak with my nephew alone," I said out loud so that He could hear the words.

"Oh – Vesta, that makes sense now, given her clothes," my God muttered softly as she left us to wait behind the wall that separated this *ambulation* from the rest of the villa, where we would stay the entire day until it was safe to come out that evening. "You hardly look the part of that incarnation," he added.

Once we were alone, I motioned to a seat I had brought outside for Him. "My Lord, if you please, I have questions."

"That's all you ever call me for, child. I would appreciate offerings for other reasons," he said with a smile, but I could see the coldness behind his watery eyes.

I quickly bowed down, rising only upon his word. I never forget what he is, no matter how many guises he may take on. "I shall try to do better, my Lord."

"I'm teasing, little one." I just looked back at him silently until he sighed, "You are too old for your age."

31

I would have rolled my eyes at such a comment, given what he had just said about comparing me to Vesta, but instead I pressed on with my question. "I think I am tired of this world, my Lord?"

His normally serene face clouded, then he sighed. "Have you lost your faith in me, little one?"

"Not in you, my Lord; in myself. I can barely choose a good servant; how can I find a good family?"

Enki was still for a few moments, then he stood up, water rushing beneath him, pouring over walking stones and into the plants. "Let me evaluate this Vibia, then, and offer you advice you must heed."

Vibia came to me when I called her through the bubussunu that I fed her regularly from my wrist. She came and looked at Enki warily for a moment but stood still when commanded. While not born a slave, they had been part of her life, so she knew what to do even if it grated against her personality.

"She looks a bit like you; real blonde hair is very odd for these Romans," Enki stated, and I saw Vibia stiffen. Rumors of her paternity had haunted her since her birth but being chosen to serve the temple had freed her family of that shame. Unfortunately, the rumors had arisen once more when she had been accused and cast down into a living grave as an example for her sisters and the world. I'd found her in that grave, pulled her up, and healed her, and all I asked in return was that she be as a big sister to me.

"You chose those who have fallen onto hard times, who are not much older than you, whom you think can love you as a mother or a brother might," Enki stated as he ran his cool damp hand over her face and down to her neck. "You need to pick one who has the experience to be a parent, not a playmate, not a slave," he finished.

I flinched as he snapped her neck and let her body slide to the floor. I couldn't move; I couldn't look at him until he was crouching down in front of me, his eyes like swirling pools staring into mine. "I will find a better one. Stay here until I return."

I hid myself inside the villa for many nights, feeding on the slaves only as much as I needed, knowing that, if my Lord did not return soon, eventually I'd need to move on without an adult to navigate Rome properly. But it was the hot season, and many of the wealthiest citizens

32

were away, leaving only the weak, the infirm, and the necessary behind. Since I was content to leave the slaves to their own desires during the daylight, they proved reliable if quiet in the evenings.

I was sitting with some of the maids weaving when one of the slaves entered, announcing that my uncle had arrived to care for me. I didn't have a proper majordomo; he had gone with the family to their country villa, but the doorman had stayed, chained to the door, and the younger butlers with nothing to do now took turns keeping him company.

I stood up, prepared to fight if the family of those who really owned the villa had come, when a finely dressed gentleman with oiled black hair and liquid eyes entered. I felt my knees start to bend, but he rushed forward and took me in his arms. "Oh, my niece, I came as soon as I could. I am so sorry your illness prevented you from traveling this summer."

I looked into my Lord's eyes and nodded. Enki had returned to me, and I had been foolish enough to fear he might not.

"Are you well? Are these slaves treating you as befits a Roman?" he asked, casting his gaze about as the maids and the boy who had introduced him all stood, their hands clasped in front of them, bowing their heads. While I, a child, might be easy to appease, this nobleman who claimed to be their master's brother was a large man, and I could see from his dress and his form that he presented himself as a man who knew military service. Here was someone they should fear. I wondered if my Lord might not be in the form of the man he was claiming to be. I saw only Enki in different clothes and with an odd hairstyle, probably because he wished me to know his game, but perhaps the slaves saw a more complete disguise.

"I am well, Uncle; please do sit down. Fetch us wine!" I instructed, sending the slaves scurrying out of the room and leaving us in peace.

Enki still held me but released me enough to look into my eyes. "Inna would be pleased with your actions, little one. You have held on to this villa despite your fragile form." He sat me down in one of the chairs and took the sole couch in the room to recline upon, as is proper only for the men in such a household.

When the slaves returned, he made up stories, or perhaps they were the truth, about the girl I was pretending to be, her father, mother, brother, and elder sister, who were relaxing, though bored, he added, with country life. The slaves moved in and out with wine, figs, cheese, bread, and some poultry quickly prepared for him. Several stood around the room awaiting our pleasure, but, of course, this merely prevented true conversation.

When my eyes started to droop as the sun rose outside, my "uncle" picked me up and declared he would see me to bed. I could see and hear the maids reacting to this, but he merely ignored them and carried me to the room I had taken from the previous inhabitant, since the windows were covered in wooden shutters and heavy curtains, unlike any other room in the house. "I will inspect things during the day," Enki called out, and that caused another stir among the household, who knew their freeloading daylight hours were at an end.

I must have been asleep because I recall hearing his voice. "Wake up, little one. You don't need to sleep; it's just habit, one I need you to break right now for me."

He was crouching and looking at me when I opened my eyes. "There you go, little one. Now stay there," he commanded as he went to the door. He raised his hand and outlined the frame, causing a layer of water to appear and cover the wood. "That will give us more privacy."

I nodded silently and gave him my attention.

Enki looked directly into my eyes. "I have found you a suitable wardum, an arammu-wardum, someone who can offer you the love that you seek," he said.

I stood up, but my Lord simply pulled me back to my bed to sit next to him. "Not yet; she has duties to finish, and then you may claim her."

In three nights, my Lord had tired of playing with the slaves, and we had found our way to the Temple of Vesta, which I had avoided since rescuing Vibia. For all their claims of sanctity and their focus on the Holy Flame, the Temple was busy much of the time with the most mundane matters, citizens sending messages to and from it at all hours of the night and, I assume, of the day.

Their leader, the Virgo Vestalis Maxima, was in her 50s, having decided to remain in the service of her goddess rather than accept a wealthy marriage, though as we watched over the course of a week, she received one such offer, to which she commanded her secretary to respond in the usual fashion.

I get bored easily; call it the remnants of my youth. I should have thought that Enki would become bored, but perhaps he did things more interesting than mere spying when he hid me away during the daylight and went about as a priestess after tying her up for me to feed from when I awoke. He told me little, and I was starting to debate questioning him when he shifted from Vestal into what I recognized as a Mercury guise and told me to hurry but be quiet.

"The Maxima is about to indoctrinate a novice into the ranks of priestess. A replacement for Vibia, I heard, one Maria Aemilia, age 19, so a bit older than the previous one, and apparently well trained in the rules of what not to do, if you catch my meaning. This will also free up the Maxima herself," he added with a smile.

We watched the formal ceremony from the shadows, sending my former meal out to stand in her place, looking a bit dazed but completely unaware of what had happened over the past week. The Pontifex Maximus performed the rites in unison with the Maxima. After this the Pontifex Maximus left immediately, for even he should not be inside the most sacred space without a valid reason.

After some time of congratulations among the sisters over the promotion of Maria, the Maxima told everyone to return to their duties and retired to her private chamber.

We watched her do her evening prayers and then sit to read, but the scroll could not hold her attention, and soon she was gazing out into the night. She was an impressive woman – age had not bent her; her black hair was braided in the traditional form, with only a crown-like band of silvery gray to mark her age at a distance.

Enki took me by the hand and pulled me through the door, announcing loudly, "You do not seem like a woman who is content to stay here in service to a minor goddess."

The Maxima stood up swiftly and turned her gaze to us, one hand at her throat, the other on the back of her chair as she moved to put it between her and us. "Men are not allowed here!"

"I'm not a man," Enki said as he stepped forward and took a pose to display his winged shoes and hat for her. He stood there as she glared at him for a few moments. "You aren't quite sure, that's refreshing," he exclaimed with a stomp of his foot and called up a tiny pool of water under him.

"And not Mercury, either," the Maxima pointed out.

I stood there until my Lord pulled me alongside her. "What do you see when you look at this child?"

The Maxima blinked at me. I had not clouded her mind in any fashion, leaving her to see me for what I was. I had been too shocked by Enki's actions to do much. "Some child you have abducted, no doubt," she spat.

He tilted his head to one side, sending droplets spraying over us, but was silent for a few moments. "I'm called Enki by this child here; she is called Ningai. I am a god, or deity, or force of nature; I'm not that picky about it. She is unique, the first of the *Akhkharu*, the embodiment of every child who's lost her family, you could say."

"What kind of word is *Akhkharu*?"

"Old, much older than your Latin."

They stared at each other for many minutes until my Lord bade me leave them to talk as adults. Even though it annoyed me to be dismissed again because of my form, I scurried from the room to wait in the hall outside her doors.

I waited for some time, and then the doors opened, and the Maxima stepped out. I glanced around her but saw only the emptiness. "What have you done?" I asked her in the firmest voice I could manage, but if she could cast out my Lord, what power could I use against her?

The Maxima knelt down and loosened her *palla*, letting it fall to the floor. "I've made a deal with your gods. I will leave my position here and devote myself to you, and in exchange they will offer Rome aid in these wars against the slaves, promising that the sacred flame will burn for at least four more centuries."

She knelt down and turned her head so that her neck was exposed. "Your god explained your life to me, and it is a terrible wrong which has been done to you, Ningai. I cannot have a child of my own, but I see that I have been prepared by my own goddess to care for you."

I frowned but stepped closer and took what she offered, hearing her gasp in pleasure as I sank my teeth in, letting her hand grip my arms as I searched through her most recent memories. She was telling the truth.

"If you are willing to pledge an oath to me, to make a Tamu, I will take you as my wardum. The aches you have now will disappear, and you shall move as though you were young once more. What is your name?"

"I am Statillia Galbaea, and I am the last of my father's line. I willingly give myself to you."

"Then drink from me, and become more than what you are," I replied.

Soon she looked at me with clearer eyes from a face with plumper flesh and smoother skin. "It will take some time, Domina, for me to resign my position here, but I am told you have a home to stay in and that your uncle is waiting for you outside."

"Come to me as soon as you can, Arammu-Wardum," I told her with a huge smile that she returned after a moment of hesitation.

With much greater ease she knelt down and took me into her arms. "I shall protect you as best I can," she promised.

"Help me find my family again; that is all I truly need."

Statillia helped me for many, many centuries, becoming like a mother to me until the daytime took her away.

*I stop and look over my people, all watching me with rapt attention. "We'll go in order, shall we?"*

*I turn my gaze to Enki on the wall, who has sat up, a grin coming over his face, and he nods vigorously at me.*

*I turn my gaze to the oldest of the family leaders, the Belum of the Gelal, who only turns away in a coquettish fashion that I know is part game and part truth. "No?" I ask, then look to her servant standing by her side, her damu looking up at her expectantly.*

"I am not a man of great words," he begs, another half-truth which is not surprising.

"Bard?" I turn to him.

He nods and comes forward, one hand pushing back his white hair. "I will tell you the story that I heard from Lucien many times."

# Courtesan

The two officers strolled through Cairo as though they owned the place. Indeed, the locals often acted as though they did by offering them the "best goods" their little shops had. Silly Europeans often didn't pay much attention to the fact that the prices suddenly were at least twice what that same shopkeeper charged his neighbor.

The younger of the two officers was leading his elder to a well-laid-out villa near the edge of the main markets. "I'm telling you, Sir, this is the finest establishment this horrid city can offer. Not the quality of Paris, but you won't forget her girls."

Lucien Gaudreau followed his junior officer but was frowning. Most military men took pleasure where they could. One never knew when one's time might be up, after all. French women seemed content to forgive their husbands these field indiscretions as long as their honor was maintained, and their families supported. To be honest, Lucien had no wife, and his children were all in the hands of relatives; he had no one's honor to protect except his own, and he wasn't sure frequenting a brothel was an honorable thing for an officer in Napoleon's army to be doing, even on his free time.

Yet he followed the younger officer inside the villa. Its opulence was surprising in and of itself, given its location and external façade. Their army had been liberating and saving Egypt's ancient treasures from the Muhammadans who might destroy them, but here in this building was some of the finest art he had seen since arriving at the Nile almost three months ago.

"Welcome to Isis' Throne, gentlemen," a lovely female voice in broken French greeted them. The voice's owner was a petite girl with a fine silver collar around her neck, a low-cut blouse that barely covered her feminine charms and an almost sheer skirt that rode low on her swinging hips as she crossed to them. "Are you here for pleasure?"

"We are," Francis replied before Lucien could. He'd just follow the experienced man's lead this time and see what happened.

Soon he was in an upper room, which was surprisingly cool given the devilish nature of the environment here. A beautiful but small-breasted woman greeted him and helped him out of his boots and coat, but then stopped and merely motioned for him to sit while she poured a drink.

He continued to sit while she cooked them dinner and served it. They ate as she attempted to converse in French, so he tried to use a few words he knew in the native tongue, and they both soon fell into laughter. After a good meal, he let her lay him down on some soft pillows and dance for his amusement, baring her attractive form to his eyes as his manhood awoke. Then she insisted on doing all of the work by straddling his hips and taking him deep into her.

Lucien slept and wondered why he had thought this was a bad idea in the first place.

Thus, it continued for a few months. Normally he got the same girl, called Nenet, but occasionally he tried others. The routine was the same each time. Basic comfort, a drink, a meal, dancing, then sex and sleep, with a light break of the fast in the morning before he headed back to his quarters. While some men might have found it boring, to Lucien it was reassuring; it felt like home, and he asked to meet the Madame in charge.

At first his girls – he was starting to think of them as "his" – told him it was impossible to make an appointment. Madame Maha – at least he got her name – was too busy. The Emperor didn't seem interested in leaving any time soon, so Lucien informed them that he would schedule an appointment at her convenience; he'd even return early in the day. That only earned a firm shake of the head, and the girls would focus on skills that no decent European woman could possibly know. When he again insisted on meeting her, at night, if necessary, they'd tell him that then they'd have to take another client, and he might lose his claims to their time. Ridiculous, since he was seeing only Nenet regularly, and the only regulars to frequent the place seemed to be foreign soldiers, he was noticing.

After a week of arguing – what type of prostitute dared argue with a client, anyway? – Lucien was literally marching through the streets much later than normal toward the brothel. He'd debated going back, and after a few days he found he was drawn there like a moth to a flame. They were probably using witchcraft on him and his fellow officers because none of them could stop going back again and again. The only way to know for certain was to see this Madame Maha for himself.

Thus, there he was, marching down the street in his dress uniform, a bag of coin hidden away, and his purpose firm. He would approach her calmly, valuing her time as a businesswoman, and if that didn't happen, he had his position as one of the Emperor's best to back up his demands for answers.

"How about this one, my precious?" a woman's voice in English drew his attention to a booth that was selling trinkets nearby. He'd learned the barbaric language under protest, to help him during his campaigns, but here it thoroughly shocked him. He paused and looked at a grandmother and her granddaughter, both in native garb, their hair covered but their skin the porcelain one would expect from the upper classes in any civilized city. The little girl turned pale blue eyes to him, which she narrowed, then turned back to her grandmother who had directed her cool gaze upon him as well.

A knot was suddenly forming in Lucien's stomach; there was something odd about those two, but he swallowed the fear and pushed on toward the brothel.

He waved away Nenet, who cursed him in some uncivilized tongue that didn't sound like the chatter he heard in the markets. He waved off every girl who tried to get into his path as he made his way to the one room in the brothel that he knew was the Madame's. Straightening his jacket and holding his hat under one arm, he knocked three times and then waited.

After a few moments of silence, he knocked again. He was about to knock a third time when the door opened to reveal the most unexpected sight he had ever seen. She wasn't as young as her girls, but her jewelry and fabrics clearly showed she controlled the money, although she was probably no more than twenty years old herself. Her face looked young, but the dark eyes that stared back at him were serious and devoid of any emotion. "Monsieur, what do you want? Are my girls not pleasing to you?" she asked, her voice rolling over him, deep and soft, like the finest sweets he could imagine coupled with the most delightful vintage he'd ever had.

Lucien's eyes glanced up and down her form as she moved more fully into the doorframe. She was short, coming barely to his chest, and yet her presence was almost overwhelming. She was ample, full bosomed and hipped, yet her waist was narrow, her feminine charms flowing like the Nile. Her skin was like the light caramel sauces his grandmother used to make for holidays. Her long, straight black hair was braided and fell over one shoulder to tease the edge of one breast. Words other than those he had rehearsed rushed to his lips, but he bit his tongue before replying. "Madame Maha, it is an honor to meet you. I wanted to thank you in person for your ladies' charms and to express the gratitude of the Emperor for entertaining his officers so well." That last part was a lie, because the ruler in question had eyes only for his dove, who pined for him back home though his sword sought many scabbards. He frankly didn't care what his officers did when they were not on the field of battle.

"As long as they have coin, we will comfort," she said and started to shut the door. She frowned when he put one foot and leg in the way, saying, "Monsieur, you presume too much."

"I have abundant coin. I was hoping I might speak with you more this evening," he began, but her displeasure only creased her face further.

"I am not for sale," she said, and with a strength that surprised him pushed him from her door and shut it.

Lucien stood there dumbfounded for several minutes. He raised his hand to knock again and then lowered it when his stomach knotted much like it had out on the street when that strange girl and her grandmother had looked at him. Unsure what to do, he wandered back to the main floor, but none of the girls were willing to take his coin that night.

Or the next, or the night after that, for a full week, until Nenet came to him with a sad smile. "You want her, not us, not really, not now," she told him simply, then walked away.

He stood there, the several days' beard on his face, unshined boots, and unbuttoned uniform jacket all bearing silent testament to what she had said. Lucien closed his eyes and prayed that he could walk away, but he found himself soon in front of her door again. As soon as his fist touched the door it opened wide to a surprisingly simple yet elegant room.

Entering, he saw that it was unlike the rooms below. No oven or cooking cubicle, no low table with cushions, just a big bed that looked European and out of place in Cairo. Low candles burned in the room, casting shadows about because there was no light, even though the moon outside was full, because the only window was a small high one that would only allow the sun to shine through onto a wall opposite the bed.

He didn't see her anywhere, but her voice reached him from the shadows. "Take off all your clothes," she ordered. It was an order unlike any he had ever received from a woman, most of whom were generally content to let him direct the action or, like the prostitutes below, to take action without words. It didn't feel right to obey, and yet he found his hat falling to the floor and his jacket soon after it.

When he was as God had created him, he started to turn around but found his body pressed by another cool, feminine form, her unnaturally strong arms wrapped around him, pinning his arms to his sides. "You come to me with coin?"

"No, no, no coin. I would not insult you so, Madame," he replied.

Her laughter sent a thrill up his spine as she released him. "I entertain for pleasure only," she stated, her voice suddenly coming from a distance. "Come to me."

He turned and saw her reclining on the bed, her full form laid out as though she were a queen or a goddess. Without concern for his immortal soul, Lucien came and knelt down to gaze upon her. "You are so lovely, beyond the words a mere soldier can express," he whispered.

"I have heard even great kings say this." She giggled again and pulled him up to her. Compared to those whom she employed there was no doubt that she was the most skilled, the most gracious and the loveliest. All thoughts fled his mind, his body reacting to her slightest touch, and his soul became the least of his concerns as she took her pleasure with him over and over. It was ludicrous – he seemed exhausted, and yet, at the end of the night she turned and made him rise again, mixing sharp pain with stark pleasure.

Lucien looked at the sun rising over the markets. He was never here this early. Normally he slept in until a good breakfast was served. He frowned and turned around. The brothel was right there, but as he took a step toward it, he froze. He was to return in two nights' time and not before, he knew. Why was that?

No answer came his way as he obeyed the unknown instructions and soon found himself back at camp, where his men taunted him for riding too hard that night, and he merely smiled and went to his tent.

She never told him anything about herself beyond vague ridiculous statements that suggested she had pleased entire kingdoms worth of dignitaries. She never asked him about himself either but merely used him for her own amusement. He received pleasure as well, but it was as though he had become her woman and she, his man. He was musing about this on one of the evenings he could not visit her and thus dreading a night alone – he still wasn't sure why he couldn't see her every night – when his personal assistant came into his tent.

The man had become rather vocal about his distrust for this woman Lucien had been visiting, claiming that Lucien was growing paler and thinner with each visit, and Lucien was about to tell the man off again when his assistant fell into the tent flat on his face. Jumping to his feet he gasped as the Madame walked through the flaps, her entire body smeared with something red. "What in God's name?" he said as he watched a pool of equally red fluid spread on the ground around his assistant's head.

She spat on the ground and stalked to him, gripping his wrist in one claw-like hand. "Gods demand our own justice," she tossed out, and then dragged him from the tent in his nightshirt.

The camp was devoid of all except a few other bodies, he found as they marched through it. He tried to demand an answer, but her growls and jerking on his arm stripped him of the will to do more than follow. The city was quiet, and not even the late-night stalls were open as she led them back to the brothel. As they passed by a fountain, though, he turned to find a pair of pale blue eyes looking at him until he was too far away to see them in the darkness.

Lucien froze as they entered the brothel, and the hanging body of one of his other officers met his eyes. The man was naked, his torso mutilated, and the whores were gathered around weeping, though not for him, he discovered, as his eyes fell on a couch at the center of the atrium and on the body of a young girl laid out upon it, her neck at an odd angle and her face unnaturally bluish.

"He was under your command, yes?" Madame demanded as she turned to glare at him. Any beauty he might have seen in her was gone, replaced by a monstrous sight beyond his comprehension. Two of her teeth were extended from her mouth, her eyes were literally glowing with fire, and her nails, usually so well groomed, were like talons.

He looked up and swallowed, then shuddered at her repeated question. "Yes, yes, Madame, he was one of my junior officers." Indeed, he had brought the man here himself three weeks back, because he had felt the man needed a break and he had wanted to give his lover's business a good client.

"You are disgusting, all of you!" she screamed, releasing his wrist so hard that it knocked him to the floor. "We offer pleasure merely in fair exchange, and he took her life in his hands and pulled her soul from her body. She was mine to use, mine to profit by, not his!"

Lucien nodded his head as he stood up slowly. The girls were silent now, staring at him, except for Nenet, who turned from him and hid her face in her hands. "I'm sorry for your loss. I will cover whatever her replacement price may be with my own salary, and you may have all his possessions to do with as you wish." The man had no bride or children, so he could pull rank and make such promises, he was certain.

"Price? Is that all you see? Money? No money can replace one of my flowers," she said with a sneer. "Payment in kind is required." She snapped her fingers, and Nenet stepped forward with a goblet she held out to him. "Drink it," the Madame ordered, and he found his eyes locked onto hers as he raised it to his mouth.

The taste was unique. It wasn't wine; it was too thick and red for that. It was cool in his throat but heated up in his stomach. It seemed to travel throughout his limbs and into his mind, sending shivers of fear and desire through each section of his body until he was convulsing on the floor.

Lucien tried to lift his head, but the grogginess he felt in his mind was making him feel languid and immovable. He swallowed and felt some sort of band around his throat. Try as he might, he couldn't even lift a hand to figure out what it was. All he could do was open his mouth and drink when he was offered more and more of the odd liquid. Then he mumbled some words upon command from that same voice that had enchanted him weeks ago, stealing his soul, he now knew, with each return to the pit of sin he had foolishly allowed himself to enjoy.

After some indeterminable time, he was able to sit up with help and blink until his vision cleared. The Madame was sitting at his side, her eyes as cold as when she had dragged him back to her business. Glancing around he saw he was on a bed in a small room with only one high window. "They will expect you to do everything my other girls do," she said, startling him.

Finding himself capable of movement, Lucien quickly checked, relieved to find his manhood intact. "How dare you keep an officer of the Emperor against his will," he said, as firmly as he could manage.

She chuckled, then shook her head. "Your Emperor left some time ago. They came looking for you but found nothing. I did hear them mutter something about your being tried for the murder of a junior officer if they should ever find you."

He sighed and buried his head in one hand. "You have aligned false evidence against me," he stated, with more horror than strength in his voice.

"Not really. You brought him and convinced us he was worthy of my house, and thus people died because of your actions."

Her honey-soft words were like the sharpest knives in his soul, confirming what his own mind had been replaying in his nightmares. She let him sit for a few more minutes until he could control himself as a Frenchman should, then when he looked at her, squaring his shoulders, she delivered her justice. "Since you caused the death of one of my best girls, you will replace her."

"What?" he demanded as he jumped from the bed and backed away. "That's insane. I'm not a woman, I'm a man, a military officer; if you require protection, I will consider that a duty to repay you," he started to babble, until she stood toe to toe with him, her face serious and set. "I won't do it."

"Some of my highest paying clients want men, not boys, not girls, not women, but men."

Impulsively he grabbed and shook her. "Let me out of here, you daughter of Satan! You shall not corrupt my body or soul."

"Release me," she instructed in a moan that sounded like passion, and he felt his hands drop to his sides. "You make your living through the dead bodies of others, and you claim I could corrupt you?"

She stepped away and turned her back to him as though unconcerned about what he might do. Truth was, after her command he found he couldn't lift a finger to harm her again. He was terrified, and yet part of him wanted to crawl to her and beg her for any attention at all. "I am the embodiment of life itself, a life that conquers even death. Everyone here lives healthy and happy lives, bringing greater happiness to those who enter in, as long as they respect the power of pleasure. But you wouldn't know about that," she spat, turning toward him. "You deal in death and follow rules to make yourself feel untainted."

Lucien felt himself cringe as she came toward him, her eyes seeming to burn again with unnatural fire. "Here we deal in life and pleasure, and the rules are my rules. Obey them, and you may find your slavery bearable. Do you understand?"

He nodded, but then added at her frown, "Yes, Madame."

"Mistress. Only clients call me Madame," she informed him.

"Maîtresse," he said in French, which earned a softening of her set mouth.

For decades Lucien lived and worked in the Cairo brothel, away from all eyes other than those of a wealthy client or one of the other slaves owned by Madame Maha. Surprisingly, a fair number of clients were wealthy women whose husbands had no time for them, but most were men whose sexual demands ate away a bit of his soul each time he served. When he started to fade away, his mistress offered him something special, an opportunity to train her other prostitutes to fight. During those days in the courtyard or atrium with sword, pistol, or just fist, he rebuilt the fabric of the body that was disgusting him each night.

In time, his female clients stopped coming altogether, and he was left with only masculine demands, so he began to fade again. He wasn't sure how much time passed, to be precise, since he didn't seem to be aging, nor did the other courtesans; he figured it was only a few years at most. With words of encouragement from Nenet he approached their owner one evening right after sunset to see if he could persuade her to use him in other ways. From bits and pieces his clients revealed when they visited, he had determined that things were changing in Cairo, and not for the better in terms of the brothel.

He was allowed into her private chamber again, and he knelt until she gave him leave to stand. "Maîtresse, thank you for agreeing to speak with me," he began.

"I'm told you are as concerned about this new Islam as I am," she simply said.

Lucien blinked at the term; he still thought of them as affronts to the True Faith, but he'd follow his owner's lead for now. "I know that my female clients have disappeared, and my own clients complain about stricter laws."

Madame Maha snorted at that comment. "I have always lived in Cairo, always, but yesterday another of my girls was taken when she went to the well for water. During the day I could not avenge her, and tonight the others have been crying out in fear, not anger. I am ...." She paused and hugged herself.

This action, so feminine, so fragile, spurred his feet to lead him to her so he could slip his arms around her and hold her to his chest facing away from him. She stiffened in his arms and then relaxed. "I am more than a mere pleasure for your clients. Sometimes we engage in more manly pursuits, and I have been training your other servants in the martial defenses. I would welcome the chance to fully use my skills in your service, Maîtresse."

"Usually, my people do not stay long in one location unless they live in solitude. I thought I could live in harmony with the akalum, but I guess all things must come to an end, even for me," she said softly.

"Do you want to leave Cairo, then?"

"No!" Her reply was shaky, and her fingers clung to his forearms tightly. "But we must do so, for I cannot protect you all now."

"You need not protect us, Maîtresse; let us protect you," he said as he took the opportunity to turn her around, so they were facing each other. She didn't appear older at all, as her dark eyes considered him. "Let me protect you using my connections back in France. Surely the Emperor will have forgiven me enough that I can at least write to a Madame I know in Paris. She may have work there until you can establish your own place. What?" She was laughing at him as he continued to speak.

"You have no clue, really, as to what year this is?"

"I suspect 1803," she laughed again, "or perhaps 1804, then? I don't understand, Maîtresse."

"It's 1937, Lucien, and Europe is also no safe place for us," she stated as though it was the truth.

Now it was his turn to laugh. "You tease me, Maîtresse, but I can see you have not aged; I see the girls and boys and myself. True, you feed us well and never seem to be ill, but it cannot have been more than a few years."

Her face remained slightly amused, but she tossed something to him from her bed. Unfolding it, he realized it was a journal or paper of some sort. Reading it with his newly learned knowledge of the native tongue, he saw that it claimed it was indeed January 13, 1937. It was talking about some elections and some group calling itself The Muslim Brotherhood.

His face drained of color as all the lies he had told himself these many years exploded in his consciousness. Swallowing, he looked at her, letting the paper fall to the floor. "You are really a demon or a witch then. I thought, I'd hoped ...." He slipped to his knees.

"Stay focused," she ordered softly, and her words burned through his shock, making him look up at her. She was holding her wrist down to him, and it was bleeding. He could smell it, just like the goblet he got once a week. She was a demon, but as the scent overwhelmed him, he didn't care. Her blood was cool, as it always was in the goblet, but it tasted more intense as he suckled, and she stroked his hair with one hand. "You've been punished enough. Now I have new use for you, Lucien. You are going to help me save us all."

They were standing on the railing of the private boat her friend Gaius had helped her find. Madame Maha called him a bastard, but one who had connections she sometimes needed. Another friend of hers named Cornelius had had one of his children help them with the appropriate documents for travel to what Lucien still thought of as the untamed new world. Apparently the Akhkharu, for he had learned that was what she and her friends were, felt that Rio was a safer place for them all at this time. The other slaves in her service – her wardum, he learned – were nervous, but he merely stood by her side, looking at the approaching coastline.

Here he would learn another new language and new customs, and as a man of action he'd prove his full worth. Then, maybe then, she'd take him to her bed again and not merely feed him from her wrist. Perhaps the Portuguese had gotten things right in their little corner of the world, because as the news reports that he now consumed like water told him, everywhere else was heading straight to hell.

*Bard stops his tale and gives a bow toward Maha and Lucien, then turns and bows to me, so I give him a smile before turning to my audience.*

*"While we all now live in harmony, driven by love, love was not always there from the start, as you see. Though for some of us, it was the only thing that drove us. Will you tell us how you found your Arammu-Wardum?" I ask the Kashshaptu elder.*

*"I would be delighted. I remember as though it were happening right now,"* begins the whispering voice.

# Guardian Spirit

I've been watching her for so long that I feel I could say the next words that come out of her mouth before she does.

"Unhand me, or I'll tell my father and brothers," she hisses at the minor aristocrat who has visited their camp and feels he has the right to corner her and demand a more private entertainment than the dance she performed a few minutes ago.

His words almost urge me to reveal myself to come to her rescue. "Call them, and we'll settle a price, then, if you insist."

Now she does not need me to protect her.

"I am no whore, sir, and you would do well to remember that, or my grandmother may inquire of the spirits about you," she retorts, and then smiles as the bastard's superstitious fears make him hesitate. That moment is all my dark-haired beauty needs to hurry back to the campfire.

There, with their colorful wagons surrounding her on three sides and her multitude of extended family, she can safely dance. I know men, though; I know them all too well, and as her body blossoms into womanhood she shall need more than matriarch, father, mother, brothers, and cousins to guard her honor.

Then she will need me to protect her.

My Beauty has power; she's had it since the day she was born.

At first, I followed this family merely because I needed a diversion. When you have seen as many moons come and go as I, diversions become welcome if you wish to keep going and not merely stand out in the sunlight until you turn to ashes. This family's lot is not an easy one, given their bloodline and their nomadic ways in a world where nations are competing for land and scholars are competing with the Church for hearts and minds. While those groups may all fight with each other, they unite on one cause: the despised gypsy.

The matriarch of the family has some minor magicks, coupled with a knowledge of herbs and a fine mental flair that preys upon those who come to the outcasts for entertainment and hope. When I heard the name they gave this newborn who reeked of so much power that it called to me, I shuddered: Chavi, "girl," simply "girl," almost an insult to what she could become. But then as I watched and saw how much the matriarch, the patriarch and the family protected and guided her, I suspected they meant it in a loving fashion. As the only girl born of that mother, as a rarity in their small community dominated by men, she must be protected by all.

I couldn't agree more, so I kept close, following the band from village to village, from nation to nation, from tongue to tongue. My plan was simple: Follow until the child was a woman, then rescue her from a loveless coupling with a cousin to continue their heritage. In her I could have an equal, one to teach my craft to, one to spend each daytime with away from the sun, one with whom to spend eternity without the chains of blood to bind us.

This family knew not how many of their enemies I had laid low, enemies who came to them late at night, quenching my thirst and sparing the Roma from my hunger in the process. Let it suffice to say that often they are targeted by the superstitious who would have attacked me even more eagerly than they plotted against the wanderers.

Only once did they spy me watching them. It was the girl herself; she approached me late one night, and her grandmother pulled her back to the firelight, the crone's still-sharp eyes sending not daggers but something odd in my direction. It was a surrender I saw in her eyes and heard in her voice when she approached me hours later. "When will you take her, Spirit?"

"She is not old enough," I whispered back in their native tongue, which caused the matriarch to pale and cling to the charms about her neck. "Give her this," I ordered just as softly, for we need never raise our voices to be obeyed, as I tossed a carved bone charm to the ground at the matriarch's feet. Then I left, knowing it would be worn the next night, and it did indeed show up on the girl's flat bodice.

The years passed, and the little girl blossomed into My Beauty and drew crowds of men to the traveling camp. This did not please me, but I made myself watch night after night, week after week, as they tossed their coins and clapped their hands.

You see, I know men; I know them as well as I know myself. Content most will be to watch and fantasize, but some will always want more. If they have the audacity and the will, they can persuade others to follow them in their evil schemes. That is how my father pretended to be the sun god, and how that band of cursed seamen stole my isle from me. Do not let the winners tell you about history; winners lie.

I was living on my mother's father's estate with our servants and slaves; surrounding us were the local villagers to whom we owed protection in exchange for their loyalty. Then the men came, saying they were great warriors from Ithaca on their way home from the war. All men think the war they have fought in was some great moment, but we Ogygians knew this had been merely one among hundreds of battles around the world as it fell apart. It had been falling apart since my grandfather's age.

My maternal grandfather, that is. I never had a father, but the villagers believed the story their lord had told them about my mysterious birth, so they respected my mother's right to rule in her own stead since her father's death.

These warriors did not.

The rules of hospitality dictated that we invite them in and feast them for a few days while they replenish their ship. The rules of hospitality also dictated that they give us gifts in return, though their captain claimed that some curse from one of the jealous gods had destroyed all the wealth they had acquired in this great battle. He claimed that other gods favored him, but I did not believe him, and neither did Naida, the village wisewoman who had been my teacher. After they overstayed their welcome, she called them on their manners.

Their leader was a wily man who crafted lies as casually as we could tell when it would rain or turn a calf still in the womb. To him they gave the title of lord and captain; us they called witches, as though that were a bad thing. I was amazed as this liar turned the minds of the village men against us with his tales of battle over the beauty of one woman. Why would anyone believe such a story? Naida told me that men often do not listen with their minds.

When the village men turned on us their women started to avoid us as well, and I knew why, though my grandfather was never a harsh master to blood or vassal. They came to us in secret to heal their bruises and wounds, and we learned a terrible truth. Their husbands were not the cause of all of these.

Naida prayed to the Earth Mother to protect us and cast these warriors from our midst. When the ground shook a few days later, those men claimed it was the god who was chasing them, trying to drive them from our island, and they moved into our home to protect my mother and her servants from his wrath. What could we do? We were not the women of the steppes whom we'd heard fought and hunted alongside their men, driving forth any that harm a virtuous maiden.

Those warriors valued no woman's virtue except those they told us about who waited for them at home. I wondered how many tears those wives would have wept if they could have seen their husbands grabbing our women and sometimes our young boys to press them into alcoves, where I overheard screams or giggles. When the bastards started arriving, the men of the village were no longer suckered by the tales of battle. They rose up, but they were little match for the warriors, who sealed themselves into our home.

This liar then turned his eyes to me, declaring that they could not leave until I was properly wed. Until there was a lord here to guard us against such disrespectful dependents, he would stay, he said. He told us he was married, and he sang of the wisdom, beauty, and skill of his bride, left over a decade ago with his own son. When he came to my bedroom in the darkest of nights, he had forgotten his role as husband.

While I may have been weaker in form, my skills with herbs and my way with words allowed me to drug him so I could escape. I looked down over the ragged cliff into the water, knowing I must jump, when a voice pulled my attention from the water. It was a beautiful woman; one I'd seen with Naida a few times when we went herb gathering at night. Naida claimed, though I did not believe her then, that this Hermia, as she called herself, was the most powerful witch on the island. When I pointed out that I had never seen her before, my mentor told me that it was because she wished it so.

She spoke, and I had to tilt my head to hear her, for her voice was so quiet, and yet her words seemed to dive into my very soul. I confessed all that had happened that night to her and reaffirmed my need to jump, thus depriving that liar of any claim to my body or my grandfather's estate. Through my tears she whispered to me, holding me in her arms as my mother used to do, her embrace and words so calming that I barely felt the sharp penetration of my neck and my life slipping away.

For one week, my mother and my mentor thought I was dead. The villagers searched for me while my new mother taught me some basics and denied me food so that I was like a savage animal upon my return to the estate. Hermia came to exact her own revenge upon some of the men but primarily to watch me as I tore them to pieces with my newfound strength, the blood vines that were now part of my body rippling forth to strangle and bind. When in my bloodlust I turned to one of the female servants, my new mother stepped in front of me and commanded me back. She told me again of our Ummum, the Mother of our Night, who created us to exact vengeance from the beginning of time, and this reminder of our purpose cooled my wrath.

My mortal mother knew not what to do, though she was grateful the liar and his surviving men fled. I stayed there with my two mothers then, learning, and weaving spells around the isle so that we could live in peace. While we never tire of our company and sisterhood, two of our kind cannot live together for more than a few years, so soon I was left alone with new servants.

But that was my past, and I need to focus on my present.

Much like the liar and his warriors, My Beauty's admirer has no true admiration for her. It has been two nights since she rebuffed the aristocrat's advances, and he has returned late at night with some allies. I easily control the four men through my whispers, their minds so full of lust that they are open to me without much effort. Four, however, are too many to be consumed all at once, so I drag them back to my haven and drain them, storing their blood in vessels I've had constructed for such occurrences. Had I a slave with me I would have sent her – for I refuse to have male wardum – back with the supplies to my main haven, but I have not had one for centuries, and my home is nations away. Lean years make one too conservative about saving the blood, and this time it almost costs me My Beauty.

I feel the presence of something old and powerful near my cave, but when I turn, I see only a blonde child standing there, so out of place in the woods all by herself at night. Then I feel the girl's pale blue eyes opening up my soul and rummaging through my memories. Yet every fiber of my being screams that this is no child, and my words catch in my throat when she speaks softly to me. "Have you abandoned her? It is a horrible thing to be abandoned by the ones who claim to love you."

Suddenly My Beauty's overwhelming fear washes over me like the most powerful tide, and the mysterious child ceases to occupy my thoughts as I hurry past her. The trees, shrubs and underbrush fall from my path as I run, but I can smell the blood, the smoke, growing with each step.

A horde of villagers is in the camp, and I do not need to see to know what they are doing, for they are doing what I have seen men do to such outsiders for millennia. I rarely use my full power because it is rarely needed, but now I tear my cloak from me and bare my tattooed arms and legs, crying out as loudly as I can: "Leave before you die!"

Only a few of the men have the common sense to guess what I am, and they flee, dropping their murderous gains behind. The rest, a good several dozen fools, pause, then rush toward me with torches, farm implements, and weapons raised.

I chant the ancient words of curse and praise, calling to my old gods, Artemis, Ares, Athena, Cybele, Hecate, and even Father Helios, hate me as he must. Each vine on my flesh worms into life and shoots forth from each limb, impaling each man through throat or groin or heart. Other vines sprout forth from Gaia as she drinks in the spilled blood of the family, and those I now avenge them upon.

As I thus judge some of the men, their cohorts turn to aid them, slashing at the vines and inflicting injuries to my body that I absorb as best I can. They die as all men do, thinking themselves such kings yet behaving as such animals. I survive, as I always do, by releasing that same animal instinct. They forget that the female of the species is always far more deadly once she is pushed.

Limping, I search the camp, one heartbeat echoing in my ears, praying again to the gods that it is hers that still pumps. My Beauty is hiding, and her dark eyes widen when they see me.

"I know you," she whispers, and I coo back softly, "Yes, I am sorry I could not save them."

As I slip, she finds some inner strength and catches me, my bu flowing from the wounds I cannot absorb onto her dress and skin. *I should warn her from it,* I think; *I should steady myself and lead her back into my haven,* but I find her heartbeat overwhelming as she helps me sit by the fire.

"I have never seen a woman do such things as you, not even my grandmother," My Beauty says as she sits down and wipes one bloodstained hand across her mouth, grimacing when she tastes my essence. "What is this? You are hurt?" she mumbles but tastes more of it from her other hand.

I want to say "stop"; I want to grab her and order her to wash it off. This is not what I want; this will not give me a sister I can teach my arts to, nor a lover I can share the daylight within darkness, yet something inside me knows it is too, too late.

Four nights later I watch her finish cleaning up the camp without a word from me. As all her people do, she mourns, performs the rites, then moves on to what is her best chance of survival. She told me on the second night that honor binds her to repay me. If such fantasies will ease her through this transition, I am content to let her believe so.

I look up at the new moon and know she is secretly watching me. "We will take one wagon, so gather all you can, and I will return shortly," I tell her. Another would have to lean in close to me to understand, but as her own voice has softened, so too have her ears become attuned to my whispers. In time, there will be no need for spoken words.

I take one of the horses and return to my local haven to gather my own meager possessions. As I lift the containers of blood, I laugh at how the gods have played with me. Yes, we will need much blood for the rituals, but first we need to get home, and that will take weeks. Her sense of honor should bind her in that time, but if we do not hurry, the power she has may lash out, fueled by my bu.

I suck up my tears as I hurry back to the camp. She would have made a truly amazing witch, but now she will languish as a mere wardum forever. As I pause to watch My Beauty wonder at her own new strength as she loads the wagon with supplies and goods from the others, I know that cannot be her fate.

"Mistress!" she calls out with a bright smile as I step into view.

I shake my head, and she sighs but says my name, so delightful to my ears as her soft voice forms each syllable. "Calypso, I'm almost done," she repeats with a gentle smile.

I cannot bear to let the lie pass my lips, so I merely smile and tie the horse I have brought to the back of the wagon she has selected, the best of the four. These weeks' travel back to Ogygia can be her solace before I must rip her world apart to fully claim My Beauty as my own.

I have never been good at holding my emotions inside. The limitations on speech that we each inherit with our transformation into Kashshaptu upon our reemergence has helped with that, as have the years, but being so close to My Beauty and knowing we can never become full lovers, true sisters, is shattering my resolve to protect her.

Obviously, I have to tell her what I am, but she doesn't believe me until two weeks into our journey, when the supplies I've laid up run out and I take us to a small farmhouse. As I drain the hired farmhand down to unconsciousness, she just stands there staring at me, her dark eyes wide and frightened. I think she might run then; she could, since the full bonding has not yet formed, but instead she swallows and steps forward when I lay his body on the straw of the barn where I captured him.

"We must hide the body, or they'll know," she whispers even more softly than my bu was forcing her voice.

"He isn't dead, Chavi," I tell her gently. "He'll wake up tomorrow and have a vague memory of something wonderful and intense," I explain in vague terms.

"But I saw you, I saw what you did," she whispers back, edging closer to me.

"I'm very skilled at this. I've had a long time to practice," I say and turn toward the barn door. "Come, we need to be at the next inn before sunup." At this level of bonding, she cannot refuse such a direct command, but she keeps looking at me the rest of the night.

"Where are we going?" she asks me a few nights later as we near a port city. A fully bonded wardum wouldn't ask that question; they'd merely know already.

"My home, one of them – my original home, you might say," I whisper as I take a seat by the fire she's set up at the center of our camp.

"You are wealthy then, an heiress?" she asks, and for a moment I frown as she threatens to fall into a stereotype for her people. "We are two heiresses then, traveling the world. It's exciting, Mistress," she concludes, adding the title and smiling at me with her lips, but her eyes still express concern.

She's right; we are similar. We are both women trying to survive in this man's world, both technically alone without family or friends.

I have never considered those I have changed as true family; after a few years they must go out on their own to survive and find a new coven. I was hoping with her ... but best not to dwell on what cannot be.

In a few more days we are on a ship to my isle; the fisherman we hired is looking at us suspiciously, but my control over his mind is just enough to make sure we get there, and he remembers nothing. I could have crushed his will completely, but I have been cautious of what I show My Beauty.

She will be so devastated so soon.

The boat drops us off into the waiting arms of my other two wardum and my last child, Ena, who has spent almost two decades in charge of my estate. They say nothing but take our trunks and Chavi's hands to lead us back to the safety of our marble walls.

The house proper has been rebuilt over the centuries, and it looks like Ena has made a few changes. Our silent consultation informs me of all that she has had done and reassures her that she need not leave yet. She has been one of my most needy damu, but given how I found her, left for dead in Dublin after her pimp beat her, I am not surprised.

The other two wardum move to take Chavi to prepare her for what lies ahead, but she refuses and looks at me. "You must go with them. They will help you because I cannot," I say softly. My child shows me some letters that have arrived for me during the past several years to distract me from My Beauty's screams.

After meditation and consultation with my own Shi, Ena and I prepare the vessels, herbs, inks, and knives. So many knives, so much ritual to be observed. These are the moments when I wish I had been left for dead or taken by another family, but then I see how they struggle so with each other and within themselves, and I know our way is best.

My friend Maha – for if I have any friends, it would be that Gelal who has heard tales for longer than I have myself been in the Night – tells me that the legends which describe how we become vampires and how we create our blood-bound servants reflect the first Shi or parent of each family. Thus, to become one of us, we must show promise in the realms of the goddesses and spirits, but then the paths of mistress and slave diverge.

We Kashshaptu are creatures of tragedy; we are saved from an act of suicide by our Shi, who has been watching us but not interfering in our lives. Our suicides have various triggers, though in all we feel that we are refusing to submit to the will of men and taking that final stand for our lives by ending them. For my original people this made perfect sense, and it was a strong man or woman who would take the honorable path instead of submitting merely to survive. By doing so, we prove our ability to become the nobility of the Night Kingdom.

Our servants, though, we rescue, often from lives of continued servitude to males or, in the current millennium, to the dictates of the Church. The mere fact that they had to be rescued proves that they are not strong enough to fully wield their own lives, no matter how skilled they may be in the feminine arts of magick. To prove their worthiness, then, they must be stripped of their old life in all ways, their old life sacrificed so that a new one may be reborn. My friend claims that the first of our servants was left as such a sacrifice, her skin removed, and her body left as a corpse for the witch the villagers thought of as a demon.

My hands shake as I lay down the last of the knives, and my dami almost touches me in comfort before leaving me to do as I must. To let My Beauty continue to partake of my power without a strong bond threatens the entire family as well as herself, and I did pledge to protect her should she need it.

I cannot protect her from myself.

A month later I am sitting in the twinkling of the stars on my marble roof when My Beauty comes to me. Her gown is subdued now, simple, her right wrist and the right side of her neck revealing the living tattoo I inscribed on her newly grown skin during her month-long ordeal. The black fuzz on her head is bare to the night breeze, and I am shocked when she smiles at me.

Normally the ritual strips the mortal of all the sorrows of life but at the cost of the joys as well. Our slaves are the most loyal, but they are not as happy as those who serve the lesser families. I've never asked, of course; I have merely assumed, because I cannot imagine never smiling, never laughing, though it may well be years before I myself can again.

Our thoughts flow together; I do not bar mine from her, and she stops when my sorrow hits her. One lone tear leaks from her eye as she kneels down in front of me, placing her hands on my knees. She radiates happiness, a sense of purpose and, surprisingly, a sense of freedom as well as she wraps her arms around my legs and leans toward me.

"Thank you," she whispers so softly before she places her lips on mine and kisses me as I have not been kissed in centuries, if ever.

As I surrender to the kiss, I feel my chair and our bodies rise up just a bit. I'm not doing it. Then I realize that she is not merely my slave, and my kiss grows in passion at the forbidden thoughts I have of making her my sister and lover in all but formal name. In concert with my desires, she melts against me, and we move just a bit higher into the darkness.

Chavi breaks the kiss for only a moment, then almost growls, and we spin to the left just slightly as she reaches up and pushes my shawl from my arms, sending it cascading to the rooftop below. I catch her face in my palms and look at her carefully. "Are you sure? For once we do this, we are connected even more deeply than now."

*Yes, Mistress,* her thoughts come to me as she turns her head to nibble at the cold flesh of my hand. Her feelings flood to me via our bond, and I see through her eyes the repulsion she's felt at the idea of men and their hard, angular bodies while her gaze lingered over the women in the towns who scurried out of the gypsies' way.

My Beauty's deft fingers unlace my bodice, opening it to reveal skin that has not seen the sun for centuries. She reveals my breasts slowly, gently, one at a time, pushing the fabric away but not removing it from my body. "Perfect, far better than mine," she whispers, but before I can contradict her, for I have seen every part of her form, recreating it with each cut and each chant, she encircles one ruddy nipple with her mouth.

I groan as she works her tongue along every crevice and line, teasing it into a taut pucker and making my thighs start to tremble. When she takes a breath, I hold her with my gaze and use one edge of a nail to cut a small wound on the other nub, drawing her attention to the scarlet that forms there quickly. She licks her lips, then suckles me as a child might, though with an increasing fervor like what I have heard tell of in bardic romances.

The sky seems to lighten as she works, and for a moment I fear the sun is rising, then I realize it is merely my own passions opening my eyes to the Great Mother around me. Everything seems so much clearer, so much sharper, more so than when I allowed myself such pleasures in the past. Though it was millennia ago, I know what will transpire as My Beauty reaches to gather up my skirt.

I use words because I know they will drive my will firmer into her mind, where she is accessing forbidden skills to dance us in the air. *Picture me on the divan below, laid out for you to taste; picture us there reveling in our desires.*

Slowly we descend, and soon I am indeed lying on the seat, my skirts pushed up and my undergarments tossed aside. My Beauty has discovered the secret we all hide beneath our layers of cloth, and she smiles as she looks up, her nose, mouth and chin covered in my blood, my bu, my precious fluids that course through all our tissues.

"Am I doing it correctly, Mistress?" she whispers, and I know why she asks. What all those men had wanted from her was either to be the first, or one of many – it was about her body, not her. I want only her desire, so I nod and spread my legs further, displaying myself to the gods who created us.

Following instinct or our spiritual bond, she licks each ridge in long languid strokes, then flicks her tongue's tip on the button at the top, making me gasp. She repeats this teasing until my legs are shaking and I can hardly separate our thoughts as they mingle. Trying to steady myself I reach out to grasp her dark hair, dusting only over the new fuzz on top and reminding me of our new positions. As she tickles my channel with her eager tongue, I can feel a burst of energy erupt from me along with a squirt of my bu into her open mouth.

She is mine, mine, and no man's; My Beauty belongs only to me. That knowledge should sadden me, given my hopes and dreams for a lover and sister, but instead her shining dark eyes and blood-smeared face reassure me as she cuddles up into my lap.

"I want to feel that way, too, Mistress," she whispers.

I am hers as well.

*"I still am hers," Calypso adds softly as she turns to me for approval before returning to her family in the gardens.*

*"Every one of us today found our hearts opened by those nearest us, even if we fought it with hatred fueled by the bubussunu that runs through our veins. Isn't that right?" I ask my most difficult descendant as he sat frowning with his fellow berserkers.*

*"I ain't tellin' no tale, and not you neither, stupid git," he orders his wardum, who merely shrugs and gives me a sad look.*

*I turn to Bard, who is now grinning as he takes his place. "This is a truly fun story to tell, but to do it right I shall have to affect his funny language and horrid accent," he insists.*

# Useful Tools

Most of the traffic just stepped over or around him as Jamie sat glaring at the sidewalk, his legs pulled up to his chest, his right cheek still sore from where his mater had slapped him before his da kicked him out. His left cheek still stung from the tattoo he'd gotten and the punch his da had placed there when they tore off the bandage he had been supposed to wear for a few days.

"Wot the 'ell is this?" His da's face had been redder than he'd ever seen, his voice shriller than he'd ever heard, and his little sister had run faster than ever before from the kitchen the moment things started happening. Things had been "happening" there a lot as the economy had changed and jobs were threatened. His da's dark eyes had widened as he recognized the series of numbers, and his fist flew, sending Jamie staggering onto the floor. "Look at wot yer son's done, Martha!"

His mater had come and crouched down to look at him. Her mouth moved as she read the numbers off silently, then with a look of deep sorrow she slapped the other cheek and ran from the room in tears.

"Look wot ye did, ye stupid git! Wot were ye thinking?"

"I did it to honor grandda. Ye all just ignored wot he went through, wasn't right," Jamie had begun to say as he stood up.

"Been through? Yer grand never talked about it, we weren't supposed to talk about it, we just fit in here so it never 'appens again."

"Forgetting makes it 'appen, ye can't forget," Jamie had yelled back.

"It's a sin, ye know." His mater's soft voice had made both men turn to her. "Not supposed to mutilate yer body."

"Grand's was," Jamie had started to say when his da punched him again.

"Ye did this to yourself! Yer grand did not! How dare ye compare yourself to him! Get out! Get out!"

It was a common enough threat, but this time his mater had just turned away, saying "I have no son," and Sis stayed out of the kitchen. So, Jamie left, and that had been three days ago. The locks on the flat had been changed, and no one would come to the door when he rang the bell. When he began to yell, the nosy neighbor called the cops, who said he must be a sick bastard to do that to his face. Since he was legally an adult, his parents were within their rights to kick him out, and they'd be within their rights to press charges.

So now he was sitting and despising the world that had tortured his grandda and made it impossible for any of them to talk about it. As he was playing out variations of his favorite Nazi-killing fantasies, something bumped his leg, making him look up.

A little lass with blonde hair and pale blue eyes stared at Jamie from where she'd fallen, then got up and ran off faster than any human he'd ever seen, her tattered coat flapping about. His stomach felt like he'd been punched, and his breath was shallow for no reason, so he started to recite some punk verses he favored to drive away the terror that seemed to grip him. Jamie was rubbing his eyes when a shadow fell over him. Peering up, he saw a male figure in leather and denim, his face covered with piercings and his mouth disfigured. The man crouched down and smiled, showing the worst teeth he'd ever seen.

"Little bitch led me here on purpose, trying to throw me off her scent," he said in a strange accent that sounded a bit like the Americans in those westerns his grand used to watch on the telly. "Not sure what she is, but you – you are giving off some stench."

"Oi!" Jamie frowned and climbed to his feet as the man stepped back and stood up, his arms over his chest and a look of amusement on his face. "Go home ye fucking Yank!"

"Home? Boy, my home is long gone, those damned wetbacks took it long before yer granddad was born. Oh, I say something that got you even more riled up," the man said with a twinkle in his eyes.

"Ye shut up about me family!" Jamie said, and he threw a punch only to watch the man dodge with a chuckle. That only made him angrier, so he started lashing out with fists and feet until the man had him in a headlock and slammed him against the nearest building.

The man took a deep, loud sniff of him and then used his tongue to lick Jamie's tattoo and neck. "You know, sometimes we just take someone so another family can't get him, fuck up their plans. But sometimes we find someone very special, with so much rage, so much self-loathing, that we just know it's gonna be fun. You and I are going to have some fun," the monster growled, for surely no normal man could have so easily disarmed and pinned Jamie.

Jamie tried to wiggle away as the creature licked him again, and then he felt two stabs of a knife in his neck and pain greater than he'd ever known. Then something cold and primal seemed to be seeping into him just as the night became darker than he remembered.


The Xul, that's what his vampiric da called their kind, lived by a set of rules, though they'd never call them that, Jamie learned quickly when he woke up the next morning in an abandoned building by the river. You got rid of everything that tied you to your past that wasn't part of your body. That meant your name and your family. Your Shi, your creator, gave you a new name unless you could make a good case for him not to, and Jamie had nothing left to lose, so he gave it up easily. "Swaggart" was a bit of a joke, though it was a solid enough name in some parts of the island. Now he had to prove his bragging rights by walking into that house and getting rid of some other ties.

Damon was right there watching him with his arms folded over his chest again. The Texan followed him inside after he ripped the door from its frame, surging with his new strength and seething with anger over being kicked out, belittled, and ignored. He went inside and didn't bother with the lights, his eyes blazing with another gift from the Texan.

Swaggart tilted his head and heard his da's footsteps coming down the stairs. Burning from his humiliation, the vampire raced around the corner and caught his mortal da in the throat with a fist, knocking him up a few steps. As the old man tried to breathe and stared in horror at him, Swaggart stepped up to straddle his head. "Not so 'igh and mighty now, huh?" Then, using one booted foot, he crushed the mortal's head and continued up the stairs to find his mortal mater screaming at him.

"Wot did ye do to yer da? Oh, my God, Jamie?" she was saying over and over, and that just made him angrier.

He grabbed her and shoved her against a wall, making his little sister scream and shut her own bedroom door. "Don't ye remember, mum? Ye don't 'ave a son!" With that he ripped her head from her neck and tossed it down to Damon standing at the bottom of the steps.

The bedroom door could be shredded within seconds, but the open window and empty room told the story. "Balls! She's run," he said to his Shi when he stepped out to find the other, letting the blood from murdering his mother run into his mouth and over his face.

"Then get after her, boy! No one gets away from us! Go!"

They ran back into the bedroom and jumped from the same window, landing at a run after the screaming lass, who wasn't that far away in her bare feet and nightie. With supernatural speed they caught her before she could get to another house, Damon jumping in front of her, so that she backed up into his dami.

"Jamie, please," she whispered, then screamed as he lifted her up over his head and threw her across the street to land with a crunch. "Jamie," she kept whispering as he stalked to her and crouched over her.

"I'm hungry," Swaggart said, glancing at his creator.

"No children; our bite changes automatically," Damon warned.

"No children," he repeated, then snapped her neck so he could feed at his leisure. In his mind he saw that pale blue-eyed blonde girl, but he pushed that thought down deep to follow his Shi again.

Swaggart became efficient, an odd quality for their kind, Damon told him on several occasions. They never stayed with one hive for too long because his Shi had a thing about being "trapped." Of course, if they had stayed with a bigger group, the English vampire wouldn't be alone now, his creator only a bit of ash he'd managed to collect in a bottle before he'd turned to smoke after some religious zealots found them. Some humans did know that Akhkharu existed, though their ideas about them were a mixture of myth, pop culture, and fact. At least they'd taken out most of those dozen religious bastards before Damon lost his head and Swaggart got revenge.

Now he was sitting on the sidewalk again in another city watching the akalum walk around like they owned the place. Stupid krauts. Have all the fun you want now, because soon the slaughter will start. They had come to Berlin to have some fun, which had really been his plan for the past two decades, but it took a while to convince the Texan that it would be a lot of fun. They'd only managed to take out one small neo-Nazi group when the monks had found them. Maybe the monks had been watching the illegal gathering too, but they'd insisted on interfering. He'd get them next, but for now he wanted a good target. He had to learn their codes so he could find them, and after a few nights he spotted one to follow.

Revenge should have made him feel better, but it never seemed to. Swaggart terrorized Berlin for a few years. The media was so embarrassed by the affiliations of those he killed that they rarely reported on them. That started to annoy him more. These people refused to take responsibility for their past, hiding it from their eyes, never discussing it … it reminded him of others from a lifetime ago, but he could never quite see those faces clearly in his mind. Then he saw a newspaper article about a gang of neo-Nazis back in London, and he ate his way back to his homeland.

The place was basically unchanged as far as he could see. Still no flying caravans, and there was another fucking war the damned Yanks had gotten everyone into, and the out of work blokes just hung around getting munted. Now some of them were flaunting their little swastikas and shaved heads, so it didn't take long for Swaggart to hunt one group to an abandoned warehouse. The old hives were gone, and he didn't want to waste time going through the initiation for another one when he could take out this handful of wankers.

When he exited, covered in their blood, piss, and beer, he ran right into a man standing staring into the open door. The bloke fell, the notebook and pen he had been holding floating to the ground. The stranger was maybe in his late 20s, blond, blue eyes, darker than you might expect, and built like a lorry. The vampire frowned and snatched up the paper, placing his foot firmly on the man's chest. "I saw what you did," the man said.

Swaggart snarled, then looked at the notebook. He'd learned their damned language in that damned city, and now he kicked the kraut back against the building. "Ye here recruiting, ye fucking bastard? Not in my city!" he ordered, hauling the man up to his feet.

"No, no, I'm reporter, reporter," the man said, fumbling in a pocket, which Swaggart ripped open as he took out the sought-for item. It was a journalist's ID like he saw on telly. The man's name was Karl Van Houster, some fucked-up kraut name. "Reporter," the human said, and the vampire picked him up and carried him inside the warehouse, holding on to the back of his neck.

"Seen wot I did?" Swaggart said. The man nodded but didn't answer; neither was he getting sick. The Akh was impressed so far. "Ye gonna write this for yer paper or telly or whatever?"

The man shook his head.

"I should kill ye, make sure ye don't talk," Swaggart said, licking the kraut's neck on his way down as he made him kneel.

"No, no, I help you," the man said, but it didn't sound like an attempt to plead for his life, which made the Akhkharu stop. "I track them, all over Europe from Berlin where this group begin. I help you find more, yes?"

"Why ye want to help me? You're a kraut too," Swaggart growled.

Now the man did something that made the Akh release him and take one step back. He started to cry – no, not cry, weep; he was weeping like a man who'd seen his entire family killed and had nothing left to live for. "Holy shit," Swaggart said as the man started babbling about sins and crime and penitence. He dragged the man to a nearby old pipe that had at one time had water running through it, then used some handcuffs he always had, just in case he wanted to take a bit more time, to chain him to it. Then he went back and found the man's caravan and equipment, returning it all to the warehouse where he could look at it at his leisure.

Damon had complained about technology, but Swaggart tried to keep up on it by stealing their victims' stuff and mucking about with things until he could use it. That was a good thing, given what this bloke had in his backpack and caravan. Two different cell phones, a tape recorder, a video camera, and something that looked like a small computer but required a password to use. "Oi!" he called as he came over and kicked the man's foot to get him to wake up. "What's yer password?"

"Look, I can help you, I saw what you did," Karl began until Swaggart knocked the wind out of him with a kick to his chest.

"Password!"

The kraut swallowed, then took a deep shaky breath. "No," he whispered, and Swaggart narrowed his eyes. "I can help you. Get you more information than you could ever get on your own. You want to take them out, right? So do I. We can help each other."

The Akhkharu snorted but didn't lash out physically again. Revenge was proving slow-going at best. Damon hadn't been much interested in his dami's vendetta, and once he was solo, Swaggart was relying on newspaper articles and information he could beat out of folks. For now, he just set the computer by the kraut, who couldn't use it with his hands chained, and went to paw through the rest of his things.

Turned out that all of the articles he'd read in Germany were by this reporter, this Karl bloke, and he was tracking the flow of information and money between the Fatherland and other nations where neo-Nazi activities weren't strictly outlawed. Swaggart thought for a few minutes, his eyes watching the kraut's as they stared at each other. Damon had had a few slaves over the two decades they hunted together. They were called wardum in some freaky old dead language, and if you gave them your blood without taking theirs, they became sort of supermen, stronger, faster, and better than the average meal. Plus, they seemed to really need the blood or bu something or other that came from a vamp, so they'd do whatever you wanted. He'd never seen one last more than a year, though, before Damon got bored or they hit a dry spell in the hunt, and then he was just another takeaway. There was something in Swaggart, some stupid moral part left, that rebelled against the idea of enslaving anyone, but he also didn't want a kid, which is what he pretty much figured he'd been to Damon for the first decade.

He stood up and rummaged in the warehouse until he found a length of heavy chain. He broke open one link, then went to the kraut, ordering him to his feet. Once the bloke was on his feet, he wrapped the chain around an ankle and re-bent the link to lock it, then did the same with the other end around the pipe. Then he took his keys and undid the handcuffs, one of his few possessions, and returned them to his leather jacket. "Ye can do yer work, but don't ye dare contact anyone or call anyone here, or I'll gut ye like a fish!"

"OK, OK," Karl said, shaking and rubbing his numb hands.

Swaggart fetched the backpack and its human supplies and tossed them at the kraut's feet. "I'll be right over there, watching," he said, pointing to a dark corner where no sunlight could reach him.

Karl just nodded and dug into his backpack to get some snacks. The vampire watched for a minute then just shrugged and headed into the dark. The chain was several feet long, so he'd be able to get any of that mortal stuff he might need without causing a commotion. Last thing Swaggart needed was to be awakened during the day when he was almost helpless to do much more than cower in the shadows.

That thought made its way into his dreams. Pop culture said that vampires were the undead, but that wasn't quite true. Yes, to make a child you brought them close to death, then replaced their blood with your own, plus some stuff that Damon had never really explained. Let the bookworms and politicos worry about that shit, just never bite anyone you don't want for a few decades, was his education. So Akhkharu dreamed, and desired, and wished for things, just like they did when they were human, but most of what they wanted was subordinate to blood, and, in the Xul's case, violence.

It kicked ass to be a vampire, certainly, but it was limited to the nighttime. Imagine what he could achieve if he had a man in the sun tracking down these Nazi bastards so he could take them out as soon as the sun set. In his dreams, Swaggart killed dozens of clubs and saw visions of some old man he thought was his grandda smiling in approval. Damon had failed to purge him of all his mortal ties, because every time he looked in a mirror, which was rare but still happened, he was reminded.

He watched the kraut for several minutes after he woke up. He was eating something and typing away on his computer every now and again, then writing down something in that notebook of his, probably in that damned language, too. "Oi! Ye use the Queen's English now! No more of that kraut scratching!"

Karl looked up toward him and narrowed his eyes as though trying to find him, so Swaggart turned on his night vision that had his eyes blazing red, which made the bloke turn pale and swallow. "OK, OK," he called back.

He gave him a few minutes to write something new, then the Akh stood up and rushed over to crouch in front of him, grinning when the man just swallowed and stared at him. Swaggart bent down and took a deep sniff of the man, noting he was starting to get a bit ripe from fear and captivity, and feeling pleased when Karl flinched but didn't plead or try to move away. He did something unexpected and actually leaned toward the vampire when he ran one jagged fingernail over his cheek. "Ye still want to help me, Karl?"

"Ja, yes, OK," he replied. His breathing was different – faster, but not from fear, and Swaggart blinked once before standing up.

"This is how it's gonna work. You're gonna be my bitch, do wot I say, when I say, and I'm gonna give ye a gift in return and not kill ye until ye piss me off."

"Gift?" the kraut's eyes went wide, and the vampire hit his forehead with one hand. Damned language.

"A present, a reward for service you're gonna do me," Swaggart explained.

Karl smiled, nodding his head as he struggled to his feet only to be knocked against the wall by a punch.

"I didn't tell ye to move, bitch! Stay there until I say ye move!"

The kraut's eyes were shining, but not with tears, as he sat back down in the same position. "Yes, Sir," he whispered, his face turning a bit red.

The Akhkharu swallowed now, as the response seemed to stir something in him that hadn't stirred in some time. He could do rape and torture with the best of any hive, but that's the only time he did it, in the hive, on behalf of whomever was head, usually for some sort of party or initiation rite. His own arousal was more from lust than anything happening around him, but as long as the others didn't know, he could do what needed to get done.

Right now, though, his jeans were feeling a bit too tight. Unsure of what to do in such an unexpected situation, he rolled up his sleeve and bit into his own wrist. "Drink it!" he ordered, holding it out.

Karl sat up, but didn't stand, and took the offered wrist. "I knew it," he whispered before placing his mouth over the wound and sucking. As his lips and throat worked, Swaggart felt his pants getting tighter and tighter. He had never fed someone before, and he hadn't noticed such a reaction in his Shi, but then again, now that he thought about it, Damon usually fed his bitches in private or from a cup or something. Too late for that now, but at least he had the strength to pull away in a minute or so, when he figured the kraut had had enough.

"Burns, huh, bitch?" he asked with a chuckle as his slave started shaking and twitching.

That lasted for several minutes, making him nervous until Karl opened his eyes and smiled. "OK, OK," he said with a dopey grin.

"Don't get all happy, cause ye gonna be busy, very busy, bitch." Swaggart motioned for him to rise, and when he did, he ripped the chain in half. "Come on. We need a base of operations where ye can do yer human shit."

"I have house," Karl said as he gathered up his stuff.

"Ye mean I," Swaggart thumbed his chest with a snarl, "have a house, don't ye bitch?"

"OK, OK," the kraut said again with another smile. He caught the keys in one hand and followed when the Akh led the way. After stowing his stuff in the trunk again he looked at Swaggart and tilted his neck to one side. "You need?"

The vampire shoved him hard against the caravan. "Not from ye. Not from ye ever," he said, though he leaned in and pushed his slave back further to the auto. "I'm fine for tonight. Let's go see my new house," he added before stepping back and jumping over the caravan in one leap.

"OK, OK," Karl replied, making Swaggart's head start to ache. He had to teach this bloke to talk better.


The flat – it wasn't really a house but a two-bedroom apartment – was in a nice part of town, and that was a problem, the Xul thought immediately. Upon seeing the telly, the sparse furnishings, part of the rental agreement, and lack of windows, though, he thought it might be brilliant. No one would look for the monster killing Nazis in an area this nice.

Karl had contacts around the world. He'd won a few awards for his reporting in Germany and was respected among his peers. Another potential problem, but perhaps for the future when he tired of the kraut.

His information was amazing. He had one wall covered in maps with numbers written on it, a bigger map of London with four clubs identified, though one he crossed out as soon as they entered the place. The Akh crossed his arms over his chest and considered the map once he finished giving the place the once over. "Three more of them?"

"That I have found so far ... Sir," Karl added, with a grin that made Swaggart glance his way. "According to my research, though, there may be one or two more on outskirts of city. I have not found them yet."

"We'll find them," the Akhkharu replied, then growled as he realized he'd included the man as though they were a team. Wheeling around, he shoved the German against the opposite wall, knocking the wind from him and getting a moan that didn't sound quite right for his trouble. "Why ye targeting yer own people like this? I thought all ye krauts stuck together."

The wardum did something quite unexpected; he shoved him back, and Swaggart was so surprised that he released him and stepped away two paces. "They are not my people! Some of my family died in the camps, you know these camps?"

"I think I know summat about it!" Swaggart yelled back, slapping his cheek with the tattoo.

Karl stepped forward and reached out as though to touch it, but the Akh growled and jerked back. "OK, OK. I see this before. It is camp number, yes? Had cousin and aunt who went to camps, they were undesirables," he added with a sigh.

"Wot ye mean? I thought only Jews were slaughtered?"

The German's eyes filled with tears. "It is great shame, that, but no, others, for politics or race or mental reasons. Idea of master race, you know it?"

Swaggart spit on the floor at the expression. "Fucking bastard! We didn't talk about it much growing up. My grand's," he said, motioning to his cheek again.

They stood silently for several minutes until the wardum slipped his jacket off and tossed it to one side, then stepped forward and spread his arms out. "You can hit me if you want," he offered, and Swaggart's mouth fell open.

"Wot the 'ell is wrong with ye! First ye don't run when ye see me, then ye don't plead for yer life, and now ye offer me a punching bag of ye! I'll hit ye when I want; I don't need yer bloody permission, slave!" He was feeling so confused right now. Nothing was going as it had with Damon's wardum or other Xul's akalum or slaves. God, couldn't he do anything right?

"OK, OK," Karl said letting his hand fall to his side.

That expression again, it was going to drive him batty. If he beat him, though, the bastard might think he was doing it because he had asked. Instead, Swaggart turned and went to the better of the two bedrooms and slammed the door. Then he paused, opened it up, and said "This room is mine, ye stay out!"

"OK, OK," the kraut's voice replied, just loud enough to be heard through the door.

The Akhkharu started upturning furniture and tossing clothes on the floor in a rage until he found this box under the bed. Inside was a set of German, British, French, and Italian, he thought, magazines with men in them. Men in leather and rubber, men in blindfolds and wearing cuffs, men being beaten and fucked by other men. Oh, balls. Of course, he'd have to enslave some pervert; just what he needed. After a few hours of reading, though, he realized that he might try something

76

unusual with the kraut in the other room. The wanker wanted it rough, then he could earn it, he decided, as he fell unconscious with the sunrise.

Swaggart had just finished off the last member of another Nazi club when he heard a scream that sounded too masculine and too familiar to escape his notice. Taking a big whiff, he smelled his slave, where he'd left him to watch for any runners, but then he also caught the scent of another vampire. With a snarl he ran from the room and ploughed into the other Akh, knocking him from his wardum. The two struggled, piercings clicking together, leather squeaking against leather, fangs and claws ripping at any exposed skin, until Swaggart ended up on top of the other Xul's arms, pinned above his head. "Don't ye touch my stuff!"

"Yours? He ain't marked. Figured he was a mistake, thought I could use a bitch," the other laughed, so Swaggart punched him several times, then re-pinned his arms. From his smell and taste, he was about his age, maybe a few years younger. "You gotta mark him, idiot, or you lose him," the other whispered.

They both glared, then Swaggart stood up. One of the other rules they existed by was that Xul never killed other Xul and never took another's property if it was appropriately marked. "Get out of 'ere!" he ordered with a shove, and the other monster ran off with a nasty chuckle. He probably had a hive and would come back with them to claim the unmarked slave.

"Sir?" Karl was standing next to him, looking at him with those intense blue eyes, a bruise forming on his chest that showed where his shirt had been torn open. "Sir?" His wardum's eyes that reminded him of paler ones from another time that he could barely see in his mind.

"Hey, you're a pervert," Swaggart began with an insult, but the kraut only nodded with a sad smile. "Ye know where we can get ye inked, pierced and collared this time of night?"

"OK, Sir. You come with me," his slave replied with a wider smile that Swaggart immediately regretted earning as the wardum picked up his stuff and escorted him to the auto.

The place they went to wasn't like the one where he'd gotten his own tat, and Damon had done most of the piercings Swaggart could now boast. Normally Xul did it themselves or stole things, but in the three weeks he'd been using him, Karl's money had proved very useful. Less time scrounging on the streets meant more time scouting out new clubs, tracking lone Nazis and kicking arse.

Karl turned to him when the bird behind the counter asked them what she could do for them and the vampire tried to explain what they wanted. It was a big order, she said, and they'd have to come back over several nights, but they could do it. They'd just taken out another gang, so Swaggart justified this break in his mind as doing what was necessary to continue his work. The fact that the kraut seemed to get off on the attention didn't bother him half as much as it probably should have.

The wide metal posture collar paid off when they ran into other Akhkharu, Xul and others, who quickly crossed the street away from them. London had a huge night population, something Damon had called a Kingdom or something like that. Swaggart frankly didn't care as long as none of them got in his way. Two hives tried to coerce him into joining them, but once they found out what he was doing – the newspapers ate up the murders like candy – they just snarled at him and let him be. He'd never been much for the fun of violence on its own, something he knew had deeply disappointed Damon, just as his mortal da had been disappointed in him for failing to earn A levels and dooming him to continue the family's working-class status.

Not that it mattered now, as they hid and watched the huge meeting at one of the last Nazi groups near London. There had to be at least 40 of them, and their leader had the smell of a politico and ancientness about him, which made Swaggart punch in a wall back at the flat.

"Sir?" Karl asked as he put their equipment away and just watched from a distance.

"Ye stupid wanker!" the vampire turned but stopped himself from throwing the punch. They'd settled on a nice weekly reward ceremony, and he didn't want to mess that up no matter how angry he was. "They got a Akh in the lead!" he yelled and kicked an ottoman across the floor.

"I see, this is problem?"

Swaggart snorted. "Yes, is problem," he mimicked back, then sat down on the couch. "I think he's stronger than me. The followers I could do when they come and go, follow them home, ye'd find them for me, but the politico would just find me. Likely kill me then take ye as a snack. Not that I care about ye," he added as his slave sat down on the floor in front of him.

His wardum grinned but said nothing.

"Balls! I'm a failure again!" Swaggart yelled. He flinched when a large hand came to rest on his knee.

"No, Sir. Only fail if you don't try," Karl told him, which reminded him of something his Grands used to say when he was growing up.

Swaggart thought for a moment, then placed his hand over the other's. "Ye ain't gonna coast this time. Ye gonna get into it with me."

"OK, OK," his slave replied, and when the vampire made his repeated sound of frustration, they both laughed.

"We must be smart about it, Sir," Karl pointed out after a few minutes.


The solution was obvious but disgusting. Adding the swastika to Karl's face was an added sign of his commitment to the Fatherland, and his native look and tongue made him a star candidate for their organization. The view of it only increased the intensity of the weekly reward sessions from Swaggart's side, and with bu running through him, the wardum could take it pretty easily. When they were done with this, when they'd killed them all, they'd get it removed, the vampire told them both. In two months, they had enough information to make an attack if they were careful.

They waited until a new moon, which was when Xul had their own little rituals and rites within the hives. Swaggart had no idea if the superstitious crap he'd heard was right or if the greater darkness would give the Sarrutum any extra powers, but he felt damned strong as he sliced through another Nazi in the building. Off to one side he heard Karl using his gun and his sword alternately as the vamp tried to cut his way through to the headman, who was glaring at him.

"How dare you interrupt our naming ceremony!"

"Looks like a party of sick fucks to me!" Swaggart yelled back, hitting one man who came at him in the throat and following through to sever his head from his neck.

"I will enjoy killing you, monster," the other Akhkharu said as he took off his robe, letting it fall to the platform he was standing on.

Karl had locked all the doors, and out of the corner of his eye, Swaggart could see him shooting anyone who tried to get the two doors opened. Since his slave was armed with several guns now, the sword at his feet, most of the bastards were staying a good distance from Karl, cowering from him as the bodies started to build up.

That was the last thought he had before the other Akh had him by the throat and up against one of the columns in the room. Attempts to break the other's hold proved futile, and he started to feel his flesh and bones sever around his neck when the other vamp burst into flames and screamed, releasing his grip. Staggering back on his hands and knees, Swaggart watched in horror as the politico's body continued to burn until it was collapsing in a pile of ash that turned to smoke.

He had only a moment to wonder what had happened when three Nazis piled on him. Rage exploded from him as he ripped them limb from limb, and shots rang out around him as the rest ran screaming into Karl's bullets or fell at Swaggart's feet as he lashed out with every part of himself.

It was only when silence fell that he heard another odd sound from the platform. There was an altar there, a concave vessel that he stood in front of in two bounds. He just stood there staring until Karl joined him. "Baby? What?" his slave asked, wiping a splatter of blood from his face.

They had decided that either they both died tonight or everyone in that building died. The baby was part of everyone, but Karl gasped when Swaggart lifted it from the altar to stare at it. "I'm sorry, luv," he whispered.

"Stop!" a child's voice cut through the air, and Swaggart dropped the infant back onto the altar where it started screaming. He could sense a wave of power rush over him and taking a deep whiff he scented an exceedingly old vampire somewhere.

Spinning around he saw a child-sized shadow. "I helped you. You owe me," she said.

"Didn't ask for yer 'elp!" he yelled and jumped off the back of the platform to get a better look at her, but the ancient's power was so strong it was making it difficult to focus his eyes. She seemed to have blonde hair and pale blue eyes, and was dressed in an oversized coat, a rucksack hanging from one hand.

"Most of your kind will die, and I won't be sorry for it, though he helped me when I needed it. If you leave the child and any other innocents, I'll let you leave here now," the ancient child told him.

"If I don't –" His words were cut off as he found his body tossed up and slammed into the ceiling, then back down onto the floor.

"Don't doubt I'll destroy you where you lie."

Swaggart pushed himself up to his knees and glared. "Don't much like little ones anyway," he mumbled. "No big deal to leave 'em be."

"Good. There will be others you mustn't allow to come to harm."

"Who?" he said and glanced up as Karl joined him to kneel on the floor.

A wave of energy seemed to strike him, making him bend over backwards with a scream of raw primal pain. He vaguely heard Karl pleading for him, but his mind was afire with a swirl of images, all surrounded by a weird glow. As suddenly as it had started, it stopped, and he found himself in Karl's arms.

His slave led him from the barn and back to their hidden auto. Behind them the building burst into flames. "Drive, just fucking drive," he said softly.

"Who was that, Sir?"

Swaggart just shook his head for several seconds. "Someone I can't fuck with." That's when he decided they'd be better off allying themselves with hives as they continued their journey of vengeance. She never said he couldn't do that, and maybe, just maybe, she couldn't find him, among others.

*"But that didn't happen," Bard concludes to the laughter of the audience.*

*Jamie, Elder of the Xul, snorts and gives the wardum a two-finger salute that has his own family laughing louder.*

*"That's a tale for later, perhaps tomorrow, if you are willing to return," I tell the audience, who immediately quiets and looks at me. After a moment they*

*start agreeing to return again to hear more tales after tonight, but we are far from finished.*

*"Not all of us are creatures of action, though we are all passionate," I proclaim, turning my eyes to the Allamudi group, whose elder, Cornelius, quickly closes the book he's been reading when our eyes meet.*

*"I know that you won't tell your own story, but I warn you that Bard may reveal deeper arousal than that found in your books."*

*Slowly my dearest scholar turns to his own most beloved servant. They just stare at each other for several moments before Cornelius sighs and motions for us to continue.*

*"I pieced this together from the writing of our honorable Cornelius and the tales that Jack has told me. Again, I must use some slang you may be unfamiliar with, but bear with me," Bard urges us before launching into his next tale.*

# Lost in Translation

Cornelius hummed a drinking song that was well over one thousand years old as he cleaned the hundreds of cases that housed his most valuable property: his tablets, scrolls, and books. As he moved, his old robe brushed the stone floors, sending slight whirls of dust building around them that made the old Akhkharu sigh. Protecting his precious writing meant doing the terribly boring work of maintaining the converted cave system, but truthfully, he preferred reading and rereading, patching up, and preserving the literature far more than mere dusting or checking the few mechanical systems he had set up.

He was alone, as he had primarily been for 1500 years. His numerous damu sent him akalum whenever they sent him new acquisitions, and he had a kataru, or alliance, with another of his family at the local universities and colleges within the region to send less-promising scholars who would not be missed his way from time to time. In exchange, Cornelius translated anything difficult, and they took all the credit. Other than to keep himself functioning for his passion, he rarely used his vampiric abilities and thus rarely used any bubussunu, so his hunger for anything other than knowledge was low.

As he worked through the glass cases, he picked up books and looked at his favorites. His current one was an account from the Fifth Crusade that any number of historians might give their souls for, though only one had given his life to bring it to Cornelius. The mortal had not needed to act like a jackass, but when he insisted on money for his trouble instead of simply being allowed to live, the Akh had had no choice but to hold him captive and feed on him over the course of three months. The fool's incessant screaming had forced the elder vampire to remove his tongue, a task he found distasteful, and which frankly only made the screams wordless and less noisy until the man gave up and fell silent.

That had been a few months ago, and he had had no visitors since then. Thus, when a knock came on the door at the entrance of the cave, which was marked with a state government sign warning that the cave was unstable, Cornelius assumed it was another meal sent by one of his allies. He put the small book back, shut the door to that case, and slowly made his way over. Mind-controlled humans would just stand there as long as need be once they'd knocked on the door.

Cornelius paused when another series of three knocks sounded on the metal door right in front of him. Ah, that suggested his visitor was one of his damu's wardum bringing him a new text. That hurried his steps a bit, and soon he had the seals on the door opened and was looking at an odd young male.

Granted, the boy was tall and broad, but his clothing and hair seemed childish as he stood there in pants that barely came to his knees, a simple shirt with long sleeves, and a pair of hiking boots with no hat on his odd blond spiky hair. At least he had the common sense to carry a big flashlight in the darkness at this time of night. The boy smiled at him and said, "Dude, sorry I knocked again.[1] Thought you might not have heard me."

Cornelius tilted his head to one side and considered what stood before him. This wasn't a wardum; there was no trace of anything supernatural about the boy. He was about to rip the creature's throat out when it spoke again. "Professor Weston said this was a hairy favor, that you'd be all fear and that, but other than a damned difficult to find inlander place, the hike was good."

---

[1] My simple attempts at using minor surfspeak comes from Trevor Cralle's *The Surfin'ary: A Dictionary of Surfing Terms and Surfspeak*, Berkeley, Ten Speed Press, 1991.

"You," Cornelius drew out the word with a sneer, "know Professor Evan Weston? I doubt it," he added and started to close the door until he was overcome by surprise as the boy literally slipped inside, barely pulling the backpack he wore with him.

"Chill, dude, you might trash the goods I was sent with," the boy said as he turned and flashed a brilliant smile the Akhkharu's way. "Oh, dude, you're going to think I'm derel, so here," he said as he fumbled in the pocket of his short pants for a folded envelope. The boy paused, then shrugged and got down on one knee to offer it on the tops of his palms. Someone had attempted to teach him some protocols, though the grin and eye contact were annoying.

Cornelius snatched the envelope and walked a few steps away so he could read it and keep an eye on this intruder, who stood up and looked around instead of waiting for permission to rise. Inside the envelope was a formal letter of introduction from his dami, who currently called himself Evan Weston, professor of Literature at Boston University. The boy was named Jack, and even though the professor gave his surname the older vampire dismissed it from his mind: akalum and wardum didn't need such lofty identifications as far as he was concerned. Such a "need" was a sign of their foolish overpopulation, which threatened the very survival of his precious literature and resulted in the bastardization of the art of writing and enlightenment of reading.

The letter said that this boy had just finished a dual degree in Classics and Library Science, which made Cornelius snort in disbelief as he noted that the intruder had turned and was craning his neck to try to see further into the cave system. The letter further claimed that the boy had graduated with highest honors in both fields and that Evan hoped his Shi might find some use for the creature in exchange for his advice on one of the texts he'd sent.

"You, Jack," Cornelius said sharply, which made the human turn around and look directly at him. "Give me the texts."

The boy nodded his head and slipped his backpack off to set it on the floor. He unzipped it as he knelt and carefully took out each wrapped item, then handed it to Cornelius until the vampire had a stack in his arms. "I can carry the rest inside, dude," he offered but was stopped by a growl. Frankly, these weighed nothing, even though the Akh didn't look particularly strong to the unknowing observer.

"Leave now," Cornelius ordered as he headed further into the cave. "Shut the door securely behind you."

"Wait, dude, ah, mister," the boy said as he jogged to him and stepped in front of him. The boy was lucky the vampire was not hungry right now, and he seemed completely clueless to the danger he was placing himself in by demanding further attention. "Professor Weston said you'd have a job for me. Right?"

"Wrong," Cornelius simply replied and stepped around the boy.

In a few minutes he heard the door shut firmly, so Cornelius set his new acquisitions down and took out the text he was asked to lend his expertise to. The text in question was actually a four-page photocopy of something that flew from his hands at the unexpected voice behind him. "Dude, that wanks because the prof promised me you'd have this rad job for me. I've got a small place, and I've totally done the R&D and found some sweet spots for dawn patrol ..." and then the human gasped as Cornelius wrapped one hand around his neck and lifted him from the ground.

The Akh's full power was shining forth like a cloud across the sun, his lips pulled back to reveal his fangs, his fingernails extended and digging into the stupid mortal's soft neck. All it would take was a flick of his wrist and the annoyance would end, but the whispered words made the vampire pause and loosen his grip enough to clarify what he heard.

"Ati Me Peta Babka," the boy forced through his throat and lips. He was repeating the Sumerian password that Cornelius' damu used to signal potential wardum material. He gasped and sat on the floor when the Akhkharu tossed him. The boy was muttering as the vampire approached. "Grim situation, not derel, won't be drilled," he muttered, and this only made Cornelius order him to shut up if he couldn't speak sensibly.

"Periculosus locus, non bardus, mos non deficio," the boy said in broken Latin through his coughing. "Ianitor, patefacio vestri porta mihi."

86

Cornelius paused, and his intense anger faded as his body took on its more mortal-seeming form. "Your Latin is atrocious," he stated.

The boy stood up on shaky legs. "Docui mihi," he said as he took one step forward, his eyes now watching warily.

Cornelius narrowed his eyes again and waved at the scattered four pages of photocopies. "Put them in order, and I will consider not tearing you limb from limb."

"Totally fear," the boy whispered only loud enough for an Akh to hear, but Cornelius said nothing as he watched the mortal pick up the pages and start looking at them carefully. There was no title page, and thus the only way to sort them was to read the beginning and ending of each, then attempt to put them into the correct order.

In only a few minutes the boy offered him the pages as he had the letter of introduction, but this time he turned his eyes away. Cornelius took the pages and was surprised to find them in order. "Come," he ordered simply, then turned and returned to his big desk where he had set the other books.

Then he sighed, imagining what sort of filth the mortal might have on him. "Supposedly you have some training with libraries, so go clean up and put on the appropriate gloves to move these," he ordered again with another wave toward the small bathroom he had been forced to get to accommodate any akalum he had staying with him for more than a day.

The boy went to the open area, then glanced back with a shudder, but took his time to clean up his hands, lower arms and even slid down his short pants to clean up the mess his terror at the vampire's anger had caused. Most Akhkharu were more sensitive to smell, but unless it was a direct danger to his precious texts, Cornelius paid such things little heed. The boy returned with a pair of clean cotton gloves like the vampire wore. Upon one simple set of instructions and three trips, the boy had delivered the new materials to the sorting table and put them into four piles based on their subject. These were all in Greek and Latin; Cornelius assumed this had been his dami's attempt to make him interested in the boy. But that wasn't what truly interested him right now as the boy's movement stirred up more dust.

"Remove the gloves, then clean this floor," the Akh ordered as he continued reading the photocopied pages. They were an odd mixture of French, German, Latin, Greek and Sumerian, like nothing he'd seen before, in a passage about esoteric and forbidden knowledge some unidentified author claimed to have discovered on a trip to a newly unearthed Babylonian site. Forbidden indeed, because as he continued to read, he realized that this mortal was talking about the Ummum, the mother of all Akhkharu and their own legends about themselves. Cornelius frowned at a word that couldn't be what he thought it was, for it wasn't "woman" at all but "girl" that was written in the text. He'd need to re-examine some reference materials to decipher it more fully.

For a moment he recalled a strange little girl he'd met while escaping from Constantinople as it was falling for the last time out of Christian hands. As he'd fled with two servants and one dami at his side, they'd seen a woman and a girl traveling toward the City, neither of whom had paid any attention to their pleas to turn away. He could feel the girl's power, stronger than his own Shi had wielded, when they had passed close to them. The child's eyes had met his with a bright smile as she said, "You must go much further to be where you are meant to be." Shaking his head at this odd memory, the Allamudi returned his attention to the words that seemed driven into his mind.

As he was absorbed in his task, he was oblivious to the boy working and casting furtive glances at him that began wary then turned annoyed and finally angry. "Dude, um, Mister," the mortal said, his voice bringing Cornelius's attention to him as the boy stood there, his clothing and person wet and messy. "Your floor and the walls were hideous. I'm gonna need to pop some to deal with this shit in my head."

Cornelius just shook his head, not completely certain he understood what the human was complaining about, but he did notice the floor. It was shiny and clean, more so than he'd seen in years, and when he took a sniff, it smelled clean, but not in any fashion that might damage his precious texts. The Akh turned and looked at the walls around him and noticed they were also clean. "This area is acceptable, but you need to do the rest."

"Done," the boy replied as he folded his arms across his chest. "You been in the pages there for about five hours, Dude ... Mister," he added.

"Follow," Cornelius ordered as he took off to examine the rest of the cave. The boy was correct in that he had cleaned the parts of the system he could access, but when the Akh took out a key and opened another door and pointed, the human just made a sound of frustration.

"No, not until you agree to give me a job. A real job," the mortal insisted in the best English he'd used to this point.

"Real job?" Cornelius repeated as he stepped closer to the boy. "Explain what you think a real job with me will entail."

The boy swallowed but then lifted his chin up and continued. "You know, regular hours, regular tasks, a chance to do what I was taught to do, decent salary, benefits, time to catch the waves. Prof told me this wasn't paradise, but hey, I got waves, so it's better than Beantown."

The Akh studied the human for several seconds, then nodded. "Go get your possessions, then wait for me by the entrance. I do not tolerate being spoken back to," he added when the boy opened his mouth as though to speak more.

Cornelius went to one of his locked sections where he kept his other non-text possessions and opened a large trunk. He took out one of the many coins he'd collected over the years and studied it. No clue what it was worth today; he determined it might be a good week's salary, and if not, the annoying human could become lunch or mindless without much effort, thus protecting the Akh's holdings and existence. As he walked back to the mortal, Cornelius sighed, wishing foolishly that the texts he was looking at were correct.

"Take this and trade it for what you can. Return tomorrow at midnight," Cornelius simply said as he handed the boy the coin. "Shut the door securely behind you," he added, but did not move this time so he could make certain the human did as instructed.

The boy nodded, mumbled something that sounded like "Ionic," then left, slamming the door hard as he did so. Cornelius rubbed his head as he went to sleep. Whatever language the boy was speaking was odd, but his Latin pronunciation and grammar were like fingernails on a chalkboard. He'd just have to beat better English into him if he decided to keep him on as help, with more beating to fix his Latin before he'd even consider claiming him as a wardum.

Jack went back to the beach and retrieved his board from the little hut he'd rented the day before. His stomach was rumbling, but the sun rising over the morning waves was too tempting, so he pulled on his dry suit. This wasn't ideal, but it was better than living in Beantown, he consoled himself as he took off into the water, where he knew he would not be completely out of his element, as he had been in the weird scholar's cave.

A few hours, a shower, and a change of clothes later he was eating a pastry at a shop in the nearby town and studying the coin he'd been paid. It had some Latin on it, but the quality of the images was not Roman or well made, though it was in great shape as far as he could tell. He asked the cashier if there was a museum in town and then headed off on foot toward that place.

The lovely at the cashier's desk at this small museum looked at his coin, didn't charge him admission, and pointed him toward the director's office. It didn't take much more than a flash of the object to get him invited in to sit while the man cooed over the coin and called up some colleagues.

An hour later, Jack was on a bus to a city a few hours away to meet another museum curator who attempted to convince him to donate the coin. When they wouldn't pay him for the coin he sighed and left, only to be whispered to outside by someone in a suit. "Look," this other man said, "I know a company that deals with private collectors of such things. For a reasonable commission, I can get you a meeting with them, since you said this was part of your inheritance."

That was the lie that Jack had told, and he wasn't completely sure why he'd lied at all. Something about his old professor and the weird guy in the cave made him feel like he needed to lie about them. They felt off, but still, he couldn't pull himself away. He made an appointment to meet with this guy and his colleague back in town the next day, so he didn't need the bus. As he got back on the bus and studied the little coin, he felt like this might be one strange but potentially profitable job for a while.

Over the course of the next few nights and days, his profit predictions came true, but the guy in the cave got weirder and weirder. The coin turned out to be a 6th century piece that the private collector paid him almost a thousand for after his new buddy's commission. When the weird dude asked him if it proved a worthy weekly salary, he could only stutter and say, "Yes." With this cash he could afford a bigger hut, but primarily he started dreaming about the new board and gear he could get.

The weird guy told him to call him "Master," which was not going to happen as far as Jack was concerned, so he simply waited to be noticed and finished assigned tasks silently, which seemed to please the freak. He could think of him as "the boss," but not "master," though he never said that out loud; the creepy feeling he got when he was around Cornelius made him careful to keep his emotions in check.

Jack got to see the rest of the cave, which was this massive system designed to preserve an amazing collection of rare books. Yes, the temps and humidity in the cave were fairly consistent, but when Jack offered some suggestions, the boss just hushed him and told him to work.

Besides cleaning the floors and walls, which desperately needed it, Jack also had daytime errands to run the guy's clothing, also very weird, to the dry cleaners with another old coin he had to trade again. Seemed like the dude didn't have any modern money and lived entirely off the grid, which would be cool, except he also didn't have any food or anything to drink but water from the little bathroom sink. When Jack mentioned that he got hungry and thirsty while he worked his boss only stared at him, then muttered something about the "weakness of humans" and agreed to let him bring some things in as long as he made sure not to infest the place.

After a month, Jack had over $3000 in a new bank account and had finished cleaning everything he could and getting into a routine of keeping it all to the boss's harsh criteria. Every night, the boss also gave him a section of text to translate, and Jack figured it was to test his skills. Without a dictionary, though, it was a bit slow. Most of the texts he'd never seen before, and they were strange in content; some of the words weren't even in Greek or Latin but some other languages that seemed

91

to be in a distantly related linguistic group that had been transliterated into Greek and Latin scripts. When he finished with a text, copying the unknown parts on a separate piece of paper, the boss offered him a goblet, again some old looking thing, full of the oddest wine he'd ever tasted, though the taste grew on him with every glass.

As the months rolled by, Jack found himself more engrossed in the texts and pleasing the boss and less concerned about having to skip out on beach parties early or being too tired to do dawn patrol each morning. He got a simple cot and started to move his few possessions into the cave, in a small empty section that had a door that locked on it, though he wasn't given the key. One morning as he ate his pastry in the coffee shop he visited each day, he was surprised to see the guy who arranged his coin sales for him. "Jack? Where have you been? We've been dying to know if you want to sell any more of those great coins but haven't heard from you in over two weeks."

Jack shook his head. "Sorry, very busy at work, you know. Here," he fumbled in his jacket pocket and found the last four coins he'd been paid, which the man took from him immediately.

"Your uncle must have been some eccentric. Every coin is from a different time, a different place; you are so increasing my side business," the man confessed. After slipping each coin into a plastic baggie the man frowned at Jack. "Are you feeling all right? You look pale, like you aren't getting much sun."

"Night shift is a bitch," Jack simply said, and the coin dealer shook his head.

"If you were to sell all your coins, I think you could just retire and spend your days in the surf, wouldn't that be ideal?"

Of course, he didn't really have all those coins, he got only one a week, but the ideal wasn't sounding so ideal anymore, and that made Jack stand up suddenly and run from the coffee house into the mountains.

Cornelius awoke to find his new servant staring down at him. The Akh had been expecting a series of questions, but then again, the human seemed so easily manipulated and controlled that he'd started to believe he might not need to tell him for several years when the image in the mirror showed the face of a 23-year-old instead of a much older man. "What have you been doing to me?" the boy asked.

Cornelius stood up, and the mortal stepped back instinctively, the bu in his system making him unconsciously acquiesce to his master's desires, though he still had not learned the proper protocols. "Ask me in the correct manner, and I will answer you, Jack." The Akh had begun to use his servant's name after the third bonding ceremony. While other families might use complex Tamu, or vows, his merely required acknowledgement of their dynamic and a series of annual tests to prove the slave's continued intellectual value. And the ring – he had a nice ring he'd give the boy if only he'd fall in line.

The boy just paused, then he started to shake until he was yelling. "That is totally uncool! I'm out of here!"

Cornelius just watched as the mortal stormed out and slammed the door behind him. He did briefly wonder how many days the mortal could last without his presence and bu but dismissed the idea as he picked up a recent addition to compare it to a few others he was using to trace this prophecy about the Ummum and her return. He was convinced now that their creator was indeed a female child, and now all that remained was to figure out which form she'd appear in at the Time of Revealing.

Cornelius ignored his servant's presence and words until the boy said the required terms with a choked voice. "Master, please, what did you do to me? Please."

The boy was kneeling on the floor, tears rolling down his cheeks, holding himself as he shook. It had been over a week, and the Akh was indeed impressed with the wardum's self-control. One of the big problems with such blood-bound slaves was that they needed to be in contact with their vampire owners on a regular and consistent basis. With age and training, one could create a trusted servant to do one's work miles and miles away for days at a time, but even then, they required contact of some form. It was one of the great limitations Cornelius saw with having mortals as servants at all, but other Akhkharu could never be fully trusted beyond the general outlines of any kataru; by their nature they were each independent and dominant forces to be reckoned with.

Cornelius waited for his servant to plead for information again before he bent down and picked the boy up, one of his stronger-than-mortal hands on each of his arms, so he was holding the mortal upright but denied his feet the floor to stand on. "I gave you what you wanted, Jack. A job, a job unlike any you could possibly get outside in the human world."

Jack swallowed and whispered, "You aren't human."

"No, something I revealed your first night here, but you were too stupid to run away then, and now it's too late, my wardum," Cornelius stated as he set the boy on his feet.

"Wardum? That's a word in the text you had me copy. What does it mean?"

Cornelius chuckled as he considered the man before him, still trembling. "I think you are clever enough to have pieced it together from the words around those statements. Of course, if you aren't," he continued, and as he spoke the Akh pierced one wrist with a long sharp fingernail and let his blood pool there, "I can always send you away."

The mortal was staring at the small pool of dark crimson. "That's what you were giving me," he said slowly as he willed his eyes to move upward to meet his boss's face. "It's like a drug, and you've enslaved me. No wonder they didn't answer my cries," he whispered as he stepped forward.

"Who?" Cornelius's curiosity got the better of him.

"First, I called out to Jesus, figured he made my mom happy, and I'd been baptized and all of that, right?" Jack explained as he stopped and fell to his knees before the Akh. "The urge to come back here was so strong, so I went to the waves and called to Kahuna, who I always figured was really a metaphor, but even a classic day couldn't keep me away from here, from you ... Master," he whispered as he looked up at the blood now dripping from flesh to the floor.

"Drink," Cornelius said, and the mortal took his wrist and lapped at it hungrily. Usually, they didn't need bu more than weekly or monthly, but that was if they were in their Bel's presence; more time away meant the thirst grew. The Akhkharu muttered the final words, pledging himself to use this slave well, until he pulled his wrist away, willed the wound to close, and silently slipped the simple gold ring onto the boy's right index finger. Immediately the wardum bent his head to the floor and licked up the drops there before sitting back with more tears streaming down his face.

"Smile, Jack; it is a rare honor you've been given to serve one of us. So few of you know we exist beyond your silly stories."

Jack forced himself to smile and stand up to follow his master to the desk, where he was going over his latest projects. "Master?" At a glance from the Akh, the wardum continued, "I think I need something else from you, please," he pleaded as he turned the ring on his finger a few times.

Cornelius almost sighed. Ah, yes, the senses of wardum were increased, as well as their desires for all forms of contact with their owners. Frankly, it seemed like a waste of time, but the few wardum he'd had over his many centuries were all the same, male or female; they needed that intimate touch to ground them from time to time, a fact that the Gelal exploited in a disgusting fashion but which all families used to their benefit. Given that he did not have another mortal presently, the Akh realized he'd need to make contact himself, which meant putting off the next section in his text a bit longer. But the boy was young; how much time could he need?

"Let us be civilized about it, then," Cornelius announced as he grabbed his wardum by his wrist and dragged him to his sleeping alcove. "Remove your clothing while I light the candles," he instructed.

There were only a few large candles on stands to be lit, and the mortal already wore little clothing, so soon he was naked in the shimmering flames. The Akh considered his new slave in his full form for the first time. He reached out and cupped his face, pinched a nipple, gripped an upper arm and thigh, then turned him and considered his backside before turning him again to find Jack's manhood at half stance. At least his wardum appeared to be in good physical form.

"I've never been with a guy before," Jack whispered as he swallowed and looked down to find himself even more aroused at that admission and the possibilities of what they might do running through his mind.

"You begin by removing my clothing and folding it respectfully," Cornelius ordered as he had his own slaves when he had been a mere mortal, and early in his dark existence when physical matters still stirred his own manhood. Now he might be aroused from reading a complex piece of literature, but his last wardum had been well over two centuries ago when he'd first set up this repository. The wardum had proven himself so capable that he'd been killed by a rival Akh, so Cornelius had sworn to his damu at the time that he'd never take another fragile mortal as an assistant. That his child would ignore his oath and send this boy to him might have been compensation for his inability to find a worthy grandchild for the line.

The young wardum worked quickly to disrobe his master and fold his robes, trousers, and undergarments, then stepped back and sank to his knees. "Master, you are awesome," he said as he looked at the well-built body of a middle-aged man who stood straight and firm before him. The only problem was that the Akh's own groin was not aroused, and Jack looked up with a worried frown. "Does my body displease you, Master?"

Cornelius tilted his head to one side and considered the words. "Your actions and attitude will impress me more. Take my member into your hands and feel it, then use your lips and tongue on it until you stir it to firmness. Do you require further instructions?"

The boy was blushing as he reached up and shook his head. "I can figure it out, Master. I know what feels good to me, I've seen porn," he added with a slight grin that seemed more like the original Jack who'd shown up at the cave at the end of spring.

The first thing that Jack noticed was that his master was not circumcised, though if he really were a vampire, he could be hundreds of years old, and that wasn't common in the distant past unless you were Jewish or Egyptian, but he looked more European than Middle Eastern in descent. He touched the cool, soft flesh and was rewarded by a slight movement of the organ. "Master, you got lube?" Jack asked, knowing that dry stroking was a huge turnoff to him and assuming it was for other dudes as well. In the pornos guys just used spit, and that gave him an idea when the Akh didn't reply.

Jack lowered his mouth to the soft flesh and used his tongue to get it wet, his hand sliding up and down as he got it moist, until it was poking out and bobbing with each stroke. Without instruction, he tightened his lips over his teeth and opened his mouth wide enough to slip the tip into it. The extra skin moved back and forth; it tasted bitter for a few sucks until that disappeared, and Jack found a good rhythm he hoped his master would like. The Akh, however, was just standing with his eyes closed, his hands on his hips as his member was worked.

The boy didn't have many skills, but he did manage to keep his teeth under control and breathe after each stroke. Previous wardum had taken themselves to brothels and learned skills during their service for their own amusement, Cornelius believed, but frankly this was more for the wardum's benefit than for his.

When he was hard, Jack sat back and smiled. "Never thought I'd want a guy to plow me," he said with a grin as he stood up. "I've never, you know, been on that side of it," he added with a swallow.

Plow sounded like an old term for intercourse drawn from agricultural cultures to Cornelius's ears, and he wondered what this mortal could possibly know about growing food, since all he ever talked about were the texts and the waves. "There will be pain, Jack. The first several times there will be pain, especially because I am not prepared for such interactions," the Akh cautioned his servant.

The wardum paused, then snapped his fingers and went to his shorts, where he pulled out a few little packets. "I got these yesterday in a drugstore when I was trying to keep you off my mind," he admitted. "Thought maybe I'd meet a lovely, but no, you're pretty much what was in my mind, Master."

Cornelius looked at the square but did not move to take it. "What is it?"

Jack frowned then he chuckled. "I'll show you," he whispered as he tore the small square and took out a circle of rubber that he stretched a bit. Then he put his mouth back onto the vampire's cock and got his master erect again before slowly rolling the condom onto his shaft. He wasn't particularly skilled, but he knew what to do from sex ed, pornos, and personal experience on himself. "It has some slick on it so you can plow more easily, Master," Jack said as he blushed a bright red.

"Slick?"

"Lube, to make it easier, safer," Jack continued as he stood up on shaking legs. Without another word he turned and bent over his small cot, placing his hands at shoulder width and his legs equally spread.

It has been decades, but Cornelius doubted mortal men had changed much. He placed a cool hand on each of his wardum's cheeks and let the human's heat warm him up before parting them to view the back opening. They'd discuss hygiene later, the Akh decided as he positioned himself and started to penetrate his servant. He went slowly but steadily, holding the boy's hips to help him cope and slowing down further when Jack's voice or breath hitched with pain.

Once he was inside and their balls were almost touching, the wardum shuddered. "Damn, totally, god, totally insane," Jack whispered as he glanced back to find the vampire regarding him.

Cornelius frowned. "Sexual penetration affects your mental health?"

Jack rolled his eyes and nodded. "Totally, in a good way, Master." They remained still in this position until Jack groaned. "Please, Master, please, I think I want, I need you, more," he mumbled.

The vampire nodded, and holding onto the boy's hips, he began to thrust in and out, never fully exiting the mortal's hot core completely as he did so. The condom on him decreased his own sensation by a small amount, but frankly Cornelius never came for his own pleasure but for the satisfaction of his slaves, since their bond created a strong need for connection that he himself did not share. As the boy's sound turned from moans to groans to gasps, the Akh decided he'd had enough, so he angled his own hips to start hitting that spot deep inside that caused all men to spend quickly.

The result was that Jack stopped all movement and sound and just looked back at the vampire as his prostate was pounded over and over until he literally stood up and shot over the cot. Cornelius wrapped an arm around his wardum and helped him stand as he calmed down. "Master? What was that? What did you do?"

Cornelius smiled slightly as he pulled out and let the boy fall to the cot. "You have a lot to learn about your own body, Jack. You have ten minutes to clean up, then I want you to look through the Byzantine philosophy collection I have. I want summaries in two months, and it is extensive." With that the Akh pulled up his trousers, then left.


Two months later, Jack knelt on the cave's floor as his master examined his summaries. He had not given the assignment his entire life, but he'd worked on it every night from the time the master awoke until he slept. Being wardum, which was what he was now – more than a mere human, he'd learned – had a lot of advantages. First, he never felt ill, which meant he never had to miss work or the beach. Second, his stamina seemed to have increased as well as his ability to focus, so he was able to accomplish more in less time.

Thus, the days he could spend on the waves until he could barely move, grab a few hours' sleep, then drive up to the cave. Eating took some remembering, and he only got serious about it when the bros started harassing him about turning into skin and bones and not being a decent shark meal.

"For a brief scan of the materials, this is acceptable," Cornelius said as he handed the handwritten pages back to Jack. "Your next assignment is to start reading the texts."

Jack took the sheets and nodded. Byzantine Greek could be either easy or difficult to handle, depending on the writer and the quality of the text, but frankly he didn't know what good his reading them would do his master. He stood up, followed the Akhkharu to his desk, and took a deep breath before speaking. "You sure you don't have anything else you want me to do, Bel?" He'd learned some of the more appropriate terms for the Night Kingdom these past two months and found his master more approachable when he used these ancient formalities.

Cornelius blinked, then looked at his wardum. The boy still dressed in an atrocious fashion, and his speech was barbaric, but he was as intelligent as his dami had promised. "You may take the evening off if you like, Jack; begin reading tomorrow night," the vampire offered. Allamudi knew that intellectual value had to be nurtured by both tasks and relaxation; they thought of themselves as the kindliest of masters.

"Really? Well, there is this luau tonight down on the beach … Would you like to go with me, Bel?"

t took the ancient Akhkharu some time to process what his servant
had just said, then he sat back and considered the boy. "Go with you?"

"Sure. You ever been to a luau? It's rad, lots of lovelies and bros,
insane food, dancing, killer drinks. You could, you know, hunt," Jack
offered using some of the terms he'd learned in his studies about his
master's people. They really were a people with a mystical past, rules
and norms, an evolving language, and even a set of laws that governed
them when they lived in the cities among their akalum, or prey.

All that study had been hideous on some level, yet it made so much
sense on others. Several historical events made more sense when you
thought of vampire overlords manipulating human populations and
dictating bizarre trends in culture. Human beings were obsessed with
issues of reproduction, food, and populations because they meant so
much to their secret masters. That they had to remain a secret seemed
odd to Jack, but he knew at some primal level that he wasn't close
enough to his master to ask those sorts of questions.

Cornelius thought for a moment. It had been a while since he'd
hunted; something deep inside him called out when he considered it.
He had finished with his dami's translations and sent on copies to a few
other scholars he respected; if the boy was willing to risk offending him
by this luau, he'd give it a go. "Yes, we will go to this luau of yours,
Jack."

Jack left his master by the fire, where the vampire seemed content
to observe the lovelies and bros interacting in what he'd whispered was
a "peasant's mating ritual." With that statement, Jack had started to
observe his friends and their dates with new eyes. Everyone was very
drunk and luckily not stupid enough to go out on the dark waves. He
had only had one beer and had brushed off two lovelies who had tried
to scam him as he stood by his master unless he was filling his plate
with more food. He and Cornelius were different from everyone else,
and here on the beach he felt that difference more strongly than when
they were in the Akhkharu's cave.

"Bro, who's the fossil you brought?" one of his surfing buddies
asked as Jack picked up a plate of food.

100

"That's my Bel ... boss, my boss," he caught himself. "Cornelius Bel," he lied to cover his earlier slip.

"Your boss? As in the inlander who paid for that killer board you just got?"

Jack nodded, suddenly feeling especially uncomfortable here among his peers with his master just a few steps away. Surfers bragged about their skills on the waves and in bed, but dudes never did it with dudes, so Jack considered it a grim situation he was now in. To combat that he started alternately insulting and praising his buddies' skills, dragging out every memory he had of their adventures and his own elsewhere.

Jack spun around as a cool hand dropped on his shoulder. The fossil was talking to him, no, his master was talking to him, and he focused on the vampire immediately. "We must go now, unless you intend to bed one of the ladies here?"

"Ladies!" his buddies repeated with some rude gestures that said lovelies returned as they started threatening to leave unless the men paid more attention to them.

Jack glanced at his watch and saw that a good hour had passed. "Yes, Bel," he said and only when his buddies and his master made a noise, did he blush and look at the sand and say, "Yes, Mr. Bel, I'll see you home safely, Sir."

As they walked away, wardum and Akhkharu, Jack heard his buddies make rude speculations behind his back about his "work" that ranged from his being on a short leash to his being a slave to his being his boss's own lovely to plow. He couldn't tell them they were wrong, so he just felt his face heat up as they walked to the parking lot.

They drove to the cave in silence, and Jack followed his master inside, stopping only when the vampire put his cool hand on his face. "The luau was not to your liking, Jack? I found it most fascinating."

"I'm glad, Bel, I'm very glad. I, um," and Jack took a breath as the evening caught up with him, leaving his head spinning and his heart heavy. "Could I stay here during the day, Master, while you slept? I could get more reading, cleaning, organizing done. I promise I won't bother you at all, and I'd go to town to run errands and do all the stuff we need."

Cornelius smiled and put his hands on the boy's shoulders. "You are welcome to expand your education here, Jack, or elsewhere as well. Come, the sun will be up soon, and I can tell from your breathing that you desire closeness."

"Yes, Master, I do," Jack admitted as he followed his Bel to his sleeping chamber. Inside he could feel himself becoming dismo, and that only bothered him slightly as he felt the waves drift further from him.

*"I have more respect for you," Maha chuckles lightly as soon as Bard finishes the tale, causing all in the garden to erupt into laughter.*

*"These are amusing tales," Enki says as he hops down from the wall. My descendants know of him, though his full power he never reveals to them. Most of them think of him as another supernatural creature like Ziusudra, and he is content to let me keep his secret.*

*Enki walks toward me and sits in the front row, the ground growing moist beneath him. "I believe now it is your story again, Ummum."*

*"Yes, though, Bard," I call to my other wardum as Jon glances at Enki, then at me, "do you have the strength to repeat Jon's tale?"*

*"Ah, Jon's tale, is it, Bel?" the older man asks as he nods. "Your strength in me allows me to keep talking for as long as you all wish, if," and he pauses and looks to the others, "you would like to learn more about your creator and her arammu-wardum."*

*"Ain't fair to leave em out," Jamie replies as the others agree.*

*"This, then, is what Jon has told me," Bard begins.*

# Orphans

Jon had kicked the discarded beer can for almost a mile when he finally stopped and just sank to his knees. "I can't go back," he whispered as his slacks soaked up the puddle he'd landed in. His head ached; his stomach ached; he wouldn't have been surprised if his soul were aching as well from the longing he felt. Four months ago, he'd been his Bel's arammu-wardum, his personal secretary, his confidant, and his lover, all while working from home as a highly paid computer programmer.

Three months ago, he had quite literally been kicked out onto the streets. Montesarat was moody, so Jon had just gone to his private apartment and waited. And waited. And waited.

At the end of the first month, he'd telephoned the main house, but he'd been hung up on. Two weeks later a letter he'd sent had returned unopened. No one had answered the door when he'd visited at the end of two months.

Starting to feel desperate, Jon had started waiting around the main house, harassing anyone who left it. Most had run away when he'd talked to them, but he wouldn't just allow them to ignore him. Finally, Sara, who had served Montesarat longer than he, had confronted him.

The Master thought that Jon had cheated on him. There'd been reports that he'd been seen at gay bars, and even a letter from a rival Akhkharu claiming he'd had sex with him. Nothing Jon said mattered to Sara because, as she pointed out, all that mattered was the rumor that something had happened. Since they'd suspected that it was all a lie, he was allowed to continue his mortal job and keep his apartment, but one word to anyone about vampires and – she drew a finger across her throat sharply.

Those concessions meant nothing to Jon. Mortal life? Over the next year his 25 years in service would start to show in his body as he'd age to his actual early fifties. How could he explain it to the mortals he must interact with on a daily basis? He'd have to move if he decided to live. Right now, he was too confused and hurt to think beyond the next few seconds.

Jon stopped crying when a familiar echo reached his ears. Someone else was crying. He stood up, his damp slacks clinging to his legs, and looked around. He was in a park, one fairly far from Montesarat and from his apartment as well. The cry was feminine and childlike. Without much thought, he headed toward the direction of the sound.

Both thoughts had been correct. A young girl, maybe six or seven years of age, was sitting on the ground by a park bench crying. Her light brown hair was in loose braids, and she was wearing a pink dress over light blue leggings, a white sweater tied around her waist. A teddy-bear-shaped backpack was sitting next to her, and she cradled a rag doll in her arms. She stopped crying and just looked at Jon as he approached her.

Jon crouched down to look directly at the child. "Are you lost?" he asked, amazed and worried slightly when she nodded but didn't seem afraid of him; didn't parents warn their kids about strangers anymore? "I'll help you find your mommy, then. Do you know her name?"

The little girl shook her head, and Jon noted how pale she seemed. "Do you know your daddy's name?"

"I don't have a mommy or daddy," she said, and her trembling, slight voice filled him with intense empathy.

"I'm alone, too," he said as he opened his arms up to her.

She came into his hug and let him pick her up, laying her head on his shoulder. "My tummy's hungry," she whispered, and he felt his heart ache.

"You should eat something," he said. "I can take you somewhere." Then he stopped as fangs sank into his neck. He felt the erotic rush of the bite leave his knees weak, as he sank to them. In a few minutes, the drain of his life force left him unconscious.

Jon woke up to the sound of a child humming. He opened his eyes just enough to see his attacker sitting next to him on the ground; she was humming to her rag doll. She still seemed sweet and innocent, and he was unable to be angry with her; she had to survive, after all. "Generally, it is better to ask permission before you take blood from someone," he stated as he sat up.

Her brilliant blue eyes glanced at him, then she tried to scramble away. She was fast, really fast, like some very old Akhkharu were rumored to be, so Jon only managed to grab her doll and backpack while she bolted away. "You're faster than me," he conceded as he walked to the nearest bench and sat down, his new possessions in his lap.

He wasn't thinking rationally, only acting on instinct, because his logical memory would have told him that no Akh takes another's servant, especially a dishonored and dismissed one. He felt so empty, so alone; he knew she felt that way, too, because it couldn't all just be an act or his desperation playing tricks on him. It just couldn't, because that would be too much to bear. He waited for a while until he was sure she was still around and within hearing range. He held the doll up to one ear and nodded before announcing, "Lucy says she misses her mommy."

"That's not her name," a child's angry voice replied somewhere behind him.

He held the doll up again and laughed. "Lucy says that you don't love her."

"I do so love her. Her name is Mary," the child replied, and she sounded closer.

Jon had, as far as he was concerned, nothing to live for except maybe this opportunity, so he pretended to listen to the doll again. "She says that if you loved her, you wouldn't have run off." He turned around to stare straight into the small vampire's eyes, "'Cause you'd know that I just want to help you."

They stared at each other for several minutes until he held the doll out toward her. "It's Mary," she insisted, snatching it from him.

"Are you sure?" he asked as he turned to watch her circle the bench a few times before she sat next to him.

"Mary," she repeated firmly, hugging the doll tightly to her chest while she eyed her backpack, still on his lap. "Sam," she added with a nod toward the teddy bear's form.

Jon nodded and pointed out the doll, the backpack, his own chest, and then the vampire and he said their names, "Mary, Sam, Jon, and?" He paused, then spoke more like an adult. "My name is Jon."

When she didn't answer he pretended to listen to the teddy bear backpack. "He told me your name, but since Mary lied to me about her name, I can't be sure. Would you tell your name? Please?"

The little vampire frowned but replied, "Charity," after a few silent seconds.

Jon smiled, nodded, and handed her the backpack. "Charity. That's a nice name. I know what you are and why you bit me. I want to help you, I know how to help you, I've helped your kind before," he added gently. He wasn't lying, really; she was just a child, after all, and perhaps didn't even know what she was or how careful she really needed to be. The night kingdom was powerful, but only so long as they hid in the shadows and the fantasies of mortals.

They just sat there in silence for a few minutes, then Jon stood up, a bit wobbly on his feet from the drain of blood, but the remnants of Montesarat in his flesh, mind, and soul were healing him still. "Look, I'm going to go grab something to eat, then head home. You are welcome to join me, Charity. I really do want to help you." With that he left.

He got several yards away when a small, cool hand slipped into his bigger, warmer one. He smiled down at her as they walked to a nearby café, where he got a huge sandwich and an extra-large soda pop with an extra empty glass and plate for appearance's sake. He chose a quiet corner so no one could comment on whether or not she was eating. As he ate, she chatted to her doll in a language he couldn't completely understand, but it sounded a bit familiar, almost Sumerian, the language of all Akhkharu. He hadn't been expected to learn it beyond the basic phrases that populated the night kingdom that he knew secretly ran everything.

Then when he was almost finished, she took the empty glass, bit into her own wrist, and bled into it so it was about half full. Jon's eyes focused until all he could see was the red, his ears focused on each drop, his nose picked out the special scent that vampire blood possessed, and his tongue could almost taste it. She licked the punctures closed and slid the glass toward him. "You want this," she said clearly.

Jon just looked at it, then at her. "Charity, do you know what this will do to me?"

She nodded. "Mary remembered first. It's been a long time for me since I needed it. But I'll be a good girl, I promise. I'll take care of you if you take care of me." Her voice was almost pleading.

Vampires do not plead, they do not weep, and they certainly never ever beg anything from a wardum, ex-wardum, a blood slave, abandoned slave. *They should also never be small children,* he countered mentally. Vampire blood, as far as he knew, was all the same, and it would solve one of his biggest problems as well as create another set of them if he accepted her offer. The blood, or bubussunu, bu for short, only created half the bond required of a wardum, and he didn't know what family she was or what else she'd have to do to him, but right now she was looking seriously at him, waiting for him to make a decision, needing him to make a decision, it seemed. As he sat there, he felt safe and needed, something he suddenly realized he'd never felt with Montesarat.

Jon drank it all down quickly, then set the empty glass on the table. His head spun for a second. It wasn't true; bu wasn't just bu, but what hers was doing to him was unclear. He smiled at her, stood up and offered her his hand. "To home then, Bel?" he said, adding the honorific because it gave him comfort to use that title again. If she knew how to do a contract and continued to give him her blood, by the end of a week he wouldn't have any choice but to call her by that title. Part of him was anxious for that, and another part was terrified of the possibility.

"Yes, Daddy," she beamed up at him as she scrambled out of her seat, dragging doll and backpack behind her. Her use of a title for him made him blush and glance around at the mostly empty café. Joining the night kingdom basically eliminated any option to have kids unless the master commanded it. It felt subversive to have her call him what was almost a forbidden word.

They walked a few blocks, then took a taxi to his apartment. It wasn't grand, but it did have an empty room – a small room, but then she was rather small. The entire place had been set up with darkened windows just in case Montesarat had decided to drop by; he never had. As Jon watched the little vampire look around, he realized he wanted her to like the place. No, this was not the original plan for his life, but it was starting to feel good.

It didn't take much convincing to get her to take a bath, but he had to lay out an old T-shirt and shorts because he saw her clothes really needed washing. In fact, the clothes in her backpack were dirty as well. He ended up throwing clothes, doll, and backpack into the washing machine. She was clearly capable of bathing herself, a point she made clear when she shut the bathroom door then handed out her clothes to him before shutting the door again.

She didn't have a lot – a comb, some hair accessories, a few old coins, and a small children's reader dated 1928. Could she be that old? How had she survived alone for that long? When she walked out in his old clothes, one hand holding up the shorts that threatened to fall off, he knew how. She survived because she played into the natural desires of most adults to protect children.

She had combed her hair but not re-braided it, so he could tell it was blonde, not brown. Her skin looked even paler than before. He doubted he needed to check her for fleas or ticks; what would they live off on a vampire? The mere idea of wardum bugs made him shudder. She watched him do laundry, but soon the sun was up, and she fell asleep. He laid her on the couch, tucking a blanket around her before going to bed himself.

Jon slept for a few hours then got up and moved around. He did a check-in at the computer company then headed off to buy some things for her. Goodwill first; it was easy, quick, and cheap. He got a few outfits for someone her size – he'd looked at the tags on her clothes – and a small bed with sheets. It was easy to set it up in the empty room.

She was awake when he returned, even though the sun would still be up for another hour or so. This surprised Jon, because he thought that older vampires needed more sleep, but then again, maybe a century wasn't old for Akhkharu, though Montesarat had never told him his age, so he had little but pop-culture references to go by. She hid at first, then came out and looked at what he had purchased. She tried everything on and helped him make up the tiny bed. As soon as the sun went down, he asked what she wanted to do.

"I don't know. Usually, I'm figuring out how to eat, where to hide the next morning," she confessed as she watched him eat a light meal. She was sitting on the other dinette chair and pretending to feed her doll as he ate. "I do what I have to do," she added a bit defensively.

Jon leaned back in his chair. "You have options now; I'm here to help. You could keep hunting as you have been, and I could just watch in case you needed me." She just shrugged at that suggestion and kicked her feet back and forth.

"I could get you blood from a butcher or a blood bank; some vampires, or Akhkharu if you know that term, find that easier, if not as tasty." She stopped kicking, but still didn't look thrilled at the idea.

"Or we could work on getting cooperative people for you to feed from. Maybe nannies, babysitters, tutors; I don't know. I'm not used to working with someone ..."

"... Who isn't an adult?" she finished his thought. "Your previous Bel was an adult; he could do adult things." She didn't seem angry at the facts, but Jon swallowed anyway. He so did not want to even think about doing adult things with her. She seemed to understand the discomfort her statement caused and quickly spoke again. "Is there someplace nicer than a park we could go to? It would be nicer than what I did before," she asked seriously.

Jon thought for a few moments then nodded and stood up. "I know how to find out what is open this time of night. I can search using my computer."

She followed him, and they collected information from the net for about fifteen minutes. Turned out that there were many kid-friendly places open until 9pm or so in the city; probably to help out working parents who needed to shop or wanted to spend quality time with their kids. There were also more general businesses like grocery stores and gas stations open 24/7.

They were getting ready to leave for the mall when Jon paused. She looked up at him with a questioning expression on her face. He knelt down so she didn't have to look up at him; it didn't feel proper that way. "Charity?" he asked, then paused again. She did nothing except continue her questioning look. "Last night you gave me your blood, and we need to talk about that."

She blinked at him. "Did it make you sick?"

Jon shook his head. "No, no, not sick, not at all. But for the next week you'll need to give me more of it. And we'll need to make a contract; I'll need to take a Tamu, make a promise to help you," he tried to explain. She was frowning, so he hastened to add, "After that, it's just when you feel I've earned it, your blood, your bu."

"Why?" and her child's voice made it seem like such a silly question, but Jon made himself answer seriously.

"It will bond me to you, make me more focused on caring for you, helping you, make me more obedient to your will," he said out loud, but added silently, *and get me over Montesarat faster.*

"I thought you wanted to help me?" She seemed hurt, not angry.

"I do, I will, but," and here he was at a loss to explain, so he fell back onto an arrogant adult reply, "this is how things are done in the night kingdom, so we must do it".

"Night kingdom?"

"You are a vampire; Akhkharu is what your people call themselves, or Akh, though that sounds a bit like the Egyptian term for life, so perhaps it's a joke. And there are lots of manners and rules for how vampires and their helpers should behave. If they don't, they can get into serious trouble," he added.

"Oh," she said and walked past him to sit on the couch. "I don't know those rules and manners. Can you teach me?"

Jon turned around but stayed on his knees by the door. "Yes; everything I know, I'll teach you. If I don't know, I can find out," he agreed immediately.

Charity thought for a moment, then stood up with a firm nod of her head. "I need a glass, then."

Jon fetched a glass about the same size as the one at the café and knelt down again in front of her. She bled into it and handed it back to him.

As he drank it, she stroked his hair and shoulder, and whispered more of those exotic words. He wasn't sure what the words meant, but when she told him to repeat a few, he did, merely noticing that his skin warmed and she seemed to grow cuter and more precious afterward. They took his car to the mall and shopped until it closed; she used the women's restroom to hunt in and left it feeling very full, she said. Jon was surprisingly happy as well as he watched her fall asleep the next morning.

The next day Jon arranged to do all of his work from home. The company was used to him needing a lot of time to himself, so they agreed, though he might have to come in for special meetings. The goal was to be at home with her during the day so he could protect her; that was a concern he'd never had with Montesarat, who had at least six wardum serving him at any given time. Charity had only him, only him, and that made him grin as he watched her sleeping, smoothing back a stray lock of hair that had fallen over one cheek as she slept.

Their days varied over the course of the next week between various public venues they could go where they could pick up one or two items and she could feed. With every evening that passed, every feeding of her precious blood, and every strange word they exchanged, he was more certain that his first Bel had been a mistake and had been mistaken. He wasn't sure what he felt toward her, but he knew deep in his heart he couldn't leave her, not even if Montesarat asked him to return to his bed. He ripped up all the letters and trashed all the gifts his former master had given him to prove to himself that his loyalty was truly transferred to the precious little one he gave piggyback rides to as they walked from his car to whatever business she felt like hunting in.

She wasn't hungry at the end of the week, so they went to the public library and got a few children's movies before returning home. "Jon?" she called to him softly as he was messing with the DVD player.

"Yes, Bel?" he immediately reacted, then swallowed and smiled. "Charity," he corrected.

"Is tonight the last night we have to do that Tamu thing?" she asked as she stood next to the couch with her doll clenched in one hand and the glass they'd been using in the other.

Jon's eyes narrowed for a second. It hadn't seemed like he was pledging himself to her, but then again, his connection to her seemed very strong now. "Yes, after tonight it will be entirely up to you when or if you allow me to share your blood," he agreed.

She nodded but set the glass on the coffee table before climbing up onto the couch. Charity looked at him, favoring him with one of her gentle smiles for a moment before she bit into her wrist and held it out to him. "This way tonight," she said, and her voice sounded older, steady, and commanding.

He didn't even bother to stand but simply crawled the few feet to her and knelt, looking at her and the pool of scarlet forming on her wrist. He took her slender limb in his hands, and as he was about to lower his mouth it hit him. Swallowing, he looked at her, all the fragileness of her small frame, and shook his head. "I think the glass would be better," he began.

"No," she said, and he stopped, not moving, not breathing. Her eyes were serious, as steady as her tone. "Arammu-Wardum, feed from me," she ordered him.

A dozen reasons spun through his mind urging him to not touch her in such an intimate way. None of them could compete with her command, and soon he was lapping at her wrist, her other hand in his hair, her exotic words rushing through him. He finished to rest limply on her lap, gazing up at her, almost unable to move. "I have a gift for you, a nice lady helped me get it at the mall last night," she told him as she reached into a pocket. She fished out a little jewelry box and held it out to him.

Jon blinked as he set back still dizzy from the flood of new power that seemed to almost be flowing from her into him and back again. It was too big for a ring box and he swallowed as he remembered Montesarat giving him something to mark him as property after they had done a Tamu. "Do you know what this is?"

She nodded as she popped open the lid to reveal a beautiful bracelet for a man.

It was simple, not as flashy as his old one had been, but even thinking of it made him remember how Sara had literally ripped it from his wrist that night she'd told him he'd never be welcomed back. Jon started to tremble as he took it from the box.

"I had it inscribed," Charity added. "The lady helped me a lot, even though none of them remember me or this," she confessed with a chuckle.

Jon looked on the inside and found the inscription. *World's Greatest Daddy, Love Charity*. Looking up, Jon slipped it over his hand, and when it touched his wrist, it seemed to shrink a bit, something that should have unnerved him yet didn't. "I love you," he whispered.

"I love you too, Daddy," she whispered back with a giggle.

That was what he became, her beloved and adoring daddy. He spent each day working to buy her the best toys and clothes that any little girl might want. Most evenings he helped her hunt, feigning the need for some kind-hearted woman to take her into the women's rest room because obviously she couldn't go into the men's and he was so afraid of child molesters these days, surely you can understand that Ms.? They went to movies, plays, museums, or anywhere else she wanted to go, and always his darling got whatever she wanted.

Jon had once thought about having kids, 25 years ago, until he'd discovered the night kingdom. He'd always been rather domestic, as his mother had said, and he found this life with her was just what he hadn't realized he'd needed to make him feel fulfilled. After a few months of bliss, he was a bit shocked when Charity called him by his name again and not the beloved "Daddy" that made his heart swell up in pride.

He was giving her a piggyback ride through the park on their way back from the movies when she commanded, "Put me down, Jon." He obeyed automatically but reached for her hand as her feet touched the grass. A chill went through him as she shrugged off his hand.

"Well, well, you can sense us," a man's voice surprised Jon, but Charity only placed her feet in a wide stance and held her fists at her sides. Out of the shadows came one of the other vampires from the city, followed by another. "You're to come with us," they said simply.

Charity didn't reply immediately, so Jon stepped between her and the two others. "I don't think so," he said, daring to look at one of the Akhkharu in the eyes as he spoke.

The one he was looking at just smiled, then backhanded him so strongly that he flew back a few feet to laid on his ass.

"Jon! Daddy!" Charity yelled as the other one picked her up and literally started to carry her away.

"No fucking way!" Jon yelled as he jumped up and ran after them. Of course, Akhkharu move much faster than even the best wardum could, but somehow Jon kept them in sight as far as the mansion they were headed into. He stopped and swallowed. Montesarat's place. Only a moment of hesitation, then Jon bolted up the walkway and burst through the door.

Sara was standing there, her mouth open in shock. "What do you think …" she began, but he just pushed past her and into the main room where the local vampires held biannual meetings.

Charity was there, and Montesarat was staring at Jon when he came in to kneel at her side. No one said anything for a moment, giving Jon time to glance around. Damn, the most powerful vampires in town were all here, staring at Charity like she was a freak. Jon turned to Charity, their eyes at the same level, when he knelt. "I'm here, Bel," he said clearly, and she placed one hand on his shoulder but never took her eyes off his former master.

"I thought it was a joke," the elegant vampire said as he glanced around at the disapproving faces of his peers. "First he fucks someone without my permission, then he stalks my house, and now he couples with a child," Montesarat stated, drawing angry glares and exclamations from the others.

"No," Jon stated clearly as he turned to look up at his former Bel. "Don't you dare say that about her."

Montesarat turned and sneered. "Oh, please, we both know you only think with one head, boy," he tossed out. Before either one could say something more, another Akhkharu stepped forward. Jon didn't know these others well except that they were important, but this one had been to Montesarat's home many times to discuss formal kataru, or alliances within the night kingdom.

"Sexual perversities are not our concern," she stated clearly. The others in the room agreed, so Montesarat stepped back and yielded the floor.

The speaker looked seriously down at Charity and Jon. Jon met her eyes, as did his tiny Bel. "Who is your Shi, child? Who created you? Who is your mother or father?"

"I don't have one," Charity replied calmly.

"Come now; we know this must be so confusing for you, with only a mere akalum to guide you."

"Jon isn't akalum," Charity stated. "He is my arammu-wardum. Do you have a problem with that?"

"What?" the speaker replied, but she was drowned out by exclamations and calls for both Charity and Jon to be killed immediately.

"Leave the room, Jon," Charity told him.

He looked at her, seeing that seriousness in her eyes, hearing her steady tone, and even though he didn't want to leave he found himself standing, bowing, and backing out of the room. The last thing he saw was that the speaker had fallen to her knees, her face paler than even a vampire's should be.

Once the door was closed behind him, Sara started yelling at him, but he quickly put a hand over her mouth, surprised that he was stronger than her, and leaned against the door. Both wardum's eyes widened as a series of screams, curses, and sounds of destruction reached them through the thick doors. In a few minutes everything was quiet, so Jon released Sara.

"What the hell happened, Jon?" she demanded. She was sweating and breathing hard, one hand to her chest as through she'd been stabbed. Terrified, Jon opened the door again and ran inside.

He slid to a stop, his shoes slipping on the blood-covered marble floor. Around him were strewn limbs decaying quickly into ashes, and the blood beneath his feet was starting to hiss and turn to smoke. There at the far end of the room he saw his little one sitting on Montesarat's favorite chair. The vampire who had asked her about her Shi was kneeling at her feet.

Jon moved forward slowly, finding it difficult to breathe and see in the rising ash and smoke. As he got closer, he could hear the female vampire stating over and over, "Ummum," as she rocked back and forth on her knees, her hands clenched before her and her head bowed as though in prayer. Charity's lovely pink overalls were stained red, though that, too, was clearing in a cloud of smoke.

"Charity?" he asked as he stopped a few feet from her. She was holding her doll in one arm, her teddy bear backpack on the floor in a puddle of gore. Jon stopped and vomited as he recognized the head of his former master at her feet, turning to ashes under her pink tennis shoes.

In a few moments he regained control and looked at her again. She was petting the female vampire and cooing to her in that exotic language she used, but Charity paused to motion him toward her with her doll. Jon stepped up, then knelt at her feet. "Bel," he whispered as he lowered his head to her kicking feet.

"It's going to be all right now, Jon. I promise," Charity told him. "Isn't that right, Marina?"

"Yes, Ummum, everything will be as you desire now that you have returned to your children," the female vampire replied.

Jon's head was spinning, and he moved on his Bel's command without much awareness or thought of his own. A few nights later, he was standing on Montesarat's balcony looking at the moon when Marina approached and stood next to him. An Allamudi, she had been the chief law keeper in the city. "Ma'am," he said softly but didn't move.

"Five thousand years," she stated. "She's been watching us the entire time, judging how we've lived, how we've treated our own kind, your kind, the rest. She isn't happy," Marina said with a forced chuckle.

"We'll go to the children's museum; that always makes her happy," Jon stated, but glanced back when Marina's laughter increased and turned dark in tone.

"You don't get it do you, you stupid mortal?" she gasped in frustration. "She is our mother; she created us, and she is going to kill us all."

116

"She wouldn't do that," Jon corrected as he turned to lean back against the railing.

"Oh, maybe not, maybe she'll just remake it all in her image, that will be even worse, worse for your kind. The gods who made her hated humans; she'll fulfill their desire as much as hers. You'll see, if you live that long," Marina told him, then stopped, her face frozen as Charity ran onto the balcony and into Jon's arms.

As he lifted her up for a piggyback ride, Jon locked eyes with the Akhkharu and said firmly, "Anything my little girl wants is good. It's good," he emphasized. Without another word he carried her back inside the house to decide what to do with the night.

*The entire audience is looking at me now. The oldest of my damu know that my "name" changed often over the millennia, but the younger ones have known me only as the Ummum or Ningai. I smile at them to let them know that it is fine to be confused, to be uncomfortable, because I've been that way myself. But I say nothing, only move on to the next in our timeline.*

*The Sarrutum.*

*Most believe that finding a worthy child among the Xul was my greatest challenge, but my royal children can be much worse. They have always been the ones to plot against me. Thus, when I catch Natalie and Niibori's eyes and they meet them with blushes, I am reminded that their oddities are what drew me toward them.*

*The wardum speaks for them both, as she often does. "If it pleases you, Ummum Ningai, we would be honored if the Bard told our tale, both of them, for he has skills we do not."*

*Manipulation is not lacking with them, but I agree with a nod and turn to Bard again, who merely claps his hands and gives the audience a grin. "This is a tale of outrage, inversion, and betrayal, but also of love."*

# Acquisition

Niibori Takayoshi smoothed down his exquisite linen shirt then tucked it neatly into the perfectly tailored trousers. He glanced back at the servant kneeling to shine his shoes, made to perfectly complement his suit and some of the others he was taking with him. The other servant handed him a red silk tie with the house logo on it, and he tied it around his neck in a subdued knot that exuded confidence and power. Then he allowed this same servant to place the cufflinks on his wrists and help him into the perfectly cut jacket.

As he studied his reflection, faint as it was, he saw an elegant, authoritative business executive of about middle age, with a slightly receding hairline of still quite black silken strands, a smooth face, and sharp, intelligent eyes with a hint of tiredness. Exactly as his Shi had made him. His suit, however, enforced the message of competence by its perfect design, the finest craftsmanship, and the subtle hint of creativity. Exactly as he had designed it.

As he allowed the servants to slip his shoes onto his feet, he closed his eyes and recalled why he was going to all this effort in December.

"Niibori!" The shout caused him to stand up and bow at the waist as he waited the few tense minutes it took for his Shi to enter his office. "There you are. Always drawing, always drawing," Gaius chuckled, with a slight disapproval in his tone that made Niibori tremble just a bit. He jumped slightly as the bigger man put one cool hand on his shoulder and looked over it at the table and his sketches. "How soon can that one be ready?"

"If you approve, Gaius-san, it can be finished in three weeks," Niibori said softly, never raising his head, though his mind was starting to boil at this intrusion into his office. Of course, his office was at the ekallim of his creator, so in reality nothing was truly his, save perhaps the clothes he himself had made. Byzantines were even stricter with their children than his mortal parents had been, but Niibori had had no choice but to adjust over the centuries since his creation.

"Excellent, then that will give you time to finish it and to make yourself aware of the particulars of this business contract."

Niibori's head shot up as he looked straight at his vampiric father. "Sir?" he asked, using the Western term that he knew would please his Shi.

"Yes, I'm sending you to America – Los Angeles, so not that far from here, really. To Bradford Sensible Designs, an up-and-coming house in the field of women's business clothing," Gaius replied as he sat on the edge of the drawing table.

"Me?"

"You aren't refusing this task, are you?"

"No, no, Sir," Niibori quickly replied, ducking his head and shoulders again in a bow. Too many beatings over the past century and a half had made him unlikely to openly defy his creator, but it had not honestly curbed either his curiosity or his sense of unworthiness.

And this was why he found himself at the end of the twentieth century in his old Katsura estate, which had been taken by this Gaijin he was forced to serve as a son for eternity. Centuries ago, the Katsura clan had adopted him as they adapted to the new Imperial order. His family had served the emperors for generations as royal tailors, and Niibori had been hoping to succeed his grandfather in his position when the revolution came. He had been curious when the Westerners came to the court to meet the new emperor, so he had gone to watch, against his grandfather's wishes. He wasn't actually good at hiding, and when the politician had seen him, he had felt certain he would be executed. In a sense he had been, as Gaius had met with him in private, drained his life, revived him, and made him swear his allegiance to the family.

119

It didn't matter – not your skin color, your eye shape, your religion, or your native soil: Business was family, and family was business. Niibori had never been the man in charge, so that wasn't a change either. But what really caused his pain was this feeling growing inside him like a cancer that he really should be the one in charge, at least here in Japan, in Osaka, where Gaius clearly was not comfortable. That was a new hurt. The old one was being denied his own culture while being forced to live within it. Outside the ekallim's walls he could fully embrace his heritage no matter how much it had changed, but here he had to be careful, because even little slips might send the elder Akhkharu into a rage. Or, as Gaius put it: "I gave up my heritage for this. Do you think you are better than I, boy?"

Niibori didn't know much about foreign histories, but he was pretty sure that his Shi had not given everything up, merely combined his Christian-Latin background with the Akhkharu foundation. Today Gaius had seemed pleased enough with himself to let Niibori's earlier - *san* slip by without a belittling comment or physical reproval. Niibori was grateful but worried about what this meant.

"It will be an excellent business alliance," Gaius continued, oblivious to his dami's anger. "Women will always want clothing and be willing to spend well beyond their husbands' and fathers' means. How we could possibly be descended from one is unbelievable," Gaius muttered, referring to a legend Niibori had heard a few times from the occasional visitor to the compound. "So, make it work," he ordered before leaving.

Niibori swore again, then growled at the servant fussing with his trouser leg, sending the man – all their wardum, his Shi's wardum specifically, were male – scurrying out of his room while his fellow slave bowed and exited in a more dignified manner. Niibori sighed at his faint reflection and looked himself over once more before heading to catch the limo. His job was clear: Make a marriage of sorts with this American designer of women's fashions to complement their own offerings and get an "in" to the wealthiest country in the world.

Natalie Bradford straightened out her nylons and smoothed down her knee-length cobalt blue skirt and matching short jacket, the latest her family's design house would be offering on the New York runway in the spring. Peach pumps and silk blouse added an extra bit of femininity to the ensemble without detracting from the solid, authoritative lines that could be loosened or tightened via some clever designs her younger brother had created a few years ago. The modern woman was both an intellectual powerhouse and a sensual delight, so these new suits could easily go from the office to the club in a few minutes.

Sensible jewelry designed by her younger sister complemented it all, as did the light leather briefcase her mother had given her as an early Christmas present. Turning, she double-checked her nylons, as did her maid from her place on the floor. "Looks perfect, Ms. Bradford," the woman said as she stood up, but Natalie just frowned as she turned back to the mirror. Her sandy hair was swept up into a loose French braid; her makeup was subtle and highlighted her light gray eyes and her pale skin to the fullest.

She lingered over her blouse for a moment more. To leave it unbuttoned this far down, or to do up one more button? With a frown she did up another button, still angry at her father's final comments to her the previous evening.

"Never forget to use all your assets, Nat, darling. That's why I chose you over Richard this time," her father had said as he patted her back a bit too long in his farewell hug after dinner. The brother in question was still scowling at her later that evening, practically ignoring all attempts at polite conversation, until their father had banged his fist on the table, which had only made their mother hurry to get dessert.

She had been so shocked by her father's words that she had just stood there for a few moments after he had left. "He means your boobs." Richard's voice had startled her, and she had turned to find him at her side, glaring at her chest. "If I had them, I'd be on the assignment," he'd snarled.

"Oh, for God's sake. You do over half the business meetings. Why do you want this one; why do you always take offense when Father chooses me?"

"This is important, little girl," Richard had said as his eyes swept up to meet her, but Natalie held his gaze. "If we can make a deal with

Takayoshi Fashion, we can get an inside track to women's fashion in the East. So many companies competing to get into that market, but this will give us an edge. Your ... assets may give us an edge, and that pisses me off."

He'd backed off and smirked. "It should piss you off more. Boobs over brains; why can't you see that?" With that he'd stormed out of the dining room, leaving Natalie breathing in shallow pants as she'd felt her legs start to collapse under her.

The truth was that she was as capable as Richard if not more, but as Mother had explained it, Father was a bit old-fashioned about some things. Even though she had the better degree with much higher grades and stronger recommendations than her older brother, Natalie knew he'd be named CEO while she'd play at president or merely have a place on the board. She wasn't creative like her other siblings, and she wanted so much more than to design the products; she wanted to place them in the hands of women around the world. Surely a woman could understand how to do that better than a man.

Her father had never been fully convinced by her arguments, but given what her paternal aunt told her, his using her talents at all was a huge step from their own father, who had started the business sixty years ago, just after World War II. Granddad would roll over in his grave if he knew they were trying to make an alliance with the "yellow menace," as he had still called them when he was alive and would go off into one of his rants about the dangers lurking just across the Pacific.

That was ridiculous, since this was nothing more than a mere business arrangement. It was foolish to get so torn up about old propaganda about the "slant-eyes wanting to rape good American women and pollute our blood." It wasn't as if this was the Middle Ages, when Natalie would have to marry a foreigner to get a business deal. She'd use her savvy and knowledge to win this merger, she decided as she did up another button on her blouse.

Research was one of her best talents, but while she could find out a lot about Takayoshi Fashion, she couldn't find out much about this Niibori who was coming, though obviously he was one of the family, given his surname. All of her connections and time on the net hadn't even gotten her a photograph of him. In fact, no one seemed to know who was really in charge of their company, even though Niibori signed all the contracts, from what she could piece together. The only really useful information she could gather was that he suffered from a rare allergy to sunlight and required a special diet that his own people would take care of. Even this necessary information had only been offered to them once the meeting had been fully arranged.

Therefore, beyond the basics of how Japanese companies did business and the basics of Takayoshi Fashion, she was walking in blind. With an audible sigh, Natalie undid one of the buttons on her blouse again and reached into her bra to arrange her assets nicely.


Natalie bowed just the exact amount one should to a new business associate, and Niibori paused for a moment, then did the same thing. "Takayoshi-san, it is an honor to meet you." Her strong yet feminine voice made him blush slightly as they both stood up.

"I am honored to meet you as well, Ms. Bradford," Niibori said as he held out his right hand and shook hers with his.

He took a seat at one end of the conference table while she remained standing, and her assistant handed out folders to him and the wardum representatives, who accompanied him to this first meeting. Gaius made sure they lived in a world of men, and thus to Niibori's eyes Ms. Bradford might have been the most beautiful woman in the world as she explained what their company hoped to gain from a merger and how they could improve profits for both companies through this plan. He was certain she was dumbing down a few of the concepts, but her smile and poise kept him captivated enough that he didn't care. It was clear that she had done her research, and while his needs were being catered to, no attention was drawn to them, even his need for his own "energy drink" while the rest of them ate a meal delivered to the artificially lit conference room.

When his own companions had asked all of their business questions, she turned directly to him, and Niibori found himself fixated on her light-colored eyes. "Takayoshi-san, do you have any questions?"

"No, no," he replied after taking a moment to adjust his gaze to look respectfully at her shoulder, not her chest or her eyes or hair, which were like a dream he could never have had before now. "I am in charge of the design of our clothing lines. I will have questions when I see your own designs," he added, feeling his cheeks heat up as she arched one eyebrow ever so slightly.

"Excellent; I have that scheduled for tomorrow afternoon. If it would please you, gentlemen ..." It sounded a bit like a question, but something inside of Niibori said it was more of a command. "I've made arrangements for a nice dinner, then courtside seats at a Lakers game."

The men in the room seemed thrilled, but Niibori only nodded and worried that he had no clothing to go to a lake in. One of the wardum who accompanied him explained in the limo back to their hotel and helped him simply hang up his tie and jacket for the evening. "Takayoshi-sama, it will be fun; an amusement that these Americans do so love," the wardum explained when Niibori frowned at his reflection.

"Hai," Niibori agreed and let himself be led off into this new world of loud steak houses and even louder sports.

The wardum and the mortal businessmen were enjoying themselves, but Niibori found himself bored. Soon, though, he felt a warm and gentle touch upon his hand. He turned to find the light eyes of his hostess looking into his. "I apologize, Takayoshi-san. I did not mean to insult you by bringing you to this event," she was saying, and he found himself looking at her lips as they moved, wondering what they would taste like against his own, listening to her heart pound the precious akalum through her body, and unconsciously stroking her thumb with his own as she let it rest on his hand.

"I am not one for such entertainments," he replied. "It is very loud."

She smiled and stood up, releasing his hand, and turned to one of her own aides for a moment, who nodded but remained seated. "I can fix that," she assured him as she motioned for him to follow her.

She led him to an elevator that went up to another level and then into a small room that was well-furnished. "This is our company box; it's one of the smaller ones, but then normally we only use it for special occasions," she explained as she walked over and hit a button that stopped all sound from entering the room. "There, is that better?"

"Hai, yes, better," he agreed as he came and looked down over the center of the court. He could see the wardum now interacting more casually with the mortals, and he smiled. At least they might have a few hours of relaxation, then, even if he could not. A dutiful son was more a slave than a slave at times, he felt, but he could only feel good for the three who traveled with him and jealousy when his hostess sat on a couch at the middle of the box and patted it for him to join her.

At one time he had been married. A lovely girl, only a girl, Kaya, who had died during the birth of their only child, a son who had not lived many months after that. That loss may have been the real reason for his curiosity so many generations ago that had led him to this moment here. Now that girl, that wife, that Kaya, was but a faded memory as he found himself chatting with his hostess. She seemed interested in his designs, intrigued by his company's refusal to do women's clothing, and amused when he pointed out a flaw in their own business model of not attempting to do men's fashion.

"Which is why our company would be a good match for yours," she pointed out with a smile as she patted his hand, which had somehow ended up on the back of the couch as he'd turned toward her during the conversation.

As her hand rested on top of his, Niibori watched her lips move and the steady angle at which she held her head, relaxed yet poised, as though ready for something at any moment. Kaya had rarely looked at him directly, rarely touched him; he had had to make every initiation in their relationship. He did so because he was a man; it was a man's place to be master of his house, master of his wife, master of himself.

Right now, he didn't feel like the master of even himself, though, as he listened to her and answered her questions, asking polite ones in return; he decided that not being master might not be so bad in the hands of a competent and capable master.

The next evening, after a tour of the Bradford studios, they all ate at an expensive restaurant where Niibori just sipped his dark wine, laced with blood that one of the wardum had brought along and slipped into his goblet. If the Americans were offended by his not eating, they said nothing, though Ms. Bradford did smile at him a bit sadly throughout the meal.

When his stomach grumbled near the end of dessert, one of the wardum glanced at him and then excused himself and left. A few minutes later when that man returned, Niibori excused himself and went to the men's restroom. In the third stall, as they had prepared, he found an unconscious man propped up in the corner. Locking the door behind him, the Akhkharu quickly fed, then left the man crumpled on the floor, feeling a bit dizzy but sprouting an erection he could deal with as he saw fit.

In the hallway he nearly collided with another man carrying a child in his arms, a young girl with blonde hair and pale blue eyes who looked right at him. "So sorry," Niibori started to say when his gaze met hers. He felt his stomach clench as her power washed over him. There was a rumor going around the ekallim that an entire ruling class of the Night Court had been removed by a child on the East Coast, but where exactly he couldn't remember.

"Excuse me, sir, I'm terribly sorry," the man replied, but the girl kept staring at him until he couldn't look at her. Niibori remained frozen to that spot until the two left, then he leaned against the wall trying to collect himself. Where had the wardum who had been sent with him gone? After a moment he spied the man exiting the bathroom he'd just left, his hand on his neck, his face a bit white. Niibori damped his fears down and straightened his tie.

Upon returning he noted that the table had been cleared and only Ms. Bradford remained, writing on a credit card receipt. She looked up with one of her bright smiles and rose when he approached. "The car should be waiting outside," she said as she led the way to the coat rack. Niibori had been watching American men closely during this trip, so as she reached for her mink, he took it gently from her then held it out to help her into it. "Thank you, Takayoshi-san."

"Please do call me Takayoshi-kun, Ms. Bradford," he replied as he set the shoulders of the fur onto her own slender ones.

"Let us see if this merger happens," she replied carefully as she turned to him. He bowed slightly at her response then motioned for her to lead the way to the car. The entire flight back to Osaka he worried that his Shi might say "no," even though he had been the reason behind this visit.

Natalie smiled at the signed and faxed copy of the contract between her family business and the Takayoshi company. There were two names on the document, Niibori and then this "Gaius," which didn't sound at all like a Japanese name. But what did she honestly know about the Japanese? Perhaps it had become fashionable at some point to give out Western names to children, though she would have thought daughters would be more easily given such names, since as far as she could tell they were still decades behind in women's rights issues.

She looked over as the fax machine spit out another sheet of paper. Only select people had this private line, so she prayed it was not an emergency to draw her attention from this great victory that she could rub in her brother's face. Natalie took the new fax and blinked at the handwritten message. The English wasn't perfect, but it was quite legible, and she could grasp the message quite clearly.

Niibori Takayoshi had invited her to dinner in Tokyo to celebrate the merger, entirely at his own expense.

She sat back and twirled one strand of her hair around a finger as she thought about this. She had been impressed by Niibori during the visit. He was a powerful man and yet very unassuming, almost shy. He was a brilliant man, and yet he'd asked her questions in return, not merely answered hers or bragged about his talents. Even though she'd unbuttoned that one button on her blouse and touched him a few times, she'd never caught him looking below her face, and he had certainly never made even a subtle sexual comment. In short, he'd managed to treat her as a business colleague as well as a lady.

Natalie smiled as she called for her secretary. Grandfather would have been horrified, but she was accepting his invitation, because it was just business, after all.

Natalie woke up in the first-class cabin and stretched. Excusing herself, she went to the nearby lavatory to clean up and fuss with her makeup and clothes. Given his allergy, she doubted that Niibori would be picking her up from the airport himself, but she wanted to look presentable, nonetheless. "Takayoshi-kun," she said to the mirror, trying the new name out with a smile. While she may have been thinking of him with his personal name, they were only business

127

partners now, and the Japanese were particularly concerned with language propriety.

She was wearing comfortable travel-business attire, also from their new line, so it only took a few minutes to get things straightened and adjusted. A quick once-over with a premoistened towelette and a brushing of her hair, and she was ready to exit as soon as the plane touched down. Her father had been so pleased by this merger that he had given her the choice to stay in Tokyo a few extra days if she wished, along with contact information for a few excellent hotels. Her secretary had a list of places she might wish to see in the city if she stayed over. She reviewed that list now as the plane started prepping for landing.

As she had expected, he was not there to meet her personally, but two other men were – a limo driver, who took her luggage and stowed it immediately, and an impeccably dressed young man, who bowed deeply and opened the limo door for her. This second man explained softly that he was to see to her every concern while she was in Tokyo and that Takayoshi-sama hoped she might stay a few days longer if she enjoyed dinner this evening. He introduced himself as Udo, with no surname, so she was stuck with using the more familiar term for him, which he oddly did not seem to mind.

The hotel was one of the finest in the city and had been on the list her secretary had given her. Her room was a penthouse suite, and Natalie's mouth almost fell open when they entered it. She looked around while Udo put her clothing away silently then came back to stand by the door, his hands clasped in front of him, and his head bowed. Natalie's eye twitched a bit when he just stood there. When she inquired, he asked permission to stay in the attached servant's quarters during her stay so that he might fulfill his master's orders to assist her during her visit.

She agreed, a bit worried to have a strange man in her suite from a culture where one of their comic-book heroes was a rapist, or at least that was what she'd heard years ago on the nightly news. There she was, thinking with her grandfather's prejudices again, so she frowned and went to check her own bedroom in the suite.

All of her clothing had been put away neatly and the bed already turned down. She went back out to the main area of the suite and called to Udo, who immediately appeared a couple of feet from her, hands clasped, and head bowed as before. Natalie gasped softly at his speed then shook her head. The Japanese probably took service to a different level than in the States. "How long until my dinner with Takayoshi-kun?"

One of Udo's eyebrows twitched a bit, but he merely informed her that it was a good six hours before dinner. Natalie dismissed him with an order that he wake her up in four hours, then she returned to get some more sleep to help fight off jet lag.

Natalie sat up when someone touched her exposed shoulder. "Forgive me, Bradford-sama," a soft male voice said, and she remembered where she was. "You instructed me to wake you now." Udo backed away on his knees and bowed his entire body down to the floor. Slightly freaked out, Natalie hurried from her bed to the bathroom, not thinking of grabbing any clothing on the way.

Which proved to be a problem when she was done, but she focused on combing out her hair first, then put on a hotel bathrobe and went back to her bedroom to find Udo standing there, hands in front, head bowed, and one of her dresses, with matching undergarments, complementary shoes and accessories laid out on the bed. "This is most appropriate for dinner this evening," Udo softly declared with another deep bow.

Natalie blinked, surprised; not even her own maid back home took this initiative, and for a moment she was suspicious. "Why did you do this?"

Udo bowed again as he spoke. "I want to help you make a good impression on Takayoshi-sama."

"I see," Natalie answered, then she frowned. "Wait for me out there, then, while I get ready. I don't need your help with that," she commanded with a slight huff of displeasure.

Truth was that this was the exact outfit she had been planning to wear, and it unnerved her a bit that the servant had figured that out so easily. It was not something she expected from someone working for a men's fashion design house.

When they arrived at the restaurant, Natalie smiled slightly when she found that Niibori was dressed in a suit with accessories that complemented her own attire. They looked like a couple as she sat down in the chair he pulled out for her, and for some reason that didn't bother her in the slightest.

They made pleasant conversation; he, laughing lightly at her attempts with Japanese and she giggling as he asked how her holidays had gone. For some reason she felt extremely relaxed and at ease with him, and by the end of the evening he asked her to use his personal name, and she gave her permission for him to do the same. Thus, it was no surprise, really, when he escorted her back to her hotel suite and paused at the door to kiss her hand while Udo stood a few feet down the hallway.

Feeling as though she was in a daze, Natalie didn't bother to close the door but did turn to find Udo locking it behind him before he bowed and resumed what she was now thinking of as Udo-normal position. "You told him which dress I was wearing, didn't you?" she asked as she handed him her mink coat and stepped out of her shoes.

"Hai, Bradford-sama."

"I'm surprised you know so much about women's clothing," she said, giving voice to that hours-old thought now, as she was coming down from what by all other standards was an incredibly romantic evening.

"I was instructed to learn about your company and women's clothing so that I might assist you during your stay," Udo replied, then glanced up just briefly. "Takayoshi-sama wishes to know if you would stay for a few more days."

Natalie smiled at this question and the fact that it was coming from a mere servant instead of the man himself. "Yes, I think I would like to stay, but only if Niibori will continue to be my host," she added before retiring to her bedroom. She did not hear Udo's sharp intake of breath at her familiarity with his master nor the slight smile that graced his face when he made the call to share this good news.

Niibori smiled as Natalie went to her bedroom in the hotel suite, then turned his attention to the wardum waiting silently across the room. Udo was new to Gaius's holdings, a young man who had turned out not to be as entertaining as the Byzantine would have liked, so he

130

had handed him over, even if he couldn't transfer the bond fully. He had been a gift for this merger, and Niibori was using the slave well, considering this may have been the only other person in his Shi's holding he had trusted in any form in a century and a half. As he walked closer the wardum bowed down to the floor silently and waited.

"You've done very well, Udo," Niibori said firmly but in a quiet voice.

"Arigatou gozaimasu, Takayoshi-sama," the wardum whispered back as he knelt up but kept his eyes averted.

"Walk with me; Natalie-chan will take some time to prepare for sleep, and I have need of your confidence," Niibori ordered as he walked away, fully expecting the wardum to fall in step behind him.

Once the men were on the roof looking at the Tokyo skyline glittering in the night, the wardum knelt again and waited while the Akhkharu thought for a few moments. Niibori took a deep, unnecessary breath, then spoke simply. "I will ask for a marriage contract with Natalie-chan. You will find out how Americans do this."

Udo looked up, his mouth opening a bit, then he returned his gaze to the rooftop. "Hai, Takayoshi-sama."

Natalie was attempting to eavesdrop on the living room from the kitchen, but her mother was proving to be a formidable opponent, as she insisted on making a clatter as she put the dishes in the dishwasher, even though they had staff who should have been doing that. "Mother!" Natalie hissed softly from her place by the swinging door.

"Natalie, you're always such a big help to me in the kitchen," Mrs. Bradford said far too loudly, which only made her daughter sigh and step away from the door to perch on a stool at the breakfast counter where she'd grabbed her breakfast and lunch for most of her school years.

Her mother messed around with the dishes some more, then turned on the washer, tuning out any chances they had to overhear the conversation in the other room. With a smile she sat on another stool and spoke softly to Natalie. "We'll know what they're talking about soon."

131

Natalie rolled her eyes and glared at the swinging doors. "Why would Niibori ask to talk to Father in private? I've been in charge of the entire merger from day one. We open our first boutique in Osaka in two weeks. I could answer any concerns he or his father has, not Dad."

Mrs. Bradford just smiled and put a calm hand on her daughter's arm, giving it a slight squeeze. "Sometimes men need to be a bit old-fashioned in order to feel good about themselves."

Before Natalie could parse what that meant her father walked through the swinging door. "Amelia, my love, I think it's a lovely night out and we should take a walk," he announced.

Natalie just watched in shock as her parents exited quickly without another word, leaving her in the kitchen. She thought for a few minutes, then put some tea on and went back out to the living room to find Niibori standing there looking nervous, though he tried to hide it when he saw her. Over their six months of visiting each other, talking on the phone and even in email, once he had consented to learn how to use email, she knew him well enough to know something important was on his mind.

"Niibori, is there a problem?" she asked as she stopped within arm's length of him but did not reach out.

He looked at her seriously then shook his head. "No, it is as I had hoped. Your father's answers fulfilled one half of my desire for this evening, Natalie-chan."

Without another word, he reached into his suit jacket pocket, took out something, knelt on one knee, and looked up at her with the strongest and most purposeful expression she had ever seen. "Natalie-chan, would you be my wife?" He revealed a small box and popped it open, holding it on the palm of his hand.

The ring was elegant yet simple, bold yet feminine at the same time, and Natalie gasped, clutching her hands to her chest as her heart pounded. Men needed to be old-fashioned sometimes, huh? As in he needed to ask her father's permission. It was a big step for her father to move so far from his own father's views, which meant he was exceedingly happy with the business merger.

For Natalie, though, this represented more than just money. She had been feeling romantic urges for Niibori for some time now, and though she knew it was not proper for a lady in his culture to openly pursue such a relationship she had tried to drop subtle hints. Now those hints had paid off in more ways than she could have imagined. Then she frowned as she thought about what he might think such a union would represent.

"My oldest brother will have the majority of stock in the company, Niibori; I can't bring controlling shares," she explained, but he only stood up with a shake of his head and slipped the ring on her left hand.

"This is not about business, Natalie-chan, though you are a skilled negotiator, a brilliant strategist, and a lovely woman," he said firmly, looking directly into her eyes. He almost made her believe every word, and she chose to banish all doubt as she smiled at the ring and leaned in for their first passionate kiss.

The wedding was a whirlwind of activity, and within two months Niibori and Natalie were in a cabin in Anchorage, about as far from their parents as they could manage and still have a decent level of customary luxury. Natalie had paid her maid to follow in her employment and was staying in a room on the other side of the elegant little rental while Udo, in his ever-normal position, was waiting in the main living area.

Their first-time making love was as sweet as it was fiery, and Natalie giggled as Niibori lay down next to her, propping himself up on one elbow so he could nuzzle her breast again. "It was very good," he declared when he laid back. He wasn't even flushed, nor had he been breathing hard, so Natalie could only go by his words and the twinkle in his eyes that he had enjoyed himself as much as she.

"It will get better the more practice we get," she suggested as she turned onto her side to consider her husband.

"I am a man of perfection," Niibori declared, not quite getting the English expression correct, but Natalie knew what he was saying. "This is practice I will never dislike," he added with a grin as he leaned down, captured one of her nipples in his mouth, and laved it with his tongue until she moaned then pushed him onto his back.

Natalie straddled her husband and waited as he looked up at her expectantly, content to let her take the lead for a few minutes at least. "Let me do some of the work. This is a partnership, after all," she commented as she reached back and found him just as hard as he had been mere minutes before.

Using her hand to stroke him a few times, she made sure he was ready, then lifted up her hips to angle herself over his cock. Locking her eyes on his, she guided him inside and took him deep until his balls were pressed against her rump, and she moaned, adjusting to the new position.

Niibori used his hands to steady her by placing them on her hips and let her bounce on him for several minutes until he joined by thrusting upward. When he had been a mere mortal his lovemaking had been a brief thing, once a night or once every other night as his duties in the palace allowed. Kaya had never complained, as a good wife of her generation never did, but he knew that this prolonged passion felt so much better than he remembered that he hoped Natalie was enjoying herself more than she might enjoy becoming a mother.

When she had brought up the subject of children weeks ago, he had not told her the horrible truth, and he suspected that her dismissal of condoms tonight was a sign of what she wanted in ten months' time. Pushing those negative thoughts aside, he tried to ease his guilt by taking her hands in his and wrapping them around his throat.

Natalie's eyes were closed as she felt her arousal rise, and she barely registered her hands being moved until she felt something hard bob under her palms. She froze when she opened her eyes to find her hands wrapped around her husband's throat, his own on top, urging her to squeeze. "God!" she gasped and pulled away, scrambling off the bed to tumble onto the floor before scurrying up to grab a bathrobe and hold it in front of her. "What the hell are you doing?"

Niibori just looked at her in shock. Kaya had been surprised by his rougher desires in that they were directed toward himself, but she had only silently complied with his commands, choking him during intercourse, beating him with a shoe, or tying him tightly after a stressful day at work. Surely his confident, American bride would welcome this chance to have power over her husband if his submissive deceased spouse had happily learned the necessary skills.

"I enjoy it, Natalie-chan," he said as he sat up, not bothering to cover his erection from her view. "I offer my body to you, as I said in our vows, for all things," he added, hoping he was explaining things clearly.

She looked horrified and stepped back, pointing at him with one finger. "You are never going to touch me like that!"

Niibori blinked, then stood up, grabbing a robe for himself, since it was obvious that he had not explained well. "No, no, Natalie-chan, never, never, will I touch you in this way. I wish for you to hurt me in this fashion."

"For the love of God, why? What is wrong with you?"

Niibori sighed and let his shoulders sink in sorrow. "So many things," he whispered. A few minutes passed in silence, then she stepped toward him, not within easy reach, but still he hoped it was a sign and spoke again. "Always have I had this longing for strong women. So rare, but you," he explained, pausing and looking up to catch her watching him warily, "you are strong. Americans know so much, they see so much, I hoped ..."

She stepped up and put her hand in his, causing him to look up. "I know some things; I've heard some things; played around with it; who hasn't?" She forced a giggle out of her mouth. "I love you, and I can see how hard this was for you. I love you," she whispered and moved even closer to pull him into a hug. Without shoes she was only an inch or so taller than he, so she could easily rest her head on his shoulder. "I don't want to hurt you, Niibori."

He smiled into her arm and stroked her back, attempting to send reassuring thoughts into her mind, but he had learned months ago that she was resistant to vampiric powers of that nature. "You won't," he told her firmly, "unless you say no."

Natalie sighed, then pulled back so she could look at his eyes as she agreed to try. "Let's hold off on the choking thing, though; that really freaks me out." When he nodded with a weak smile she added, "I've always wanted to see how red your butt could get from a spanking, though."

Niibori's face broke into a huge grin as he pulled her back toward the bed. "I think very red," he whispered softly.

The honeymoon lasted two full weeks. Fourteen days of discovering some love-play that they both could enjoy, though it required compromises from each. Natalie called it their "third most important negotiation," and even if he didn't fully grasp the modern meaning of that expression applied to their sex, Niibori was happy to finally have found a woman who seemed to be interested in his more unique desires.

She was constantly amazed at how quickly any marks, even bruises, faded, and this mystery added to her increased harshness during those moments when they got rough. For his part, Niibori kept his secret for as long as he could, fearful that all too soon they might be confronted by the reality of the Night Kingdom. He only hoped that none of the wardum who worked for this company that they had rented the cabin from would think it worth their effort to tell anyone what they had surely seen and heard. Udo tried to run interference, but since he was the only one to be trusted with blood acquisition, he could not stand guard the entire time.

In an attempt to place some distance between himself and Gaius, Niibori had recently taken an apartment, saying that he was constantly bothered by the junior Akh and new wardum. If they wanted this merger to succeed, he needed quiet to design. Thus, he took Natalie back to this apartment when they reached Osaka, and they eagerly anointed the place with their passions.

"You know, I didn't think you had the balls to keep secrets from me," interrupted a voice on their second evening, and Niibori turned to face his Shi, placing himself in front of his bride.

"Who the hell are you?" Natalie demanded as she looked over her husband's shoulder at a man who was clearly not Japanese and yet was difficult to place in any ethnic or national group she knew.

The man stepped closer as Niibori tried to hush his wife without looking away from his creator. "Gaius-sama, please," he said softly. His Shi's slap sent him sprawling over his bride, giving him what he hoped was some way to protect her as he had hoped his verbal submission might.

Taking an obvious deep whiff of the room, Gaius stepped back with a look of disgust on his face. "At least you were wise enough not to change her or bind her without my permission. We'll just call her dinner, shall we, my number one son?" he taunted as he pulled the female from under Niibori and hauled her to her feet while she struggled.

"Let go of me, you bastard," Natalie ordered as she slapped this person who had interrupted them. He merely laughed and literally threw her across the room to go crashing into a wall. She moaned and tried to get up but could only watch as her husband fell to his knees and grasp the other man's legs.

"Gaius-sama, please, she is ebebu, ebebu," Niibori pleaded, using the one ancient term he hoped might save her life, if not his.

His creator growled but did not kick him away, then his face broke into a cruel smile. "I suspect she is, at that. They are all so innocent, all of them," he said, then he turned his eyes down toward his child, "but you are not."

Natalie tried to figure out what was going on. This man that Niibori was pleading with looked younger than him, and yet he'd used a suffix of profound respect and even submission. She tried to stand again but could only manage to crawl a few inches. She felt like some of her ribs may have been broken, and her head seemed to be swelling.

"Arnum," Gaius simply said, and his dami released his leg and nodded silently. "This punishment will be threefold, for your betrayal endangers me, the business and the Sarrutum." He waited until Niibori was looking up at him. "First, call me properly as you should have, asking me for forgiveness."

Niibori shuddered. He had hoped that his submission using his own culture's words might be enough. While he had already referred to Gaius as his Shi, he knew that what the creature really wanted to hear was a display of a deeper submission, one he had not given since life had left him. He glanced at his bride and saw her pained expression as she attempted to crawl toward him. This was his fault and his alone; honor dictated that he do what was necessary to save her. "Abum," he beseeched, adding, "Father," so she would understand, "I am your dutiful son."

"What?" Natalie moaned as she heard and stopped moving. In shock she watched as the stranger bit into his wrist, then offered it to

Niibori, who took it in both his hands and seemed to suckle his blood. "Oh, my God."

"Do not be foolish enough to cry out to the gods, stupid woman," Gaius snapped, pulling his wrist from his dami's mouth. "They may hear you, and then you are surely in even worse trouble."

"Abum," Niibori said as he wiped his mouth on the back of his hand. "What are the other penalties?" Drinking his blood did nothing at all other than symbolize his submission. Unlike with mortals, for Akhkharu one's bu could only be used to heal or feed; it could not bind another vampire's will, though it did strengthen the mutual sense of place and time that all Shi and damu shared.

Gaius smiled and showed his fangs to the woman, making her gasp and lower herself to the floor before looking back down at his feet. "Second, you will make her your wardum. Cover her up, and we will leave to begin." Without another word, he left the bedroom.

Niibori shut his eyes. To think of his strong Natalie broken then bound to his will – it should have been his goal; it should have made him happy, but instead it made him bow his head in shame. He couldn't save her from slavery, but he could help her right now.

He crawled to her as she whimpered and tried to move. "Natalie-chan, baby, it will be fine. I will never hurt you," he lied to her as he bit into his own wrist. "Please, this will help you, please, it will ease your pain, I swear."

She seemed in shock as she took his wrist, cringing at the taste. Her eyes rolled up in her head a moment later and she clamped down tight with her teeth, making him gasp. At this first level it would start to heal her, and he could start to direct her emotions, maybe. He had never met someone resistant to the mental powers of the Akhkharu; he hadn't known they existed, but he prayed he could at least calm her from the weeks ahead in the ehus, where his Shi trained future wardum by breaking their wills through deprivation and humiliation.

She followed him silently, clinging to his body as they entered the ekallim. He almost sobbed as they neared the ehus, but then followed as they walked through the hallway into the ritual room that each Sarrutum was required to keep for the sake of maintaining the family cult. Two wardum in the room took Natalie from him and made her

138

stand in the place of submission while his Shi motioned him to the domination spot in front of her.

"But," Niibori began to ask as the local Sarrutum Kalum who oversaw such matters stood behind Natalie and whispered in her ear. Niibori took the offered bracelet of metal and placed it on Natalie's wrist as she and he both repeated the Tamu they were being forced to take. When they finished, and only they and Gaius were in the room, Natalie drew back her hand and slapped her husband as hard as she could, surprisingly hard, as she looked at her hand.

Gaius chuckled. "That is three. She must serve you, but she is not broken to you. You must master her, but you have no skill in this. Let's see how long you can survive," he added before leaving.

That night he sat next to her on the floor, letting her beat him in rage as she called him names and cursed him, always with "master" falling from her lips. She beat him for three straight days and nights until she was exhausted, then he cradled her in his arms and cooed to her, promising that they could do this together. She was his strong American bride; he would never see her otherwise, and he would always be her loving and proud husband. But as the sun rose outside on that fourth morning, he felt his heart drop as he fed her again from his wrist.

Natalie leaned back and wiped the bu from her lips. bu, that is what he told her it was called, but it looked just like darker, thicker blood to her. She let him hold her and make the absurd promises that gave him comfort, stroking his arm and hand as he did so.

Her heart clenched and her mind raced, but she had exhausted herself in her angry outburst. Anger had never gotten Grandfather or Father to notice her; only calm, purposeful demonstrations of her ability and skills. This monster, this Gaius, he might be a lot like those other men in her life. She just had to be able to do this well, whatever this was.

"I'm OK now, Mast..." she stumbled over the word that felt like it was being ripped from her subconscious.

"Sama, Niibori-sama," he replied, turning, and taking her face into his hands. He looked terrified, she realized, and that should have shocked her after learning what he was. Yet it didn't as he continued to

139

explain his suggestion. "It's how wives have addressed their husbands for centuries, old-fashioned now, but maybe," he trailed off.

"Niibori-sama," she said simply, and that fulfilled that pressing need she felt to obey and submit to him without making her stomach churn in protest. She kissed his cheek as he bent his head and cried again into her shoulder. "It will be OK, Niibori-sama. We're smart, we're creative, we can do this," she whispered to reassure them both.

"We can, because of you. Did you know that women are stronger than men?" Niibori began to tell her the story of the Akhkharu creator that he'd heard, amending it with legends of valor and survival populated by heroines from his own era. Soon Natalie was settled against him, content for a moment that he feared would pass too soon.

*"Did you know that the girl was the Ummum?" the new Allamudi asks as Cornelius tried to hush his eager damu.*

*"I did not; how could I, even with her power?" Niibori asks, turning to me and bowing before continuing, "Where I was from then, we had only rumors."*

*"I didn't interact with all of you in the same way. There wasn't always a need for me to be ... assertive, as I had been with others," I say, shooting Jamie a glance that made him snort, but he still looks away.*

*"Sometimes it was easy to see what needed to be done to encourage you toward this pairing that has allowed us all to flourish," I explain. I look to Bard, who was now standing with his hands clasped behind his back, his shoulders bowed, and his eyes watering already. "We need not continue if you do not wish," I tell him. I feel Jon's arms slip up from my elbows to my shoulders before he slips them around me in a hug that was both fatherly and like that of a lover.*

*Bard turns to me with tears on his cheeks. "No, it is time to be honest about what we did. About what she did, for I was merely a tool," he states as he looks over the audience. "What I'm about to tell you will seem beyond possible. Please believe me that I have many lifetimes of experience to share, and not in your Akhkharu way."*

# The Stranger at My Door

"Of course, someone comes to the door just as the oven beeps," Sara thought, quickly turning off the oven and opening its door a bit as she called out, "Just a minute!" She looked through the peephole and saw a man perhaps her age or a bit older dressed in a charcoal gray pinstripe suit, the full three-piece kind that one wears on formal occasions.

"Yes?" she asked without opening the door.

The man smiled and held up his hands to show he had no weapons, or at least none visible in them at the moment. He was carrying an envelope, though, in one hand. "Are you Ms. Sara Barkley?" he asked, his smile a bit wary now as he blinked at the peephole.

"Yes; who are you?" she returned his question as she studied him more closely.

"I am called Daedalus Montgomery, Ms. Barkley," he introduced himself with a nod of his head, then motioned with the envelope toward the door. "May I slip this through the mail slot, Ms. Barkley? It is a letter of introduction."

"Well, what's the worst thing an envelope could hold? Enough to close down post offices and schools," Sara thought, but there was something vaguely familiar about this man at her door, so she agreed, and he slipped the envelope through the mail slot. She turned on the extra lights outside her townhouse, too, both so she could see him better and so he could see around him better. "Thank you very much, Ms. Barkley," he said as he looked at the lights.

Sara examined the envelope and paused. The handwriting looked familiar. Opening it up, the same handwriting read: "I talk to myself often enough – I suppose I might as well write to myself. Yes, this is a letter from you, from the future. Just accept it for a moment and keep reading, OK?" Sara blinked, because the wording sounded just like her, and the handwriting – this was her handwriting, but she had never written this. "The man outside is my associate, Daedalus Montgomery. He won't harm you. In fact, he is here to escort you to your meeting on campus this evening. It is exceptionally important that you make it there on time." It was signed in her full name.

Sara opened the main lock but left the two door chains on as she opened the door to get a better look at the man. He had dirty blond hair pulled back at his neck into a slight ponytail, and his clear blue-gray eyes looked back at her. In fact, since he could now see a bit of her as well, he stepped back and muttered something under his breath. "What did you say?" Sara asked with a frown.

"Sorry, Ms. Barkley. I said that you look just like you do now, I mean, will look," he added. Daedalus glanced behind him, then turned back to the door. "May I come in? I promise I mean you no harm, but it isn't terribly safe to have this conversation this way, Ma'am." He sounded worried, and his smile was faltering.

No, outside at nighttime wasn't safe anymore. The murder rates in all the major cities around the world had skyrocketed in the past decade, but world officials were hard-pressed to determine the cause. There was a time when terrorists were the big cause of fear; now it seemed to be individuals and gangs who never claimed responsibility, never used the fear to promote themselves publicly, and yet managed to force everyone into isolation and carrying weapons. A look around revealed that he was alone, though her eyes blinked upon seeing a little girl standing across the street looking at them. Too bad, but parents really did need to look after their children better. She wasn't Sara's responsibility; only this stranger at her door was. "All right, but I know self-defense, and I will kill you if I have to," she warned him.

Daedalus paled a bit but tried to smile more. "I understand, Ms. Barkley; I certainly do."

He came in and waited for her to shut the door and relock it before he addressed her again. "I was a bit concerned, only a tiny bit," he added quickly, "that your ritual wouldn't work. You were correct, as always."

Sara studied him another moment when suddenly her stomach growled. The vaguely familiar stranger swallowed and stepped back. "I was just getting my dinner out. Want to join me? If not, you can come to the kitchen anyway, because you're not hanging out in my home alone," she told him as she walked to the kitchen, where her pizza had gotten a touch too brown but at least had not burned.

"Pizza?" he asked as he followed her, then he shook his head. "Of course, you're eating food, why not pizza?" he whispered as he took a seat on one of the barstools at the kitchen bar that separated the cooking area from the small dining room. Then Daedalus looked around at the small townhouse. "Very nice; you inherited it when you came here for school, right?" he stated.

"How did you know that?" Sara asked as she set the pizza on the counter and got the cutter out.

"Did you read your letter, Ms. Barkley?" he replied. When she nodded, he smiled. "You told me yourself, or rather, it was one of the many off-hand comments you've made to me over the years. I remember everything you tell me," he said with a bit of pride in his voice.

"Right," Sara muttered. "Well, since you are my associate, why don't you use whatever skills you have to get us two plates and then some drinks?"

Daedalus simply stood up and started looking through the cabinets until he had two plates and two glasses. He put the plates next to her, then went to the refrigerator to see what drinks there were. "No alcohol; might not be wise, given where you need to go tonight," he explained as he returned with the quart of milk.

"Where is that?" Sara asked as she took the plates holding slices of mesquite barbecue chicken on a self-rising crust to the bar's counter. She then moved one of the bar stools across the floor so she could sit and keep her eyes on him.

"You're going to meet the English professor you've been having an affair with, Ms. Barkley," he said simply as he turned to return the milk to the refrigerator.

Neither of them said anything then for a few minutes as they waited for the pizza to cool and considered the odd situation. "I apologize, Ms. Barkley; that was a crude statement for me to make. I should not have made it," Daedalus offered. He swallowed and looked down at the table, the color draining from his face a bit as he turned a simple ring on his right index finger a few times.

"No, I just, well, the letter, you, you are a stranger after all, yet familiar. I mean, no one else knows about Professor Weaston, so you must be …"

"Who the letter says, Ms. Barkley?" Daedalus finished her sentence. "I've been with you – the future you, that is – for well over three decades, so I do appreciate how odd all this must seem to you," he explained.

"Three decades? Did I adopt you when you were born?" Sara asked with a chuckle.

"No, no, I'm not sure how much to tell you; you didn't cover that question," Daedalus frowned as he looked at her.

"Normally if something's important to me, I'll make it clear; otherwise, you've got a brain, use it," she said simply.

That got a nod and a grin from him. "Exactly! You are you, completely." He glanced at his wristwatch and seemed to make a decision. "All right, we have some time to kill, so I'll try to explain, if you promise me that you will indeed keep your rendezvous, Ms. Barkley."

"Of course I'm keeping it," Sara replied. She was planning to break up with the professor, and it couldn't be put off, not one more day, regardless of what this … person told her.

"I come from the future, specifically 75 years in the future. The world is no longer in the hands of human beings," he began to explain, but that statement made her laugh out loud.

"You're telling me aliens have taken over – 75 years in the future – when I'm over 90?"

"No, not aliens," he replied with a slight smile. "You would call them vampires; they call themselves the Akhkharu or the Akh for short."

"That's the dumbest thing I've ever heard," Sara said as she picked up her milk. She didn't tell him to leave, because something in her stomach and her mind was suggesting he was telling the truth. It was like a new sense was operating in her that was letting her gauge his motives, and his motives were sincere – or else she was going insane.

Daedalus nodded with a shrug. "Luckily, they generally just use their family names, the names of those whom they can trace their lineage back to. Your family is the Allamudi, the scholarly family. There are others as well; all of them can trace their ancestors back to the Middle East, among the first human cities."

"Such as?" Sara prompted him with her tone and body language. If nothing else, this was taking her mind off the breakup with Evan that night.

He thought for a second, then said, "The Kashshaptu are the family that use natural magicks born in their blood and the blood of others. The Gelal are the family that control others via physical pleasures. The Sarrutum are the family that manipulates human enterprises, often political matters. And the Xul, they are monsters, pure and simple."

Sara's mouth had fallen open as he talked, so now he reached across the table and gently lifted her chin up, his face and hers both taking on a slight blush at the touch. "It's overwhelming; perhaps I shouldn't tell you more, Ms. Barkley."

"No, no, this is, this is, I don't have a word for it," Sara replied. "This is just amazing, and if it's a very clever prank, I'm going to kick your ass and the asses of everyone in on it!"

Daedalus blinked and sat back up straight. "I would never kid with you about these matters. You saved me from the Xul. I consider this mission merely a small repayment as well as my duty," he said so sincerely that Sara was shocked into nodding.

"Ok, say I believe this vampire story, but tell me why I should believe you are from the future. Time travel involves all sorts of freaky logical problems, and probably just plain old laws of physics that can't be broken, so why should I believe you?" Sara countered after a moment of awkward silence. He said she'd rescued him, but now he was here to protect her? How did that work?

"There was this old television show you mentioned to me, called Quantum Leap, I believe," Daedalus offered and then smiled when she leaned forward with a nod. "Using the knowledge you and your Shi have gathered," Sara stopped him with a question about the unfamiliar word he'd just used. "Shi is the one who brought you back from death, recaptured your soul in your body, like a parent," he explained, then continued, "you mimicked that fictional show to create a time passage within your own lifetime so that you could send me back to make sure you get to your meeting tonight."

"Why would that be in doubt?" Sara asked, seeing a logical flaw in his story.

"Others may be able to do what you have done, and they are enemies of your family. Besides, you said I was here to escort you to this meeting in your past; therefore, you must have sent me back to do so," Daedalus countered simply. His wristwatch beeped. "We need to start out so we can get you safely to your meeting, Ms. Barkley," he announced as he stood up. "I will clear things here while you finish anything you need to do."

Sara found herself leaving the familiar stranger alone in her kitchen as she went to brush her teeth and change into better clothes for the walk to campus. She had had a car at one point, but it had been vandalized a few nights ago after her last class of the semester. Evan had a sabbatical in Scotland for the next three months, so it was the perfect time to break things off with him. She couldn't justify continuing to see him when frankly she doubted the reasons for her interest in him and in English literature. It would add a year to her degree, but she just wasn't happy thinking of a future teaching writing and literature anymore. Plus, Professor Markus seemed to think she had potential in astronomy and physics.

Sara let Daedalus put her denim jacket on her for their walk and then went with him out the door. She turned on her flashlight and made sure her door was securely locked, then joined him at the bottom of the steps. Sara paused and stared across the street, where the young blonde girl was still watching them; she was alone, and then a man not much older than Sara joined her and took her hand. That man was crazy to be out at night with a child that young; it was like sending smoke signals out to the gangs. Not her problem, so Sara shook her head and led them off.

They walked in silence for a few minutes; campus and the English building were about fifteen minutes away at a casual pace that would not draw attention to them. "So, you and I in the future. What's the story behind this associate thing and me rescuing you?"

Daedalus sighed. "Perhaps I used a strong word there. It wasn't a Wonder Woman sort of rescue. Rather, it was sort of a pet shop situation," he said softly.

"Pet shop?" That didn't sound good.

"Vampires rule the future; most of us humans are either cattle or pets, but some of us survive outside the system unless we are caught. I got caught, and then, well, you acquired me before something else did, something quite nasty."

Sara stopped walking and looked at him. "I bought you like a dog?"

Daedalus literally put his hand on her arm and urged her along. "It's all quite normal in the future; it didn't make you a bad person," he offered.

Sara paused, then, at his tug on her arm, she moved to keep up with him. He seemed nervous now, and she noted that he was glancing around them as they reached the gates of the campus, where a guard asked for their IDs. Whatever Daedalus showed him looked blank to her, but the guard acted as though it were a student ID and let them pass.

"Still, it's all terrible," Sara finally said, referring to the information about how he was her associate or pet or some such horrible thing. "Isn't there anything I can do to make it, well, I don't know, better?"

Daedalus chuckled a bit. "Sure," he said off-handedly, "you had me at the fourth week; honestly, you did."

Sara nodded and repeated the information softly to remind herself. Doing so made her ignore the most direct route to the English department, the path she was supposed to take. She and Daedalus were both surprised when they ran into one of the political science faculty who was out for a walk and dinner – but this dinner, the professor decided, was better turned into a dami, a newly created vampire, once he'd easily dealt with the unfamiliar wardum, or slave, with her. What better way to mess with some other family's plans than to take their desired dami from them?

The world spun, and Sara was standing in her kitchen again. The oven's timer was beeping, and the doorbell was ringing. She looked down to find herself in the same clothes she'd been wearing before she had left for campus that night. The clock said it was 6:47 p.m., the same time when it had all started before. The oven and the door kept complaining, and Sara frowned. "Just a minute!" she yelled toward the door as she took the pizza out of the oven and turned it off.

When she got to the door, though, she saw an envelope lying on the floor as if it had been put through the mail slot. Again, it was addressed to her in her own handwriting, but the letter inside was slightly different: it made a comment about "smack him if he gets disrespectful." Sara was frowning as she undid the strongest lock and opened the door, so the chain locks were still in place.

Daedalus was there, and he grinned at her, adding a little wave. He looked different. First, his hair was shorter, a buzz cut, and he had a trimmed Van Dyke. To add to the entire look, he was wearing jeans, a blue-gray sweater, and a long black leather jacket, and from what she could see he had hiking boots on. This was not the same formal stranger she'd met before, but it still looked like him, and his voice had the same tone when he spoke. "So, you gonna let me in, Sara, or what?" he asked as he held up his hands with a wounded puppy look playing across his face.

"Oh, yeah," Sara said as she closed the door so she could undo the chains to let him in.

He stepped in past her with a grin and a glance around. "I'm surprised that you let me in so easily. You're usually more cautious than that. Guess that's why I'm back here, huh?" he theorized with a wink. Before she could reply he stepped really close to her and breathed in deeply. "You look and smell so very nice," he whispered.

For a moment Sara thought he was going to touch her, but he stepped back, continuing to sniff the air. "Is that barbecue? Oh, Akhkharu Ilati, I would give almost anything for some good barbecue," he said as he moved to the kitchen.

"Akhkharu Ilati?" Sara repeated as she followed him.

Daedalus smiled at the pizza, then raised his eyebrows at her. "Sort of a religious phrase, you could say," he told her. "I heard your Shi mention once that you knew a lot before you crossed, but I'm impressed with how well you're taking this entire thing." Then he motioned to the pizza and clasped his hands together as though begging.

"Sure, you can share it with me if you get the plates and drinks," Sara added quickly as he grinned. Apparently, she was remembering the time shift, but he wasn't. Of course, now that she thought about it, the earlier him had mentioned that she'd done something in the future that enabled him to travel. Maybe this was connected to her, and thus she could sense the time shifts. Of course, he was the one traveling, so why didn't he remember?

"No problem," he agreed as he went to nose around the cabinets, more quickly than last time. He came back with two plates and two glasses. "Do you know how long it's been since I've had pizza? I know what it is, seen vids of it, but it's all got to be healthy food for the best blood," he commented as he went to the refrigerator.

He turned around with a grin as he noted the beer. "Oh, oh, oh, is this what I think it is? Oh, Sara, you are such a naughty girl. I knew it all along," he added as he brought them each a light beer.

Sara grabbed the beers before he could open them. "Healthy food, huh? I don't imagine you'd deal well with this, then," she said as she took them back to the refrigerator.

As she passed, he moved behind her and shoved her against the refrigerator. "Right now, lady, you aren't my Bel; you're just a human, not even a wardum like me, so you don't get to decide what I can and can't eat," he growled. He turned her around and openly leered at her, even licking his lips in a vulgar fashion. "In fact, I'm thinking, given the power that is mine right now, I might get a chance to do a little something I've been thinking about for three decades." Sara glanced at the one hand that he'd placed right next to her head, pinning her in place. A small padlock was dangling from his wrist, and it caught her eye, so she almost didn't see what he did next, except that the lock moved slightly.

When he leaned in to kiss her, Sara brought her knee up and thrust it sharply between his legs while driving her clenched fists into his chin, forcing his head back with a crunching sound. She ran away from him and into her bedroom, where she locked the door, muttering, "Four weeks is apparently not nearly enough."

She grabbed her purse and a jacket, then unlocked the gate on her window as he slammed himself against the door. By the time Daedalus looked out that same window at her running down the street toward campus, another creature was moving quickly to intercept her. Her screaming was cut short as she felt her own life force drain from her quickly and something cold and nasty seep into her body. As her eyes closed, she thought she heard a child's voice say, "No, that's not quite right."

The world spun, and Sara was standing in her kitchen again while the oven timer was beeping. Same clothes, and the clock read 6:47 p.m. again. No doorbell this time, and she frowned as she kept one eye on the door and turned off the oven. As she took the pizza from the heat and placed it on the counter, she heard a knocking on the door. It was three solid knocks, then nothing.

She took a deep breath, took a kitchen knife in hand, then went quietly to the door and peeped out. The man there was facing away from the door; his dirty blond hair was a bit long, and it hung down around his face and over the collar of a long-worn trench coat. He seemed to be wearing gray trousers under them and scuffed dress shoes, but it wasn't until he turned back toward the door that she recognized him as Daedalus, again with facial hair, though this time it wasn't neatly trimmed and well-kept. This version also looked extremely worried, almost afraid, as he finally reached out and rang the doorbell.

"Yes, is that Daedalus Montgomery at my door?" Sara asked as she opened it all the way this time. She kept her hand with the knife ready behind her back just in case. She blinked, noticing for the first time that the strange little blonde girl was standing across the street, staring at them with a frown. How long had that child been out there alone?

Again, it really wasn't her problem, so she turned her gaze back to the man as he blinked, then fell to one knee and offered the envelope to her with shaky hands, his eyes on her doorstep. "Yes, Mistress, as commanded," he whispered.

She paused, blinked, and began to process what he'd said and how he was acting, her face reddening slightly in shame. This was definitely not the same man who had come to her door twice before. "Get up; the neighbors will see," Sara said quickly as she stepped back and opened the door further. "Get inside, come on," she urged, and he scurried inside to kneel on both knees, not directly before her but off to one side.

"You knew I was coming, Mistress? I am in awe and so unworthy," he whispered as Sara shut the door.

"What the fuck?" Sara thought as she locked the door. She stood there and read the letter, but this time it introduced him as her wardum. Another weird word that made her frown. "What's a wardum?" she asked.

Daedalus paused and blinked, then answered simply, "I am your wardum, Mistress. Your slave, Mistress," he added as he bowed his head lower.

Slave? Not pet, as the first Daedalus had said; of course, maybe he'd been lying or downplaying things. The second version had said she wasn't his Bel, so she asked about that term.

"Lord – there used to be a feminine form of it, but it hasn't been used in many centuries, so you have taught me, Mistress. You prefer the English term of female ownership, correct, Mistress?" he inquired as he glanced nervously around him with his eyes only.

"Sure," Sara replied as her stomach grumbled loudly. "I have a lot of questions for you, but right now I'm starving," she said as she turned and headed toward the kitchen.

She heard him following along after her, making some odd swishing sounds, and when she turned around, she found Daedalus had shed his coat and rolled up one sleeve on his light gray sweater. He was frowning and muttering something as he raised, then lowered, his arm, so she asked him to speak up. "You are as you are, yet you are not. I would offer myself, but, Mistress, I am confused," he said.

Offer himself? Vampires, blood. Sara's eyes widened a bit. "No, no, pizza and milk," she suggested, recalling what the first version of him had taken from the refrigerator. He lowered his arm, and although he was not looking directly at her, she got the feeling that he was watching her carefully. "Get two plates and two glasses, and we'll eat while we talk; that's an order," she added when he hesitated.

"Yes, Mistress. Where are they?" he asked and waited for an answer. After she indicated the correct cabinets, he went to them in a blur of movement, returning to kneel at her feet before she had barely removed the pizza cutter from the drawer. He wasn't breathing hard or anything, just kneeling there with the glasses resting on the plates he held on the palms of his hands. Sara bit her lip as a glint of thick metal was revealed around his neck, not quite fully hidden by his ratty sweater.

"Will I move that fast when I'm, you know, changed?" Sara asked.

"More quickly, Mistress," Daedalus informed her. He stood when directed and put the plates and glasses on the breakfast bar. "Wardum are mere shadows of the Akhkharu," he added as he went to retrieve the quart of skim milk.

"But you are stronger than or faster than other humans?" Sara said as she started placing some slices on the plates.

"Yes, wardum do not age, do not get ill, are stronger, faster; we tire less easily and can withstand greater extremes, Mistress," he said, adding the title, but glancing directly at her. "We, in return, serve with all these gifts, without question, and with our very souls the Akhkharu who bound us."

"Am I making you uncomfortable with all these questions?" Sara asked as he returned the milk to the refrigerator.

Daedalus stopped at the question but didn't turn toward her. "You wouldn't ask unless you were supposed to, unless you had, Mistress." His voice sounded a bit uncertain, and he did not move for a few seconds.

"You know I'm not your Bel yet," she replied, because his wariness was starting to unnerve her.

"You are always Mistress," he stated firmly as he put the milk in the refrigerator and shut the door. "I am only as you made me," he added when he had joined her for pizza. He didn't take a stool but simply stood, waiting.

"I made you? You mean like I trained you or educated you after getting you away from the Xul in the pet shop?" Sara asked with a half-smile. He paled and backed up a step. "That didn't happen? I mean, I want to make sure I do what I'm supposed to do," she added lamely. It was starting to make a creepy bit of sense to her now. Each time she learned something more it seemed to change him. What if it changed her as well?

Daedalus looked up slowly until she could see those gray-blue eyes, not clear as before, but dull, directly looking into her eyes. "You are Xul, Mistress," he said matter-of-factly.

Sara let the slice of pizza she held fall to her plate. Xul are monsters; that's what he told me. "No, no, Allamudi, scholars, it's supposed to be scholars."

He closed his eyes and sank to his knees again. "My fault, always my fault, you told me, but this time, I promise, Mistress, I will protect you until you reach the office, or I will die trying, as I deserve."

Her head was spinning with confusion. No, she had tried to make it better – she didn't know what exactly she was trying to make better – and it was getting worse, so she tried a different set of questions now. "Stand up, Daedalus; eat something, and answer my questions. Be honest with me," she added, worried that the first version and the second had neglected to add details that were necessary for her to hear. She was being given a chance to make things better for herself and for this man cowering on the floor. Until she did so she might be destined to replay this night over and over again, and that did not appeal to her in the slightest.

Daedalus stood up and took one bite of his pizza, a slight smile at the edges of his mouth. What did Xul do to their slaves? Did they torture them? Did they give them decent food? His attitude, clothing, and body language suggested she was not going to like the answers, but she had to know. "How did I make you? Tell me … everything, well, a lot," she amended as her stomach started to knot.

Between bites and sips he recounted the tale of how she had acquired a young man whom she turned into Daedalus Montgomery, a name she gave him that replaced some name he didn't remember. He had been born akalum, or food for the Akhkharu, but those who controlled the farming village where he lived had been defeated in battle. There were many battles between the various families of vampires. His town had been rounded up, and the men of his age had been sent off to be chosen by the victors. She had challenged another for him when she saw him; she had won.

For some time, she kept him isolated from anyone else but her and her hive of other Xul, who beat him, raped him, withheld food and water from him, and constantly told him that he was nothing unless she said so. She herself had broken each of Daedalus' fingers as her Shi, or father, made him watch; she called Daedalus an arrogant bastard, but he swore he didn't know why, and from time to time, when he did not fully succeed in a task, she would yell at him further and have him tortured more. That had been his life for three decades when he'd been called to her and her small circle of intimates. He had been sure he was destined to be akalum again, but she told him about this mission.

Sara had slid to the floor as he recounted his life to her. She was just sitting there when he knelt down in front of her. "Mistress, I'm sorry if I upset you. I only told you the truth. It isn't bad, it really isn't. You are Bel, Akhkharu; it's just the way of things. You are the most beautiful and gracious of the Xul; your kindness I never deserve; I, your slave, serve you humbly and thankfully; and you grant me life."

But she wasn't listening anymore as she muttered over and over, "There has to be a better way to do this; there has to be a middle ground."

By the time she had calmed down enough to leave her apartment they had to run all the way to campus, where the guards had just locked the door. Daedalus watched nervously while she called for Evan, but he didn't answer. Another woman whom Sara called Professor Anika was leaving the gated campus. Daedalus sank back as he recognized the witch; he was so terrified that he couldn't speak as she entranced his mistress and once more marked his failure in his mission with her

154

whispered words: "You are destined to keep repeating this night until it is perfect. Let me help you just this once."

Sara put her hands to her head as the beeping from the oven caught her off-guard again. Then, a few seconds later, came one ring of her doorbell, held down a second or two to draw her attention. Damnit! Am I never going to get this right? Blindly she turned off the oven, then rushed to the front door. Cautiously, she opened it to see what new Daedalus she had created and if that strange girl was still across the street. The girl was actually on her side of the street now, just one house away, staring at them in a fashion that was making Sara's skin crawl, but she made herself turn to the man at her door.

His hair was short, like the second version's, but his face was clean-shaven. He was wearing a long black leather coat over a three-piece charcoal gray pinstripe suit, his dress shoes were shined, and the hand that was resting on the side of the door when she opened it looked well cared for. His face, though, seemed a bit too pale as he looked at her and blinked. "Ms. Sara Barkley? I have a letter of introduction." He got the soft words out before collapsing in her arms.

She struggled to pull him inside and lock the door behind him. She checked the steps again for anything he might have left, jumping as a shadow fell over her. That young girl – blonde hair, pale blue eyes, and teddy-bear backpack – was standing on the steps. The girl shook her head, muttered something under her breath about limited attempts, then ran off, leaving Sara blinking until she saw another shadow around the corner that terrified her into her townhouse.

Sara took Daedalus' coat off and loosened his tie so she could check his breathing. He coughed a bit, and she sat back on the floor across from him. "Ilati, I am so sorry, Mistress – Ms. Barkley," he amended as he sat up straighter. He looked at his missing coat lying next to him and reached up to find his shirt opened a bit, the tie just dangling loose around his neck. "Wow, you already know why I'm here, don't you?" he said, though his voice rose at the end as if it were a question and not a statement. His voice, though, was really more of a firm whisper, hardly audible unless she was close to him and yet not trembling with fear as the previous version's had been.

"Yeah, I've been replaying this a lot tonight, Daedalus Montgomery," Sara said.

"Ah, that might explain my rough ride, then," he speculated with a grin as he stood up. He offered her his hand, and she let him help her up. "Would you mind, then, if I called you Mistress? I know I'm going to at some point, but if it makes you uncomfortable, I'll try to refrain," he promised.

Sara considered him and his words for a few seconds before she nodded. "Do what is comfortable for you. You might be distracted too much from escorting me tonight otherwise."

Daedalus smiled more widely and made a small bow. "Impressive," he whispered as he picked up his coat and folded it over one arm, glancing at his wristwatch as he did so.

"We have time for dinner," Sara told him as she motioned to the kitchen.

"I thought I smelled something interesting," he replied and then stepped out of the way so she could lead them to the kitchen. He moved in front of her and pulled out a stool expecting that she'd sit down. Sara did so, then just watched as he put his coat over another stool and quickly went through her kitchen to find plates and glasses as well as the pizza cutter. She gasped when he simply reached in the oven and took the pizza out with two bare hands.

"Mistress?" he asked as he set the pizza on the counter and came to her. He didn't resist, flinch or pale when she took his hands and looked at them. On the back of his right hand was an odd tattoo winding up from his wrist; it looked like roses on a vine, and the ink seemed to move on its own. Red and painful-looking blisters had formed on his palms, but then right before her eyes the blisters receded, and the angry red burns faded to a healthy pink. "Oh, sorry; you have potholders, don't you? I should have used them, but ..." She released his hands, and Daedalus put them in his pants pockets as he tilted his head to one side and laughed. "You know so much that I'm just falling into old habits, as you said I could," he reminded her. "And you eat like me because currently you aren't Akh, so I should get your food," he quickly added as he turned back to the pizza.

"I'll get drinks," Sara offered but didn't move, because she wanted to see what he would do.

Daedalus put the pizza in front of her and shook his head. "No need, I'm here. You'll learn soon enough that you were destined to be served, not to serve," he added with a wink as he walked past her.

"Is that something I told you when I was brainwashing you?" Sara bitterly speculated. She had figured it out while version three had been talking. Whatever these vampires did to control their servants, their slaves, it involved brainwashing, and then – what was that called? – Stockholm syndrome came into play.

"Whoa!" he said in a normal tone of voice and made some noise that urged Sara to rush toward him, only to find him cautiously balancing the milk jug via its handle on one finger. "Almost dropped it. Brainwashing?" he repeated in his softer tone as he steadied the container and brought it to the bar. "You mentioned you had been having this, this meeting with me, I assume, Mistress, multiple times tonight?"

"Yeah, and you've made it quite clear that Akhkharu basically torture and brainwash their slaves, their wardum, in order to get their service," she explained as he poured the milk.

He didn't return the jug to the refrigerator but instead looked at her seriously. "That is correct for some of the families and for some Akh, but not all; it's really not necessary if you choose your servants wisely." Daedalus folded his arms over his chest as he continued, his voice soft again. "Perhaps this is my ego talking, but I think you will choose your servants wisely. Learning how you wish things to be done, allowing myself to be recreated as a new man, and accepting my submission to you was not easy, I admit that, but I do not believe it was torture or brainwashing. Think of it more as a transformation into what I should be."

He put his hands on the bar and told her a few more facts. "This world you live in right now is on the edge of a massive upheaval. It will probably be very violent and confusing to you. You've told me that becoming Akh is that way, that the vampiric world seemed that way for you at first. But for me, I was born into a world controlled by Akhkharu, one nation at a time, sometimes one city block at a time, falling into their hands, often being traded back and forth, or won with death and fire. There was nothing to brainwash for. I had three roles open to me ...”

“Food, slave, or on the run,” Sara interpreted.

He chuckled softly and nodded his head. “This is an extraordinarily strange conversation,” he said after a moment. “Yes, and I’ve been all three. I know which one is best,” Daedalus added as he picked up a slice of pizza and began to eat.

They ate in silence, and then he cleaned up as she headed to her bedroom to get ready. After she cleaned up a bit and pulled on a different pair of pants and a shirt in the bathroom, she squeaked when she found him waiting in her bedroom. His tie was retied, and he was just standing in one corner with his hands behind his back and his head slightly bowed. He looked up at her squeak and frowned. “May I make a different clothing suggestion, Mistress?” he asked.

It didn’t seem like a come-on, and he didn’t seem afraid of her; he seemed like he belonged where he was, making the suggestion he was, as if he lived almost intimately with her, assisting her with her clothing and caring for her personal affairs. Sara nodded and blinked as he went through her closet and brought out a pair of jeans, hiking boots, a tank top, and a button-down shirt. “I think you’ll be more comfortable in these, given what you, the future you,” he amended with a smile, “has told me about tonight.”

Sara nodded. “Ok, well, I guess I can do what I have to do just as well in those clothes as I can in these,” she said as she took them, but he didn’t move. “Turn around, or wait out in the hall or something,” she ordered.

Immediately he turned away from her and looked at the floor. Sara considered this version as she changed. The entire thing was still ridiculous. Vampires, her becoming a vampire, and him, right, sure. Only one way to find out: get to her meeting, or she feared these snaps back and forth in time would leave them both more than merely confused and with burgeoning headaches.

“Let’s go,” she said as she bent down to lace up her boots. She heard him sigh, but he just smiled at her and waited for her to lead them to the front door. He put on his own coat, then chose her denim jacket for her.

He even offered her his arm as they walked, and Sara found she felt comfortable enough with him to take it. They walked quickly and, in several minutes, had made it through the main gates of the campus. "How did you show him that blank piece of paper and get him to believe it was a student ID?" she asked when they were too far for the guard to hear.

"Suggestion, something you will teach me in the future, because you have amazing mental powers. Rather useful with mere mortals." That sounded a bit odd to Sara, but she just nodded and accepted what he said for now.

As they neared the building where the English department was, Daedalus stopped and put his other hand on hers, resting in the crook of his arm. "Mistress, problem in the door there," he whispered.

Sara didn't bother asking how he knew; he was fast, he was ever young and strong; it wouldn't surprise her if his senses were heightened as well. She watched and saw a shadow move inside. "There's another way, through the tunnels," she whispered back.

Soon they were running into the science building and toward the tunnel when something jumped over the side of the stairs and blocked them with a scream out of hell. Sara felt her heart freeze, but Daedalus pushed her back up the stairs. "Run!" he ordered. He pulled something from his leather jacket and sprayed the creature, which screamed and tore at its face.

He bounded up the steps behind her and apologized as he went past her, only to tug on her arm to encourage her to move faster. "They can sense me, I'm afraid. They like to try and steal future damu from each other."

"Damu?" she asked as she hurried as fast as she could; thank god she was in these boots and not her dress shoes.

"Children, you might say," he explained as they went past the fourth-floor door.

"No, in here," Sara ordered as she pulled him back down and opened the door. "This is the same floor one of my professors is on; we have to warn him, or maybe we can hide in his office," she quickly stated.

Daedalus paused to ask, "English is that way, correct?"

"Yes, we'll get there soon, but we can't let someone else get hurt," Sara insisted, even though his question also made her pause. This would only take a few moments, and she could call Evan from here to tell him that she was on her way, but this – she pulled on Daedalus' arm – this had to be done. He didn't argue, but he did resist for another second before hurrying after her.

He followed her until they were in the room where the upper-level astronomy classes met; Professor Markus had told his students he could be found here most nights. She had come back here a few times in the past semester as she found herself in another physics course, confused over why they were more exciting than Shakespeare now. "Professor Markus! There are criminals on campus! We're being chased!" Sara explained as the professor came around the giant telescope.

Sara's smile faded as her professor got too close to her; there was something odd in his eyes and the tone of his voice. "Don't worry. They aren't going to hurt you. We protect our own," he said before spinning her to face away from him with a strength and speed he did not look like he should have.

Sara felt her life draining from her, replaced by something powerful, primal, and eerily calming. She glanced sideways and saw Daedalus moving toward her as though in slow motion. She reached out one hand toward him, but some odd shimmering in the air pulled him from her as the world turned black one final time.

*Bard ends his tale suddenly and falls quiet. After a nod from me, Jon goes to him and helps him sit down in a nearby chair. The others just look at me as I pull my thoughts together. "He was right when he told Sara that things were about to change. I accept responsibility for that," I tell them, and my eldest damu exchange glances, but I continue, "and I am not sorry for it. I will try to tell                    you                    ..."*
*"I can do it," Bard's voice cuts across mine. I turn to find he's pushed past Jon. He takes a few steps, then kneels at my feet. "You've both told me so much about it that it almost feels like I was there. Please, I can do this, Bel."*
*He never calls me Mistress, and I have never asked him to do so, just as I have never used the name Sara gave him. In the audience several of the Gelal are wiping their eyes while the Xul toss them disdainful looks that their leader*

*cannot manage at this moment. Jamie meets my eyes and gives me a single nod. My most difficult one has become my most honest counselor, so I heed his wisdom and turn the tale over to Bard.*

# End of Days

"Still no further comment from the governor on the situation in and around Boston." The newscaster on television set down her script and frowned at the camera and her viewers. She spoke in a firm, icy voice, and the camera shook a little. "Normally I don't go off script, but this, this is unacceptable. An American city has been surrounded for weeks now by hordes of people who refuse to speak to the press and somehow block all our attempts to find out what they want. Now the National Guard has placed itself between the city and these hordes." The newscaster pointed her finger at the camera. "Governor Milcrest, shame on you. I hope the voters kick your butt out of office at their earliest opportunity."

"That might be a while," Marina said softly as she sat on the floor next to the feet of the chair her liege and lady was perched on, her tiny baby blue tennis shoes dead still as she watched. The child said nothing, so the other vampire turned her attention to the national news again.

Another reporter on the screen was interviewing the mayor of Boston, Gary Bilton, a once-portly man. Marina had met with him shortly after the Ummum had revealed herself, insisting among other things that he watch his diet and exercise. That and the stress of his job had made him much thinner in the three years since. Right now, he said exactly what he should.

"The fine people of Boston should not worry. Food, water, energy, all of these continue to flow. That Bostonians must stay in the city is merely a temporary situation. What better time than to support your local restaurants, museums, and businesses? We've become too reliant on external powers for too long. The power is within ourselves; it has been all along."

"Mr. Mayor, what do you say to your critics who claim this is all part of a doomsday movement that the fundamentalists have been attempting to orchestrate for decades? They also claim that you are secretly a member of one of these groups and that you are hoping to start World War Three right here in America to cleanse it of sinners?"

The mayor laughed and shook his head. "Those cults have been around for a long time now, ever since their founders learned they couldn't stop advancements in civil rights or health care, or the overthrow of the business monopolies in favor of the planet." He held up a hand when the reporter tried to speak again. "I know that unprecedented violence has shaken this world as well. We are putting a stop to that by protecting this city and its voting public. The people of Boston will be safe as long as they stay in our wonderful city."

"Is that what you promised him?" Charity asked softly.

Marina froze for a moment, then looked up. "Yes, Ummum, I did tell him that it would be safe for them all inside the perimeter. Those who have allied themselves with you have infiltrated the National Guard. They will control them, and they will hold the line, or die trying." On the screen other big cities were being flashed, with scenes of random vampiric attacks everywhere. None were as well organized as those gathered here in Boston. Marina's spies had found out exactly who these few were and what they were capable of, but so far, she could not convince Her to do anything about it.

"It never works out quite as you want it," the little Akhkharu whispered as she looked away.

Just as Marina was about to reach up to touch her, the Ummum's arammu-wardum entered with a loud announcement. "Darling, everything is ready for the move … What are you watching?" He stopped and looked from the vampires to the television, then reached out and turned it off, prompting Marina to leap her feet and snarl at him.

"How dare you turn that off, slave!" He was the reason she was unable to influence the Ummum as she should. Three years had taught her that while She was indeed immensely powerful, Her mind was still that of a child. Her actions had been understandable, but there was only so long Marina could hold off the numerous Akhkharu who demanded vengeance for their Shi or damu, only so much she could do to control the local human population, and only so much one vampire could do without Her full support.

"She only gets upset when She watches this stuff," the wardum countered boldly. "Unlike you, my first priority is Her."

"Stop it!" Charity was between them, glaring up at them, so each adult backed up and knelt down. "It's time to leave," she said simply before gathering up her rag doll and teddy-bear backpack and heading out of the room.

"Things are going to change, slave," Marina growled as she stood up.

"Yes, and if you keep upsetting Her, they are going to change for the worse," Jon pointed out as he stood and then followed after his mistress.

Marina turned the screen back on; another reporter was interviewing a group of people in Boston itself protesting outside the mayor's residence. All of them held signs proclaiming that it was the end of days and that the viewers needed to repent. No one watching seemed to notice that soon after the sun set, one of that group was pulled back into the darkness, never to be seen again.

Around the world the scene repeated itself, Marina knew as she turned back to keep watching. One of the cameras on the tents outside the city zoomed in when a well-dressed man emerged and headed straight toward it. His smile was cold and calculating, and the very fact that he would allow himself to be telecast now made the Allamudi swallow. She took her cell phone and started calling the necessary numbers right away, starting with the highest Sarrutum on the council that she had convinced the Ummum to accept. "We need to convince Her to make a decision. We need to do it now," she added when he expressed some doubt. "Turn on the international news and you'll see why."

She was channel-surfing and shaking her head as reports started to come in of foolish citizens attempting to engage the groups camped outside the city. In some areas the encircling hordes merely backed off, if it were night and the Akhkharu in charge could step in. In the sunlit areas, the servants and followers, who were often oblivious to the true nature of their leaders, were coming into violent contact so frequently that the BBC was keeping a running tally of those dying in what they called a "bizarre movement" attacking cities worldwide.

"We're moving; we're going to try to draw them away from the entire city if we can. Two days; talk to your people, and we'll meet in two days," Marina was telling the councilor on the other end of the phone. "Just remember, we have to be careful about how we push Her to decide."

Jon wanted to stretch or drum his fingers on the arm of Her throne, but he held himself still, letting his eyes remain focused on Her hands clasped in Her lap while Her allies debated what to do next. Four of the five families had members here; only the Xul were missing, and when Marina had last talked to his little girl about that, Charity had merely said it was sad when grandchildren have no respect for their elders. Privately She had told him that She had already taken care that they would not completely die out but wouldn't expand upon it. He knew enough after three years never to push Her to reveal more of Her powers or past than She volunteered. The last ally who had pushed Her on such matters had been a pile of ash moments later.

He let his eyes wander a bit over this throne, which was really just a big stuffed chair She had liked in the new esharra they had moved into just two nights before. He couldn't keep it all straight. His former master had called his mansion – the house they had previously occupied – his bitum, so the wardum assumed this new term was a more powerful statement. As long as none of them made Her angry tonight, another day and night would come. Maybe, just maybe, they could go do something She enjoyed, like a disc or a board game.

Politics had always bored him. He imagined it shouldn't, given the amount of violence being reported on the news that She had insisted on watching and listening to, even when they had been moving. This was all so unlike the Night Kingdom he knew. So many vampires coming out with their followers, just tempting everyone to notice them. Why couldn't things go back to how they were before?

Then one of the other Akhkharu said something that made Jon turn to look at the group. He could not have heard correctly, and then She spoke, and he turned back to Her. "I will think on it. Please go now; enjoy the rest of your evening," she said as she slipped off the chair.

The other vampires glanced at each other, bowed, then left, Marina following them and assuring them that they'd have a decision soon. Once the big double doors were closed, Jon knelt so he was face to face with Her. "Did he suggest that you all tell the world what you are?"

"Yes, I've been thinking about it," She confessed as She stood up and motioned to Her throne. "What would happen if we did, Daddy?"

He blinked and then stood up, sitting back down on the chair, letting Her crawl up to sit in his lap. "I've always assumed that you'd be hunted down. You know, like the Inquisition."

She actually smiled at his comparison. "That wasn't about us. It never really is," She added with a sigh as She lay against his chest, resting Her head on his shoulder. "This is a big decision. Bigger than any I've made before. They want me to fail."

Jon frowned. At one level She was right. He suspected that several of Her so-called councilors were just waiting to see if she had a weakness they might exploit. Others, though, like Marina, seemed to be true believers, but they still used their positions to gain Her favor and turn that into their own power. He chose the middle course for his answer. "I'm sure that some would like to see you make a mistake, but if you do, they may all pay for it, so they'd better pray you make a good choice."

She sat back and looked at him with a serious expression. "Thank you, Daddy!" She cooed before giving him a kiss on the cheek, hopping off his lap and running toward the doors before She paused and turned back to him. "No one is to see me or bother me, Jon," She ordered firmly.

Jon stood automatically and bowed slightly. "I understand, Bel," he said as he followed after Her to guard the place she was headed. It turned out to be a section of the basement, behind the extensive wine cellar the previous owner had abandoned when the Guard had come to take up their positions around the city. This mansion was on the edge of the city, with few neighbors, and the line of soldiers just a few football fields away. The hordes were now moving closer to the edges of the mansion's grounds, but She didn't seem concerned, though Her allies always looked relieved when they made it in for the nightly meetings.

She stopped and looked up at him, so he knelt again. "Whatever you hear, whatever you see or smell, don't come in," She instructed him before entering a small room She'd set up and had the only key to. The heavy wooden door and the stone walls should block most sounds, but Her comment made him shudder as he took up his position to just stare at the door. When Marina found him a half hour before sunrise, he repeated the Ummum's commands, and the Allamudi nodded and left him to his watch.

She had made this room all by herself when they had moved in. She didn't even let her arammu-wardum help her set things up. He wouldn't have understood why things had to be done in this way – why that sign had to be made with her bu, or which object had to be aligned in each of the four directions. No one had really taught her, but in those rare moments when she'd been in need, each of these things had been there in some fashion. Her still childlike mind had figured it all out centuries ago, and whenever that small space was arranged, He came and sanctified it before disappearing again.

Charity had had a feeling for some time now that things were happening just like He had said so long ago, so she had spent an entire night setting up this private room. Near the east wall was a small stove. She lit it, then went to the little fridge she'd just stocked a few nights ago and took out the now-dead lamb. Cracking the tiny window above the stove, she placed the lamb on it and lit it, letting the smoke build up in the room and leak out the window. With a glance at the door, she hoped Jon would obey her. He did, almost all the time, but if he thought she was in danger …

She put those thoughts aside, knelt down at the center of the room, and began the chant her parents had always used when they asked for the blessings of the gods.

"So, a lot of pink today." Enki's voice startled her for a moment, as it always did. "I remember when pink was a boy's color, a lighter version of red, the color of blood and warriors. Inna will be pleased," He joked as He sat on the floor right next to her.

Charity was silent for a moment until He nudged her with His elbow. Then she giggled and snuggled into His open arms. "Thank you for coming, my Lord."

"Hey, that was some fine smoke you sent up. Since I'm the only one paying much attention these days." He shrugged.

"I never want to disturb you," she added softly.

"Never, child, never. Remember," He said, pulling away so He could tilt up her head with one hand and gaze down at her with His sea-colored eyes that swirled with the power of all the waters, "you are my favorite creature ever. You have made things so much more interesting than they could have been. You and your offspring. We were thinking the rising sea levels might bring us some much needed quiet, but the rest seemed to have finally gotten that under control."

She listened politely, but inside Charity was tense and anxious to ask her question. One did not rush gods – even if one was like unto them, one was not them. She'd seen enough of her grandchildren destroyed by the jealousy of the Seven who had blessed and cursed her. So, she listened and looked at him and couldn't help but smile. He was wearing a blue T-shirt with "Save the Sharks" on it, a pair of cargo pants, and sandals, and his hair flowed over his shoulders, where it constantly moved like the never-ending waves.

He caught her eyes and waved at himself with one hand. "You like? Some idiot pissed off his girlfriend, who burned all his clothes, so they're mine now." They giggled for a bit, then Enki frowned. "You know what you need to do now, so why am I here, little one?"

"You know what I did to save Jon, right?"

"I saw. Blowhards deserved it. It's like Nin said. Not all of them are wise or respectful, and after so much time I'm sure most don't remember you. Which is mostly your fault for living in the shadows," He added, chiding her gently yet poignantly.

"I know – it was … easier," Charity replied as a blood tear started to fall from her eye.

"Shhhh ... none of that. You're the big Ummum now. Have to act like the mommy sometimes, yes?"

"Yes," she agreed. That had always been the problem. Her only younger sibling had died before his second birthday, so her experience with children was limited. Her damu and their offspring, her offspring, were not technically children. When they looked at her, she could tell they just didn't believe it, not yet. "Do we tell the world what we are? What happens when we do?"

"Do you think those near the cities, in the cities, are going to keep this quiet much longer?"

"You've seen what's happening, then?"

"Of course, we all see it; I'm just the only one who still cares. The rest figure that if it all burns, so much more stuff for them, huh?" Enki sighed and ran his hands through his hair, flicking off the beads of water that trailed along his fingers. "I'm the only one who seems to remember how much we need all of you. So, you have to be the Ummum now, step up and make it about you, so you can be in control."

"How can I be the Ummum when most of them only see me as a child? I don't want to have to hurt them all again."

Enki was frowning now, eyes whirling with the storms of the oceans. "I know what to do about it. I will contact the Zagmi of this group who wants to be your council of elders, though most of them are not that old, as you know. Then that priest will speak my words at your next meeting, and their confusion will cease. When it has, you will need to find a respected mortal to speak for you all, someone most of the world trusts." The ancient god chuckled as He considered the matter. "Oh, I know just the person to really set things atilt."

Charity frowned, then smiled as He looked at her. In a moment he evaporated, and she fell unconscious with the rising sun.

"Kima Parsi Labiruti," the priest, the Zagmi, commanded as he walked into the throne room ahead of Charity. Each person who followed her, save perhaps the Arammmum-Wardum, knew this was a sign to recognize her authority, though in fact it was something quite different, and this particular Sarrutum priest would never utter such an ancient phrase unless he was convinced of her identity and power as the Ummum. To Charity's eyes a bluish light seemed to emanate from her now, entering each person in the room, sending them to their knees as she walked in. Behind her, Marina commented softly about the appropriateness of things finally, but Jon remained silent.

In her dreams, she had seen a vision of what she needed to do, a fulfillment of something she had been doing for years, but it would take years longer to accomplish. It was all so tiring to think about, but the Akhkharu were not supposed to get tired. As she turned to look at the council now, she realized again how different she was from all of them. There were others ... she'd call them to her later when this was settled.

"I have made the decision." The vampires looked up at her now. "Be prepared, for an announcement of our existence will come very soon."

"How? When?" one of the three Sarrutum in the room started to ask when Charity set her gaze on him, causing him to swallow.

"Prepare yourselves, your damu and your wardum. When it comes, we must step forward."

"Others will not like it," one of the five Allamudi other than Marina pointed out. "Mortals and our own kind both."

"If we don't do this, surely others will, and they will not care how many die," another scholar added.

"There will be war," one of the four Gelal added, then looked down and away from Charity's gaze.

"We stand with our Ummum. Let war come," came the whisper from one of the three Kashshaptu, and her whisper was repeated by her sisters until the entire room was echoing with the acclaim of the council.

Charity forced herself to stand tall, but her hand twitched at her side, for today she had come in her most simple clothes, her dolls, and other childish comforts back in her suite. Tonight, she had to be the Ummum. Later, alone, she could be herself again.

Jon ran his hands through his hair after Marina and the Council had left. There had been a flurry of activity after the Pope had made his announcement. Vampires had been known and tracked by the Vatican for years. It was the End of Days, he had said, but we should not see these creatures as agents of the devil but of God, sent to guide us when we have failed to follow Him. It was insane, crazy, that the representative of God on Earth would say such a thing. Christians might like to think of themselves as the one true religion, but he imagined the others would disagree.

As they continued to watch the news, the anchor almost gaping at the viewers in shock, reports came in from other religious centers of the world. One by one, the leaders of the world's religions came forward and gave a variation of the exact same speech. Jon stepped forward, his mouth also open, until he was standing right next to Her. "How did you do this?"

She slipped Her hand in his and tugged on it, so he'd glance down at Her calm smile. "I didn't, Daddy. The gods did, or one god did in this case. You can't tell anyone that. They lost their faith a long time ago."

Jon frowned at this vague reply but just swallowed as he sat down on the floor to keep watching. She sat down on his lap and watched silently as well. Outside he could hear the phones ringing, but that's what the scholar was around for, he decided after a few moments. His place was here, regardless of what happened.

Whatever happened would be good. It had to be.

If that's what his little girl wanted, it had to be, he just kept telling himself as various political figures now either started denouncing this farce or tentatively supporting it.

Around the world the groups that had gathered outside the cities made themselves known, but instead of easily taking over, one by one they were confronted by armies, police, and other local forces, sometimes controlled by Akhkharu inside the cities and sometimes by mortals who felt they could retain their authority. The counter on the BBC now started clicking into the thousands, then tens of thousands, as the human race tried to fight back, finding their weapons and their soldiers were not truly theirs to command.

Jon shuddered as a drop of bubussunu hit his hand, its familiar power seeping into his skin. A look up confirmed that She was crying, so he pulled Her to him and cuddled Her in his arms. "You'll figure this out, you'll see," he told Her as he rocked them both, stopping only when the door opened.

"Ummum?" It was the Allamudi's voice, so he released his princess, letting Her use his shirt as a handkerchief for Her tears, so She could stand up. "I have the President of the United States on the phone, as you asked," Marina said. "Do you want to talk to him now?"

"No, tell him that I will meet him tomorrow night, but he must control his troops and order the governors to stand down, or I won't come," Charity replied.

Jon glanced up over his shoulder to see Her, chief of all Akhkharu, smile. "Of course, Ummum," Marina replied. "I'll make sure he appreciates the gravity of the situation."

He looked up at Her as She turned back to him, Her face a mask of intense self-control. "Marina will help me best with this, Jon. But I need you to support me, or I can't do what has to be done."

"Of course, Bel; I'll serve in any way you require. Just ..." He bit his lip but continued when she motioned for him to do so. "Don't forget yourself in all of this. Please."

Her grin lit up his heart. "I won't, Daddy. I'll make sure we keep many playmates and their mommies and daddies around for a long, long time."

Marina watched from a distance as the Ummum spoke with the President. The man let her crawl onto his lap and look into his eyes. Within moments he was enthralled, something only Gelal and Kashshaptu seemed to be able to do with such ease. Instead of the jealousy or inadequacy she had felt over the past three years, she felt pride.

She was poised to be the chief advisor, Her right hand, and Her voice to the rest of the world. Marina had been preparing as well, these past few years – studying every culture and government, their successes and failures, the reports on what was healthy for people and what made them the most productive. The Ummum disliked making decisions, she could tell, but that meant She'd be open to friendly, supportive advice like Marina had been giving Her all along.

Marina smiled as her name was called. She stepped forward and inclined her head slightly for politeness' sake. "Mr. President, it's an honor to meet you. I made sure my people voted for you in both terms."

The President paled and ran a hand through his mostly white hair. "It's always a pleasure to meet supporters, especially ones who come so highly recommended."

Marina smiled and then knelt down to listen to Charity when her hand was tugged at. "I'm trusting you."

"I will not fail you, Ummum," she replied softly.

She stood up as soon as the Ummum left the room to take a seat opposite the President's desk. "Our first concern is the well-being of the American people, as I'm sure is yours, Mr. President. As I'm sure you are aware, other nations are falling into chaos, something we want to avoid."

As they discussed her "suggestions" over the next few hours, they were interrupted by reports of governors declaring independence, military units denouncing the Presidency, and fighting breaking out around the country. As the man grew increasingly distracted, Marina walked over to the small bar and slit her wrist, bleeding into a tumbler. This was a bold move on her part, but things were rapidly deteriorating, so it had to be taken. She knew she could explain it all if she needed to later.

"Mr. President, please, do take a moment and have a drink."

He looked at the tumbler and swallowed. "It won't hurt, I promise. In fact, it will make things better – you'll be stronger, wiser, and more sure of yourself than you were when you ran for your second term." When he didn't move, she shrugged. "Either this or watch it all burn down around you. You know it will, too. At your primal core you've seen this before; you know what time this is. You can fight us; you can let the world explode into chaos, but how would that benefit the American people?"

"God forgive me," he whispered as he took the tumbler and swallowed it down in one grimacing move.

Marina repeated the age-old phrases her Shi had taught her and that his Shi and his before him had passed on. With her encouragement, his body and mind doubly numbed by bu and Charity, the President repeated his part of the Tamu and held out his right hand for her to slip a gold ring onto.

When she was sitting again and he was looking at her with expectation but also confusion, she smiled. "Now, let's work on saving as many people as we can."

The Ummum might want to recreate the world in Her image, but the Allamudi had learned over these three years that what She wanted wasn't necessarily as bad as Marina had first feared. It was, however, going to be extremely difficult. If she could manipulate things correctly, there might only be a 40 percent loss of life before things settled down into the nice stable feudal pattern that she'd determined would work best.

*"What I want right now is for you all to retire before the daytime comes,"* I tell them all as Bard stands up with Jon's help.

*"But there must be more,"* one of the Kashshaptu states in a whisper as she looks up at me with pleading eyes.

*"Please do tell us more, Ummum; it is very interesting,"* one of the Sarrutum adds as he leans toward me.

*Soon every one of the younger Akh is voicing their desire to hear how we went from the end of the Day period to our current days and nights of harmony. They are all children of the new order; they do not remember the pain and chaos of those decades. These will be difficult tales to tell, so I hold up my hands, and they all fall silent.*

*"In three nights, we will meet again, and Bard and Calypso will tell us more."* As I allow Jon to lead me away, I see her step up and converse with him. I trust that they will make the truth palatable to hear.

# Night

# Another Night of Tales

*Jon helps me change my clothing as we wait for all of my descendants to arrive in the garden once more. Over the past two nights I've met with the elders, and most of them prefer that Bard tell their stories rather than take the stage themselves. Given that these will involve so many different versions of the same events, one family meeting with another sometimes by my design, sometimes randomly, it makes sense.*

*"Bel?" the storyteller in question addresses me after I call out permission for him to enter. I can almost see him as the younger man he once was as he stands up after bowing. "This will be a challenge," he confesses.*

*"If you aren't up to it ..." Jon begins, but he stops when I raise one hand.*

*"I'll offer again to let them tell their own stories, but I do appreciate your craft and care in this matter. If the new ones want to learn, let's teach them," I point out. The truth is that some disturbing stories have also made their way to Jon and Bard over the past few days. The aid from the gods may be showing its dark nature, and that is a problem that even Enki claims he can do nothing about.*

*"Thank you," Bard says, but then he chuckles. "It isn't that I don't know I'll do a good job – I'll be entertaining, informative – it's just that some of it may shock people. I thought about editing some of the details; I'm certainly not including everything," he hastens to add. "What I say may upset some elders, some of the damu."*

*I pat Jon's hand and then go to my other wardum to place my hands on his shoulders; the rare contact makes him grimace and look away, but I force*

177

him to meet my eyes with a gentle touch of his chin. "It might be good to shock some of them, good for them to realize how bad and difficult it was."

"Will they see the good in it, Bel?" Bard replies, and I can feel the fear radiating from him. That is actually good, because for the first decade of the new world he'd been under suicide watch. Fear of their anger means he wants to live, that he's found purpose in his role as our Bard.

"I won't let anyone harm you," I assure him.

"No one would dare," Jon adds as he joins us, putting a comforting arm around my waist.

If we could stay here like this forever, I might be content, but soon one of the servants comes to tell us that the families have arrived.

I step out to find them all seated as they were three nights ago, but with Enki now front and center, his face mischievous. I bow to my Lord and then address my descendants. "Have you come to hear more of our story, all of our stories?"

They agree, and their demeanor shows their natures. The Sarrutum are attentive but hold themselves straight; Niibori sits in front of his damu with Natalie by his side. The Allamudi have notebooks out, and one is even holding some reclaimed technology on her lap, though she wields a stylus rather than a keyboard, while Jack sits with the other wardum and Cornelius watches his children from their center. Jamie and Karl are among the pile of Xul sprawled out not far from Enki, who keeps glancing at them with a twinkle in his lapis lazuli eyes. Almost mimicking them are the Gelal, though their sprawling is more entwined, their gazes lingering on their partners or rising to meet mine, with Maha and Lucien watching from the back. Chavi is taking notes as well this evening, though Calypso and the rest of the Kashshaptu are merely attentive; I can trust that their story will be told by the head witch herself.

Those whose behavior has caused me concern over the past week are not looking directly at me, so I decide to watch them closely tonight. "Tonight, Bard and a few others will continue the story of how we all came to live here – mortals, wardum, and Akhkharu together in one replenished world. It is a story of pain, a tale of destruction. I require that you all listen with open minds and hearts," I add, piercing with my gaze one malefactor who dares glance at me.

"Of course, that is the only way to listen," Cornelius states, earning nods from most of those in the garden. Yes, I will watch closely, I remind myself as I step aside for Bard.

*"Tonight, we begin with peace that quickly turns to conflict, not long after the last tale,"* Bard explains.

# Bodyguard

They had pretty much settled in Rio. Aside from the veneer of Christianity, it was a liberal place for the business, and for several years their exotic offerings had been available for any income level when Madame Maha determined it was allowed. Then it had happened, and the world had started to crumble around them. It had begun in America, where the people had valued their freedoms a bit too much and thus fought back a bit too hard when the Akhkharu had revealed themselves. When Night Courts from around the world had sent their warriors to surround Boston to take out a threat they called the Ummum, the humans had responded in kind. As it had been night, the mortals had fallen quickly, alongside those who had come to conquer the child-mother of all Akhkharu.

In the few years it had been since that time, which Maha had been calling "The Mother's Return," Lucien had learned more of his mistress's past and people. Every girl, boy, woman, and man associated with the brothel was fighting for her or his life as the horde of monsters swarmed over the city. Armed with the finest sword she had been able to find him from the Far East, her strength flowing through him, and with devotion born of bu and pleasure, he was standing on the roof with the one he served, listening to the slaughter below.

"We have to help them," she ordered, but her power was tinged with fear, and he'd had centuries to grow in his own authority among her household, so he ignored it. When she moved toward the stairwell to go down, he grabbed her by the wrist. "I can save them," she protested.

"Too many of them, Maîtresse, and what is more, you told me these monsters seem immune to your charms. My duty is to protect you."

She gasped as the cover locked over the stairwell moved. It shook violently until it split into pieces and a blond-haired, blue-eyed man with a scar on his right cheek jumped up and stared at them. He wasn't one of her kind, but in a moment another man, wiry where this first was solid, and pale with a series of numbers tattooed on his left cheek, fangs distended, and dark hair in a bob, followed. "Ain't this a treat then. I find the lady of the 'ouse 'erself," he said with a mock bow.

"I warn you, Sir, we shall not fall as easily as those below," Lucien made himself say as he stepped in front of her, his katana drawn.

The monster advanced, then stopped, his body flinching back, his eyes wide. "Bloody 'ell!" He turned to his wardum with a snarl, and the slave seemed to melt into the threat. "Watch it, you wanker! You!" He turned back to the Gelal he had been hoping to impress his hive leader with. "Jump off the roof and 'ead for the airport. We ain't there yet, so get the fuck out. I 'elp you once for 'er sake, but not a second time, so bugger off!"

"Thank you," Madame Maha said as she moved to stand at Lucien's side, putting a hand on his arm. "I understand now," she added before taking his wrist and pulling him to the ledge to look down. The jump wasn't a problem – only three stories, which was nothing for either of them – but Lucien looked back with a growl when he heard a sound and saw the monster's wardum cowering on the floor as his master beat him, screaming curses.

"Come, we start over," she said, then jumped.

A few nights later, Lucien put one hand over his mouth as he watched her writing a letter. They were staying at an oasis as close to Cairo as they dared go. There were no other Akhkharu here, and the few people who lived here fell easily under her power once she had taken their chief the night before. Now they were in his tent and staying as his guests.

She paused in her writing to look up at him with one arched, elegant eyebrow. "You disapprove of this course of action, Lucien?"

If the Emperor had asked him during a briefing, he'd have told him the truth in guarded language. If she had asked him in her bed, he'd have told her the truth with honeyed, cautious words. Right now, he was guarding her, and while her essence running through him charged him to be careful, his duty demanded the truth as well. "I am concerned, Maîtresse, that this will draw attention to you when we are merely two."

She looked at him with her dark eyes, tinged with hints of sorrow and mischief, but said nothing to answer that claim directly, as he had feared she might. Something inside him knew she'd shared herself with the Chief to get this shelter. "That's why I'm sending these letters to my Shi, if she is still among us, and to all my friends and allies. And this one," Madame Maha said reverently, holding up the one she had been laboring over for the longest time, "is for the Ummum Herself."

"Did She not destroy an entire city's elders and then turn her attention to an army of hundreds, slaughtering them as well? Might this not make Her come here, Maîtresse?"

Madame Maha shook her head, but he could see a slight tremble in her form. "No, She has more pressing matters than merely a child who wishes to rule one city in Her name."

"As you say, Maîtresse," Lucien whispered as he bowed his head before tuning his eyes and ears for anyone approaching the tent.

In the weeks they waited, she slowly extended her control over the entire oasis, and Lucien knew as he waited outside the tent, listening to the sounds of her pleasure and feeding, that she had claimed others to her service. He could not fault her, not truly; she was not his in any sense, and yet his back tensed up as their voices reached a new note in their passion. He recited some poems he had always used to control his temper and ease his mind, first during his military training and then later at his more than a century in the brothel before finding his current place as her bodyguard. He inclined his head slightly, a smile tugging on one edge of his lips, when the man exited with a stagger, his face a bit paler than when he had entered.

Lucien had always stayed the full night and into the day. None of them did.

"Lucien," her husky, gentle voice came to his ears, and he smiled as he pushed back the tent flap and entered. "Come to me," she commanded, holding up one arm and the sheets with it to reveal her shining feminine form reclining there, waiting for him.

He came, shedding his clothing as he moved, keeping one dagger in his hand until he could place it safely under a pillow within easy reach. Again, he lost himself to her pleasure as she used him not for mere food but to sustain her in much deeper ways. They cried out each other's names and titles over and over until the sun saw her unconscious and him about to fall likewise into exhaustion. Thus it was every night, until tonight, when a stranger walked into the tent.

Lucien grabbed his knife and sprang to his feet at the foot of the bed, barring it from the desert nomad, who stood staring at him between his layers of protective clothing. "Hail, you must be Lucien. I am Ranjan, servant of Lady Eden. I mean you no harm," the stranger declared, holding up his hands to show they were empty, and turning slowly to show that he carried no sword.

"Eden, the Shi of Maîtresse?" he asked softly, his mind turning over the letters.

"Yes," the other man simply agreed. "I am sent to tell you that my Mistress will arrive in two nights' time. I had hoped to make it before sunrise, but the sands slowed me. I humbly apologize," he added with a deep bow.

Lucien relaxed just a bit. This was their first word back in weeks, and her creator would at least be more powerful than Madame Maha was, so if nothing else it strengthened their position here. "You are welcomed, Ranjan. May I offer you some refreshments?"

The other wardum shook his head. "I cannot. I must report back to the caravan if I have found Maha and she is willing to accept Eden in two nights?"

"Of course," Lucien looked back at his sleeping lady and sighed. "I cannot speak for her," he began, but the other man's eyes went wide at this news. "If you can wait until sundown, she will agree, or not."

"You are not her arammu-wardum? She introduced you as such in her letter."

"Her what?" That was a phrase he was unfamiliar with.

"I see," her guest replied slowly. After a moment he unwrapped his head covering to reveal his darker skin and shining brown eyes. "Then I would indeed like refreshment while we wait. And some sleep, if you can show me a place away from the sand," he added with a brilliant grin.

"Certainly," Lucien said as he grabbed his trousers and slipped them on before opening the tent flap and issuing a stream of orders. Soon her guest had drink, food, and a couch to lie upon in the same tent so that they would be there when Madame Maha awoke. As Lucien returned to her bed to sleep himself, posting guards at the entrance as he always did during the bulk of the day, Ranjan chuckled. "Do you desire something else?" Lucien asked.

"No, no, only I think you are what you do not know you are," he said mysteriously.

Lucien rubbed his tired eyes with one hand, but soon sleep overtook him as he cuddled against her cool, naked form.

Lucien awoke later and made sure that Maha's guest was fed again and given a chance to bathe, joining him primarily to keep an eye on him rather than allow him to wander the camp. In their time eating and bathing, he learned more about Akhkharu society than he had in centuries from her. Attempts to hide his ignorance failed, and he watched the Indian's concern grow as they spoke, but he made no comment on it.

So, Lucien decided to investigate a bit more through his own questions in the hopes of knowing the full range of allies and enemies she might be facing in this newly darkened world. "How long have you been in the employ of Lady Eden?"

Ranjan's left eyebrow rose slightly, as did a chuckle in his throat. "I have been honored by her embrace for well over half a millennium now, I believe. Time is difficult to track with Gelal, as I'm sure you've noticed yourself."

Lucien took a deep calming breath. This truly was an eternity of service he seemed to be captured in, but at least her guest appeared to be in good form and mood. "I thought it was merely a function of living indoors most of the time, but it is common to lose time with them?" He didn't mention how he came to be Madame Maha's bodyguard, and he hoped he wasn't asked, for now he felt even more ashamed of it than he had the night it happened.

"Well, it may happen with all of them, but with our ladies the pleasure is what blurs the years. Do you not agree?"

"Pleasure, certainly, but also duty; I am not merely a plaything."

"Interesting choice of words," Ranjan commented, then sipped the wine they were drinking as they soaked in the cool bathing pool. "I was, at first, a mere plaything, as you say. There is no shame in it. To begin as akalum, to begin as distraction and food, then to prove your worthiness for something more, is that not what all men must do from the day they are born?"

"That is an intriguing way to consider our lot," Lucien agreed. His mind went back to his military toys as a child, his drilling daily as a boy, his lessons in tactics and strategy, his entire adult career, even knowing that his future marriage was decided by his Emperor because he was a capable officer with a promising future. For the first time in longer than he could remember he wondered what had happened to his children and put a hand over his eyes in shame.

"Your lady wishes to live in Cairo," the Indian changed the subject, and Lucien controlled himself and looked up. "Currently a Sarrutum controls it, which is no surprise, but I hear he has not fully accepted the arrival of the Ummum. Perhaps that will be her opening."

"She sent a letter to one of that family, group, I do not know the appropriate word," Lucien stumbled. "She has not heard back from him."

"Yes, she mentioned this in her letter to Eden. I would not hold out much hope for him."

"You know of him?"

"The Night Kingdom is a small realm in terms of the lords and ladies who rule it. Also, we visited the Far East some time ago and had the displeasure of meeting him. He clings to certain human biases that he should have left behind with the beat of his heart," Ranjan commented, then finished off the wine. "She also said she was writing to the Ummum?"

"Yes, it was a bold move, but one she felt was necessary."

"Indeed," the Indian replied as he stood up. "The sun will set soon, and I must meditate before greeting your lady."

Lucien was dressed, with his katana at his side and a new firearm he'd been practicing with on the other, sitting on her bed, and watching his mistress's eyelids flutter, then open. She smiled at him, then frowned and sat up, clutching the sheet to her bosom. "You have a guest, Maîtresse, a servant of your Shi, Lady Eden," he whispered as she nodded, calling softly for her robe.

The Indian had knelt on one knee after his meditation and remained with head bowed, one hand on his chest, one hand brushing the rug covered ground, even now when she stepped in front of him. This was not something Madame Maha had taught Lucien to do, but then again, he had never met anyone else from her people outside her own household until this morning.

"Hello, Ranjan," Madame Maha said as she smiled down at the kneeling wardum. She let Lucien approach and watch them.

"Lady Maha, I bring greetings from your Shi, Lady Eden, and from me as well," he added with a smile, though he did not look up.

"Has she sent you with word of my petition then?"

"She comes herself, Lady, traveling again now that the sun has set. I should hasten to her for this final leg, and she will arrive tomorrow night around midnight, if that pleases you."

"It does please me. Go then. Lucien, tell the others to give Ranjan whatever supplies he needs, even a fresh mount."

"Of course, Maîtresse," he replied with a bow before leaving to do as instructed. His sharper ears, though, picked up a few phrases in the tent as he walked away. Apparently, he would be educated tonight on the appropriate way to greet another vampire, and that knowledge made that long-forgotten knot in his stomach reappear.

Once the Indian was on his way and they were alone, Madame Maha told him that things were a bit different for meeting another Gelal.

Each family of Akhkharu had common abilities, but also specific ones that wardum needed to be wary of. For Gelal, it was considered a sign of infidelity to look at a vampire other than the one you served. Physically, Gelal could inspire lust more certainly than any other feeling; their voices, too, could ignite passion. On their side, Gelal were forbidden to touch another's wardum or akalum, because via the merest contact servants had been stolen and feuds begun.

None of this surprised Lucien, who knew full well the power his lady commanded with just a glance, moan, or caress. Thus, it made perfect sense to kneel, because this redirected one's natural gaze away and put one's body out of easy reach. If a member of their family were to forget this etiquette, he was expected to bring it immediately to Madame Maha's attention. He was never to raise his hand or a weapon to another Gelal, not even their slaves and food, but to allow them to mediate it among themselves.

When he inquired about other families, she merely said that she hoped he'd never need to interact with them on his own, and thus he should trust her on such matters. "Is there such animosity between your people, Maîtresse?"

Her dark eyes looked away before turning to him in all seriousness. "We are territorial creatures, and insular as well, clinging to our ancestry and our habits in substitute for our lost lives. I fear this new revelation to the world is only going to increase this competition, unless the Ummum can act wisely."

The guard at her tent flap stuck his head in at that moment to announce that a messenger had arrived. Instinctively Lucien moved to stand in front of her when this breathless person, a woman by her slight form, entered and bowed, an envelope on one open palm. As soon as he took the offered paper the messenger withdrew without a word. "See that she has food and drink if she wishes," he ordered the guard watching. "Madame Maha may have questions for her, so do not let her leave."

"Too late, Sir," the guard said.

"What?" Lucien stepped toward the door but stopped as soon as the familiar hand clasped his wrist. "Maîtresse?"

"Give me the envelope and let her go. We should not interfere with Her orders any more than I would want my commands to you disregarded," she said simply.

"Of course, Maîtresse," he replied, handing her the envelope.

She raised it to her nose and breathed in, her eyes widening. Then she licked the seal that closed it, and Lucien knew it was probably made of bubussunu, just like the emblems she placed on her own letters. "It's from Her," she whispered as the envelope fell from her hands.

Lucien bent and picked it up, feeling it tingle, even though he made sure not to touch the blood seal. So, this was what the Ummum's power felt like, even at this distance in a mere letter? No wonder the armies that amassed against Boston had fallen so quickly, his military mind determined. At her urging, he carefully opened it, then read it out loud.

"It is very short, Maîtresse, very short. She writes in your native tongue, see?" She peered around his arm at the envelope and nodded. "It says, 'Forgive my poor skill. I wish I could go home. Go to your home, Maha dami of Eden dami of Abel dami of Shag-ad who was my own. Retake your home in Cairo.' That's all it says, Maîtresse."

She took it from him and held it to her breast as blood tears streaked down her face. "We are going home, home," she whispered softly.

The Lady Eden agreed with this understanding of the letter, and the next night at sundown they left with a small caravan from the oasis toward the city in question. The Lady Eden's voice had a different accent, but Lucien made sure not to look at her or even focus on her voice for long. The power he could sense in the letter from the Ummum was much greater than this other Akhkharu's, even in her presence, but he could sense that a Shi had greater power than the child.

Protecting them from the sun during the day, right outside the city, required cooperation from all the wardum and akalum who traveled with them. There was a steady stream of people leaving the city, and as they straggled past, they often paused to glare at their two tents surrounded by armed men and women. "Be alert!" Ranjan called out as he hoisted a machine gun to his front and stared at a group who had paused too long until they moved on. Similar lines of people had approached the oasis during the past few days, but until now Lucien had told himself it must be a pilgrimage or vacation. Here, seeing their bent bodies and frightened, angry eyes, he knew things were eerily the same in Cairo as they had been generations ago when they had fled the rising tide of conservatism.

Human beings, in Lucien's experience, tolerated a lot until they couldn't feed their children, or the aristocracy got too blatant with their wastefulness. He wondered if the vampires were prepared for the backlash when things got too out of control in this new world of theirs. He assumed that decapitation worked on them as it had for hundreds in Paris. With that thought he moved closer to his mistress's tent and planted his feet firmly to protect her.

The Caliph of Cairo, an Akhkharu who had ruled behind the scenes for generations, was not pleased to see the Gelal, but he could not reject the Ummum's letter openly once its identity was confirmed by his underlings. "Your former home is no more. It was destroyed in the Purge many years ago, not on my command," he added, though his sneer said otherwise.

"We have a place to stay while we rebuild. You will allow me to rebuild, yes?" Madame Maha said as Lady Eden simply watched from the shadows of the reception hall.

"If you have a place, then why rebuild? It's not like the food needs work now; we'll take care of them," he added as one of those who served him scurried to him with a goblet and then hurried away.

"Because She told me to go home, and that is the location of my home. I intend to obey the Ummum," Madame Maha merely replied, though Lucien could see the other vampire pale a bit at her words.

"Just do not interfere with my business," he snorted to cover his fear. Then he waved them out, and they left with a shallow bow to show their strength even in his power base.

"Was that wise, Maîtresse?"

"I hope not. I'll go insane if I have to see him in charge of this city for generations to come," she confessed, slipping her cool, caramel hand into Lucien's.

Yet she leaned back into his arms a generation later after taking her pleasure from him and let out an unnecessary sigh. "Still worried about this new Caliph, Maîtresse?"

She shrugged, and he kissed her bare shoulder. "You did work hard to help him remove the former. What concerns you now?" he asked.

"Not him, Lucien, not him. He sees the wisdom in being concerned about the akalum here, listening to their needs, controlling their access, and he leaves us alone for the most part. I just find their games tiresome."

Her Shi had left after a few years, the political maneuvering finally wearing her down, Ranjan had confided in Lucien on a few occasions. Her own damu came and went, visiting and bringing news of the rest of the world and how it was settling down now that the Xul's most powerful hive had been laid low, they claimed, by the Ummum herself. This city had been divided up between the families via a kataru a few years ago, and recently the previous ruler had been dislodged in favor of a more personable leader who cared not what they all did as long as there were no disruptions of the commerce of blood and flesh from Africa.

"Then what is wrong, Maîtresse? I can tell something is wrong, and you know I have a duty to correct whatever that is or go mad trying to figure it out," he teased softly. Since settling back in Cairo, they had grown closer, her memories of the past seemingly replaced by the newer joys of not having to hide what she was from those who served her and those who frequented her home.

"I am to represent Gelal on the City Council, but they require something from me first." Her voice was tinged with an emotion that made Lucien tense up, but he kept his arms around her and waited silently, stroking his fingers up and down her smooth skin and breathing in her scent. "They require that I declare my arammu-wardum, so they know whom to schedule appointments with and whom to flatter, I suspect," she added with a tight chuckle that was lacking in amusement.

Lucien froze. He had learned what this arammu-wardum was. An honored position among a vampire's household, the servant in this position was considered second only to her among her people, answering only to her, and serving her in all things. It was a sign of deep trust, and love, if the Akhkharu could feel such a thing.

She turned in his arms and drowned him in her eyes for a moment as she asked if he'd heard questions about her in this regard. He closed his eyes, then nodded just slightly as he opened them again. "Yes, Maîtresse, they assume I hold this position, but I make no confirmation of it; I merely go about the tasks you set me," he hastened to assure her.

"I see," she said softly. She detangled their limbs and climbed from her bed, picking up her robe as she did so to slip on. She stood still for a few moments, facing away from him as he remained where she had left him on the bed. "Would you like to be my arammu-wardum, Lucien?"

The question made him cringe. In the decades since his capture, he'd replayed his introduction of the murderer into her household over and over in his mind. The junior officer had had complaints against him from numerous citizens and natives wherever the army was encamped for more than a few nights. These were always dismissed by higher officers, so when the man had asked him for a recommendation to the greatest brothel in Cairo, he had merely said yes and brought him. He had bought into the idea that all soldiers needed relief and that any harm they did was minor compared to the stability they created by their presence. Alone in his cell, between clients, he had accepted the responsibility for that girl's death.

"I am not worthy of that title, Maîtresse, perhaps Fayola. You bought her when we first came back here, and she has been a great comfort to you, I think," he suggested quickly.

Madame Maha turned and considered him. "That's a suggestion only an arammu-wardum could make," she observed, and he shuddered as she approached him. "Why would you say no when you fulfill this role already? I feel the hunger in your body when we make love, I see the concern in your eyes for me at all times, and your devotion is proclaimed with each word you speak."

Make love? He had never considered her taking pleasure from him as anything reciprocal, though he greatly enjoyed it as well. He stood up and knelt in front of her, his face turned up so he could soak in her gaze. "I am your bodyguard, your slave, in all things, but," he swallowed and closed his eyes for a moment. "I brought death into your home."

He flinched as she placed one cool hand on his cheek. "I forgave you that a long time ago, I think."

"You did?" he asked, opening his eyes to test the truthfulness of her words. Her entire body was leaning toward him, her scent like Nile lilies at night surrounding him, her bu racing through his body. "You never told me, Maîtresse."

"No, I suppose I forgot to, with everything that happened. I had assumed you knew, thus my offense when they asked me who holds this position in my household." She leaned down and brushed her lips against his. "I told them it was you," she whispered before kissing him deeply.

He returned her fervor with a passion only a man can feel for the woman he knows is his. For the first time in centuries, he knew as he enjoyed their pleasure in their bed that his error in judgment had been the greatest blessing he'd ever been given. Soon his confidence was playing itself out in new fields of combat as the Akhkharu in Cairo continued their never-ending jockeying for position, and she turned to him time and again to relieve her of the boredom born of authority. Lucien Gaudreau was truly in his element once more as military commander.

*Bard stopped and looked toward me. His tales have been surprising, lacking in the details we expect when Gelal are involved, yet what he chose to say had Maha leaning with her head against her arammu-wardum, while her damu glanced at her as they caressed their own slaves. This display was clearly upsetting some of the others, while the Xul were starting to open their mouths to hurl insults, so I stepped forward.*

*"Affection is the gift our Gelal offer; we belittle them and ourselves if we limit it to the mere physical."*

*"Mistress," Jon's whisper in my mind pulls my attention slightly. "May I tell the next story? I think it may show what you have said in some form. I will speak as Bard would; I shall not make it personal but there are things ... perhaps it is time to tell."*

*I look down to find my arammu-wardum kneeling at my feet, his arm around my legs. This will be unusual, though even having Bard speak at our meeting was unusual.* "Elders, if you will allow, my own would like to tell you what we struggled with around this same time."

"Better 'ave some more spicy details, that last was borin'," one of Jamie's *damu tosses out and earns the back of his hand.*

*Quickly, before they lose control, I sit down and wonder what exactly my arammu-wardum had in mind. Bard comes to sit at my feet as Jon stands up, clears his throat, and begins.*

# Substitutes

Jon took a moment to appreciate what lay before him.  She was a beautiful woman.  Her skin was like one of those creamy iced chocolate coffees you used to be able to order at the old malls that now lay in ruins or served as nests for various Xul hives.  Her lips were full and dark, parted now in a pant as she looked back at him, taking these few moments of rest before they began to fuck again.  Her face was solid, almost regal, barely showing the stress she surely felt as she plied her body in an attempt to win her child a spot in the Empress's household.  Had this been a century or two ago, she'd probably have been an R&B star, singing for the President and millions of adoring fans.  Her facial features exhibited traits from a wide range of humanity; this once could have caused her problems in the human-controlled era, but it was now the main reason he was attracted to her.  Her dark black hair was long and straight, but in that sense, she was too much like … no, Jon turned his eyes downward instead.

She had firm shoulders, a solid core, and just enough fat to make her a good breeder, all qualities now valued among the mimmum, those humans allowed to live their semi-normal lives as long as they produced enough food in the form of offspring for the masters.  Her breasts were full and still stood up in her supine position from the muscles she'd developed beneath them, probably from doing the agricultural work she'd told him about.  Jon couldn't even cup one in a single hand, and his entire mouth was required to cover her dusky nipple. Just the sight made his cock stir, so he bent down, taking one nub into his wet mouth as he thrust again into her tight, hot, moist pussy.

The woman – Victoria was the name playing on the edge of Jon's consciousness – moaned and arched up, wrapping her legs around his hips, pulling him closer. Her hands gripped his arms as he soon built his rhythm back up and had to pull his mouth from her breast so he could watch her face contort and her breasts bounce up and down with each thrust he made into her. His natural impulse was to close his eyes and relax, but he made himself focus on those very womanly breasts and her unique skin and shattering dark eyes. As he came hard, not caring whether or not her own screams were faked, he thought for a moment about making her shave her head, so he didn't have to see the straightness of her hair. When he lay on her breasts, though, and buried his head between them, he forgot about the minor similarity.

The next week, when Varonika – honestly, wasn't Victoria close enough? – brought her son to the Ummum-Ekallim, the grand palace where he lived, the woman smiled at Jon, and he smiled back. She wore a low-cut shirt that showed off most of her motherly assets and had her hair pulled back and under a scarf. She looked so exotic that Jon licked his lips, but then he focused on the task at hand and addressed the boy directly. "Welcome to our Empress's home, Brion. You have been chosen to be one of her playmates for a duration of a year or two. It is a great honor. Has your mother instructed you in how to behave?"

The little boy nodded, and his mother whispered something in his ear, making his beautiful dark eyes widen as he spoke up. "Yes, Sir. Charity likes to play all sorts of games. I like to play all sorts of games just like her."

Jon nodded and allowed himself a smile. "Excellent. Charity loves little boys and girls who can keep up with her. Think you can do that?"

"I brought some games," the little boy said as he held out his backpack. Jon took the bag and looked inside to find two games that the palace did not currently have. The mother impressed him more and more, because she'd taken his instructions to bring a gift seriously. For a moment he wondered how she'd found these, given that it was illegal for any mere human to read, but he supposed the black market could supply almost anything if one had something to trade. The thought of what she might have traded made him frown at her before he made a decision.

"How would you like your mommy to be able to stay here so you can see her now and again?"

Both mother and son looked at Jon, and then Varonika bowed down on one knee and thanked him profusely. "I'd make sure, Sir, that I wasn't an inconvenience," she added, licking her full lips, and glancing up at him. Her blunt sexual invitation made Jon's cock twitch again, but he just held up one hand and snapped his fingers.

Two other wardum hurried forward. "Take the boy; get him fed and cleaned. I will introduce him to our Bel this evening. Take this woman to my chamber and do the same for her." Jon stepped up to the mother and said to her softly, "Do not leave my chamber for any reason. I will come to you when my duties are done for the night."

"Yes, sir, thank you, sir," she whispered back. She didn't even cry or make a sound as the wardum escorted her and her son in two different directions.

"Ah, another one for the Ummum," the Allamudi who managed their mistress's Akhkharu affairs spoke behind him, but Jon didn't turn. "I notice that none of her playmates are … Caucasian, I believe was the mortal term."

Now Jon turned around. "They are the most appropriate companions available. My mistress has made no complaint to me, Ma'am. Unless you know otherwise?" he added, his voice dripping a challenge as he met the second most powerful vampire's gaze straight on. With others he might play the meek slave, but there was no point with Marina, and indeed there was a danger that she might consider herself more valuable than he in the eyes of their mistress if he didn't hold his ground with her at all times.

She made a sound and shook her head. "You play your part so well. Such the loving father. Eventually she'll see what you really want, what you all want, and then you'll disgust her. That day, she'll take one of her playmates for her arammu-wardum, and then you'll be on the street again where Montesarat left you, if you're lucky," she whispered, sending chills into his mind.

Jon said nothing and just watched her walk outside to where her own slaves were waiting to take her to a meeting of regional Akh rulers. The feelings she'd driven subtly into him using her vampiric force dissipated as she rode away in her elegant carriage. Once upon a time he'd thought he'd be strong enough to resist such manipulations given how strong his mistress was, but no, a few of the Akh could still find chinks in his mental armor. There was no way he'd tell his Bel that; it would make him less of a good daddy in her eyes, and his heart turned cold at the mere possibility.

Jon carried his little girl in his arms and into her playroom, where her five current playmates were already lining up the toys and games for her to choose from. "What's his name?" she asked him in her high-pitched but gentle voice.

"Bryan, though it's not spelled as you might expect; it's B R I O N," Jon said as he set her down right outside the archway to the playroom and knelt down in front of her.

As he straightened the straps on her pink overalls she frowned. "How come so many different spellings? Why do humans always write things down so much?"

"We don't have a brilliant memory like you, darling," he told her as he wet his thumb and rubbed a tiny spot of blood from the corner of her mouth. He didn't mention that humans still played with spellings as an act of defiance against their vampiric masters, because eventually he was certain another Akh would, and then she'd have to do something. He'd seen her "do something" more times than he wished to in the century since that fateful night when everything had changed.

"Have you decided what to do with Zack?" he asked softly. The boy in question was a happy kid with a round moon face like his mother, whose name Jon had already forgotten. But for all the companionship he had provided in the past two years, it was obvious he was now "older" than Charity and forgetting his place as he confused physical size with power and authority.

She looked over her shoulder and then turned back. "A party, then, back home. He's nice, but I have all I need." Jon knew she was referring to her akalum, housed in their special quarters here in the palace, where they might serve from the age of 9 or 10 to their mid-teens before she tired of them. What happened to them after that was a matter that he and Marina decided, because frankly, once she lost interest, Charity stopped caring at all. As far as Marina was concerned, such teens made excellent gifts, and Jon had given up decades ago in attempting to convince her otherwise. He tried to choose his battles wisely given his position in the new world.

"I'll take care of everything," Jon said before she ran into the room to play. When he saw her with her playmates, he could almost believe he was still nothing more than her special daddy, but soon one of the other wardum escorted the new boy, Brion, to his side, and that illusion was shattered.

The children all stopped and looked, as the new playmate held onto Jon's hand. Charity stepped forward while the one called Zack looked away. Even kids knew when their time was up. "Charity," Jon began as he came and gently pushed the new child toward her, "This is Brion. I think he's brought some games you didn't have before, didn't you, Brion?"

The little boy shuddered but nodded his head and held out the two boxes. Charity snatched them up and laid them on the floor while the others, even Zack, gathered around. "Oh, Ants in the Pants?!" she giggled at the name, and that started the rest of them laughing. Then she looked at the other. "Rock 'em Sock 'em Robots ..." she read slowly. She knew what robots were, but none of the other children would. Why have robots when you could make a human your slave with a mere word or threat?

She looked up and planted her blue-eyed gaze onto the boy who would soon leave. "Zack, you and Brion show us how the robots work," she commanded simply.

The new boy looked at Jon briefly but then sat down as their mistress unpacked the box and read them the instructions. Jon stepped back as he watched and instructed the other wardum to prepare for Zack's going-away party, find his mother, and bring her to it at the end.

The party was the next night, and Jon had worked in close proximity to his Bel for a few hours as she oversaw the decorations and packed a basket with presents for Zack and his mother, Ushi. She even fed him some of her bu directly from a wrist, and that made him horny as hell, a feeling he unleashed on a very grateful Ushi when she met him privately before the party.

Where Varonika met his thrusts with eager panting, clasping her dark legs around him hard, Ushi let her soft feminine form lay languidly under him, the only signs of her enjoyment being her string of endearments and entreaties for him to continue harder and faster. Both women, though, were round in all the right places, and both loved to have Jon bury his head between their thighs and fondle their ample tits. Taste, fondle, and thrust he did, riding out the high in his body that such a recent feeding created.

It wasn't enough to wipe the full desire for his Bel from him, though, so before he went to the party, he ordered Varonika to disrobe so he could fondle her more and even use her breasts to jack off once more, leaving her face covered in his jism and her eyes a bit wide in shock. "You can wash off after I leave," Jon ordered as he hurried to the shower to get ready for the party.

He lathered, rinsed, and repeated three times, cleaning every centimeter of his body, setting the jets to their most intense spray. He tried to focus on setting up for the party, making a mental list of whom to yell at should anything be out of place, any treat displease, or any music disrupt the atmosphere. Not that any of the playmates would express anything other than utter delight, but She might, and if She did, there was no help left on Earth that could save the target of Her wrath.

After the massacre in Montesarat's mansion, there had been only a few times when Charity had become enraged. While he kept it well hidden under his strong belief that his little girl was perfect, there were moments like tonight, when the bu that ran through his body and the formality of the other wardum all wearing expensive uniforms made his happy family life almost shatter. One could never tell what might set her off, and he knew that he wouldn't survive if that rage were directed at him. As he stood and watched the children play in the festively decorated ballroom, he prayed he'd washed away the scent of sex. That was a topic they never discussed beyond her early statement that he was used to doing "adult things," because he doubted she even felt any stirrings that might be called "adult." Because they had never discussed it, though, he had only his own guilt and fear to feed the thought that she would disapprove, and yet he couldn't stop himself; he could only channel that sexual desire into better venues.

His blood turned to ice when she ran toward him to jump into his arms and slid to a standstill just a foot from him. Her nose twitched and wrinkled, and she bowed her head slightly but kept her gaze on him; he could feel an icy chill roll off her, but his feet remained planted on the floor, his knees about to buckle beneath him, when he was saved by a boy's call for her. She took an unnecessary breath and spoke to him in a low voice that made him crash to his knees in front of her. "I'll see you alone after the party, Jon."

As she turned to run back toward her playmates, Jon felt his arms gripped by two pairs of hands. He looked up to find that two of the wardum were holding him. "You need to wait in her room, sir," they said, but the honorific sounded like a taunt. As he followed, he noticed Ushi looking at him with wide, terrified eyes.

Jon looked down from her office to the steps three stories below. He could probably survive the jump with no injuries, but then he'd be a runaway, and a quick death wouldn't be in the cards anymore. In the hours since he'd been escorted up here and locked in, a fact he could also have dealt with easily given his bu-increased strength, he'd had nothing to do but think. Jon ran scenarios through his mind of all the ways he'd seen wardum punished and killed ... quick was best. Though he bet he'd have to be very un-daddy like to earn that.

He'd seen his father cry once in his entire mortal life. His sister had been dating an abusive jerk, and when the threats and the reasoning hadn't worked, their father had broken down into tears and just begged her to dump the bastard. Jon would have crawled on broken glass for his father at that point, promised to be straight instead of bi, or even joined the Marines, but not Cara. Cara only laughed and walked out the door, never to be seen alive again. Would Charity do as his sister had done if Jon begged her forgiveness?

He heard the door open, and his sharpened senses told him it was his Bel. One deep breath, and he turned around to face her, shocked, though he shouldn't be, that she'd moved silently and quickly enough to be standing on top of her formal desk. She always stood on it, because sitting behind it only increased the awareness of how small she was; on the desk she could look down on anyone.

"Jon," she said, driving home just by saying his name the fact that this was serious.

He stepped from the glass double doors and stood in front of her, looking at her pink tennis shoes. Jon made a mental checklist of what he had written in his files, hoping her next daddy would know enough to follow the notes and schedule he'd made. Children needed structure, after all, or they could get upset easily, and no one wanted the Empress upset again.

"Jon." The repetition of his name made him look up, taking in the rumpled state of her party dress, but happily no spot or scent of mortal blood. She'd saved her anger for him, and he was almost grateful.

He drew in a ragged breath and met her eyes rimmed in tears. Wait, were they his tears or hers? No, they were hers, he realized as the pink drop fell down her cheek. His selfishness, his stupid libido; he'd made her cry. A good daddy never made his baby cry. "I'm so sorry," he managed to sob out as he fell to his knees.

A few moments passed, and he flinched when something touched his hair. Looking up he saw her sitting on the edge of her desk, reaching down to pet him. "Why?" she asked simply.

"I, um, I, I'm stupid," Jon replied with a sigh.

She was wrinkling up her nose in that trying-to-think-it-through way before she spoke. "I thought you liked other men. I smell them on you often. Why do you smell like women tonight?"

Jon would have fallen down if he hadn't been on the floor from the shock of her statement. She knew about his sexual encounters with men? He tried to be equally discreet about those as he was with the mothers he coupled with, but they were also members of her staff, and other wardum; if they smelled like anything, it would be of her in some way. Bu penetrated every part of a mortal slave, and when he and another man had just been fed it increased the passion of their fucking.

But the mothers were plain akalum and smelled only human, and that had been his error. However, being bisexual meant he rarely felt completely satisfied by only male partners.

Then a thought, a tiny hope, occurred to him as he knelt there looking up at her. "I should have never ... done adult things without your permission, Bel," he whispered.

Charity blinked, and one pink tear fell onto his face. "What?" She hopped off the desk and looked at him. "Oh, Daddy, I don't care about those things."

Jon now blinked. "What?" he repeated as he wiped the tears from his own eyes. Now he was completely confused and afraid to assume anything. "Bel, please, be clear with me. What things don't you care about?"

"Adult things, you know, sex," she said and rolled her eyes. "I'm small, not stupid. I've lived in one-room homes most of my life. I know what adults do," she insisted; her voice sounded tired, as though it was something she knew about, perhaps had witnessed even, but found both boring and silly. "Adults are so needy," she added after a moment.

It was ridiculous, and Jon burst out laughing. It was so ridiculous that soon she was laughing, too, and they ended up on the floor laughing together until Jon could barely breathe. He froze as she sat up and leaned over him, her blonde hair fallen free from her braids to touch his face. Jon felt his body shake from desire, but he made himself lay still.

"I'm not adult; I never will be; the gods willed it so," she whispered in that tone that was a sign she was about to give him a rare insight to her origins. "Adults are needy, but they need other adults. I just thought you didn't need a woman. Mommies can bring horrible things if you aren't careful," she barely said as she sat back to rest her head against the leg of her desk.

Jon turned to his side so he could watch her. "What do you mean? Mommies bring horrible things?"

Charity closed her eyes for a few seconds, then shook her head. "No, she didn't bring it. The men brought it. She was like me," she said, looking at him with her blue eyes.

Jon thought for a moment. One thing had always bothered him about Marina's claim that Charity was this first vampire, because shouldn't Sumerians be, well, darker? "Please, Charity," he said, using her name on purpose, and she tilted her head to one side, looking at him seriously, "tell me so I can be a good daddy, a better daddy," a better slave, he added silently.

"My mother was from far away; her people had been nomads, and some said they came first in ships on the distant waters, but we only knew the southern sea and the mighty river. Her eyes were like the rare beads and flowers, her hair like the sun, but her skin didn't like it much, and her people covered themselves with fabric from head to toe. I had to do the same, though I did not turn as red in the sun."

Jon nodded and reached out to hold her hand as she continued, saying far more now about her past than she ever had in the century plus he'd been with her. "You mentioned men," he reminded her when she paused.

"Adults are so needy," she whispered. "They have to have whatever another has, they forget how to share, and they fight so when they don't want to share."

It was true, he supposed. In many ways he and every other mortal had wanted to blame the world on the Akh, but the truth was that they merely played into natural human desires to control and manipulate. At first it had been secretly, then more openly after the first battle, but the methods they used were primarily mortal – guns and bombs, knives, and hostages. Akh didn't stop wanting all those adult things; they merely had more power with which to take them.

"They killed everyone, including mommy, except me," Charity finished and squeezed his hand. "Don't make me say more," she sobbed and fell against him.

As any good daddy should, he just let her cry it all out.

Jon stopped as he opened the double doors, and he smiled as the men and women in the room all turned to him with smiles on their faces. It had taken some time and some words from the Empress, but now one parent of each of her playmates was also staying in her esharra in this special area where they all thanked Jon daily for giving their families this opportunity.

Jon entered, letting each masculine hand grip his shoulder or feminine fingertips caress his hair for a few seconds as he walked with a purpose to his favorite, Carina, who was sitting just looking at him. He rushed the last few feet and swept her up into his arms, her long straight blonde hair spiraling around them before settling over them as he drank in her crystal-blue eyes.

As he laid her down on the silken bed and parted her own silks from her so he could devour her creamy skin, he calculated when it might be a good time to ask her to become Mommy now that his little girl had selected her daughter Lana to be her forever big sister. Right now, though, he could only moan as she stroked his hard cock, guided it to her moist center and then thrust upward to surround him.

*"Ilati!" Jamie exclaims after Jon finishes, making me blush. The rest of the gathering is silent as I stand up.*

*As he'd been on the night he talked about, my arammu-wardum is trembling when I approach him. He looks at me, and then at the floor. I reach out, slip my hand into his, and turn my gaze out toward the audience. "There is nothing wrong in what has been shared. You Elders know what I once was; you know of the sacrifices that were made. Just in case you wonder, no, he doesn't have a harem anymore," I toss out with a chuckle.*

*Next to me I feel Jon start to shrink in embarrassment, so I've had my revenge. Before I can even turn toward Bard, my dearest Xul has his hand in the air. "Oy, talk about me again. I'm least as interestin'," he adds with a wink.*

*He knows that his dami is in the most trouble, so perhaps this is his attempt to appease me. "Bard? Do you have a good tale about our dear Xul?"*

*"Indeed, though, Sir," Bard states as he stepped forward, "it may not show you as a pure hero."*

*At that, the entire Xul pile breaks down into laughter, allowing Jon and me time to retreat to our seats to listen and watch. Only a glare from Enki quiets them down, and at my god's motion, the story begins.*

# Mates

Swaggart was singing as loud as he could as Karl drove on through the night. They'd stopped yesterday at a good-sized village and made arrangements with the agent of the local vampiric lord – or in that case, lady – for gasoline and some supplies for Karl. As long as they kept to themselves now, they could milk the system for as much as they wanted and not answer to anyone. The wars had lasted a good decade, and the hives they'd traveled with had been decimated after being outlawed by the Ummum herself, or so her agents had told everyone. He wasn't too sure about it all. He figured most politicos were in it for themselves, as always. Every Akhkharu was turning into one of those true suckers, living off the fat of the land, as his grands used to say.

The old man was one of the few things he could remember from before his everlasting night. Didn't hurt that he still had the ink on his cheek. When the lyrics gave way to some truly nasty instrumentals, he looked at his driving slave and smiled. They'd had to do a few "jobs" for a boss in the last big city to get the car but seeing his wardum's smooth right cheek made those seem like nothing. Karl caught his look and smiled, so the Akh slapped him playfully. "Careful, Sir, or I may lose control of the car," the wardum replied with a grin as he blushed deeply.

"Fucking drive," Swaggart ordered with a chuckle before launching back into the next verse. As he sang, he started to frown as the words became slower and slower until they stopped with an eerie

205

silence. "Wot the 'ell?" he said, snatching the CD from the player sitting between them on the seat. It looked fine, but when he tried to tune in some radio nothing could be heard – no music, not some lame propagandistic shit the nearest bitum wanted, not even static.

"Batteries, Sir?" Karl suggested, motioning to the back seat with his head.

The vampire launched himself back and rummaged through their bags. "Bloody 'ell, only these recycs which probably need recharging." He smacked the back of his slave's head, forcing the man to swerve to avoid going off the road. He had given up limiting the beatings to reward days over the years. He needed an outlet for his rage, which never seemed to die down, and Karl was obedient regardless, perhaps even more so, as his perverted desires tended to make him. They both won, as Swaggart released some ever-renewing rage and the wardum got horny.

"No, Sir, I recharged them last night; they should work."

"Useful, obedient, often know-it-all prick," Swaggart thought as he tried the batteries, tossing the older ones out the window. "They'd best work, cause if I have to go without Johnny, Jimmy, and that Nico, ye can go without any snogging or fucking until we get more batteries."

"OK, OK, I make sure to keep them charged, Sir," Karl replied.

"Venus in Furs" came back on with a bang that had the vampire howling along again as he climbed back in front.

They drove until they reached the next sunrest where they could take a room, buy a refreshment, a plump blonde who came with her own tap, and spend the day. After sending the bint away, Swaggart fulfilled his promise to his slave with a rough leg over, and then fell asleep, knowing the kraut would set everything up for nightfall.

It went the same way for weeks and weeks as they tried to get across what was once called Canada. No home, no hive, no prospects for any kind of official stability; he might as well see what was left of the world, Swaggart had decided a few years back. Karl was a fount of information about old roads and cities, most of which still existed, though with much smaller populations. They'd heard a while back that something like twenty percent of the humans had been slaughtered in the wars with almost an equal amount dying from the loss of infrastructure and the necessities of life that came with that. Neither said it, but they both had a terrible feeling that this truce was gobshite, so they kept their eyes and ears peeled.

The next decent sized city, Regina, had only one guard on the main road into town, but when they saw her on her horse both men glanced at each other. Witches – not really what they wanted to run into, but it was ironic, given the name of the place. Karl turned off the car, and Swaggart got out only to find the female vampire glaring down at him. "We don't want your kind here. Keep going," she said in her soft voice.

"Just 'ere to trade, not to stay in yer lovely 'ome," he said, looking away. The last hive they'd hung with had attacked a village in Scotland where these witches were in charge, and only he and Karl had somehow survived out of pure luck. That was the last time they'd done more than sense their kind and cross the road.

"I doubt you have anything we need or want to trade, monster," she replied.

Swaggart began to growl when Karl's voice interrupted. "Excuse, ma'am, please, OK? I need some supplies, and my master could use some refreshment, OK?"

"Stay on the highway, and you'll find a sunrest where you can get what you need. If you keep heading east, though, make sure you turn south around what was called White City. Do not continue east," she ordered them.

Swaggart nodded and got back in the car, and Karl drove to the described place. Once they were in a room, purchased with some jam from a previous trade, both men gave the room a once-over, then sat very close together on the floor, their heads bowed forehead to forehead. "Wot they trying to 'ide?"

"Maybe there just aren't rest areas to the east; maybe the road's been destroyed, Sir?"

"Nah, that bint back in Swift Current and the bloke in Moose Jaw both said to stay on 1 all the way. Everywhere we been, the information been the same. Yer maps say the same, right?"

"Yes, Sir, it's true; it's just … the way she said it."

"Mind games, it's what the bitches do best." Swaggart held his head for a moment as a series of bright lights and whispers wiggled through his brain.

"Happening again, Sir?"

The Akhkharu nodded as the pain lessened. "Mum wants us to check it out, I think," he speculated, and no pain returned. "Yeah, yeah, guess we got another job we don't get paid for."

"I pay you, Sir," Karl said, slipping his big hands under the vampire's shirt and running his fingers down to his button fly.

"Wanker," Swaggart muttered as he lay back and closed his eyes.

Across the highway was a series of barriers. Now faded, they had clearly once been official province property but were now set up in four rows across all the lanes. A sign declared this was White City, but another one, made of wood, pointed south with a warning that there were no rest areas further east this way.

Swaggart swore and got out of the car as soon as Karl pulled up to the barrier. Using his senses to the fullest, he looked around the barrier and saw a perfectly functional highway, just starting to grow over with grass in places. "We can get around this, it's bloody flat," he yelled at the car.

"No, Sir, only car we have, so hard to trade for," Karl countered, making the Akh swear further. The vampire knew it was true. Most folks traveled by train, horse, wagon, or other things. No one was making automobiles now, and they only made gasoline to support the cars currently owned. It wasn't that they were concerned about the environment so much as that factories now only made what vampires wanted, and most didn't bother with driving. Most seemed content with their fiefdoms now, settling down with their own private stock.

"We're going this way!" Swaggart ordered as he hopped back into the car.

"Other way back a bit, Sir," Karl said and pushed the map they had on the seat between them toward the Akh. "We try to go to ... Pilot Butte."

The vampire chuckled at the mispronunciation. "Always leave it to the pervert to focus on the arse again," he said as he waved his hand back in the direction they came from.

Sometime later they were looking at another city sign, another roadblock, and the same advice to go south. After idling for a bit, the wardum agreed, and they hit the dirt to go around the block, both men swearing, since it felt like they were driving over bricks. Once on the other side the slave got out of the car and looked it over. "Can't take it again, Sir, OK?"

"Fine. We just rip apart any blockade we find along this way," Swaggart agreed as he looked toward the horizon, which seemed to be glowing with a faint, eerie light.

The new road led to a deserted town called Pilot Butte, according to the sign hanging from only one chain. Driving through it, they could see empty buildings, overgrown lawns, dead animals, and people who seemed to have been killed years ago, from their remains. "Bloody 'ell. Wot the fuck 'appened 'ere?"

After a few blocks, Karl stopped and put the car in reverse. The vampire had learned in his time with Karl so far to trust his slave on such things, because the kraut, ancestry or not, had a good head on his shoulders that rarely steered them wrong. They went back to the beginning of the city limits. "Sir? Would you write down the markings you see on the buildings on your side? I think something happened here, OK, and if we track it ..."

"We can figure it out," Swaggart finished the thought with a nod. "Aye, give me some sheets and a pen," he ordered. Slowly they drove, stopping at every house so that each could write down what they saw. After a few blocks, Swaggart growled. "No one 'ere, and we're wasting petrol. Let's pick one, and we can stash the auto and stay inside while we check this place out."

"We need to check it out, Sir?"

Swaggart nodded slowly, as the light glow he'd seen earlier along the road was touching everything in town slightly. He hadn't asked for this signal fire, but she'd given it to him anyway. It was a joke in most of the hives, the idea that a child had created them all and the innate cruelty of children far surpassing adults. She was the Ummum; he was pretty sure of that, and whenever he'd tried to turn away from the signs, they'd found themselves in deep trouble within a few nights.

"This one," he ordered, pointing to a house on his side that had the least amount of spray-painted letters and numbers of any home so far. They pulled up to the garage, and Swaggart got out to pull the door open, grimacing when he heard the electronic lock grinding away against his strength until it broke. Inside was a hybrid minivan that made him grin and look back at Karl. "Oi, check our new ride."

The wardum turned off the car and got out to check it over. It wasn't locked, so soon he had the manufacturer's booklet in hand. "Likely better than this, but not very, ah, cool, OK, Sir?"

"Neither was that," the Akh said, pointing to the station wagon they'd gotten back on the west coast. "I'm cool enough for it regardless," he added, punching his slave in one arm. "Pull ours up beside it. Looks like the garage used to hold two. I'll go pick the lock on the house."

Inside it looked like the people had just up and disappeared. Most of the food they found had gone bad, though some Karl packed away, claiming the preservatives might have saved them. There were books, games, clothes – all women's and girls' – bedding, linens, pots, and pans. Everything you'd need if you were the single mom with three daughters staring back from the pictures on the walls. No glowing in here on their stuff, but when Swaggart stepped out he could see it around them, though now that he looked, it was stronger on some houses than others.

"Stay 'ere and sort through things – transfer some shit to the van, figure out what the graffiti means. I'm going out to look around," Swaggart said and left before his slave could protest.

The first thing he did was open the neighboring garage and house and found them both in a similar state of abandonment. The SUV was not going to be better in terms of gas mileage, but at least he found a few containers with petrol that he made a mental note about. Also, on the mental list went the fact that the clothes looked like they had been gone through and there were both men's and women's, boys' and girls' items left behind.

He covered a three-block radius of houses, finding similar conditions, though in some he found the remains of bodies that looked as abandoned as the possessions left behind. Swaggart didn't know enough about human anatomy, but if the clothes were a sign, each of the deceased had been far older than the other members of the household whose photographs confirmed had lived in the same houses. He carried a few bottles of wine he found back in the house they were crashing in, knowing that some vampires liked to drink from intoxicated akalum, so these could be traded.

The next night they investigated together further into downtown. Downtown was in some ways even creepier, because the stores were all locked and nothing seemed to be missing. Normally that would be enough to have Swaggart celebrating as he busted open windows and doors, but the next block of houses confirmed it. Whatever had happened here, it had happened at night. Only the local police department showed signs that were promising, because the gun cases were open, and some seemed to be missing. There were no signs of a struggle anywhere in town, though, except for the elderly remains, which Karl pointed out all seemed to have their heads and necks angled oddly.

"Something came here and took everyone away quickly, Sir," Karl said as they settled into the police office as a sort of base.

"That's fine by me," the vampire said, jimmying open more drawers in the desks and pawing through them. "Not such a bad place to hole up for a bit. We can loot and trade in another town."

"No people," Karl whispered.

"Yeah, yeah, I'll need blood, I get it, I'm not daft, ye wanker. We can trade for that, too."

The wardum only sighed and walked out of the building, leaving Swaggart blinking before bolting after him. "Don't ye walk away from me, ye bastard! I didn't give ye permission. Ye're still mine to do with as I want," he said, forcing the bigger man to turn and face him. "Wot? Bloody 'ell! I ain't that pissed at ya," he said when he noticed the man's tears. In their century together he'd never seen the German cry, or even beg – at least not in a bad way.

"No, Sir, not because of you, OK?" Karl replied, wiping his eyes with the back of his hands.

"Then wot for? These poor sods? Maybe they just, I –" The Akhkharu threw up his hands with a snarl. "I know it, I know it! Wotever done this could come back, right?" At the other's nod, the vampire just shrugged. "Fine! We figure it out, we take it out, we can't, we move on, like we always do."

"You see it, Sir?" Karl asked, pointing to his own eyes.

"Aye. But I'm doing this for me, not 'er!" he yelled unnecessarily at the night sky, which seemed to respond with a rumble of thunder. "Gonna rain," he muttered and headed back inside to play with the multitude of weapons they had found.

They stayed for a good week, long enough to gather what could fit into a hybrid police SUV – better fuel efficiency than the station wagon and more armor than the minivan, a lot of dried and preserved food for Karl, batteries that still seemed to work, other potentially useful tools and trade goods, and new clothes, plus a few extras. The former reporter did some research during the day and discovered some mentions of a new community not far away that had been looking to expand in the darkness of that terrible end of days. He also worked out what he thought the graffiti might mean, and if he was correct, it meant someone had come here and taken away most of the people in a very organized fashion. The best way to test the theory was to move on to the next town.

Between towns was the remnant of an Indian reservation that still showed signs of life, but the people there refused to open their doors when Karl or Swaggart tried to ask questions. Whatever the Ummum wanted from them didn't show up here; apparently these natives weren't in danger or dangerous. So, they drove on to Balgone, which should have been a decent sized place but was cleaned out just like Pilot Butte had been. Here the highway continued east to St. Joseph's, and another road went northeast toward Edgeley, and a third ran straight northward toward some place called Edenwold. The signs were strongest straight north, but they continued on old highway 1 into an abandoned St. Joseph's, then there was another blockade across the road outside of Qu'Appelle, which was run by more politicos.

After a bit of trade – at least these weren't afraid to let them in as the witches had been – they got a chance to talk with some of the local Akh, wardum, and akalum who worked and lived there. They weren't specific, but all said they'd be best off continuing east or going south; no one suggested they stay there, though the local Kur-Bel was thrilled to know that towns further west were lootable. He just gave Swaggart two big tanks of petrol and a healthy-looking young man to take on his way.

The Xul spent the entire day awake and staring off to the northwest through the walls of the sunrest they were staying in, while his meal just sat tied up and stared back at him. As soon as the sun set, Swaggart turned his gaze toward the mortal and snarled for Karl to pack him up in the SUV. The vampire insisted on driving tonight.

As soon as they were across the blockade and out of the sight of Qu'Appelle's guards, the Akhkharu turned them off the road for a bit and headed back toward the number 10 road, heading northeast. The man in the back seat made as much noise and fuss as his bound and gagged condition allowed, but neither master nor slave in the front paid any attention as they drove until they reached Edgeley. It was as deserted as the previous villages and towns, but not clean. Buildings were missing windows and doors, some halfway or entirely burned down, and there were human remains strewn throughout the blocks as they drove. The human in the back had grown deathly quiet in the back seat, his eyes glued to the front window, until a sight at the largest building downtown made the Akhkharu slam on the brakes.

Both vampire and wardum got out of the car and stood silently until Karl turned and vomited into the street. Swaggart walked forward and shook his head as he tried to figure out the dozens of charred skeletons hanging from streetlamps or on posts driven into the ground. When his boots hit something and he looked down to find the remains of a hand next to the remains of an arm, and so on and so forth, his rage bubbled up, making everything go blood red.

The first thing Swaggart saw when he could see again was his slave's face frowning down at him. "Bloody 'ell! Wot happened?" He stood up from where he was sitting on the ground, his back against a building – correction, the remains of a building. A look around didn't show the damned strung-up bodies or those poles that also held them. Or at least he thought he'd seen such a thing a moment ago; it had seemed so real.

"Sir, are you yourself now?"

"Wot? Who else would I be, ye stupid git?"

Karl swallowed, and Swaggart noticed he was holding a rifle in his hands, clenching, and unclenching his grip. "You got angry … again," the wardum said slowly as he backed up a step.

The Akhkharu took a step, then looked down at a crunching sound beneath his foot. Bones? There were bones everywhere his eyes could see. "Wot 'appened?"

"You," Karl replied, then swallowed. "You've told me that you rely on me for my smarts many times, OK?"

The vampire rolled his eyes up from the bones to his servant's face with a frown. "Aye, only damned reason I keep ye around, it is."

"OK. Then listen, please, Master."

The title made Swaggart take a step back. He might call the kraut a slave from time to time, but something inside him still rebelled at the companion title applied to him. He preferred frankly just being called by his name, though the wardum rarely did so, for his own perverted reasons, he told himself. The vampire nodded slowly but remained silent.

"You destroy it all, entire center, dug up all bodies, ripped them down, it went on and on for hours. I take auto and the boy away then come back to watch. Then you came here and just sat down."

Hours? No, no, it had been minutes … Pulling his hand over his mouth he found it covered in dust and dirt, and a look down at his clothes confirmed it was filthy with it. It happened sometimes. Sometimes he lost control, got so angry that he lost hours. During his time with Damon, he'd heard stories of Xul who'd lost so much control that they found themselves out in the sun, which, depending on their age, might immediately turn them to ash or merely set them on fire for a painful destruction. It was the constant threat to all of them: that internal rage that seemed to well up from nowhere and everywhere.

214

"Shit," he whispered, and they both remained silent. "Ye did the right thing getting away," he added with a nod. The rage was why Xul wardum rarely lasted long. Some monsters never bothered with acquiring them, because they learned they might snap at any time and destroy them. Better to simply play with your food or have a few to serve the hive, so that if one went sixes and sevens the others could step in and protect the collective. That was over now; no more than two Xul were tolerated in any area for more than a year or two.

Swaggart reached back and steadied himself against the remains of the wall that, now that he thought about it, was probably a bigger mess than it had been before his fit. "Fuck! I thought I 'ad it under control."

"It has been years, Master, but this was very bad, OK?"

"I can see," he agreed with a forced chuckle. "Looks like I won at least," he added with a grin that faded when his wardum merely frowned.

They stayed that way until a glimmer of sun showed over the horizon. Without a word, Karl grabbed his arm and led him to a stable building where the akalum was tied to a chair, his gag removed, and most of their gear was stored. "You stay here, Master," the German ordered, leading him to a chair.

"We gonna talk about how bossy ye getting, lad," Swaggart promised weakly as he felt the ancient curses tugging at the edges of his mind.

When the Akhkharu awoke again at sunset, he knew from the smell that he was not alone. Karl's scent he knew well by now, and even the akalum they had recently picked up could be sensed, but there were two other humans as well. He woke up with a growl, only to find his wardum kneeling at his feet, his arms wrapped around him.

In front of him stood the akalum and then two old people, their skin wrinkled and leathery looking, wearing clothes reminding him of something on the telly a lifetime ago. "Who are ye and wot ye staring at?" he growled, but when he tried to move, he found his servant was trying to pin him in place.

"Please, Master, listen to them. I bring them to help you, OK?"

The vampire was shocked beyond words at this behavior and the tone in his slave's voice. So shocked he could only stare as the akalum began talking.

"Karl told me that if I help you, you may let me go, but I do this for my people, for all people," the young man said. "These are two, um, spiritual leaders, you, we can call them Elders, of the First Nations, or so we were called once. All of us are merely the People now, the free people; we band together to survive your kind."

"So, wot?" Swaggart said in a low, shaky voice.

"We know what great evil is happening north, in Edenwold," the akalum stated.

"Edenwold?"

The two fossils started talking in some gibberish, and the vampire growled but did not try to move.

"The Elders say that they have seen you in the spirit walks. They know why you are here. They can help you control your soul so you can fight."

"Soul? I ain't got no soul, I'm undead, yeah?"

The akalum seemed to translate that, and after the old folks spoke again, he conveyed their words. "You are wrong. You all have souls. It is untrue that you are undead – you were near death when the …" he sighed. "This is a hard concept to translate. When that which made you what you are happened. It is old religion, old magick, old strength passed from one to another."

Swaggart blinked, surprised, and yet as he thought upon it, he felt it must be true. He'd killed enough people to know what that felt like, smelled like, looked like. Everything had gone black for him, but he never truly felt himself leave his body or see that fabled great light of heaven or the fires of hell.

The old people were speaking again, then the akalum spoke once more. "They can help you find a new spirit guide to ease your soul, compete with the anger and the mission."

"Mission?"

"They say that the Old Young One gave you something that is driving you, they can see it in their own spirit walks. It is terrifying,

216

because it is so old, but so young," he added with a shrug. "That's what they explained before, I have no idea what it means."

"I do," Swaggart replied. "Oi, get off," he told his wardum. "I ain't going all nutters on them, I promise," he added when Karl just looked up at him.

The wardum stood up and then stood at his side as the vampire rose to his feet. "So ye gonna help me, huh? Wot if I decide to attack yer people after?"

The akalum said something to the old folks, and the woman stepped forward and reached out toward Swaggart's face. He stayed still as she ran a shaky hand over his fangs, then patted his cheek and spoke to him in words he couldn't understand. "She says that your center shines. And the Old Young One holds you captive, so you will not attack those who are not a threat."

"Tell me about it," the vampire muttered. Then he glanced at his wardum and nodded. "Why not? Lived longer than I would have in the factories, like I was supposed to. Wot's the worse that can 'appen now, eh?"

The akalum translated again and then started to back up until the old man grabbed him. The three started yelling at each other, and it was making Swaggart growl and the hairs on the back of his neck stand up until Karl stepped in and raised his voice. "OK, OK, you make him angry, he kill everyone, OK?"

The akalum translated, and they all grew quiet.

"Wot they say to ye that set ye off?" the vampire demanded in a low but firm voice.

The akalum ran his hands through his hair and sighed. "They said you'll need help. Since I was already given to you, that's me."

"Wot? Talk sense."

"They say you have to make me like you because the enemy is too great for just you. You have to make me a vampire."

"Oi, I don't just go around cranking out pups whenever," Swaggart replied. "Ye just get two monsters, then ye won't be able to 'elp at all."

"They say that they'll anchor my own spirit guardian before you change me and after they find yours. They say I won't be what you are, they say I can be a warrior for my people, protect them here. I say they're crazy," the akalum added.

"Whole world's crazy," Karl replied, and that got the vampire to chuckle.

"Well, now, what's yer name then? If I'm gonna be biting ye and birthing ye and all of that."

The akalum sighed. "Great, you're going to go along with them. Fine, you can call me Enli, it's my tribal name, and it will remain my name," the akalum insisted.

"Sure, sure," Swaggart agreed with a nod. That sense in his mind glowed with a new feeling at the name, which seemed to please Her or whatever She'd left in him.

The rituals took nights to do. As they crouched on the edge of the compound, where people were working on farms or preparing food, Jamie smiled and looked at his dami by his side. He'd had to give up so much anger – over his grandfather's life, at being kicked out of his house, at being nothing more than a tool in the grand scheme of things. They'd given him something mixed in blood, then had him write down all the wrongs against him on leather, toss it into a bonfire and scream at the top of his lungs that first night. Now, while the Elders chanted, Enli did the same. The feelings of victimization needed to be examined, in a way that didn't fan the flames tainting the soul, preventing it from controlling the rage.

He'd had to give up so much shame – at killing his sister, at all the children he'd slaughtered with Damon, at his inability to control his anger. Again, they had given him the mixed drink, then he'd beaten himself with a rod as he described each action, accepting it and releasing it into the cold, dark night while the Elders chanted and Enli did the same. It didn't matter that Akh sins were greater than mortal; both needed to free themselves of the guilt, so it didn't block the strength that welled up from their first night.

He'd had to claim so much – his desires to be with Karl, his thrill at being freed from the hives, his joy at fighting on the right side. Each Elder heard his confessions and declared them good as he stood naked before them, just as Enli revealed his needs and desires. Then each one made love to his heart's desire while the Elders chanted outside the huts where both couples lay.

Finally, he'd had to reclaim his name, the one his soul had heard from the moment it became conscious. It brought him to tears saying it, but that light that drove him on toward the north, that pain that throbbed in his mind ordering him there, dulled for a few moments when he said it, as though somehow, She knew and approved. This was not a ritual Enli could participate in, but the Elders chanted his name as the Xul drained him and infused him with new strength and power.

"Jamie?" He glanced back to find his wardum motioning toward an area by a building. During the day when he slept, his servant, his lover, had gathered information from the tribes and their observations of the compound north of them. After the provincial government had fallen, authority had fallen to the villages, but the rural areas had fallen prey to a growing spiritual movement whose leader had claimed to know how to rid the world of the threat. It was a test from the false God of this world who had misled them all for centuries, this leader had said, while the true gods had turned their backs on their creations. It all sounded like some babbling a few Allamudi and Kashshaptu had been saying when the hives they used to travel with had attacked various cities worldwide – until the Ummum's decree.

By the end of the rituals, when he felt himself more Jamie than Swaggart, more Akhkharu than monster, those claims didn't feel crazy. He didn't feel crazy either, not anymore.

They moved back to the area and snapped the fence with their bare hands. As Karl made to cross over to the compound, Jamie put a hand on his shoulder. "No way, mate, ye need to stay out here and watch for us, lay down cover with that fine gun of yours."

"I want to come with you, Sir," the wardum added, leaning toward him, and nuzzling his face with his nose.

"Oi! Ye'll be nowt but a distraction, that's wot ye'll be. Stay, that's an order," he said, tilting his head up and kissing the German briefly. Before all of this ritual stuff he never dared get close to his wardum with his mouth. Too risky. But now, now he felt in control, and he hurried away after his child, who was already checking out the building.

The true believers were marked with this weird symbol tattooed on their uniformly bald heads. It made them stand out like sore thumbs. Spies for the People reported that there were maybe a hundred of these and then two leaders who were never out in the daylight. That explained their idea that he needed another vampire to help him out.

One by one, carefully and slowly, they worked their way through the camp, snapping the necks of each true believer until they got to the main building, where they could hear a male voice preaching. As they went, they told any human who noticed them to stay put, and most seemed too terrified to do anything other than what they'd been doing. Most looked numb, in fact, and Enli commented that he doubted they could be really saved.

Inside that building were two Akhkharu, standing at the front. The female just stood staring at the three wardum in front of them, and the male was yelling some garbage about the gods, who weren't happy with the quality of the sacrifices. The male calmed down immediately when the female whispered, and her words made Jamie go paler and move away. "Oh, shite!"

"What?"

"Nowt we can't handle, I hope. But the wardum are the first problem."

"No problem, OK?"

Both Akhkharu turned at the German's voice to find him crouching by them. "Oi, I told ye to wait, wanker," Jamie growled as he gathered the wardum's shirt in his fist.

"Smarts, OK?" Karl replied with a grin.

"He can help," Enli pointed out, placing his hand on Jamie's fist.

With other Xul any touch was a signal to fight, but now the elder vampire just nodded. "Ye take on only the wardum, leave the vamps to us."

"OK, OK." With that Karl stood up and purposely stuck his head around the door and whistled. Soon he was running across the compound with the three wardum following him.

The vampires waited and then went to the door where the two inside were staring at them. "We were wondering how long you were going to take," the male said as he stepped forward until the female put a hand on his back. "You've done us a favor by showing us how weak our followers are. Best to put things in stronger hands."

"Blah blah blah. Kill 'im," Jamie ordered, pushing his dami toward the male while he grinned and said, "I want the witch."

Allamudi were great with negotiations and controlling human populations. They made excellent advisors, but they were terrible in a fight. Soon the new Xul had his prey cornered and let his full strength out in a focused burst of rage. Jamie watched for a moment, then turned his full attention to the female.

"Your kind was always so FOOLISH!" She yelled the last word, and the Xul felt his knees go weak. As he crashed down on them, he blurrily saw his dami and his victim crash down as well. He tried to stand but found his limbs weren't responding as she walked toward him with a huge dagger in her hand. Suddenly she flew back a few steps, her stomach smoking for a moment, and he found his limbs under his control.

Channeling all that rage he had been drowning for decades, now narrowed into a solid core, he rushed at her, ripping her dagger and the hand that clutched it from her arm, then that arm from her shoulder. He flipped them both over, landing on her chest, then reached down and wrested her head from her body as her screaming threatened to rend him limb from limb.

Jamie staggered to his feet and hollered, "Schtum up, thou glaikit bint!"

A few quiet moments passed, then the newest vampire spoke up. "What the hell was that?"

"Kashshaptu," Jamie said as he stood up to glare lightly at his wardum standing inside the building, his rifle still in hand from when he'd shot her.

"No, no, I mean, what did you say? It sounded like gibberish."

"Oi, that's perfectly fine Queen's English, that was!"

All three men broke down into laughter as they realized what they had accomplished. The bright dangerous glow, the pulsing beat in his mind that had drawn them all here, dissipated in Jamie's vision. As the destroyed Akhkharu turned to ash and smoke, the trio walked out through the compound yelling at each person they passed to follow along as they opened up the main gate and continued walking back to the reservation without noticing how very few were following.

"Sure you won't stay? The law says no more than two Xul," Enli reminded his Shi as they packed up the SUV.

"Nah, these are yer people, not mine. Mine are back 'ome, back in London, and I think I need to check on them."

"Then Berlin?" Karl added as he shut the trunk.

"Aye, we can go to yer bloody Berlin," Jamie agreed with a grin. He shook hands with his dami and bowed to the Elders before getting in the vehicle and letting his wardum drive. After a few miles he turned down the mirror on the shade and looked at his retracted fangs, which, while still visible, were not nearly as noticeable as they had been.

"You look pretty," Karl observed.

"Oi, thou don't tell a bloke he's pretty, ye pervert," the vampire growled and hit his companion hard in the arm, making him swerve a bit.

"Careful, Sir, you'll distract me, and we'll need to pull over," Karl teased with a grin.

"Drive!" Jamie ordered as he turned on the last album The Damned ever put out and started singing along with Vanian, much to the amusement of his mate.

*Jamie is smiling now, his dami's half-serious taunts making him reply in kind as Bard steps back with a bow. These children of mine are still so dangerous, yet they are nothing compared to their original form. His first child is far away, at another of our colonies, just as those sitting here today will go off on their own in a few decades as long as they prove their value to me.*

*I smile at Bard as I nod at him and then look out over the audience again. The timeline is not as clear as in the first night's tales. But Bard has done a good job of it so far, so I reach out to him and inquire about the next one. With a nod I catch Cornelius' eye. "You still do not wish to tell us about the library?"*

*He shakes his head while his own arammu-wardum is looking worriedly around the garden as he crosses over to sit by his master. It is true that the library was both their greatest work and their most controversial. I have never* said whether or not I fully agree with what they did, but the mere fact that they are here should be all the evidence they need.

"To you again, Bard," I state before returning to sit by Jon.

# Silk Purse

Jack sat up on the roof of what had once been the Library of Congress, looking out toward the ocean, which he could not see, even with his improved eyesight. A century ago, he may have been dismo, thinking about the waves, his board, and the feeling of it all, but now he couldn't even clearly remember what "dismo" meant. Only a deep, tiny twinge flickered through his heart when he reached up to caress his buzzed blond hair that resembled his master's own haircut. He'd changed his hairstyle within a few decades of his transformation into wardum, not because Cornelius had commanded it, as he doubted the Akhkharu even noticed his hair, but because he'd caught the looks and comments other vampires and their servants had been giving him as he'd circulated within the dark venues of the Night Kingdom.

No, there wasn't much left of surfer dude Jack anymore.

He'd been replaced with someone more focused on the almighty texts that they protected and censored below. Jack glanced down and saw the flicker of light, so he stood, then bounded down the roof and the side of the building to meet his contact below.

No, Jack wasn't just some vampire's obedient slave, at least not in these moments.

The woman he met had on a hooded jacket, large dark sunglasses, and a big hat that hid most of her hair, but he knew from her smell that this was one of his contacts. They exchanged no words but only huddled together for the few moments it took for Jack to hand her the precious relic, this one entitled "Sentimental Education" by Gustave Flaubert. His contact briefly met his eyes with her twinkling ones. They both knew how ironic this book's title was. Then she took off at the same moment that Jack turned to walk back to the crypt where all the written works of mere mortals were being buried or burned.

Ray Bradbury would be horrified and proud at the same time. His novel had been one of the first books they'd saved.

Jack stopped by the mess on his way back to his master's office. The mess was a consideration to those mortals required for the grunt work of the Library and those very select few like him who actually helped with the storage. Only the Akhkharu themselves catalogued and read the books. Every now and again when an extra copy arrived Jack would rescue it, hide it, and pass it along to the underground, built unapologetically on the fictional model.

Jack didn't talk to anyone here in the mess more than necessary. It served his purpose for them all to think he was being a snob, that he considered himself above any of them, just as his master was head of this "collection project" established by Her court. The master had met Her and spoke of the Ummum only rarely, but Her minions visited regularly.

Two of these stood out in Jack's mind as he tried to hide the memories of what he had just done deep in his mind. Marina was the one in charge of this project, the biggest supporter of the laws forbidding mere akalum from learning to read or write; she hosted bonfires in villages whenever there was a sign of illegal learning, and she had no qualms about killing anyone who disagreed with her. With that thought, Jack forced himself to swallow the last of his sandwich as he stood up to continue his duties.

The second minion he remembered was Jon, the arammu-wardum of the Ummum Herself, who came to borrow books and return those previously taken so that She could be entertained. Jon was a confident man who didn't bow to any vampire, though his language was always measured and proper. Cornelius seemed quite taken by him, so Jack had worked to mimic what he saw. As he passed the closet where he and the great wardum coupled quickly on his visits, Jack smiled. He'd learned to play on the desires of others to get what he needed.

If only that worked with his master.

It had only taken Jack a decade to figure out that his vampire didn't really desire their sexual encounters, and that the passion was an act the millennia-old creature put on to keep him happy. In some small way, the wardum supposed this was a sign of how much his Bel cared, since he knew by the force of bu and the ceremonial words that bound them that he would obey regardless of orgasm or not. Jack studied how his master faked arousal and orgasm, how he moved and how his voice sounded, and he used this with other wardum when he needed information. Not often, though, because he wasn't some silly Gelal's pet.

Jack sighed as he came into the office to find it empty. He really didn't feel like returning to the stacks just yet, so he looked around, listened carefully, and eased near the desk, looking for any clues as to where his master might be. Nope, just the usual scribbled notes and the computer that hummed away, angry that it wasn't the latest in technology, though that was very slow to change these days, since vampires didn't feel the need to make it better, smaller, and more expensive every year or even every decade.

"There you are." His master's voice made Jack turn to the doorway and execute a small bow. "Have you seen the extra copies of Brendwood's translation of the collected works of Euripides, the last edition from 2037?"

Jack thought for a moment, then shook his head. "Shall I go find them, Master?"

"What is your current project?"

"Storing the Mark Twain collection, Sir."

"Please. How can that compare to Euripides? Yes, go now and find out who didn't deliver it to me on time," the vampire added with a slight growl.

"I feel sorry for that person," came a soft familiar whisper that drew both males' attention to the doorway again. The Kashshaptu who visited a few times each year to review their collection on magicks was standing there, her slave, or apprentice if you believed the rumors, close at her back.

"Ah, Calypso, you have arrived safely. Excellent." Cornelius turned back to his own arammu-wardum. "You are dismissed."

With that, Jack bowed to each Akhkharu and hurried to find where the Brendwood translation was hiding.

The two elder Akhkharu took seats while the witch's servant merely stood aside, head bowed, appearing to be oblivious to the conversation, though both vampires knew better. Calypso had been a member of the Night Kingdom centuries before Cornelius, yet they treated each other as equals, since both valued knowledge above all other things. The type of knowledge was the only difference.

As one of the powerful and mysterious Kashshaptu she barely spoke above a whisper, so the Allamudi had to lean forward a bit to hear each word. The scholar knew three stories of how the raised voice of a magick user could level cities, call forth brutal storms, and inflict death for miles around. He had no firsthand experience, but he knew better than to ask her to speak up. Too many impossible things happened in their world to risk testing such legends.

"I apologize for being a day late, Cornelius. We ran into a small annoyance on the way here this time."

"But I see you and your servant are safe, so there is no problem. Come anytime you wish, my friend; we are always open to seekers of knowledge."

Her almost translucent eyes looked directly at him. "I think that might be … unwise."

Inwardly Cornelius froze as he worried about the reported ability these witches had to dive into the mind, but as quickly as the thought entered, he forced it aside. "I appreciate your concern," he merely replied. "Which library do you wish to visit this time?"

While most vampires, wardum, and mortals thought of the Library as one building, the truth was that all of the institutions in this former human capital were under Allamudi jurisdiction. Cornelius only administered the literature proper, but he and his colleagues allowed each other the authority to grant admission to any facility, though each director could rescind an invitation at any time. Calypso had seen most of the literature about magick, the bulk of it human fictions as far as

Cornelius was concerned, and moved on to physical artifacts a few years ago, but she always checked in here first.

"I have heard new tablets were sent here from the silk lands. I wish to study them."

"Ah, I will contact Vanslav and tell him that you are on your way. When do you wish to see them?"

She stood up suddenly and smiled just slightly. "We can walk there in a half an hour, I believe; correct, Chavi?"

"Yes, Mistress," her wardum replied in her equally soft voice.

"I shall send a runner," Cornelius announced as he rang the bell to call his messenger into the room. The young male entered and bowed as Cornelius scribbled on a piece of paper then shoved it into an envelope, sealing it with his own bu. "Take this to Director Vanslav immediately, and hurry," he ordered as he handed the boy the document.

The Kashshaptu waited for a few minutes, exchanging polite small talk with him until she turned to follow after the messenger. Only after she left did Cornelius let his mental guard down. That had been close, too close, he chided himself as he opened his secret desk drawer and smiled at his next shipment, this one due for Moscow.

Now if he could just get those Brendwood copies, he could send it all on its way.

As was his method, irrational and thus perfect for his grand deception, he believed, he took out his world map, closed his eyes and poked his finger at a random location. When he opened them, he sighed. Ah, this one would be hard to deliver to, but it had been a long time since a shipment was made to Melbourne, and they must hunger for knowledge more than most places.

Cornelius stood up and frowned. Where the hell was Jack? He needed to get these copies together so he could continue building up the next storage unit for that crazy bitch who wanted to burn his precious books. Times had made even the most formerly respected of his family insane, as her deeds and words demonstrated. The Akhkharu thought for a moment, then made some changes to the work details, moving Jack into a more "important" section where currently only other vampires worked. They'd give him a difficult time, but his slave was strong and capable, and soon he hoped to be able to save more than just fiction and the classics, though Homer had obviously been the first works he had sent out to his dozens of little underground vaults run by like-minded guardians.

Jack put one hand to his cheek where the Akhkharu had slapped him. The science collection didn't even use wardum as grunt labor, and now his master had sent him here to count the copies of books. The director's assistant who had hit him was glaring down at him, and Jack could understand his anger. A wardum on such a task was a direct insult, and he feared his master had intended it as such.

"I don't believe I know better than you, sir," Jack began as he stayed on the floor where the strength of the attack had knocked him. He adjusted his position just enough to be kneeling and looked up, but over the Akhkharu's shoulder. "I am merely following orders, sir."

"You little son of a bitch!" The assistant director pulled back his leg, and Jack knew he was about to be kicked yet did nothing to defend himself, but then the director came into his line of sight.

"Jameson! Stop it this instant!" The assistant director immediately took a slightly submissive stance with his hands behind his back and turned to his boss. Vampires didn't just play power games with mortals, but with each other as well, and Jack watched closely, searching for anything he could use to his advantage. "What the hell is going on here?"

"Director Marlin, sir, this boy here came from Director Cornelius and claims he has the right to oversee my work," said the younger vampire, his voice dripping with anger.

Jack dipped his head once in silent greeting when the Director's eyes fell on him. "Yes, this is the High Director's arammu-wardum, or didn't you realize that?" The Director was looking at Jack but speaking to his assistant.

"What should that matter? I'm Akhkharu, not some slave to have my performance questioned!"

Jack jumped a bit when the Director's hand struck out and landed hard on his assistant's cheek. "You have not existed enough centuries to speak in that tone with me or about the High Director. When you speak to this boy, every word you say will go back to his master, fool."

The younger vampire paled, and Jack's heightened senses noted with satisfaction that he was trembling slightly. "Give me the letter I'm sure he came with," the Director ordered as he literally grabbed said document from his assistant's clenched hand.

After a few minutes, the Director growled. "This should have been delivered immediately to me. You are dismissed for the rest of the night. I will deal with you tomorrow promptly at midnight, Jameson. Get out of my library."

Jack moved aside slightly to let the other vampire pass, then he noted they had drawn a crowd of other Akh in the commotion. "Everyone back to work!" the Director ordered, sending his underlings scurrying away. "Follow me to my office, boy," he then commanded.

Jack rose gracefully and followed at a few steps' distance, wiping his mouth on his sleeve, grateful that his hardier form had protected him from any real damage beyond a split lip. Once in the Director's office, which was about the size of the master's, Jack took up a position in front of him, hands behind his back, feet shoulder-width apart and head bowed, while the vampire leaned on the edge of his desk to reread the letter and consider him.

"So, you had a bachelor's degree prior to your ... service to Cornelius. Then he sent you to get both a master's and a doctorate before the Blood Wars. Besides still having a beating heart and all those mortal needs, you are better qualified for this sort of work than most out there."

Jack was surprised at the compliment but decided to turn it back to his Bel. "I am grateful to be of service to my master, sir."

"Of course, you are. If only I had wardum working here instead of other Akh, how much more smoothly things would work," the Director muttered softly, but Jack's supernaturally improved hearing picked out each word clearly, though he knew better than to react in any fashion.

"Cornelius wants you to check on how many copies we have of any given work. He mentions that sometimes his own people have found mix-ups in the shipments we've sent. Is that correct?"

"I did not read my master's letter, sir. He merely told me to deliver it and do as you instructed a few nights a week," Jack replied carefully.

The Director chuckled. "He's trained you well, I see." The Director stood up and put the letter up on his corkboard by the door. An area Jack could see just by glancing upward was set up to be viewed by anyone working in this particular library.

"Follow me, then, boy. I'll get you set up in your new part-time job."

Cornelius lay on his side watching as his arammu-wardum smiled and worked to get his breath under control after their coupling. The slave had been very eager and responsive to his attentions tonight. He knew this was because he had only been seeing him a day or two each week for the past year as he worked for the natural science library, reporting to Cornelius the other few nights. When the boy's hunger was this strong, the elder vampire worked to make it particularly intense, and he noted that Jack's pale skin was showing signs of bruising on his hips and thighs already. As wardum he'd heal quickly, but for a few days he could have the marks and the soreness to remind him of this time. That was so important to mortals.

Cornelius looked back as he felt Jack's hand on his arm when he moved to rise from the bed in his slave's room. He did not allow his special servant to sleep with his others in the dorm he had set up outside the library. The vampire simply looked at his slave until the boy whimpered.

"Please, Master, please stay a bit longer. You can sleep here when the sun rises; I'll watch over you well. Please," the boy added as he placed a kiss on the arm he held, his blue eyes begging as much as his words were.

"I have a meeting tomorrow evening with the other directors," Cornelius replied as he started to rise again, then frowned when Jack held on and followed the movement by sitting upright.

"I'll make sure you are ready for it, Master," the slave promised. "It's not until midnight. The sun will set a few hours before that, Master."

Cornelius smiled. This boy was managing to do his new job well and keep up on his schedule even though he'd placed Martha in charge of that particular task. She was a good secretary, but nothing more than that, while Jack was … he pushed those unusual feelings aside as he stood up, so his cock was in front of his wardum's face again. "If you can get me aroused again, I will stay the day," he agreed.

With Jack's eager mouth, sensuous touches, and moans of desire, plus Cornelius's own amusement, the vampire was erect and back inside his number one within a half hour, before falling asleep in the boy's arms. As he slept, he planned the next shipment to Amsterdam.


Jack could see the disappointment in the man's face as he read the title. Yeah, Richard Feynman's *Six Easy Pieces* wasn't as easy to memorize as George Eliot's *Middlemarch*, but these were the books he could get now, which meant these were the books he could pass along. The man just sighed and placed it in his jacket, then took off as Jack turned away.

He walked more slowly than he had in previous years, the disappointment in his contacts' eyes starting to wear his spirit down. If the vampires didn't want humans to have these books, then they must be important, he reasoned repeatedly. It wasn't like the underground could say "no" to anything he offered. If they didn't want them, they didn't have to come back.

Jack knew it would be safer all around if they just stayed away, yet as he walked back across the old Mall, he thought about what he could get for them next.

"I know what you're doing, slave," said a male voice that made him stop in his tracks. Jack heard the footsteps approach him, but he held still, listening. "Too young, huh? I'll get an audience with Her when I bring up the traitorous activities you and your master have been doing."

Jack always knew he was risking his life by doing this, but the mere mention of "master" made him react on instinct and training. Cornelius didn't explain why, and Jack always thought it was weird, but he was trained to kill vampires, obviously not his Bel, but anyone else who might be a threat. He'd done it a few times during the Blood War, but that had been generations ago. Luckily, he still kept a bronze toothpick in his pocket. During the war they had discovered that bronze was the only human made material that could paralyze a vampire. This small amount had been a gift years ago from his master.

With old skills developed on the waves and after his service began, he spun, not even registering the identity of the speaker, and slammed the toothpick into the main vein on his neck. If the guy were mortal, it would just surprise him and give Jack enough time for a second strike; if he were Akh he'd go immobile. The speaker fell limp into Jack's arms. "Oh, shit," the wardum whispered as he recognized the vampire as the former assistant to the Science Library Director.

Quickly he dragged the vampire through a side door into one of the storage garages that lined the building he now worked in. This was where he hid the books before he got them to the underground. If this Akh wasn't old enough, he'd leave a mess behind that any vampire could sense, and then everything would be over. Jack hid the body between some pallets and took a few moments to think before sprinting off to the main library.

"Master?" Jack stepped into his Bel's office and shut the door behind him. His boss looked up with a frown. "I need you, Master."

"Oh, for Charity's sake, you can't be serious. Now?" His master's frown deepened as he flicked his gaze downward toward Jack's groin.

"No, not that, though, no," Jack quickly controlled himself. "I have to show you something; it's a security breach, Master. Please come with me," he said as he opened the office door and looked expectantly at him.

The vampire looked at him for a few minutes, then buzzed his secretary. "Martha, I'm stepping away from my office for a while. I'll call when I'm back."

His Bel didn't ask any further questions as they crossed the Mall and went into the storage garage. He still didn't ask questions when Jack revealed the body, but he did step up and remove the toothpick, handing it to Jack.

The younger Akh gasped unnecessarily, then tried to back away, but found himself blocked by the walls and pallets. "Look, I won't tell anyone, I swear. I can even help you move the books, sir; I'm very good at all this sneaky business …"

Jack jumped as his master reached out with both hands and literally snapped the other's head completely off his neck. Since the former assistant was at least 150 years old, he disintegrated into ashes. The wardum fell backwards as his Bel showed him his fully terrifying nature as he turned to face him. "Please, Master, I'll stop, I promise."

"How long have you known, Jack?" As he spoke, Cornelius's features returned to their normal state.

"I didn't know he was following me; I don't think he told anyone, Master. I never did it to hurt you, Master," Jack began babbling.

Cornelius blinked. "What did you do, Jack? What did you do?"

"They don't keep them; they just read them and then burn them; I swear it."

The Akh stepped back and looked around for a few seconds. "You've been sneaking books out? To humans?"

Jack nodded and positioned himself on his knees, his hands behind his back, his head held high. If he couldn't be forgiven, he'd put himself into a position where he could quickly be killed. "They came to me about five years ago, Master. I didn't think it would hurt anything. So much was being lost, and they created it, after all; I just, shouldn't it be read, shouldn't it be appreciated?"

The wardum was surprised that his ribs didn't crack when he was picked up and slammed back into a wall. Jack held his neck up and didn't beg as his Bel's fangs sunk into his neck. At least there would be a minor erotic thrill while his life was drained away, but within a few minutes Cornelius had pulled back and was looking directly into his eyes.

"We have to protect the books, Jack; we have to, at all costs," the vampire whispered as he ripped open the mortal's coat.

"Yes, Master," Jack replied before his breath was cut off by cold, powerful lips on his. Kissing him? He shuddered as he felt the rest of his clothing ripped off and his Bel's cold, hard shaft thrust up into him without any preparation. It should have hurt, but instead Jack was so surprised by his master's true ardor that he just moaned deeply and tried to wrap his legs around the vampire's hips.

The natural state of Akhkharu sexual activity was always violent; only Xul embraced it fully, while Gelal played with it; the other families tried to curb it or use it for their own purposes, but the ability to give into one's sexual animal was merely the same thirst that drove one to sink fangs into a vein. It could easily kill a mortal.

Jack cried out in pleasure as his master fucked him hard, pushing him against the wall, literally into the wall as the plaster over the stone cracked against his coat. He hooked his ankles together behind his master's hips, pulling himself tightly over his warming shaft and pressing his own against the vampire's cool skin. Opening his eyes, Jack was surprised to see that Cornelius had also ripped his own clothing so that he was almost nude. He never fully disrobed, even when he spent the day with Jack in bed.

"Master," Jack moaned as he wrapped his arms around the other's neck and was carried to fall on the ground, his back making a crunching sound as it hit concrete and his Bel's weight crashed into him. Soon he couldn't maintain his grip and his hands and arms fell limp above his head. Then his legs started to slip, but his Bel kept pumping into him until everything went black.

Cornelius returned with a cup of water he had managed to get by sneaking around the hallways just beyond the storage garage where he had left his slave unconscious. He had been worried at first, then when it became clear that the upstart Jameson was talking about Jack's activities and it was confirmed by his slave's reaction, he quickly spiraled through anger, pride, and lust. The boy cared as much as he did about making sure the books weren't lost, though his choice of humans for their keepers was foolish.

He hadn't felt that much lust since he'd been a century out of the grave, as the expression went. Now he regretted letting it take him over so much as he pulled the remains of his torn clothing around him. He knelt down and lifted his wardum up by cupping his head in one hand then resting it on his lap. "Jack, you need to drink this," he whispered.

His slave opened his eyes, and for the first time Cornelius noted their color: blue, a sort of sea blue, or at least what the seas looked like in the old vampire's memory. The boy blinked but obediently swallowed down the water, then licked his lips and swallowed hard as he looked directly at his master. "I understand why you are doing this,

Master. I accept it," he whispered before tilting his head back to expose his neck.

"You do?" Cornelius answered. Truthfully, he wasn't sure what he was doing. To protect himself he should have snapped this boy's neck soon after the other's, but to see him laid out so helpless yet so accepting only made the ancient creature hard again, so he urged his servant to sit up, hoping the wardum didn't notice his state of arousal.

"Jack, you should not have taken the books, whichever ones they were. It's dangerous; you know that," Cornelius began to scold.

"I tried to be careful, Master," Jack countered softly as he sat up and bowed his head. "I wanted all the danger to fall on my head alone. I shouldn't have gotten you; I should have taken care of this myself."

"Don't be foolish. There was no way you could have decapitated him as I did, which left either fire, sunlight, or a sword to finish him off. All of those would have drawn more attention." Cornelius sat down next to his wardum and smiled at him. "Arammu," he said the term for beloved as he touched Jack's hair.

The boy looked at him then slowly smiled. "You aren't going to punish me, Master? Kill me?"

"Well, we might say I just did," Cornelius pointed out, motioning to his and his slave's torn clothes and the marks all over Jack's body.

"Oh, that was a punishment? I wasn't sure," Jack replied. "I mean," and he paused and licked his lips again, "it was surprising, but I," he paused again, then blushed and moved closer to his side, "I liked it a lot, Master. It was totally awesome."

Cornelius couldn't help but chuckle. "I haven't heard you use that language in a long time," he pointed out.

"I'm sorry, Bel," Jack replied and started to move away, but Cornelius felt the urge to hold him tight to his side.

"No, no, I can't remember when you stopped using that atrocious language, but now that I think of it, it must have happened over the course of the years. It's been a good number of years by your count, I bet," he chuckled again.

"271 years, 5 months, and 12 days, Master," Jack informed him immediately.

"By Charity, you keep track that closely?"

"Of course, Master," Jack said as he moved a bit so he could look at the vampire directly. "You are my life, Bel. I won't do anything else to shame you again, I promise ..."

Cornelius cut him off with a sudden kiss, again driven by emotions he thought had died centuries and centuries ago. "You don't shame me, Jack. I don't think you ever did. I mean, look at you. Whatever happened to that ragtag boy who showed up at my cave, it wasn't my direction that changed him into the fine – no, the amazing scholar and servant I have today. I think I've taken you for granted," he whispered more to himself than to his wardum.

"No, not possible, Master. You had me enroll in university again, you expected me to learn and never offered me detailed instruction. I thought that meant you knew I could do it, unlike Martha, whom I know you had to train for her current job," Jack added with a chuckle of his own.

Cornelius stiffened a bit at that annoying memory. He couldn't remember why the woman was entitled to his blood; she had just been sort of part of his reward for choosing the winning side. While others had households of slaves, he had been content with Jack, but She had insisted he acquire more "friends," and thus he'd added a few more students and former professors to his staff. Now he realized that none of them compared to Jack. Not in loyalty, not in courage, not in capability, and certainly not in the old feelings he stirred up. That required some trust in return.

"Jack," Cornelius stood up, and his servant stood up as well, his clothing pooling around his feet so that the vampire had to look away or risk getting lost in desire again. "I've been sending books out to other libraries as well," he said as quickly as he could.

They just stood there silently until the human pulled his clothing up and tried to cover himself. "Did you hear me, Jack?"

"Yes, Master, I heard you. I think Rodney can probably fix these clothes, but we should head back," Jack continued awkwardly.

Cornelius felt a flare of anger as he grasped his most favored slave by his arm roughly. "Don't you have anything to say about what I just told you?"

"It's not my place, Master, especially given what I've done. I just …" He swallowed again until Cornelius shook him soundly. "I wish I could have helped you. Haven't I always helped with your books?"

"Yes, yes, you have, you will," Cornelius said as he pulled the now trembling boy into his arms, so their heads rested together. "You will now, and I will help you as well, but we do this my way," he insisted.

Jack smiled a brilliant grin that the vampire realized he hadn't seen in decades and decades. He saw another when a few months later he presented him with a book he'd found by chance hidden in the stacks. Who knew that Geoffrey Band's "History of Surfing in the Western World" from 2043 could make a boy so happy?

They were walking along the shoreline during an outing that Cornelius required monthly for everyone working in the Library. His reasoning came after the convenient revelation that one of the youngest vampires had surprised the former science library assistant plotting to attack the director who had fired him. In their fight, the younger one had managed to destroy Jameson, though she had suffered the loss of a limb, which was still healing. Compared to a 2500-year-old vampire, the mere century-old creature's memories had been easy to replace, though Cornelius knew he owed Calypso a grave debt for her assistance in this manner, one he repaid by giving her "extra" copies of the texts on magick the Library had.

As he and Jack walked past Akh, wardum, and mortal, they stopped to chat for a few minutes, then moved on. Jack frowned as he picked up a discarded bag on the sand. "We never learn, do we, Master?" he said with a sigh.

"Best go throw it away before the collector picks that can up," Cornelius suggested with a motion toward the nearest trashcan that someone was already collecting.

"Hey, wait!" Jack called as he jogged toward them.

"So why are we really out here, Director?" The voice of one of the other library directors made the eldest vampire turn and subtly move his body between her and his wardum. Of course, the Gelal director of the art collection would notice things; she did have a good eye, after all.

"We've been working almost non-stop for a decade, Francesca. I, for one, need a break, and I think recent events suggest that is true for many of us, easily the younger ones, our slaves, and the akalum we use for grunt labor."

The other director nodded but was glancing around him. "I don't think that's the full reason, Cornelius. Look at your boy." She waved her hand toward the trash can, so he turned to see Jack walking back with a huge grin on his face, holding his coat against the cool night breeze coming off the water. "I think you like to make him smile," and with that soft, mysterious comment she turned to leave and rejoin her own beloved servant by the fire.

Cornelius called out to his own servant, "Did you get the last of the trash in then, boy?"

"Yes, Master," Jack replied, his grin still huge. He hurried forward and put his arms around the Akh, Cornelius drawing him in tightly for a hug. Everyone had noted the change in their relationship, and rather than causing confusion or problems the other directors seemed relieved that Cornelius was acting a bit more like one of them, though no one now dared oppose Jack when he was sent on his new job of randomly checking the copy counts in every library. "Thank you, Master. I will read it quickly and get it back to you," the wardum whispered.

"It's yours, boy; keep it safe."

Then they approached the fire so that the mortals could eat their cooked meat and the vampires could taste the akalum they desired while they still had a few hours before they needed to return to the Mall.

*The tale has the Gelal in awe, giving the Allamudi group air kisses as the story ends. "Did I do you justice, Sir?" Bard asks before bowing.*

*"It may have gone that way," Cornelius concedes with a shrug while Jack leans in and whispers into his ears.*

*I can feel the tears start to blur my vision, so I stand up and focus on the audience, but Enki's glance freezes me for a moment. The things that Jon revealed, the lives that Bard lived, these all whirl in my mind, and such sentimentality can be dangerous, I can almost hear my Lord tell me.*

*After a moment I regain my control and hold up my hands to stop the good-natured discussion that has erupted over who makes for better lovers among the families, now that several secrets have been revealed. I see Calypso's smile and nod to her.*

*She steps forward, and the audience goes quiet, only moving to lean forward in rapt silence as she reveals another chapter of her long life.*

# Dangerous Education

Chavi finishes looking at our temporary home as I take the latest book out. Cornelius has been a good friend to me, though my need to lie to him is not a commentary on him but on my own coven. If only they knew these summaries and recommendations are made after discussions with my wardum, I shudder to think how they might torture her to death, though I can't say I'm fond of the idea of being staked out for daylight with my skin stripped from the muscle.

My Beauty looks a little tired from our trip. The constant demands of various border lords and their servants to confirm she is my property as we've traveled this week has worn on her emotions. I've felt it all as it happened through our spiritual connection. Normally other Akhkharu are frightened of us, but a lone witch and her slave can also be targets for younger vampires attempting to prove their worth to their Shi or to frighten others who might be thinking of entering their territory. Our semi-nomadic nature makes us targets, and if I want to keep the rights I've been given to travel to various libraries, I need to keep my temper in check.

My Beauty kneels before me and smiles, signaling that the room is free from any device or ward that might allow another to spy upon us. There was a time when this was not necessary, but laws coming from the Ummum's Council are strict about what wardum can and cannot do. We are about to break several of these. I open the book.

Chavi shifts after several minutes of my reading and her "hearing" me so that she can focus for several hours. She must remain focused on the text at hand, though she cannot touch it beyond carrying it for me, or another of our family may discover she has read forbidden material. I cannot even risk showing her the diagrams or pictures this text on eastern magick and philosophy contains, for fear someone may see it in her mind. Our power has made us paranoid, leading spies to arise among my sisters. How I wish it were two centuries past, when it was much simpler to live in the shadows.

"Doesn't that passage contradict a book we read last year, Mistress?" Chavi thinks with a small glance at me.

I smile and close the book as I consider my wardum's question. This is where my praised insights into the value of texts comes from. Chavi's memory is amazing; my bu only enhanced her natural gifts. Sadly, all discussion must be silent between us at these moments, though I can "hear" her voice as easily now as when she opens her lips. "Explain further."

"There was a text, several in fact, where the male's role was called forceful or commanding. Here it portrays it as servicing the inner goddess of the woman, worshipping at her temple. Are these not contradictory?"

"Who is active in each of these rituals?"

Now her smile widens and nods her head slightly. "I see. In each case it is the male who does the act of sex to the female, only the motivation or interpretation changes. Thus, this claim of matriarchal reclamation is a lie."

"Should we not also consider the motivation of this author and his goals for the book?" I suggest.

"He is merely lying to himself. He does not see that his new interpretation is merely phallus worship of another form."

I set the book aside and raise my skirt just enough to reveal my ankles and sandaled feet. "Are you suggesting that a phallus is not worthy of worship?"

Chavi arches an eyebrow as she lowers herself to the floor to begin kissing my flesh between the leather straps, then starts to untie them. "I do not need it, nor do you, Mistress." Her thoughts are tinged with anger from the unnecessary fondling several of the border guards indulged in while we traveled. I am about to comment or offer comfort when she bites down hard enough on my inseam to draw bu, which she laps at as her dark eyes watch me.

My Beauty has learned much, which reduces me to the status of her slave in terms of passion, as she is mine in all other things. Soon the text is forgotten as we work to make the journey's unpleasantness fade in our minds.

Reading is the least dangerous illegal activity we engage in, however. Tonight, My Beauty is standing blindfolded in the center of this room we are staying in for a few weeks, concentrating on her right hand. The tattoo there shimmers and moves, stretching out to become a vine that snakes forward and reaches to caress my cheek as I watch silently. The slippery tendril moves now to grasp a wooden peg I've set on the nearby table. It feels the object, then gingerly picks it up and hoists it to another table a few feet away.

In all this takes a few minutes, when it would merely be seconds for me. But I have never heard of another wardum being able to do this much; indeed, none can even move the blood tattoo of their own will. Who would tell such a thing in the covens? There may be many who can do this, but as My Beauty recalls the vine to her body and slips off the blindfold to smile at me, I doubt any can be as gifted as she.

"I think I'm getting faster, Mistress."

"Indeed, but hardly useful yet," I tell her firmly. Inside I do so wish to praise her, to embrace her in pride, but our bond demands this hierarchy that I wish I had never created.

"I'll try harder then. Please don't be sad, Mistress."

I lift my chin and merely nod for her to continue.

Of course, we do practice those things necessary for all slaves and masters in our world. I've created a ward around myself to mask my true power and put on long-sleeved shirt and slacks. As I walk through this lonely, depressed part of this once-magnificent city, some fool takes the bait. From his facial piercings and scent, I'd guess this is a young Xul out to make a kill.

"Yo, bitch, you stupid or what?" He circles around me flashing his switchblade, showing his ever-extended fangs. "This is my street, cunt; you got to pay a fee if you want to pass."

"Don't touch her," Chavi's soft whisper behind him makes the Xul stop and turn around in surprise.

"Bitch, this is not your fight; this just some akalum out on a walk. Tell your master he can get his own dinner, or offer me something good for this one," he says to her. Chavi is not masked, though her tattoo is covered.

"Does it make you hard to attack helpless women?" she whispers to him, and his back straightens up.

"You take off, slave, or you gonna get a beatin' down; you hear me, girl?" he yells, and the volume makes me flinch a bit as I watch.

"Too loud. Why is it that those without real power insist on being so loud?" Chavi wonders softly as she turns around then kicks back with one leg, knocking him onto his back. With no more words she jumps onto him and plunges the bronze dagger I gave her years ago into his heart, which immobilizes him.

I drop my ward, and the Xul's eyes widen as I step into view. "Kill him," I whisper into her mind.

"Yes, Mistress," she whispers out loud for his horror as she uses her increased stretch to wrench his head from his neck.

Chavi steps back to clean her dagger as I stoop to taste his blood before he turns to ash, which this taste tells me he will. "127 years; that's your oldest yet, and the stupidest Akh I've ever met, I think."

My Beauty giggles slightly as she puts her dagger into its sheath at her waist, hidden under her over-vest.

Well, defending me is a skill she should have, and not just against other vampires, some say. I say I need only truly worry about my peers, not about the humans we now rule over.

We stay until he's turned fully into ashes and they have blown away. It would be a risk to allow anyone else to know what we've done.


Eventually we must move on, after I've written my latest reports back to the central coven about the quality of books in the last library I visited. Most of these treatises on magick are ridiculous and full of fantasy, utterly worthless and thus safe to be kept in the smaller libraries. One this time has something of true value, so that will need to be returned to the central Library and placed into protective custody.

I sigh as Chavi arranges for our transport to the next library. This job is my own fault for reading too much and teaching her to do the same. During her youth, such knowledge was denied most women, especially among the semi-nomadic gypsies, unless it was their own secret scripts. That offended me, so we spent a few years working on the basics back at my homeland on my estates. My dami became so jealous that she moved out about a decade earlier than necessary, but we have mended our hearts, and she serves as an advisor to a minor warlord in the East, protecting our family's right to travel.

"The train will leave tomorrow at 22 hundred hours, Mistress," she tells me silently.

I nod, and we return to the room we rented to start packing and spend one final night of freedom before we must again put on these masks of master and slave for the trip. Even our lovemaking is less passionate as My Beauty starts to hide herself deep inside her mind, where only I can enjoy her and feel every indignity she will suffer during our trip.

The train is segregated by species and then by service. Given my Grand Council credentials, we are placed in the most prestigious car. It reminds me of the luxury one might have found in the 19th century aboard such transports. Here we are the Kashshaptu, and we find the other Akhkharu and their wardum staying far from us. Frankly, I do not care, for this allows me to place My Beauty by the window, thus offering her more privacy, and us more privacy as well as she touches my hand or arm or leg from time to time.

After a few hours the conductor, a wardum employed by whomever controls this train, approaches, and offers me a piece of paper on a clipboard. There are several names and brief descriptions, and I note none of the other passengers have yet chosen their dinner. They may not want to associate with me, but they offer me this first choice in the hopes I will not use my frightening talents against them and their holdings. This is another benefit for our family.

I turn the clipboard just enough for My Beauty to spy it from the corner of her eye, but that is all I can risk. "Any of these sound particularly good to you?"

"The artist may offer a unique taste, Mistress, if it please you."

Her subservient reply makes me frown, but I choose the one who claims to be an artist. Humans can use the trains if they offer themselves as akalum. Of course, they risk being chosen by an excessively hungry passenger, but most often the Akh on these vessels take only enough to require the mortal to be carried away to sleep for a day, and by then they have reached their destination.

Chavi rises to go fetch the man and soon returns with him, his arms tied behind him, though she would not have done this. Must be this train's rules, and I smile slightly as she has him kneel by me.

She offers me a sketchbook, and I ask him a few soft questions, attempting to block out the sounds of our fellow travelers simply caving to blood hunger. He tells me a few stories about some of his pictures. He tells me that he is traveling to Paris because he has heard there is a patron there who might like his work. I know this Akh, so I tell him to mention my name to her; I found her a book a few years ago and negotiated its release into her custody. He is much calmer than his fellow akalum when Chavi has him rise up a bit so I can lean over him and sink my fangs into his neck. His blood is sweet and full of images, something only we Kashshaptu can pull from our prey, though I hear that Gelal pull other images, and Xul feed on adrenaline from fear.

I take only enough to leave him limp, and Chavi picks him up easily and returns him to the train owner's slaves to deal with. "Go to the servants' train to eat. I can sense your hunger from here, My Beauty," I direct her silently when I can separate my own fullness from her body's needs.

She simply pauses by my seat, kneels down, and kisses my knee as she takes the token giving her permission to eat in the wardum train a few cars back. She'll clench this in one hand to show to anyone who might challenge her, but our train is classy; only the porters are likely to demand to see it.

Thus it continues for a few days, giving us a stressful yet uneventful journey until we are about two days from our final stop and the coven meeting. Everything good must come to an end; that was an old expression even in my youth, and repeatedly it proves itself to me time and again.

I sense the problem even before the yelling reaches our car. The other Akhkharu look at me, assuming that if there is a problem it must be mine, given that this train refused to allow any Xul aboard. If you can't blame one monster, blame another.

I'm walking toward the servants' car when I am met by the chief porter. "Your girl has caused a conflict," he tells me through trembling lips.

I know she hasn't; she has merely allowed her feelings to betray her and me when she was insulted by someone needing to make himself feel superior through his bullying. I have seen it all through our connection.

"I will deal with her; keep the others away," I command, using my magick to force my will upon the porter, who can only nod absently. It will last only a short time, since the screams reached the others' ears. They may well rip him to pieces when they learn what has happened.

I reach the servants' car to find My Beauty standing in the remains of her foolish victim. The other wardum are pressed against a far wall; one of them is attempting to open the opposing door, but I know what My Beauty has done to it even from this distance.

All eyes turn to me when I enter, and that is exactly what I require. "Sleep!" I ordered; my voice slightly raised so it worms into every mind regardless of any protections their own masters may have placed upon them.

"I'm sorry, Mistress," she says without looking at me, her victim's blood dripping from her hands. "He insulted you, called you a fraud and a servant of the Devil. I lost control."

I grab her by the hand and lead her out to the car where our personal possessions are stored. Quickly I pack a few of the most necessary items, and she does the same, then we go to stand between cars, watching the ground flicker by. Luckily, the sun has set not long ago, and with my recent feeding I can jump with no difficulty. She is not so lucky, and we hear her ankle snap. This requires a few moments of focused blood to heal, then we sprint back toward the last city we passed.

"They'll look for us there," she cautions without opening her mouth as I hurry us along, parting any plant or stone in our way with my thoughts.

"She lives there, not quite inside the city," I reply in her mind, sending her images of the one I mean, the one who created this world we struggle in.

My Beauty stops and shakes her head, so I must pause to exert my will. I could just bore into her mind, take control of her limbs, strip her as my coven would say she deserves for using any of her abilities against others' servants. She used so much more than a mere wardum's skills. I saw it like a slow-motion picture as it happened; it so horrified me that I couldn't believe it until the cries of the other servants reached my ears.

Yes, he did insult me. That is nothing new. Even with the Ummum revealed to the world there are old beliefs that make it difficult for female vampires and their servants to travel alone. Perhaps such sexism is part of our human DNA, never fully killed when the body passes over, or maybe it is in our souls, recaptured and not purified from our earlier sins and blessings.

What is new is that he touched My Beauty as he insinuated truths about our relationship. What is new is that in such tight quarters we have had to play this master-slave game to its fullest form for several days without end. What is new is that My Beauty lost control and doomed us both.

"Better for Her to condemn us than for others to discover us and bring shame to the coven," I insist in a low whisper, then yank unkindly on her wrist to urge her feet to move again.

For all my courageous words, I find myself immobile at the iron gates of Her estate. Throughout the ages those in control of individual families hid behind their officers and lieutenants, ruling both in secret while everyone knew that those in charge truly were not. She has no problem with us all knowing who She is now and where She lives.

I remember the stories about Her destruction of an entire government of Elders in Boston at the very beginning of what is called in our circles "the Revelation," or the revealing of our nature to the world. I've heard of how numerous wars between our people have ended suddenly with reports of a young girl who looks suspiciously like the Ummum appearing on the battlefields or in the war rooms of both competitors at the same time. We can't even do that, be in two places at once, but standing here I wonder if She can.

An intercom system by the gate makes a noise, and a man's voice greets us. "The witch Calypso and her servant Chavi are bid enter," he simply says, and the gate swings open.

There is little point in keeping up our guises here, so I take My Beauty's hand in my own, and we step forward together.

I've seen him before on the video broadcasts that are used in part to keep the masses under control and to communicate with those of us lower on the totem pole of power. His name is Jon, and he is Her arammu-wardum. Without a word he leads us into a grand house, then through many hallways until we are so deep inside the house that I'm not sure I could determine an escape route should I wish one.

I don't know what I expected, but both Chavi and I shrink back when he throws open a door and reveals Her sitting on the edge of a large wooden desk. Jon does not touch us but urges us forward with soft words that remind me of my father so many millennia ago when he wished to earn my trust and compliance.

I kneel before our Creator, and Chavi follows my lead. Several minutes pass, and then I see a pair of pink shoes in my line of sight. "Would you give up your life for hers?" she asks me.

I look up – I'm that bold, or perhaps that stupid. "Yes, without question, Ummum."

My Beauty makes a sorrowful noise in her throat but maintains some composure.

"We expect them to do so, don't we?" She asks but doesn't give me time to answer as She looks at Her own number one. "I would, too," She confesses, and this confuses me for a moment.

"Not happening," Jon says as he rests against the edge of the desk.

My Beauty puts a protective hand on my arm but thankfully keeps her head bowed low and her voice silent. She doesn't even reach out to me with her thoughts, which is good, because another message comes through loud and clear.

"They can be so naïve, can't they?" A childish voice has invaded my mind. "Yes; anything you can do, I can do better," followed by a giggle, still all in my head.

My veins turn icy with this information, because I sense at the core of my being that She is telling me the absolute truth.

"It's my fault; please punish me," Chavi whispers, and I am shocked into silence on all fronts.

The little pink shoes move just a bit until they are standing in front of My Beauty, and I can't move or speak.

"Tell me what happened," She orders, and the words start pouring forth from Chavi's mouth in a low whisper. Within minutes My Beauty is weeping, revealing our entire history from the moment the aristocrats and mob killed her family to my decision to come here. Nothing now stands between us and death.

I am surprised when My Beauty makes a sound like a soft gasp, so I look up to see our Creator holding her in Her arms, tears running down Her small face.

"We should leave them for a bit," Jon says to me and offers me his hand. I pause and look at him. No one touches us, especially not men. "It's OK; I won't bite, and I will trust, Ma'am, that you won't bite me," he adds with an easy smile.

I take his hand and let him lead me to another nearby room, where I sit on a nice chair and accept a goblet of A positive from his hand. I never accept blood from others outside my coven, and yet perhaps I am already under the Ummum's thrall and cannot do otherwise.

Jon sits across from me and smiles as he keeps his body rigid. "If you don't mind, I would join you," he says softly.

I pause and then set the goblet down. "Will my wardum be returned to me?"

He shrugs. "I don't see why not, unless you've both lied about something. She does so hate lies."

I look at him sharply but say nothing, and he smiles at me. "We can understand a bit of what you must be going through. It wasn't easy for us to be together in the beginning. Akhkharu can be distinctly human sometimes, if you can forgive my boldness, Ma'am."

I bark out a chuckle, and he shudders as a bit of my raw power echoes through the room. "Sorry," I whisper very softly with a glance at the open door.

"No, Ma'am, your kind need never apologize to my kind," he says, and I glance at him again.

The covens are so formal, and every other vampire I have met seems so into this might-equals-right view that I am not surprised by his statement. Since my life is probably forfeit, I say something entirely inappropriate. "I think that's arrogant."

His laughter starts off barely audible, then builds up until Jon is almost doubled over on his chair, his decorum completely lost, and without my being fully aware I find myself laughing too, something only My Beauty has ever seen, and then only rarely. "Wow. That was, wow," Jon says as he leans back in his chair.

I stop and am silent. Again, my voice has let my power leak through. That's what happened to Chavi; she got angry and raised her voice, and then … I close my mind to the images.

"Please, it's OK; it was pleasant, feeling you laugh; it was amazing. She is so lucky to get to share that with you," he adds, and again his words make me look at him as I have only looked at one other wardum before.

"Yes, lucky enough to follow me to her death," I barely let the words pass my lips.

"Maybe," Jon says as he stands up and motions toward the door, "maybe not." He leans toward me with a slight smile. "If there are any questions you have, Ma'am, please do ask them. I know my Bel quite well by now. I'm sure she sent us away so you could ask me questions."

I blink and take an unnecessary breath. Even after all these millennia I do that when I am worried, and I have never been more worried than I am today. Considering my worry, I decide to ask the rudest question I can think of – what's the worst that could happen at this point? "Is She playing a game with us?"

He arches one eyebrow at me and is silent for several nerve-wracking moments before smiling and leaning back in the chair. "She does like to play games. Currently she's enamored with "Chutes and Ladders" and "Ants in the Pants," but no; to treat your question more seriously, She is not playing games with you and your girl."

I shake my head, very ill at ease with this almost nonsensical answer. "I thought this would be faster; it would clear my conscience; I thought ..." I just let the sentence die because I'm feeling so confused. I feel much like I did the first century of this existence and the first decade with My Beauty.

"You thought She'd kill you, so you didn't have to worry about your own family finding out what you've done," he said, finishing my own thought. I stare at him in silence. "She felt it; apparently your girl has a lot of power – too much, in fact, for most of us mere wardum to handle."

"It was a mistake," I reply.

"Bonding her, or teaching her how to use your bu?"

I feel frozen by his horrifyingly insightful question.

He frowns and sits up straight again. "Better for you to tell me, Ma'am, than for my Bel to ask you."

What an odd way to interrogate us – I with this servant and She with mine. All of the stories we hear about Her pale in the harsh bewilderment of this visit, which if I have understood him correctly may not be our funerals if I do this right. Right would be being honest about everything.

"Making her wardum was the mistake. I had always planned on teaching her the magicks," I admit while looking directly at him, wishing to see his reaction so I can prepare myself.

He opens up his mouth as though to say something, then closes it and looks at the hallway before standing up and offering me his hand. "I'm to settle you both in a suite for now. The sun will rise soon, and my Bel will determine what actions to take tomorrow evening. If you will please follow me?"

I take his hand and then his arm as he leads me to a large suite where Chavi is waiting, sitting by a roaring fire, staring into the flames. When we are alone, I do not bother to lock the door, and sit with her, holding her in my arms, rocking her until I can fight the sun no longer and welcome the release of darkness and unconsciousness again.

I awaken to the feelings of silk and satin around me and the warmth of My Beauty cradling me. Her dark eyes meet mine as she leans in for a kiss, our bare skin touching in the flickers of light, which suggests that the fireplace has already been lit tonight.

"I'm so sorry, Calypso," she says as she breaks the kiss. Even in our most private moments she has not used my name in years.

I run my fingers down her cheek, wiping away the tears that are falling. There is no point restricting our voices here, though I keep mine a mere whisper out of habit. "What did She tell you, My Beauty?"

"Only that after tonight we need not live with secrets anymore, Mistress."

I am saddened at her return to the formal title but nod, and then catch her breath with my mouth, diving deep between her lips and into her throat, wishing I might find a way to capture and save the soul I doomed so many centuries before.

As the kiss turns to demanding caresses, a knock makes us jump. "Audience with the Ummum in 15 minutes," says an unfamiliar voice.

Cautiously I raise my voice just enough to carry to the other side of the door, holding my power in check. I do want My Beauty's ending to be swift, so I must remain calm and not accidentally attack any of the Creator's servants. "We will be ready."

Chavi is weeping uncontrollably now, and I must delve into her emotions and force her to be calm. "Kashshaptu never show our fear, only our power; be calm; we meet this together," I urge her mind.

We are escorted to a formal receiving room where She sits, Her little feet swinging back and forth, upon a thronelike chair, Her arammu-wardum kneeling next to Her, and no one else. When Chavi pauses to kneel a few feet behind me, I put an arm around her and pull her up alongside me, so we are kneeling side by side, together as I promised.

Our two hosts, our Creator and the most beloved of all slaves, exchange a glance, then She stops kicking her feet.

"Did you know that Jon was never supposed to be with me?" This odd statement makes both Chavi and me look up.

"He had served another; they say that you can only be bound to one master at a time, and if you are abandoned you can never be bound again. Adults say a lot of silly things."

She shrugs, then kicks Her feet again. "Maybe I'm just that powerful, just that old, just that everything," She adds with a giggle that is like shards of ice down my spine.

He places a hand on one of Her shoes, and She stops kicking and retrains Her focus onto us. "We broke the rules; I had to defend us – couldn't lose my daddy, my best friend, my family, now, could I?"

Is it a question I need to answer? I do because I am confused. "You did what you had to do, Ummum."

She nods. "So did you," She simply states.

She stands up, as does Jon, and they approach us. "Which is why I want you to live here with us and become our ambassador to the world."

I grab Chavi's hand in shock. "What?"

"You are safe now. I will protect you; do not doubt that I can." Her high-pitched voice is suddenly quite sober and mature in this statement.

I swallow, then bow my head. "Your will be done, Ummum."

A giggle again as She replies, "Of course."

Then She sits on the floor, and Jon joins Her. "Get more comfortable, because what I want you to do is going to take some time to explain."

I look out the window of our private carriage as we leave the following week. The libraries and universities will no longer be my mission, and the coven no longer holds sway over my life. I look at Chavi, who is checking the list of Akh whom we must find and investigate in our search for others who are "breaking the rules for the right reasons," as She explained repeatedly.

"Vancouver is quite a ride, Mistress; I hope Jon and I have planned enough day stops for your comfort," she tells me silently.

I smile and place a hand on her black-velvet-covered thigh and squeeze. "I'm sure soon you'll know how to make all these arrangements yourself."

"Of course, Mistress; only the best for my lover," she adds and blushes, looking directly at me.

Maybe one day we'll trust this driver She has given to my service, but not today; today we keep it all under control until we are safely in our inn for the day.

*"That explains a lot," Cornelius replies as Calypso finishes her tale with a bow. "Though I thought you already worked for the Ummum when I first met you," he confesses with a nod at me.*

*"Many people confused the Council's will with my own; that was my error," I admit as I stand up and put an arm around my eldest Kashshaptu, making everyone in the gardens flinch. Old fears die hard, even when most holding them are dead.*

*"I shall tell of another whose aid was paramount for our current world," I decide with a glance at Bard.*

*There are many things he could tell, but this one, given the recent revelations, feels most appropriate for me.*

*"I'm not a storyteller, so I cannot promise it will be particularly insightful; this is only what I knew, what I saw, what I stopped," I state as I pull my thoughts together then mentally connect to Jon and Bard to draw upon their memories.*

# Forbidden Aid

I think it is because I am the first that I can feel all of you, all of the time, but the degree depends upon your power. Someone out there was using a great deal of mixed power, over and over and over again. When I was a bit younger, right before Boston's demise, I had this odd experience. I hadn't felt that in years until after I had established Calypso as a liaison.

As some of you know, I was different then than now. Now I might not have approached it as I did then, but had I not, I think we would not be here this evening, none of us.

Jon carried me through the crowds around the small fiefdom deep in Gelal territory. My most passionate children are the most oddly isolated as well. The scholars share knowledge, the monsters would amass if I allowed it, the rulers make their contracts, and even the witches gather regularly in covens. Gelal can thrive in small kurs, since they have little interest in killing mortals, yet they tended to join these holdings into larger patu, where unclaimed humans flocked. If you want to find Gelal, look for happy hordes of humanity.

Thus, it was easy to find Sara and Daedalus in the remains of someplace called Florida, on the edges of the territory ironically called Loveworld. I remember visiting there with Jon, and it has greatly changed. But I digress.

As the power grew stronger, I was able to sense other powers entangled with it. Another Gelal, a Shi's power, and that of a

Kashshaptu as well. Stranger and stranger, but I kept going, with Jon either carrying me or walking hand in hand.

The Gelal may be reluctant to interact with each other often, but they are always quite welcoming of other families, even of me, though I could tell they were afraid. It had been so long since anyone took me seriously that I mistook fear for authority back then, something I will never do again. They told me that in the direction I indicated lay the fiefdom of Professor Markus, a most odd Gelal who continued his studies as though he were Allamudi and lived with his damu as though he were Sarrutum.

"This is very odd," Jon whispered to me as he tucked me into bed before dawn when we were mere hours from the esharra of this lover-scholar, who clearly had a witch in residence.

"Maybe they have learned to live in peace here," I whispered back, though the centuries left me little hope for that.

"That would be wonderful," my daddy said tentatively, trying to sound glad, but I could tell he was worried, too.

The next night a wardum showed us to an opulent sitting room and left us with a dazed looking akalum for company, but I merely took the best seat in the room and waited while Jon sat with the mortal off to one side.

"Ah," a masculine voice called out as the doors opened just a second before a handsome Akh came forward with a beautiful wardum a step behind him. Both were barely dressed, but if they thought that might shock me they were wrong – how could it, given all that I've seen? "You've taken the best seat, excellent! Saves me having to offer it, Ummum," the lord of the bitum we were in said as he stopped to bow, his slave kneeling behind him.

I studied him for a second, then shook my head. "No, you aren't the one I'm looking for. It would be your dami."

The former professor flinched, then put a wide smile on his face. "Which one? Passion pulls me this way and then that; you know how we are."

I didn't return his smile. "You aren't like other Gelal, they told me, but I can see it all now. I could just go find her," I threatened as I made to slide off the chair.

"Fetch Sara," Markus hissed at his wardum, but before she could take one step, I added a comment about the witch and the slaves as well. "Your power is more than mere rumor, then," the lover-scholar admitted as he amended his command.

We sat still for a few minutes, but that never lasted long for me, so soon I asked, "When did you become interested in science?"

Markus looked at me in surprise, then just took a seat without permission, but it was his house, so I did not mind. "I met Descartes when I was beginning my university study. I had never had the opportunity to meet the previous great thinkers, but once I met him, I knew I had to apply vigor to my studies that was well beyond that which was expected."

"I met Galileo once – my wardum at the time thought it was good to introduce me to the smartest mortals she could find. She had high expectations, and her age and personality allowed her entry into spheres normally barred to women," I offered.

"Wow, I would have given anything to meet him," Markus admitted.

"So why Gelal, then?" I was as bold in my younger form as I am today.

"It's not like we chose our Shi," he countered with a shrug. "I find I can channel my..." his eyes slipped toward Jon's for a second as he paused, "interests into study as well as feeding."

"You mean sex." Beside me Jon was making one of his daddy warning sounds as he placed a hand on one of my shoes that was probably moving back and forth again with boredom. I bored so easily then, too.

"And that rumor is also confirmed," Markus said as he looked away toward the mortal in the corner. "Boy, grab a drink, a couple, then come here, I'm thirsty."

I giggled at the adults' discomfort but stopped when the doors opened again. I climbed up to stand on the chair as Markus rose and an Akh with long flowing red hair, another Akh in a long dark gown covering all her skin except her neck, face, and hands, and their male servants entered. The Kashshaptu stopped, one hand out to restrain the wardum, but the Gelal came toward me, brushing aside her Shi, her eyes locked onto mine.

"I've seen you before. All on that one night," she exclaimed. "Daedalus, does she look familiar to you, too?"

Her servant came forward and went to one knee, but his eyes never left my face. "I believe so, or you've told me about her so many times, Mistress."

"So many times," she repeated.

"This is my dami, Sara," Markus said as he came forward.

I tilted my head so far to the side that I recall Jon putting his hands on me to keep me from toppling off the chair. "Strange that it flows through you, but he's the one moving," I said, though I didn't understand what it meant.

I straightened up and turned my gaze to the lord of this esharra. "What have you been doing, Professor Markus? I need an explanation."

Even now I can't repeat what he told me. It was a combination of science, magick, and something unique about Sara and Daedalus themselves, attuned to something else that was an unknown variable. They just had to keep trying until it was right. It wasn't just their idea; a Kashshaptu named Anika was part of it, too.

It was two nights later when they invited me to watch their next experiment that I knew and acted.

The combining of magick and science was well beyond my understanding, so I merely watched. Some of the symbols drawn in blood upon the floor generated great power, similar to that which had drawn me here. As I stared at them, I could see the world begin to shimmer. It wasn't until the machine was started up and an odd hat placed on Daedalus' and Sara's heads, she at the center of the magick circles, he in the outer ring, that the world began to bend, crack, and melt.

I picked up and threw that machine across the floor, pulling free its tubes and wires and jerking the odd hats from both subjects, cutting but not killing them, while Markus and Anika raised their voices and Jon tried to step between us. I insisted, "It's me; I've always been there through each trip, and I … You can't do it again, you won't come back, and things will … things need to be this way right now."

There are times that I must force my descendants to do my will; when I must apply my primal power to bend them to my needs. I dislike doing it because of the first ones. I did it then, and I'm not sorry that I did.

But I did reward them for giving up their experiments, even if they couldn't enjoy that reward for long.


*I stop and look toward Bard, who has turned his back on me and the audience. "You wouldn't be here with us; we wouldn't be here if you'd gone back again," I insist, my voice taking on a childish tone it has not had in generations now.*

*Bard just nods, and then he turns around, one hand wiping his eyes. "That isn't the end, though, of the stories about the Elders, Ummum. There is the final story, the one of greatest risk and sacrifice, the one that started the rebellion."*

*We both turn and look to the Sarrutum group, where Niibori has straightened up. With one sharp nod of his head, he bids Bard to begin.*

# Promotion

Niibori sighed as he tried to stand still and let his wife, his wardum, do her work and finish his tie. She moved back just a bit, then fussed with smoothing down his suit, something he had designed just for this specific important meeting, then she smiled, her blue eyes twinkling, and stepped back so he could see his faint reflection. "I think the color does well for you, Niibori-sama," she told him firmly as she crossed her arms under her chest to regard him.

He wasn't so certain as he looked at the dark purple fabric with the slightly yellow silk shirt and pocket accent. It seemed so ... gaudy, and yet it seemed appropriately powerful, much like an emperor might have worn hundreds of years ago, back when there were emperors and presidents and chancellors of mortal states. He sighed, "Natalie-chan," but she ran her hands over his arm and leaned in so he could see them both.

Natalie was dressed in a light-yellow silk dress that came to just below her knees and hugged her contours nicely, with a dark purple wrap and matching shoes. The metal bracelet on her right wrist that symbolized their Tamu shone in the pale candlelight of his room, their room, as did the diamond and gold ring on her left hand, which matched the band on his own finger. A few hundred years ago they would have been seen as a powerful business couple, the toast of two fashion worlds, and they had been. Just not now.

Now she was a complement to his power, and a symbol of his creativity since he'd designed her clothing as well as his own. That had been a test of his ability as both a designer and a businessman, as well as a good dami. The wars had almost left him an orphan, but the gods had not seen fit to free him yet from his duty to his Shi, so now he was on another business trip for the patu, or territory, of Kansai, which Gaius had won and kept through his alliances with other Akhkharu on the islands of Japan.

His Shi had been clear in his distaste for them both, and that distaste was the reason why Niibori had been chosen as one of those representing House Byzane. If he succeeded, well, that was to be expected. If he failed, that wouldn't surprise Gaius, who would have to do something about the situation that was obviously keeping him from realizing his great potential. That "something" was Natalie. It wasn't spoken, but Niibori knew it as well as he knew that the sunlight would burn him if he stayed outdoors for more than a minute or two. The elder vampire's plan to punish him had backfired, he thought, though both husband and wife felt the shackles every day that bound them in these unnatural, unwanted roles.

He was about to put his arm around her when a knock came on the door and she scrambled away to kneel off to one side, her eyes flashing in anger. "Niibori!" An elder Akh from their own family, but one of equal rank to him, walked into the room and glanced at the wardum on the floor. "You seem ready; that's an interesting choice," the head of House Byzane agriculture chuckled. "But what do I know; I'm just a farmer, so let's get this show started, eh?"

Niibori followed, knowing that his heart was following quietly behind him, her head bowed, just two steps back so that she could assist him in any way, his briefcase held elegantly in one of her fair hands, when that hand should have been in the crook of his arm. He focused on the introductions to his fellow Byzane Kataru members – their alliance was one of the oldest; Gaius claimed it went back to his first dami in the 9th century of what had been called the "common era." The ancient eastern center of the Roman world had proved fertile ground for the Sarrutum after the fall of Rome, and dozens of elders had left their mark, first fighting each other, then using the hapless mortal kingdoms around them to wage war. The only way to survive had been to turn their collective minds to money, and once that had been done, the alliance had been easy to form.

The alliance now didn't have to worry about money, because there was no longer any such thing, but it did have to worry about holding on to kur and mimmum, land and the mortals on it, as well as acquiring the means to encourage both to grow. This meeting had been called so their kataru's Belen could make an important announcement. How important was it, Natalie had asked, if they were not inviting each patu's leader, but only a representative?

As they walked behind their host and met guests, Niibori kept stealing glances down at his wardum, counting each minute here and praying she would have enough energy to repay him in kind later. He was grateful when the gong rang, signaling an end to the casual meeting and the beginning of the formalities.

An hour later, he was almost staggering back to his suite in shock. He'd heard of this before – who hadn't? – but when the witch had stepped out and walked silently around the room everyone had been on edge. That she had stopped right behind his chair on her third circle around the giant conference table had made his heart seize up as Natalie grasped his leg from beneath the table, where all the arammu-wardum were hiding.

Natalie had given up her proper position and rushed to his side when they had gotten far enough from the gathering, so she could hold him under his arms to help him walk. Of all things they might have expected, this had been the last one.

The Ummum did need an appropriate outfit to mark the bicentennial of their Revelation to the world. Who was he, one mere Akhkharu, to say no to that? But Natalie had always taken the orders before, and only from the Ummum's arammu-wardum. Niibori had never been addressed directly.

Udo looked up, concern in his eyes where normally there was only calm, as the two who had gone to represent their Bel returned. "Master?" he asked as he opened the door and, unasked, aided the woman in bringing their lord into his room. "What has happened?" Udo demanded as he turned to the woman.

"We've been asked to design some clothing for the Ummum," Natalie said simply as she knelt to remove her husband's, her master's, shoes. She glanced up to see the confused look on the Asian wardum's face. "I believe he's concerned about Gaius," she added, refusing to use any honorific for that monster.

Years ago, she might have worried that Udo would run back to his master, but as far as they could tell, he had not fed from the other vampire for decades, taking bu only from Niibori, and when secrets remained secrets and Udo demanded nothing in return, they had started to believe this meant his bond had changed – something that was not supposed to be possible.

Like Natalie was not supposed to love Niibori after what had happened to her, and he was not supposed to kneel to her in privacy and cry out for her punishment. So many things were that should not be, according to the Night Kingdom. She turned her attention back to her husband now. "Niibori-sama, let's get you into a bath for a while; you should celebrate this honor," she added when he just looked at her in panic.

It took both wardum to get him stripped and into the tub, after which they left him to try to calm himself. A vampire, even one as kind and gentle as he, was dangerous when upset, and since Udo had witnessed so much tonight Natalie couldn't risk sending him away to give her husband what she knew would calm him fastest.

"I want you to look at this," Natalie said as she fetched the packet they had been handed when this task had been assigned to them that night. "Apparently, we aren't going to meet her, just design this outfit, so we have measurements and some information. But," she continued after taking out the packet's contents, "neither of us has designed for a child before."

Udo looked at it. Frankly, it meant nothing to him – he wasn't fashion-savvy; in reality he was simply a bodyguard. He knew, though, that for over two centuries now his former master had set up his prodigal son to fail over and over, and these two had always succeeded. This entire meeting had been nothing but a chance for them to fail, because who in their right minds would think the Mother of the Akhkharu would want clothing designed by someone who didn't know children's clothing? If they failed, he failed, and he had figured out many years ago that he was no longer bound to his old master as much as to these two, not by Niibori's blood but by their honor, respect, and love. Those were things he grew up thinking vampires could not have. "Is there anything I can do to assist, Natalie-chan?"

"Keep your ears open and watch him while I try to work my contacts and see if I can find anyone who knows anything about children's clothes," she ordered after a moment's thought. She treated her job as wardum much as she had her job as corporate vice president. Natalie kept a list of other people involved in clothing manufacture and design, an increasingly smaller pool as they made deals that gained them more influence and power. She could do this because he was relying on her, and her duty as a wife demanded that she try to assist him.

Natalie looked up from her desk, where she was trying to keep track of this flood of orders, when Udo came in with a tight smile on his face. "Another one?" she asked.

"Another one?" Niibori's voice behind her made her stand up automatically, the mystical force of the Tamu making her react. "The same thing?" he asked as he took the order form from Udo's hand.

He looked over it as Natalie looked over his arm at it as well, comparing it to her list of Akhkharu who wanted complimentary attire for this bicentennial party, which would happen by the end of the year. Allamudi, Gelal, Kashshaptu, and even another Sarrutum vampire had contacted them about this service they were offering now – a service they had never advertised in any fashion. Was Gaius spreading the word, trying to set up an impossible task?

"You are not serious." Niibori said as he set the form on the table and stared at Udo.

"They came in; they filled out the form, Master; they had the same invitation in hand; I checked it personally," the male wardum swore. "They looked … horrifying," Udo added when his Bel simply stared at him.

Natalie looked at the family box and saw "Xul," but she didn't know what it was.

"I won't design for them," Niibori declared. "They are monsters; they can't possibly be invited to this event."

"I swear, Niibori-sama, their invitation was identical to the others', to your own. They looked like trash, but it was in perfect condition," he added.

"He is doing this to make me fail," Niibori declared as he thumped his fist down on the desk, causing both wardum to flinch. "I give that, that, that ..." He caught himself before saying anything that any of his mortal and wardum workers might overhear and repeat. "I give my Shi everything he asks for; I am very loyal; I work hard; why does he continually challenge me so?"

No one pointed out the obvious answer to that.

Natalie took the form. "Two men, not much difference in their physical build, a few odd body mods to deal with on the one – no," and she scanned the sheet again, "on both, but then we've had some of this with the Gelal, haven't we?"

Niibori sighed but nodded his head. "How many is this, then?"

"This is couple seven, then, but ..." Natalie put her hand on his arm to keep his attention. "There will be more. It's only been a week since She accepted your design, and someone is telling people. You will need more help. Let me get it for you."

"Yes, yes, of course, I'll sign whatever I need to sign; just deal with it, please," he added, looking back at her with longing.

"Harder," Niibori growled as the bullwhip struck. It had taken a few years to get Natalie trained in these techniques and a few more to convince her that he did not want it to crack anywhere other than his flesh. She was still tentative, so he had to exercise his power when they played these intense pain games.

The next stroke was powerful; it drove him to his toes. She must have accessed her supernatural senses that time and moved just a bit closer. In a few more he could feel his own bu slipping down his back and pooling in a tub they had placed there. They could use that to bind the new workers they needed to deal with the 19 orders they now had for more and more clothing for the bicentennial.

By drawing bu this way, they distanced these necessary wardum from Niibori and secretly bound them to Natalie as well. It was a trick one of their Gelal clients had taught them a month ago. Pain and pleasure with purpose infused a vampire's blood with a symbiotic force that could be used to make the arammu-wardum's position more powerful in the household. That client, Maha, was an Egyptian beauty who came to them herself, with her own beloved slave in tow. She had told them some superstitions about the planets aligning in a unique way on the night of this private party at the Ummum's esharra. She had told them rumors about how those invited were not the powerful and elite but an odd collection that had been personally contacted by the Mother's personal witch.

Maha had said a lot of things, and some of them were proving to be true. Both Niibori and Natalie had always felt closer after their play or sex, but by following even just a minor part of the Egyptian's suggestions they seemed to be more closely in tune than ever before.

Niibori gasped as he felt his hair gripped tightly and pulled back. He shivered as Natalie's clever tongue licked some of his bu from his back. She moaned into his ear, "Damn, Niibori-sama, this is so much better."

It was good – this part between them was always good, as was the clothing. But other things, even the most basic things between wardum and Bel, between wife and husband, had been so taxing over the decades. The Tamu forced them to do so many things they both hated, but in these moments, with the right orders, they could switch places and be where they truly desired.

Niibori growled back and jerked on the chains that hung above the tub. She responded by slapping his ass with the full power of her body, which drove him to swing for several seconds. "You're making a mess," Natalie said, tsking her tongue at him. "Maybe I'll have Udo clean it up while you're still up there."

"You wouldn't," Niibori coughed, his dark eyes wild for a second, but his cock jumped.

Natalie grabbed his organ and stroked it once. "What are you going to do to stop me ... master?" she spat out the word and slapped his now weeping rod.

"Mistress!" Niibori cried out the forbidden word, and she rushed to turn him and cover his mouth with her own. "I'm sorry, I'm sorry," he cried as she helped him down. As a word that could get them both killed, it had become a sort of safe word for them, a concept Natalie had brought from the States so many decades ago.

She shushed him softly as she helped him lie down on his stomach and fetched a goblet of blood for him to drink and speed up his healing. Brushing back her damp blonde hair she bent down and licked up the bu from the cuts her unsafe whipping had created. Inside, she treasured the word and cursed their tormentor silently.

Niibori waited in the parlor for the arrival of the third of the three Akhkharu he was making personal deliveries to. The house was impressive, rather gaudy perhaps, but also particularly Western as well, which was to be expected, he supposed, back in what had once been called the United States of America in what had once been one of the biggest cities in the world.

The orders for the bicentennial had stopped at 49 – stopped suddenly, a few months back, leaving him both grateful and determined to create 49 pairs of complimentary couture, each pair different, so he didn't bring down the wrath of as many vampires. Natalie had convinced him to see this as one way to make a name for himself separate from Gaius's. Everyone who was at this private party would surely become some of the most powerful Akh on the planet, and his name would be tied to each of them. When they themselves had received a formal invitation that brought the number of clothes to 50 pairs, he was grateful for her insisting on finding help.

He and Natalie were making special deliveries to each of the Gelal on their list; the fact that this house also had a Kashshaptu who had ordered a pair of gowns as well was just a matter of odd coincidence. The witch and the young Akh of the household had already collected their clothing, but when Niibori tried to talk to Sara, he found himself too tongue-tied to approach the subject with her. She seemed to sense his question and giggled, informing him that her Shi would be a more appropriate mentor for his task.

Did the Gelal gossip among themselves? Did this Maha who had told them about the power of sexual passion and bu have a connection to this house? That seemed unlikely, given that Natalie was currently in Cairo trying to discover more on her own. Of course, Gaius claimed to have damu all over the world. In the beginning there had been only one Ummum for them all.

Niibori stood up and walked to the window to look at the area below. It barely looked like the old New York City he remembered from fashion magazines, back when such things existed. Another of Natalie's ideas had been to restart such publications. Akhkharu were great readers, and they still sent out newspapers and letters to each other – indeed, he'd heard that some would circulate books among themselves. Natalie read and kept the books – her age allowed her to do so – and Udo, too, was useful for checking out anyone's credentials who came to their home. Niibori was even more grateful for them after the necessity to take on so many new wardum to help with this bicentennial. Most of them were young, unclaimed, and easily acquired, often in exchange for his suits and gowns, but none of them could read, which meant it had taken hands-on training before they could work the old sewing machines.

The Alu-Bel of this city had yet to collect and approve of his own clothing and allow Niibori to make last-minute adjustments. This David Markus had somehow acquired an entire city as his kur, or land, and Niibori had never heard of a Gelal doing such a thing. One might hold a section of a city, certainly, and one might always be highly placed on regional councils, but by and large Gelal were considered unable to rule because of their passions. Or so Sarrutum all said, and until now Niibori had had no reason to doubt that bit of education he'd had.

Of the dozen Gelal who had come to him for his creations – they were a clear majority – none had seemed out of control or overly sexed in his opinion. Natalie had confirmed it, and she was a better judge, since she spent more time with each client than he did. True, their clothing was rather revealing and their slaves even less covered, but they had each been focused on presenting themselves in the best way to their Ummum. The trick had been to keep their family uniqueness without feeling like he was designing clothing for whores, a very rude thought that he quickly buried when the doors to the parlor opened and an elegant Akhkharu in what looked like black silk pants, a white open shirt, and no shoes walked into the room.

"You must be Niibori Takayoshi," the other Akh said, holding out his hand in greeting.

He was a good half foot taller than Niibori, and though he'd heard rumors of the dangers of touching a Gelal, this was his client, so he shook hands and bowed. "Markus-san, thank you for meeting with me," he said softly.

The other vampire chuckled. "Of course, of course; I do want to make the best possible display of myself at this celebration." He looked around as one of the side doors opened and a beautiful woman in a long flowing black gown that did nothing to hide her form entered to gracefully kneel at his feet. "And this is Eva, my arammu-wardum, whom you have an outfit for as well?"

Niibori had to force himself to look away. The woman was kneeling so perfectly, so attentively, and yet so comfortably at the Alu-Bel's feet. Her face was a picture of rapture or bliss, a reminder of something Niibori himself felt on those rare moments at Natalie's feet when he broke down and they were able to overcome the Tamu. "Yes, yes, I have both here," he said, picking up both garment bags, something that had been specially made in-house for these deliveries.

Both took their garment bags, and the woman stood up to help her master try his suit on, causing Niibori to turn and look away. The dami had done the same thing; it was as though these Gelal had no shame at all. He heard the zipper go down and the rustle of clothing, then another zipper and more sounds of clothing flowing to the floor.

"Well, what do we look like?" Markus asked, so Niibori turned to see. They looked amazing; the colors and the cut of the fabric hung perfectly well on their bodies, and the colors were a touch bolder than the Alu-Bel's dami and her own wardum's, to show relationship. As his talented eyes traveled over them, Niibori took out his box of pins. "Just a few adjustments, if I may, Markus-san?" he asked.

"Of course, of course," the Akh said, then he did the same thing his dami had done and looked directly at his slave. "Eva, dear, you will allow Mr. Takayoshi to touch you to do these measurements."

"Yes, Master," she replied and turned her wide eyes to Niibori, who frowned, recognizing some Asian ancestry in her, though not Japanese – maybe Korean, he thought, without realizing that he was falling back on centuries-old assessments.

"You should wear the same undergarments you will wear to the party," Niibori said when his eyes noted no lines of such pieces under the gown he'd designed.

"I am, Sir," Eva said, and Markus said the same thing.

After the fitting, Markus insisted that Eva take them to their seamstress and that Niibori sit and talk to him for a while. That worried the designer a bit, but he could hardly refuse the commands of an Alu-Bel in his own home.

They sat silently for a moment over a goblet of fine vintage when Niibori almost coughed up the blood at the sudden question he was asked. "Pardon me, Markus-san, I did not understand your question."

"I think you did, but I'll repeat it. I asked whether you were looking at Eva wishing your own slave could be as devoted to you, or that you could be that devoted yourself?"

Niibori's face started to burn as he lowered his head and glanced away. "I should think the answer was obvious," he offered.

"It is now," Markus replied as he took a sip. "Don't be embarrassed. These feelings aren't that unusual. We were just men at one time, after all. Some men are born to lead, others to follow, and others to go it alone. I think you fell into the middle there," Markus observed.

Niibori found his mouth and mind frozen as the other Akhkharu continued. "I'm guessing your inspiration is not another vampire but a mortal, perhaps?"

"No, no, that would be shameful," Niibori countered quickly.

"Then who?" and somehow every word this Gelal said seemed to worm into his heart, making him feel safe enough to talk.

"My arammu-wardum, my Natalie, my wife," Niibori said softly.

There was silence for several moments, then Markus reached out and touched Niibori's knee, making him jump a bit. "That makes it difficult, but not impossible. Tell me what you know about Gelal, because clearly you came here because you think you know something, and then I'll ask some questions. Perhaps, just perhaps, I can find a way to help you."

Niibori looked up as the other vampire settled back into his chair. "I do not wish to bring shame to my family, but ..." He swallowed and then forced himself to continue, "I cannot continue like this."

Natalie was wandering around Cairo with Maha's servant, Lucien, accompanying her. The Akhkharu had asked if a few native-made beads might be added to her gown and his suit, and since Natalie knew just enough about fashion to do that task, she had agreed, in exchange for further information about this emotional bond that bu could create.

They had the beads, but she had been walking in a daze thinking about what she had been told. Natalie paused, and Lucien stopped to look at her with a sad expression. "Her English is fine enough, though your French is atrocious," he commented, which made Natalie frown and him laugh. "There, I got a response that isn't worry. I have succeeded," he announced.

He was a handsome fellow who looked to be in his late 20s or early 30s. His hair was a sun-drenched brown, his eyes almost a match, and his mannerisms varied from attentively worshipful to his mistress, to formal with other wardum and unbonded mortals she saw him interact with, to joking with those he seemed to know well. In another lifetime she might have dated him, but Natalie quickly brushed those thoughts aside as Gelal tricks.

"How can we do what she says we have to do? She has no idea what type of a hold he has over Niibori," Natalie said as her worry slipped from her mouth.

Lucien took her by the arm and pulled her into a café, where he was known well enough to get them a private alcove. "Woman, you have little grasp of strategy and tactics, so I fear you may be doomed to fail," and he held up his hand as she started to protest, "but my mistress instructed me to help you, so I shall."

Natalie nodded and leaned forward so they could keep their voices lower. It galled her that he thought she couldn't plan, but the truth was that this wasn't a business they were running; it was an escape plan, a survival plan, even a hostile takeover. Yes, thinking about it that last way helped her see more clearly than she had before. Within hours she had gathered the information she needed from her own mind and Udo's on the phone to create an attack plan with the help of Lucien, who wished her luck when he took her back to the small airport that served only Akhkharu and their most trusted servants.

On the flight back, sitting in the back with all the other wardum traveling alone, she debated telling Niibori about her plan but decided it was best if he didn't know. She had to protect him; it was her duty as both wardum and wife.

It was time to leave for their train to Old Boston, where the Ummum lived and where they'd meet her for the first time at this private bicentennial party. Natalie needed an excuse to get away for a while, so she feigned forgetting something important. "Niibori-sama, I completely forgot my shoes; I'll go find them and do a check of everything else, OK?"

Niibori had been looking for his own excuse, and he blinked when she offered him one. "Yes, yes, Natalie-chan, I should go check with Udo to make sure the gifts Gaius wants delivered have been packed. We certainly don't want any errors on this," he added with a tight smile.

Her own smile back matched his. "No, no errors, no room for errors," she whispered before bowing slightly and leaving.

Natalie ignored the part of the compound where Gaius had insisted they live for the past month. That suited her plans just fine; though his staff would be loyal, she hoped that would dissipate quickly once his corpse was rotting. Over the course of this month, she'd been using some of the bu she and her Bel, her husband, harvested during their covert play as a replacement for Gaius's own precious fluids. Udo had helped her sneak in the replacements. Niibori had gotten a bit weak, and she worried it was because of the amount she was using, but she needed these people to let her pass into the master suite without question. Right now, they were comfortable enough with both of them that they were never asked questions anymore and could move freely about the compound except when the Byzantine was around.

Udo was waiting for her in the hallway outside the master suite. He looked at her and nodded, offering her the bronze tipped wooden stake on his palms. He had a sword hidden in his coat, and if she could stake him, he was pretty sure he could decapitate the bastard who had abandoned him decades ago. Or they'd die trying.

They walked into the master suite and found the lights down – unusual for such a busy monster, Natalie thought as she swallowed nervously. True, both wardum had better eyesight than any mere mortal, but compared to Akhkharu they were blind. She heard a strangled sound off ahead, so she reached out and fumbled for Udo's arm. He returned her touch with a shrug and the sound of metal slipping from leather as he unsheathed his sword.

Together they moved toward the sound and paused when they heard swearing in something that sounded like Japanese, though not modern by any measure. Natalie's stomach did a flip as she recognized the voice. "Niibori-sama?"

There was silence, and then a dim light came up, enough to let the two wardum see their Bel standing over his Shi, the elder vampire impaled with a stake in his heart against the wall. The elder's eyes were moving, and he was struggling – if they didn't act, he would get free. Stakes only weakened them for a moment – a shock to the system, but you had only minutes to act, Lucien had told Natalie.

Niibori's mouth had fallen open, and the sword he had fell to the floor. "Natalie-chan?"

"Do it!" she ordered Udo, and he raised the sword, put all his supernatural strength into it, and went for the staked Akh's neck. This required that he meet his former master's eyes, and that underlying original bond made him freeze.

"Do it!" Natalie yelled again. She watched in horror as the other slave fell to his knees crying. She looked to her Bel, her husband. "We have to do this; it's the only way to be free."

"Yes, yes, I know, how did you?" Niibori started to ask.

With a growl Natalie grabbed her master's sword and put it in his hand. Sometimes he thought too much, was too submissive to Gaius and any other higher-ranking vampire they met. Normally it annoyed her; now it could end their lives.

"We'll do it together, Niibori-sama, together," she insisted.

She maneuvered them to stand over Udo, kicking him aside as she did so, and helped Niibori raise the sword. "Don't look into his eyes; if we have to slash several times, so be it," she ordered firmly.

It took three attempts to sever his head from his body, and they were covered in blood that turned to ash and smoke as his form crumbled. Natalie dropped her grip and ran to a corner to vomit. She'd hated that monster, but she'd never killed anyone before.

"Natalie-chan, thank you," Niibori's voice reached her, and she felt cool hands on her arms, rubbing up and down as she wiped her mouth.

She nodded as she turned around. "Thank you, Niibori; I guess this turned out as it should have – and to think I was afraid to tell you," she chuckled.

He had released her and stepped away, so Natalie froze and looked up. He looked … smaller, but more handsome for some reason now. "What's wrong, Niibori, baby, what's wrong?" she asked, reaching out toward him.

His face broke into a smile. "You called me by my first name and by a nickname," he replied. "You've haven't done that since our honeymoon."

Natalie smiled as he took her into his arms and kissed her, the ashes and smoke drifting around them. "The Tamu has been broken, then?" she asked, hopeful but worried.

Niibori frowned and stepped back. "Let me try." He focused and then bowed deeply to her whispering, "Natalie-sama, I am so pleased you have accepted me into your life."

"It worked," said Udo's voice. The newly freed couple stood and looked at the other wardum as he stood up. "I can feel it too, inside, only you, Niibori-sama and you, Natalie-sama," he grinned as he used the honorific finally for her. "I can only feel the connection with you now."

They all smiled, freed finally after more than two hundred years of living a nightmare. Then Natalie's face grew pale. "The others will know – what are we going to do, Niibori?"

With a new sense of power, Niibori stepped forward and straightened his jacket. "I'll take care of everything, Mistress," he added the word with a glance at her, his smile revealing one fang. He had already made plans for when his Shi was suddenly gone.

Niibori walked into the party with Natalie on his arm, not trailing him as most wardum were, though now that he looked around, he saw many more configurations than he ever had at the Sarrutum gatherings he'd been forced to attend. He greeted each Akhkharu he met, Natalie whispering the names he didn't know in his ear.

As he assessed what everyone was wearing, he was surprised that each outfit was his own design and there were no others. Somehow everyone invited here had come to him for their gowns and suits. He paused to exchange a hug with Markus and his dami Sara, whispering to the older vampire that his advice had helped.

"I can tell from your eyes. They glow with power," the other replied.

Niibori nodded and excused himself. They needed to get through the crowd and greet their hostess personally, though he was shaking inside.

"It's going to be fine, baby," Natalie cooed to him as she leaned in and stroked his chest with one hand.

Niibori nodded back and took her hand in his and kissed it. Before this he had always felt lost, floating in the wake of Gaius as he bullied his way through the world. His submission to his creator had always been forced, a thing borne of bu, religious dogma, and political necessity. Removing his lips from Natalie's hand, he knew he was still submitting to someone, but this made him feel like a man again, a real man, in control of his destiny.

As they neared the throne where the Ummum sat with her own arammu-wardum, he paused, caught by surprise as their Mother giggled and swung the sparkling blue tennis shoes he'd sewn for her with his own hands. Inside, he heard a small feminine voice say, "Finally, someone took a stand."

*Bard ends the final tale of the Elders, and I step forward, looking at the new Sarrutum with a smile; after my monstrous descendants, these kings were the most changed in my new world. "I knew you were the ones, but you had to prove it. You've all had to prove it," I say louder, looking through the garden audience, my gaze lingering on each family.*

*I pause when I look at my Lord sitting in front, his often-mischievous expression serious. After a moment he nods. It is time to reveal what happened beyond what the elders experienced, beyond what they saw. It is time to remind them all of the cost incurred for creating our harmonious world.*

*"New creation comes from destruction; it will always come from destruction," I add. "This tale will seem disjointed, because I changed, and my viewpoint changed," I say before telling the final story for this quinquennial celebration.*

# Beginning of Our World

I remember when the first of my new chosen family died.

In hindsight I know he was murdered, but at that moment, sitting straight up in my bed with Tina clutching at me, her voice sounding so distant in my ears, I just knew he was dead.

His name was Yemon, with no family name anymore, and he was in Kanpur, just doing what he always did, saving what few he could by taking them into his brothel. In some areas akalum were less valued than others, and this was one such place. He first rescued Anjali and made her his most beloved. Then they started to save others when they could, using their blood and acquired skills to trade for safety – things Gelal are good at, even if I did not fully understand it all.

All I knew is that I felt like someone had set me on fire.

It took Tina a few minutes to calm me down, but I refused her offer to fetch Jon. The only real reason I finally made some of my playmates my servants was so he could have a break. He is a good daddy, but every arammu-wardum I'd had before grew too needy, too connected to me, to fully be what I needed them to be. His accepting his position as daddy meant that he needed time with a mommy or two, and an occasional other man as well. It's adult stuff; I didn't care much about it until it interfered with what I wanted.

I could only calm my wardum down by telling her about Yemon and what I'd seen and felt. She didn't look convinced when I told her it was OK, but she couldn't refuse me when I made it an order for us to go back to sleep. Neither of us really did. I had never woken up during the day before unless Enki was there to remind me that I could.

I remember when the second was murdered.

I was watching my friends play in the pool while Lana and Brion were blowing up more inflatables that someone had sent me as a gift. I don't like the water much – too many bad memories – but I liked to watch them play sometimes. And my adult servants enjoyed the pool as well, so we could pretend for a while that this was a family party, maybe a birthday party – it didn't really matter, as long as I could imagine that this was what I missed.

I felt a sharp stab or slice to my neck, then I fell to the cement, though I only saw blades of tall grass bathed in blood that was turning to smoke. I heard some Gaelic and then English in my ears before I found myself looking into Jon's worried eyes. "Charity, sweetheart, can you hear me?"

"Alleen is dead," I whispered, clutching his hand, which rested on my chest.

His eyes grew wide, and soon he was yelling at the others to keep playing, though he carried me inside followed by a select few others. He laid me on a couch where he'd sit and read to us all when it was raining. Kneeling next to me, he looked up, and I followed his gaze to find Varonika, Carina, Tina, Lana, and Brion all surrounding me. "Tell me again what you saw, Bel," Jon asked me, and I knew from his tone that he thought this was serious.

I told him what I'd seen, smelled, heard, and felt. Alleen had been checking out the villages not far from Galway, doing her best to make sure they were well fed, housed, and clothed; from time to time, she'd pick one to educate, and they'd move into the city with her. She didn't do it because she needed them; most of those she sent were shipped off to others to become members of their households. The Allamudi had a fair trade in educated servants, and she was just one more cog in that machine, though a more humane one.

Someone didn't like what she'd been doing, though. As I thought back, I could almost see things through her eyes, and I tried to describe it all. She had been walking with a newly chosen boy, testing his wits, when something jumped on him and tore him limb from limb before her shocked eyes. She had never seen who wielded the scythe that separated her head from her neck, one of the three ways my people can be killed.

"How do you know all this?" Carina asked as she knelt on the other side of me.

Before I could frown, Tina spoke up. "Is this like before, Charity? Is this another bad dream?"

"Before?" Now Jon was angry. He scooped me up into his arms and dismissed everyone with orders to say nothing, just go back to the party. They didn't hesitate long, because when he's being a real daddy, no one questions his decisions.

He carried me through the mansion, pausing only long enough to tell Gavin, Tina's father, to double the guards tonight and to tell Marina absolutely nothing. Again, Gavin only nodded and ran off to do as he was commanded.

Back in my suite he set me on my bed and then sat beside me, facing me, his frown still deep. "This has happened before, then? When?"

"About two years ago, I think. It woke me up when Yemon was killed. Tina was with me, as she often is, as a sister should be."

Jon stood up and turned to my desk, where he retrieved our secret files from a secret drawer. He consulted them for a moment, then sighed. "Why didn't you tell me this when only ninety-eight showed up the last time? In fact," he continued, closing the folder now and walking to me, his face very angry, "you lied to me when you told me you knew he wouldn't be coming."

"That's not a lie!" My own anger made him flinch and hunch over a bit.

We were both quiet for a few minutes, our bond outstripping any roles we might want to play for a few minutes, and that made me more angry. With a growl I stalked out of the room and headed to my feeding room, where my sekretu and sinnis scurried to attend to me. None of them dared to say anything to me, even when they had to take the cold body away by the time I had calmed enough to remember to stop.

Word of what had happened spread throughout the esharra, and when Marina returned from her latest tours for me, she was pleased that

I was being treated with more appropriate respect. I remember that was the first time I realized I was going to have to kill her sooner or later.

The third one was a shock, because it showed me that this wasn't random. Fortaleza is a hub that Father Aperta had set up long before the Night came to the world. A good Catholic, he wanted to help the children who were suffering, and the city was just big enough to offer them a good education without the temptations of a place like Rio used to be. The Sarrutum who created him thought he'd gain control over a cheap labor pool, but instead the priest had remained firm in his convictions. I was immediately impressed when I met him in 1787, and I spoke to him frequently over the centuries. He was the first person I sent an invitation to, two decades ago, when I started meeting with my chosen few once a year.

I was playing with my friends when I had this urge to run. I remember getting up and running around the mansion, being followed by increasing numbers of my servants and playmates. I knew I wasn't in the orphanage; I knew my home's rooms were not on fire, but I felt like they were. I ran screaming until Jon picked me up in his arms.

"Father Aperta!" I yelled as I tried to wiggle out of his arms.

As I heard Jon giving orders again, I froze as my visions filled with a pair of heavy doors being flung open, and then searing pain. I couldn't even blink as Jon's face and voice drifted further and further away as it felt like I was dissipating in the rising sun. Soon I was overcome with sleep, though I was safely in my own home with my servants to protect me.

When I woke up, I could sense that Jon was lying next to me, something he hadn't done in a long, long time. When I looked at him, he was staring at me, and he sighed when he noticed I was awake. He kissed the back of my hand and held it. "Please don't get angry, Bel, but we have to talk about what is happening."

"What is happening?"

"I used some of your contacts, my contacts, in the region. Father Aperta's orphanage had a fire early this morning – in his attempt to save the children he seems to have run outside with them just after the sun rose. His one surviving wardum is on his way here to talk to you."

"Marina?"

"Doesn't know anything, or at least none of us will have told her anything," he tried to assure me. "You know that, right? You know we all love you here; we'd do anything for you?"

I just stared at him for a few minutes before nodding my head. "I know, Daddy, I know."

Such acclamations always worry me. I've had so many die for me already, even before the Night. I hope it can end, but it never seems to stop.

"Baby, don't cry. I'm sorry I upset you," Jon said as he pulled me into his arms. I let him hold me; I pretended for a few moments that he could protect me. He couldn't let the questions pass, though, and soon interrupted. "Why are you feeling it when they die?"

I made an unnecessary sigh, then pulled back to face him. "I've seen everyone at the meeting before, usually soon before or after they were changed, sometimes before they found their arammu-wardum, though most don't remember that. I keep track of them up here," I added, tapping my forehead.

"Keeping track hurts you?"

"Not usually." I tried to stand up, but he put his arm around me.

"Please don't. I know this is hard; I know none of this has turned out how you wanted, Sweetheart, but we have to talk about it. I can't be a good daddy, can I, if I don't know what's going on."

He knows exactly what works with me after these centuries, so I just resigned myself to this discussion. Adults always have to talk about things. Of course, talking is sometimes much better than just doing. It's just so hard to explain.

I screwed my eyes closed for a moment and tried to figure out where to begin, but Jon just waited. "I'm not like them," I said finally.

"I know it's hard when all they can see is your size," he started to say until I shot him an angry look.

"I don't know!" I shouted and jumped off the bed. He didn't follow; my voice, the power behind it, had left him either stunned or terrified. I calmed myself down and turned toward him with my arms hanging by my side. He'd slipped to his knees by the bed, his head bowed, silent, but I could hear his heart pounding.

"We were made differently ... it makes us too different ... they fall so far," I tried to explain.

"Because the gods made you." Jon stated, though his fear made his voice rise at the end, as though he was asking a question.

I tilted my head. I doubt he believes in the gods, not the true ones anyway, but if I told him to, he'd pretend, and he'd be in so much danger. "Yes," I agreed slowly. "I was changed for a reason. You remember I told you?"

"Yes, I remember everything you tell me, Bel."

I frowned a bit. Part of me hates it when we stop pretending. I'm not stupid; I know it is all pretending, the words we use, the game of daddy and little girl. He does better at it than most have. Of course, what I am helps, while it also makes this so hard to explain.

"Put your hand here," I ordered as I stepped forward and put my own hand over my heart. Jon lifted his hand and his head to look at me, then put his hand on my chest while I rested my hand on top of his. "You feel that, right?"

"You're making your heart beat at a regular pace. I feel it – Montesarat used to do that, too, for kicks, he said." Jon's even mentioning his former master was a sign of how scared he was, and I ran a hand through his hair to try to calm him.

I whispered the truth into his ear. "No, I'm not. It simply beats like that."

He didn't say anything for a few seconds, then his hand curled around the fabric of my shirt. "Oh, I'm so stupid," he whispered, then he released me and moved so he was sitting on the floor instead of kneeling. "You aren't undead ... you ... you're something ... uh, yeah, I don't understand," he ended.

I remained standing, though I wanted to sit on his lap, pretend we weren't having this conversation, but the third death meant this wasn't an accident. If I knew who was behind it, I'd just make it stop. I didn't know, and that meant I needed help. "You don't have to die to become like me – it just happens most of the time. Very hard to stop drinking once you start."

"I imagine so," Jon commented. He thought for a few moments, his brow furrowed, so I let him think. Knowing something myself and getting it out into words that an adult can understand has always been a problem for me. That creates bigger problems.

"Wait. I thought giving your bu to a living person made them wardum – bonded them to you – but didn't fully change them?"

"There's a point, a moment that it either changes you fully or only binds you. It's tricky. Too much life and the person bound requires more reasons to serve."

"Like a Tamu or torture?"

I nodded. Those aren't my fault. I didn't create all the stupid rituals and rites; I just didn't stop them as they were made and reused. "Too little life or no life and the person will change fully. You have to listen to the heart just right if you want to keep the soul intact."

"Not Xul. I thought that was automatic?"

Now I flinched. That one is my fault. Curses are powerful things; I try not to use them anymore. "It's a … punishment," I offered slowly.

"I remember now," Jon replied, and his face was visibly paler as he said it. He's the only wardum I ever told so many stories. The only one who could make believe so well that he deserved to know more about me. I haven't told him everything. He wouldn't understand.

"But I'm not sure why this is bothering you, Sweetheart. You are the Ummum; you should be different."

"I get lonely, and these hundred …" I paused, knowing that number was now a lie. "Like me, they have some life left in them; their souls are intact."

"Really? Is that why they seem to care more?"

"No; I know others like them who were changed right on the edge of life and death before the final heartbeat. Not everyone can still feel or want what we do." I've never voiced what that feeling … that desire, is; they would think I was crazy, just like they'd be frightened if they could hear my heart. I can mask it, and I usually do, which is the opposite of them. Even my chosen have heartbeats so faint that only I can hear them; only the best doctor's machines could measure them.

"Bel," he said, using the title, and that makes me look at him seriously. "Do you think your people are being targeted because someone knows the truth about you and them?"

"I'm afraid," I said softly. Jon pulled me into his arms and held me for a while.

"We'll figure out what we can do about it, I promise."

"I already know. No one will like it," I whispered into his shoulder.


We met somewhere different every year, and this year it was outside, in the ruins of the Coliseum in Rome, which was controlled by one of mine. They numbered only ninety-six, with the murder of another just a month back. That's two in one year, and that made me decide to make this move.

I was waiting with Jon as the others came and mingled, exchanging pleasantries and information after a year's distance for most of them. During the first few meetings they had grouped together by family, with the exception of the Xul, who had stayed away from everyone and each other. There were only three of them, and I was glad that none of them had been targeted yet.

"Ready?"

I looked up at Jon and squeezed his hand. I walked out first, and he followed. As we walked the conversations stopped, and those we passed fell in line until everyone was gathered around the big stone Jon helped me stand upon. I let my eyes move from one Akhkharu face to the next; I sent out tendrils from my mind, easing the worry that had lingered over this party since it started. After these quiet moments I spoke up as loudly and clearly as I could, holding my power in check so they were just words.

"Four of you are gone now. Taken from us, from me. I felt each one murdered here," I said, touching my heart, "and here," I touched my head. "Some of you know I am connected to you – you feel me; sometimes it isn't nice, but it is necessary."

Below Jamie rolled his eyes, but his wardum rubbed his upper back with the flat of his palm to help him maintain control. A bit further away, Calypso smiled, holding her servant's hand in her own. Others, too, smiled or shifted uncomfortably on their feet, while the rest merely glanced around trying to see what I was talking about.

"I love all of you." There, I said it, that word that we who are trapped in the Night never use except to manipulate, or in the deepest of private moments. Around me the Akh and slaves reached to one another, cuddling closer, confirming their own feelings, but also the fear that admitting such brings. "That is what makes us different. This ability to feel love. For some it was always present, the driving force behind our mortal lives. For others it was discovered as the decades ticked by. For most it was recovered after being buried under what we saw around us."

Jon nodded his head once when I glanced at him. We had practiced this for weeks, but I was feeling nervous, not because they might hurt me, but because I didn't want to hurt them. "Someone hates us for this ability. They hunt you; you know this is true," I added, off the script, when there were a few mutters of disbelief. "As they harm you, they harm me."

That made them all freeze in silence, staring at me in horror. Enki once told me that as He was to me, so to them I seemed. To admit that I could be harmed, that I could be damaged, was very risky. Before I could say any more, Jamie stepped forward.

"We can't be 'aving that. We 'ave to do summat. Don't ye agree?"

Around us the crowd nodded and started to talk until Cornelius, my head of libraries, stepped forward and raised his hands. "Ummum, you are our creator; we will do whatever you command to protect you."

"Because we love you," Sara added as her Shi and their wardum petted her arms and back.

The others began saying it, and soon it became a chant that jerked my mind back in time. My father was asking my mother what she wanted from the trade fair he and brother were venturing to in the nearby city. She told him, looking at each of us, that as long as we loved her, she had all she needed, but salt would be very useful. I started to giggle at the memory, and my laughter stopped the declarations.

I finished my prepared speech then, detailing how we must share blood together. That would do more than merely give us a sense of each other; it would allow us to determine our exact locations and share powers across distances. Maha raised her brown bejeweled arm and then spoke. "They will attack us even more if they sense we have such a close bond with you, Ummum."

"Then we fight," Calypso added softly.

"We can fight; I suspect most of us have had to fight just to be here," added Niibori as his wardum held his arm and nodded firmly, her eyes meeting mine boldly before dropping to the ground.

"Oi, that's bloody right!" Jamie agreed, and soon they were all affirming that they understood what I was asking of them.

Of course, they didn't and couldn't fully understand, since I didn't myself. Nothing ever works out as we wish. I knew that as each stepped forward to bleed into a large mixing vessel and exchange some blood directly with me. The words that Enki said so long ago that I can barely remember started echoing in my mind.

Things never work out as I plan. We were spread all over the world, and so, though we could feel the attacks on each of the next two in the course of a year, we could not get to them to save them. Instead, we each felt a bit stronger, a bit wiser, a bit more with each passing.

Except for the Sarrutum, all of these were very solitary creatures, living only with their servants, their mortals, and interacting with others only when necessary. I just sat and listened at our next party. No one was dressed in finery this time as they discussed what to do. When all the ideas had been put forth, they turned to me just as the self-appointed council did and forced me to make a decision.

In groups of two or three, I sent them off with orders to never be alone among anyone not of this gathering. Some I organized by family, and others by location. Sara was looking at me the entire night, saying nothing until all the rest had left, and then she knelt down to hug me, whispering, "I love you, Ummum," in my ear.

Later, as I stood waiting for the sun to fully set so we could return home, Jon did the same thing, and I started to cry. Though he urged me to tell him why, I could not, because the thoughts seemed like memories and like visions at the same time. I felt afraid and calm at the same time. I had this terrible ache in my stomach, a pain that seemed old, though I'd never felt it before.

"Why are they doing this?" I asked my Lord as soon as he appeared, sitting by my side.

"Well, that's a straightforward approach for you. I knew it was important as soon as the calf hit my nose, but ..." he began with a grin that faded as I just stared at him. "Things aren't working out quite so well?"

"You know it," I countered. Four of my own had been killed in the past thirteen months. The groups I'd set up weren't protecting them. Too often they turned and fled instead of fighting together or helping each other. I didn't understand it. When one of my playmates falls, the others all gather around to help her; when one is hurt, the others gather to comfort him. If you don't play nice, you won't have playmates at all. It is rather obvious.

He sat down, and I noted that He was wearing shorts, sandals, and another T-shirt – this one had "Big Kahuna" on it – and I almost smiled. Almost. "That took about 5000 years; I guess I lost the bet."

"What bet?"

"Not important," He said with a shake of His head, which sent a mist of water around us and onto the floor of the temple space I was still using in this mansion. "What do you want, Ningai?"

I was startled when he used my real name. I hadn't heard it in millennia; he has always respected the new names I've chosen as I've counted century after century.

"I know what you wanted at first. We helped you get that, but I knew you wanted something else; that's why I gave you the power to make servants."

"That isn't what I wanted," I said softly as I pulled my knees up and rested my chin on them.

We sat in silence for a few minutes. "You have to say it, little one. I risk it with the others, so you must say it, out loud."

"I want my family back."

"You can have five as your family, to replace those five you lost," He declared.

Five I lost? For a moment I was confused, then I realized what He was saying. "I can make more damu?"

"No!" He quickly replied as he looked around, then leaned over so we were forehead to forehead, His essence surrounding me as though I was floating again down the river. "There are five now whom you can choose, whom you can start over with. You know them; they have been selected among those you gathered."

I frowned, thinking over those who came every year to the big party, those I had watched when they were beginning, though most had no idea I was around. A small group seemed to shine forth in my mind's eye. "There are six, not five."

He stood up and looked down at me with a very serious expression. "You can start over with five, but you must sacrifice something to gain the ability to protect them. Some of the others have turned from you to your enemies," He added, and that brought me to my feet.

"Who are they? Give me their names, and I'll just get rid of them."

He shook His head, and raindrops as big as the buttons on my shirt flew around the room. "I have told you all I can. Be happy that not all of the others have turned from you, or I could not have come here at all. Of course, you could always ask Z," he added with a wink, referring to the first immortal the gods created.

With that he disappeared, leaving me more worried. Ziusudra has never liked to meet with me – he actively flees from me and my children, sometimes hiding among mortals, sometimes abandoning those as well. No, I'll figure it out on my own, I decided as I stood up to exit the sacred space.

It took a dozen more murders to drive me in search of him. Jon was sleeping as ordered out in the jeep when I found the first immortal back in my old cave, the first place that had offered me shelter from the sun. He looked up at me, his wrinkled face frowning. At least the gods had been kind to him in that he looked no older than he had the day he had entered the boat that saved him.

"Well, well, your kind have certainly messed things up, haven't they? What's the world's population now, the human one, less than a billion and falling every day, while those you won't control let their hunger drive the slaughter?"

I frowned and glanced around at how comfortable he'd made this old cave. "Not like you've done much to help. You could have warned them, organized them; you had time," I countered, and jumped up onto the table he was sitting at to sit cross-legged on it so I could meet his eyes.

"What makes you think I didn't? That I don't?" He finished eating his dinner and then sat back to stare at me. "Why are you here?"

"Our benefactor sent me," I said simply, and he rolled his eyes and stood up to take his plate, cup, and utensils to the washbasin he'd set up.

"Did he now? I haven't spoken to him in a long, long time. I was hoping he'd forgotten about me."

"Lord Enki never forgets," I replied reverently. This made Ziusudra laugh out loud. "They still control things – even if the mortals forgot, we shouldn't!"

My raised voice made him stop and stare at me again. "Well, no high priestess ever had a thing on your faith, did she?" He held one hand up to silence my comment, and out of respect for his greater age I bit my tongue. "What did he say? Exactly, if you can remember."

Jon found us sitting outside the next night. Ziusudra had bid me stay during the day so he could think upon our god's words. Though he claimed to have no respect for them, I can tell he was still afraid of them. Considering what blessings and curses they have brought to us both, he is wise to be. I introduced them, and Jon came over to set me on his lap, wrapping his arms around me, probably more to comfort himself than me, but I pretended otherwise, because daddies need someone to need them. At least I had learned that in time to keep my arammu-wardum all these years, the one spark of true happiness I have had in a hundred lifetimes.

"Yes, he's correct," Ziusudra suddenly announced. "To start over, you have to start fresh with each family – you know who they are, the best of the best, the ones who were driven to you by something inside them, the ones most willing to take risks, even if you had to push in one case."

"But I saw six – in the vision he gave me, I saw six," I insisted, and I could feel Jon tense behind me, though he asked no questions.

"The sixth isn't of a family, not really. She has something you will need to deal with the rest."

"What's that?"

"Time."

I called these six to me one special night, to the cave where Ziusudra had agreed to mediate if need be. His existence would be discovered if I could not begin again. And living eternally as a blood bank was not worthy of this once-faithful man. It was not worthy of my greatest enemy, who I had learned was calling himself Enmul, after my fourth. It was a lie, as are the other claims of my children's names, but the whispers had turned to screams, and even those who came to the Council did so purely out of fear.

I'd killed them all, including dear Marina, who had tried so hard to keep her place at my side for her own gain. Soon, very soon, the families would know what I'd done, and the world would turn against me.

These twelve, for I counted their beloved servants among my allies now that I saw the end approaching, frowned at me as I told them everything, right from the beginning until the elimination of my Council. At first, they said nothing, then my little monster broke the silence as he always does. "This is some fucked up shit, it is," Jamie blurted out as his wardum nodded.

"It makes sense; it fills in so many gaps in the texts," Cornelius insisted, while Calypso agreed, speaking a few lines from the oral stories the covens tell.

Maha looked to Sara, who only stared at me. "Don't you feel the truth of it, too?"

"Truth or not, there will be consequences, Ummum," Niibori, always sensible, pointed out with a bow.

"Fuck yeah, they gonna rip us to pieces. Can ya take on thousands of our kind with all their wardum – hell, their mortal armies you know they been hiding?" Jamie asked, his voice filled with fear, the first time he'd been brave enough to show it to me, though I'd always felt it.

No one said anything more until Ziusudra stepped forward. "I know I am not like you, and yet, if you believe your Ummum's story, you know I am more like you than not. The gods," he said, pausing, and no one objected, so he continued with a glance at me, "say things must start afresh – well, as fresh as they can. Each family must begin under a new parent, under her control," he adds, placing a hand on my head.

"Wait. The texts say there were five damu in the beginning," Cornelius started, thinking out loud. "There are six of us, two of you," he said directly to the Gelal.

The dark beauty put her arm around the younger one as their servants took positions near them, their arms tense, their eyes darting around those they had felt were friends mere seconds ago. "I do not know why we both were called; all of us are loyal to you," Maha pleaded, but I was immune to her influence, though I pouted.

None of this, none of this was what I wanted.

"I know why I'm here," Sara finally spoke.

We stared at each other for a while, and then I sighed, waving my arms and hands. "Out, out, everyone else out! You, too," I said firmly to Jon as he looked at me. It took Jon's greater power to force her wardum from the cave.

"You know what I did. I remember, you were there, watching, you told me I had to get it right. Do you remember?" Sara said as she took my hand in hers. "Each of us was marked forever by what we did, Daedalus and me most of all," she added, touching her head for a moment, her face contorting in pain.

I touched her and felt that shock again. "But you more than most. Why?"

She smiled; her eyes seemed duller than any Gelal's should be. "I can hold together better than he can. His body took a strain; he isn't really that old, you know?"

That made me reflect. She looked young, maybe in her late 20s, but he had white at his temples and even wrinkles on his face. He looked twice her age, and in my memories of them until I had met them recently, he was younger than she.

"If I can't be one of the final five, I still want to help. If I give you the knowledge ..."

I cut her off with a sigh.

"No, I understand, Ummum. I know that it isn't something I can teach. You have to take it into you," she whispered, and then she turned her head and offered her neck to me.

"I can't, it isn't done, it was a rule, an old rule," I said, standing up to withdraw, but she caught me by the wrist, sending wave after wave of energy through me.

"The one rule we kept, out of so many you set up," she chuckled and tilted her head again.

I saw Ziusudra in the background; of course, he had refused to leave. His eyes met mine, and he nodded his head just once, then turned away.

Sometimes we feed from our wardum, and their blood tastes different. Sometimes in battle we might feed from an enemy's slaves, and they taste intense, frightening even. Never, ever do we drink from each other, except as a token to pledge loyalty, and then only dami to sire, a repeat of the same process that created us, them. But I had expanded what was allowed when I'd bonded us all together just a few years before.

I am not us. I am alone, just as she was not one of them but all of them. She cooed words of encouragement for as long as she could as I sank my teeth into her and drank her down. I felt the memories of five lives rush through me, over 500 years of experiences, feelings, and horrors rushing through me in a matter of minutes. The pain was so intense that I could feel my mouth open, but nothing escaped until the ceiling of the cave was spasming over me for eternity.

Ziusudra was looking down at me when my mind cleared. I could smell blood – hers, mine, ours, I couldn't tell them apart. I sat up, and the cave seemed smaller to my eyes. Then I looked down and saw that I had changed.

"Well, you aren't as old as her; I'm guessing about the average of your ages, so a woman by many standards. Try her clothes – yours ripped," the old immortal says to me.

I did as he said, shaking her ashes from them, and found them to be a bit big, but at least they covered a body that my mortal sister might have envied during her lifetime. "Why –" I started to speak and clapped my hands over my mouth as a deeper voice issued forth.

"Don't know," Ziusudra replied with a chuckle. "You are a pretty thing, though; I will say that. That should make for interesting changes in your world, eh?" He laughed some more as I frowned at him.

I took a look into a well-polished platter he had and saw a version of me that reminded me a lot of my mother and sister, though my hair had a touch of red in it now, and my eyes were a bit darker. "They are never going to believe this."

"I barely believe it, and I've been watching," Ziusudra agreed. He looked around and sighed. "Nope, didn't think he'd show. Leave us to try and explain it all. Bastard."

I was about to challenge his disrespect when an exclamation of shock made us both turn around. There were Jon and Daedalus – I knew them both, one as my father looking at me with wide eyes, the other as my lover, who had stepped forward to touch my clothing and look at the smoke now drifting around us, which used to be her ashes.

"Mistress?" Daedalus whispered as he fell to his knees and enfolded me in his arms.

"Hey!" Jon was peeling him off me, and they were about to come to blows when my words stopped them. Not words of power, but words of the past. Memories from each of their lives, things only Charity or Sara would know. It took them a few minutes to accept it all, and then they began arguing over how we could tell the others.

While they argued I simply stepped outside into the night air, where my new children awaited me. One by one, they paused then smiled, and approached me to hug me or offer a kiss as one might to a mother. Cornelius asked the question first, and it took me no time to answer, as I seemed to hear a river rushing around me.

"Call me Ningai. That has always been my name."

I felt my Lord's presence surround me, and I knew I had my family now.

I simply had to protect them.


The wardum gathered around Daedalus, offering him support and to a lesser degree supporting Jon as well. None of us had ever experienced or imagined what had just happened. To lose and yet not lose their Bel, to have their lives changed after centuries of stability – well, I've experienced it enough myself to know it is difficult at the best of times. The first thing he demanded, for arammu-wardum can make demands, was that his name be erased from our memories. I asked if he'd erase her from his, but he only started to cry, proclaiming that he'd never forget.

"Then remember everything," I told him with my new voice, looking up into his closer eyes, my larger hand on his cheek. "Remember it all, help us remember it all."

My new children – well, in heart and mind at least, if not in blood – gathered around me. They asked if I felt OK, and I had to admit I felt huge and a bit exposed. Maha chuckled and said it was probably best if I do not take on their garments, at least not right now. Out of the corner of my eye I saw Jon pale and knew he was listening.

"Be a good daddy," I chided him mentally, and he turned away, his face blushing deeply. For some reason that made me uncomfortable, but soon between Calypso and Niibori I had more clothing on me. I caught myself pouting as I thought of all my pretty little shoes, pants, shirts, and jackets I'd never be able to wear again, but when I got too far into my own worries the sound of the river in my ears grew into an angry torrent. I had a responsibility, and now for some reason I felt it more strongly than before.

I noticed that after the clothing issue was settled, the five with me seemed to pay more serious attention to me. Oh, those hundred I had chosen had always treated me with respect, as did the Council before I ended it, but even among those I could see their looks from time to time, their smiles that seemed to reflect how cute I looked or how adorable my voice sounded. It was really my own fault, now that I think of it, for choosing those childish clothes. I had never had much of a childhood; we didn't really have that sort of thing when I was a real child. Jon had made it easy to forget what I was for stretches at a time. It had been my only real freedom.

I hugged myself and frowned as my arms met these new breasts, not big but clearly there, and feeling … I didn't have time for any of that. The Council's demise would be discovered. I found myself asking Cornelius to repeat what he just said.

"Of course, Ummum. Besides the physical changes, do you feel any different?"

I frowned and looked around. Auras – I knew what those were, but I'd never seen them before. Around each creature here – Akhkharu, wardum, even old Ziusudra watching us from the cave – I could see glowing lines very faintly. "I don't know. I think I see something different, around each of you." I held out my own hand and saw the lines expanding in all directions. "Around me, too."

Maha opened, then shut her mouth, until Jamie swore at her a few times to speak up. "It's only a rumor among my family, a silly thing, but given what happened ..." She shrugged. "Some said that Sara wasn't a true Gelal, wasn't even true Akhkharu, was something else."

"No, I'm sure she was one of us," Cornelius countered with a shake of his head. "She did everything that we do, didn't she?"

"She, they, manipulated time somehow; she lived as all of your families ... the memories were hurting her; the memories hurt him," I added, nodding at our servants, still talking to the now unnamed wardum, who was sitting staring into space.

"That's bloody brilliant, that is. All sci-fi shit," Jamie chuckled. "It real though, or just bollocks?"

That left everyone quiet until Calypso whispered and drew us all close to her. "There were tales among the covens of a witch who left us to cling to another family. I didn't believe it until the first party where we hundred met. Then I saw Anika. She'd been a coven leader, and then just disappeared about a century or so ago. She was a coven mother, a position only those with the greatest power could hold. It was a terrible loss to us."

"Anika who has come here with Sara's sire before?" Niibori asked with a bow of his head.

"Yes, that is her. If such a time magick could exist, she would know. She had pre-sight and post-sight before she entered the Night," Calypso added softly.

"Bring them both here. They need to know what has happened to Sara," I commanded, and for the first time in my existence there was absolutely no hesitation to obey me.

Calypso and Maha both took off together with their servants to find them while the others helped us settle down in the cave, much to Ziusudra's frustration. With my new body, his complaints didn't last as long because, as Jon put it cautiously and Jamie directly, as an adult I was much scarier.

Niibori and Jamie worked to acquire more luxuries for us by visiting or having their wardum visit the villages a day or two from us. So far there were no reports at that level that the Council's fate was causing a problem, though as Natalie pointed out, a clever strategy would be one of silence until the last possible moment.

I knew we were in trouble when Ziusudra announced he was leaving and simply held up one hand with only four fingers to emphasize that for him immortality did not mean regeneration. "Hittites will seem like boy scouts," was his muttered final comment. Of course, they hadn't been the worst by far, except for being the ones to take his finger, but I knew we had little time.

Time is a funny thing. As I prepared a sacrifice with Cornelius's aid – he wished to learn as much as he could about what he called our traditional ways – our allies returned with Sara's sire and Anika.

Markus seemed to know what had happened as soon as he saw me, but he had to deal with the unnamed wardum, who was kneeling at his feet a moment later, swearing he had not known his mistress would do this. The bond transferred, as I learned a few nights after the event, and Jon refused to comfort me because it made him uncomfortable. Sara's wardum, mine now, touched me in ways I'd only known about from a distance, whether it had been in my parents' house or in books, music, or television before all of that had faded away.

When he could free himself of the still confused wardum by turning him over to his own, Markus walked to me and took me by the arms, looking deep into my eyes before pulling me into a hug. "Thank you for ending her pain."

"It was her idea," I told him, stepping back and waving Jon back with one gesture. "We have questions to ask you, and there isn't much time."

"I know, we barely made it here, but the witches are quite impressive when cornered," he added with a glance back at the red-haired Anika, who stared at us calmly. "We aren't getting out of this, are we? Anika, I, our lovers?" He said it bluntly, but not harshly.

"I don't know," I tried to lie, to ease what the god had told me, what Ziusudra had reasoned, and what my own heart had confirmed.

"It's all right. Four hundred years is a long time; more for Anika there. We've already talked. We want to help if we can, but we need to hurry, Ummum; the world has turned against you, though they will not recognize you," Markus told me.

"You could run and save yourself," I told him, but he only shook his head and motioned toward the unnamed one.

"He told me that you ordered him to remember, so I told him some things I know about Sara. When this is done, you should all talk with him. Tell him everything; use him well. He's a good man; he'll be a good bard if you give him what he needs."

Though not destined to be one of my new family, the few remaining of those hundred came to me that next night, just in front of the hordes. All of them deserve to be remembered, even though we know little to share. All of them, all of them, kept us all safe, and for that we will now have a moment of silence.

I don't remember much about the ritual we finally did. I remember Calypso, Markus, and Cornelius consulting. I remember Jon raising his voice to me for the first time in a long time to plead with me not to do this. I remember the unnamed one telling me that I had to do it, or it was all for nothing. I remember each of my new children looking at me as they formed a circle around me, chanting.

I remember the lines shining forth, and it was like I could see exactly where to strike, and how. I remember Markus' final words to me. "Save your chosen first. It may not work for long. Sara told me that there was a limit; someone told her that, and she could feel it was true."

As the hordes descended, I watched the lines, and when the final moment was at hand, I slipped through to save each of them.

Calypso was besieged by a band of Sarrutum who had their ears blocked with something so they could not fall victim to her voice. That didn't stop my fists bursting through their ribs to pull out their hearts, so she and Chavi could decapitate them.

Jamie was impaled by blood vines and screaming banshees. They found it hard to speak when I filled their mouths with molten lead, giving Karl the opportunity to blow off their heads with his trusty shotgun.

Maha and Lucien were pressed back-to-back, and the Allamudi attempted to close their well-constructed trap of bronze daggers in each hand. I grabbed each and shoved it into their hearts long enough for she and Lucien to take their own scimitars and lop off their heads.

Niibori placed himself between Natalie and the Gelal whispering to them, reaching toward them, trying to turn them against each other. I reached out and turned their hands toward each other's skin, and soon they stood transfixed by each other's eyes so that Natalie could scream, "Fire in the hole!" and set their assailants aflame with a gift her husband had given her the night before.

Cornelius and Jack were yelling in Latin, trying to find another route to the trap they'd set up in the cave, when they were corned by more monsters than I would ever have allowed together. I simply severed the Xul's knees and left them on the ground for the scholar and his assistant to jump over before releasing a rain of bronze shards over them, impaling them into the ground, where they could remove each head at their leisure.

Even in their anger and fear, only my five children could truly cooperate, and that allowed me the exact timing I needed to make the difference.

When Natalie's gun ran out of fuel, Karl was there to toss her a fuel can.

As Niibori flinched back from a Gelal's touch, Cornelius tossed a bronze shard into the offender's heart.

As Jack's sword broke, Lucien kicked a scimitar his way.

When Calypso's vines were snapped and she screamed in pain, Maha placed a hand on the attacker and pulled his will from him.

Chavi was turning toward Jon to help him when Jamie intercepted a spray of bullets in his chest and had to submit to her whisper to pull them out later.

I am told that the battle lasted the entire night, that our wardum had to carry us into the cave to protect us not just from the sun but from a wave that appeared out of nowhere, though we know who created it.

Some will desire more details of this horrific night, but I say that our cooperation is more important, that our survival is more important.

Also, I simply cannot remember, and the war is a blur to the Elders, I'm told.

*I finish my tale with a chuckle before growing serious again.*

*"I have told you all of this because you are the first generation to ask for the truth. I have forbidden all of us, every single one of us and those who serve us, from making the same mistakes we've made in the past."*

*"Six threads through time," I whisper, "are not the only ones I can follow. Now that I know better, now that I am older, I will never hesitate to discipline my children as a good mother should."*

*"And if we should prove to be lax in your rules, Ummum?" This comes from one of those I've received complaints about, so I turn my dark gaze to hers.*

*"Then I'll just have to start over again."*

Since 1995, TJ Eckhart's fiction and non-fiction work has been challenging readers to look at themselves and their world through a different lens. *True You 101* continues Eckhart's challenge to reimagine a magic world colliding with the mortal one in regard to our true nature, one that rejects either a reversal or continuation of our everyday biases in favor of the more realistic complexities of what such a realm might be like. If you're willing to risk opening up your mind, you may find Eckhart's worlds opening up your heart as well.

You may find her at her main <u>website</u> or join her adventures on <u>Patreon</u>

CPSIA information can be obtained
at www.ICGtesting.com
Printed in the USA
BVHW041429151121
621700BV00012B/347